Praise for
TRAITOR'S DANCE

"Plenty of twists and excitement all the way to the last line." —*Kirkus Reviews*

"The writing here is even sharper than it was in the earlier Capra novels....A must read for Sam Capra fans." —*Booklist*

"I have always thought of Jeff Abbott as 'the King of High-Octane Thriller Writing,' and that has never been more evident than with his terrific Sam Capra series. The latest installment, *Traitor's Dance*, truly lives up to this hype....A great story with shocking twists and non-stop thrills. I expect nothing less from Jeff Abbott, who continues to blow me away with his unputdownable thrillers." —Book Reporter

"[*Traitor's Dance* is] all action and has a great character in Sam Capra....There's kidnappings, shoot-outs, deaths, betrayals, and twists and turns everywhere. For fans of authors like Mark Greaney, Don Bentley, Gregg Hurwitz, and Matthew Betley." —Red Carpet Crash

Praise for
JEFF ABBOTT

"A master storyteller....Those who enjoy unpredictable stories can never go wrong diving into the world of Jeff Abbott." —*Washington Post*

TRAITOR'S
DANCE

TRAITOR'S
DANCE

A SAM CAPRA NOVEL

JEFF
ABBOTT

**GRAND
CENTRAL**

NEW YORK   BOSTON

Copyright © 2022 by Jeff Abbott

Cover design by Jamie Keenan
Cover photograph by Silas Manhood Photography Ltd.
Cover copyright © 2023 by Hachette Book Group, Inc.

Grand Central Publishing
Hachette Book Group
1290 Avenue of the Americas, New York, NY 10104
grandcentralpublishing.com
twitter.com/grandcentralpub

Originally published in hardcover and ebook by Grand Central Publishing in August 2022
First mass market edition: September 2023

Grand Central Publishing is a division of Hachette Book Group, Inc. The Grand Central Publishing name and logo is a trademark of Hachette Book Group, Inc.

The publisher is not responsible for websites (or their content) that are not owned by the publisher.

The Hachette Speakers Bureau provides a wide range of authors for speaking events. To find out more, go to hachettespeakersbureau.com or email HachetteSpeakers@hbgusa.com.

Grand Central Publishing books may be purchased in bulk for business, educational, or promotional use. For information, please contact your local bookseller or the Hachette Book Group Special Markets Department at special.markets@hbgusa.com.

ISBNs: 9781538708750 (mass market), 9781538708767 (ebook)

Printed in the United States of America

OPM

10 9 8 7 6 5 4 3 2 1

In memory of Kyle Navarro
Who once organized a tailgate for a book signing

TRAITOR'S
DANCE

PART ONE

1

Austin

SAM CAPRA WATCHED THE ASSASSIN enter the middle
school gym.

Screams and cheers erupted as Sam's son Daniel sank
a basket. An excited dad next to Sam slapped his shoulder but Sam kept his gaze on the assassin. He watched
the man scan the crowd—both teams' supporters were
on one set of risers on one side of the gym—and the man
was careful not to look directly at Sam.

He's here for me.

There was no other explanation for this man to be
in the Austin suburb of Lakehaven. Sam was the only
reason.

Sam watched the man wait until the action had moved
toward the opposite basket, and then move quickly to
take a seat on the third row. Sam was certain the assassin had seen him, probably through the glass doors before
entering the gym, and would not telegraph a look toward
Sam. He wore a gray-and-red polo, close to the colors of
Lakehaven Middle School, same as Sam and many other
parents there. Trying to blend in. Not be noticed.

Strike and leave.

"Your boy's on fire!" crowed the hearty dad, Matt, and Sam just nodded and smiled. He saw Daniel glance at him—*Dad, are you watching?*—and Sam nodded and smiled again.

He glanced at the game clock. Two minutes left in game time. If the assassin was going to make his move, he'd wait for the crowd to thin—the players' parents, and the team itself, were the last to leave. Sam would have to get Daniel and everyone else clear of danger, see if another parent could take Daniel to their house, manufacture a quick little lie. Stay behind and get rid of this guy.

Or Sam could walk out right now; the killer would follow surely. And then the departing crowd might find the man's body in the parking lot. It wasn't enough time to dispose of a body. He was unarmed at the moment, but he had a Glock and a combat knife hidden in his SUV.

But the man might not take the bait, and other parents would wonder why he was bolting at the end of such a close game.

Lakehaven down by two points. Daniel stole the ball and drove toward the basket, got it stolen right back from him. Daniel's face wore that look of frustrated concentration that Sam knew well.

The other team scored; one of Daniel's teammates and best friends, James, responded with a fast score. Down two again. A foul against the other team, but the shooter missed the free throws. Sam risked a glance toward the assassin.

The man remained in place, apparently mesmerized by a middle school basketball game.

Who sent you?

Thirty seconds left. Two points down. His friend James stole the ball, drove, scored. Tied game.

Next to Sam, Matt, who was James's dad, whooped as if he were at the Super Bowl and not watching a bunch of thirteen-year-olds.

Sam's gaze locked on the assassin. Worst case: Sam killed him in front of people. It would mean the end of their lives here in Lakehaven, being resettled elsewhere by the government, uprooting Daniel's life and explaining finally to him what Dad really did for a living. He watched the assassin lean toward another parent, say something, laugh.

Ten seconds. Daniel had the ball. Attempted the shot. The ball bounced, rolled on the rim... and went in.

The Lakehaven crowd erupted into cheers; Daniel was mobbed by his teammates. In the heady celebration of victory, of the first time he'd ever made the winning shot, he turned to see his father not looking at him but staring somewhere else, lower on the stands.

"He made it!" Matt yelled in Sam's ear.

Yes. Sam calculated the odds. That meant people would be around his son—coaches, parents, excited players, and students. That meant the assassin couldn't get near Daniel. So Sam could lure the man outside into the darkness.

Now the two teams lined up for their handshakes.

Sam watched the assassin stand, clapping like the other adults. Now the man looked up at Sam. Gazes met. Then the assassin looked back at the court, stopped clapping, crossed his arms.

Crossed arms made it slower for him to produce a weapon. Sam stared.

"Wow, Daniel's improved so much," Matt said to Sam. "Did you get him a private coach?"

Sam kept his gaze on the assassin. "No, we just practiced more when I was home," Sam said. Matt was patting Sam on the back, as if Sam had scored the points.

The two teams did their walk-by handshakes. Daniel didn't look up at Sam as his team retreated to a corner of the gym and had their postgame meeting with their coach. Most of the crowd began filtering out of the gym. The assassin stayed put, no one interacting with him.

Waiting.

Sam let the words of the other parents wash over him: the excitement, the complaining about the coaching, why hadn't so-and-so gotten more playing time (it never failed to amaze Sam what parents would say in front of each other when it came to sports). One of the moms started talking to Sam, reminding him he was due to work the concessions booth next week at the A team game (Daniel was on the B team). He turned, smiled, nodded, started making his way down the risers toward where the assassin stood.

Get him out, away from everyone. On the opposite side of the parking lot was a pedestrian exit that fed out to a tree-covered hillside. Dark, quiet. He glanced over at his son, who had his back to him, and thought: *This will not be the last time I see you.*

The assassin walked toward him. Now with both hands full. One holding a red-and-gray pom-pom some of the students had been waving during the game, the other hand holding an envelope.

A peace sign.

Sam stepped toward him, away from the other parents, no one paying attention to them now.

"Mr. Capra," he said.

"I know what you are," Sam said, putting a cordial smile on his face.

"Do you?" He had a low, careful voice. Vague accent, the kind an American who lives in Europe for a long time tends to pick up.

"I saw you. In Paris. Six years ago. We were both

dispatched for the same job due to crossed wires with intel agencies. You got to the target first." He shrugged. "Clean, efficient job you did."

The assassin's smile didn't waver, and he didn't seem upset Sam mentioned such a delicate subject in a crowded high school gym. He was about ten years older than Sam, gray touching his black hair. "I moved into management in Section K, I don't do...that...anymore...Like you, I am now a fixer of problems. I need your help."

"I'm not sure I believe you. I'm leaving now with my son. Do not follow us. If Section K needs me, they can contact me through regular channels."

"Actually, they can't, Sam. Not this time. Because there can't be a trace of what this job is about. No records, no communications, no history. Completely dark."

"You show up at my son's game and you want to talk shop?"

"Get your son settled for the evening. And then walk down to your neighborhood's mailbox station. We need to talk. I mean you and him no harm." He held up the pom-pom. "Your boy's got a nice shot."

The assassin turned and left.

2

SAM WATCHED THE (FORMER) ASSASSIN head out to the parking lot through the gym doors.

The postgame meeting was done and Daniel walked up to his dad. Daniel let Sam put his arm around his shoulders, pull him close.

"Proud of you," Sam said. "Great game."

"Thanks," Daniel said, not looking at him. Sam hugged him tighter than usual and could tell it was embarrassing Daniel, so he let his son go.

"You can call your grandparents when we get home. I know they'll be sorry they missed it." Sam's father, Alex, had just been released from the hospital, and he and Sam's mom, Simone, had not come to the game.

"Okay." Now Daniel glanced up at him. "Are you all right?"

"Yes. Fine. Super proud of you." He ruffled his son's hair.

"Sam?" Matt came up to them, with James, his son. He high-fived Daniel. "I got video of Daniel's last shot, since James passed it to him...if you want it, I can airdrop it to your phone." He smiled brightly.

"Sure, thanks," Sam said. He was sure to bring out his "dad" phone from his pocket. He had another phone in his pocket that would not accept files from a stranger, that was armored and a veritable digital fortress. That was the work phone Section K had given him.

Matt sent the video file to Sam's dad phone, and they watched it.

"Great pass, James," Sam said to James, who smiled.

"I knew if I could get it to Daniel, he'd score. He was on fire tonight."

"Well, thanks for this. His grandparents had to miss the game and I know they'll be thrilled."

Another parent, a mom Sam didn't know well, hovered nearby.

"Hi," Sam said.

"Hi, I'm Annie, Hunter's mom. Great game."

"Thanks."

"Quick question, we're organizing an end-of-season party for the team—can you or your wife help with that? Should I talk with her?"

"I'm a widower," he said, and Daniel looked away.

"Oh. I'm sorry." Always the slight look of shock, because Sam was only in his mid-thirties.

Sam nodded, to ease the awkwardness. "But yeah, Annie, can you please e-mail me the details and I'm happy to help. I do have to travel a fair amount for my work, and sometimes unexpectedly, but I can do the lifting on parts that aren't as time-sensitive."

"Sure. What's your work?"

"I own a number of bars and nightclubs."

"Oh, cool, here in town?"

"No. All over. America, Europe, Asia."

"Oh. Wow. How interesting." Annie gave him a cautious smile. "Well, I'll be in touch for the parent party committee, then. You seem to be a natural choice for that."

Sam fake-laughed. "Yes. We'll all need a libation at the end of the season."

"Well, great game, Daniel. Nice to meet you, Sam." Annie sailed off to recruit her next volunteer.

"C'mon, James, let's get you to the burger joint," Matt said. "Y'all coming?"

"Oh, is the team going?" Sam asked.

"We don't have to go, Dad," Daniel said.

"Matt, could Daniel ride with you? I have to make an overseas business call and it might take a while." As a dad, he should go. The dads and moms would sit at a separate group of tables, bond, chat about their kids. Part of the experience. Normally he went, but he'd only been in town for three other games.

Unfortunately, a (former) assassin awaited.

"Sure," Matt said. "No problem. I can bring him home if you don't make it to the burger place. School night, so we'll be quick."

"Thank you. Daniel, you got money?"

"I'm covered," Daniel said. He seemed relieved.

Sam watched them leave, gave them a little last wave. Hamburgers and milkshakes. This was the settled life he'd wanted for his son, the one he'd never gotten in his own childhood.

Then he went to meet with the killer.

3

THE MAILBOXES FOR THE WHOLE street Sam lived on stood together, in a station in front of a densely wooded entrance to the neighborhood's greenbelt, which led down to a large creek and a wildlife preserve. The neighborhood was on the edge of Lakehaven, closer to Austin than the outlying suburbs.

He'd called his boss in the government unit he worked for: the Federal Intelligence Analysis Office. A man named Seaforth, who had pulled Sam from the wreckage of his post-CIA life and given him a purpose. The Federal Intelligence Analysis Office supposedly existed to help federal agencies better understand their data. It did that important work, but behind its quiet statisticians and unassuming, bland office space in DC, it also served as a front for a top-secret intel agency code-named Section K: a team of fixers, of former CIAers, of intel misfits who needed a second chance to serve their country.

"I got approached by a guy I recognized," he said to Seaforth. "The kind who fixes problems with an extremely direct approach."

"Woodruff," Seaforth said. "He just got assigned to Section K. He asked me for your contact info, for a face-to-face."

"You couldn't warn me?"

"I was told to say nothing and to ask no questions."

Sam didn't like this. "You're not involved?"

"Apparently not," Seaforth said. "It's above my pay scale. But I know Woodruff, and he's solid and reliable."

"I'll call you after I talk to him."

"No, Sam, you won't. He'll tell you not to. I can give you permission to use your resources: your bars, their financial accounts, your network connected to them. If you accept the assignment. If you don't, we don't ever talk about it again."

He didn't like this. Bob Seaforth was one of the best people Sam had ever known in intel work, and Sam trusted him. Seaforth being shut out didn't ring right with him.

"All right," Sam said.

"Good luck, Sam."

And Seaforth hung up.

Sam slipped the phone into his pocket. He could see, from the streetlight, anyone approaching on foot or by car; if you wanted to have a private conversation outside and not risk a neighbor overhearing, Woodruff had chosen well. He'd clearly surveilled the neighborhood before making his request.

He waited. The night was dark but eventually he could see Woodruff approaching him, on foot, no longer dressed in the team colors, but now wearing a dark shirt. The other man stopped.

"I'm sorry that recognizing me caused you any concern," he said. "You can call me Woodruff."

Sam decided not to say he already knew the man's name. Just leave Seaforth out of this. "What do you want?"

"We have a problem that needs your—and my—expertise to fix."

"What's the problem?"

"Markus Bolt."

The name silenced Sam. He forgot to breathe for a few moments. The night, cool, pressed against them both.

"Is he dead?" Sam asked. "Finally?"

"We're not sure. He's vanished."

"From Russia?"

"Yes. Obviously he doesn't travel elsewhere."

"There's been nothing on the news."

"We have this information from a source inside Russia, a solid, high-placed one. Bolt dropped out of sight from Moscow two days ago and no one realized it until yesterday, their time. No sign of foul play so far, and we didn't snatch him, so we're assuming he's running. The Russians are frantic to find him. They've said nothing publicly, of course. Not sure if the British or the French or the Germans know, and we're not sharing this news with our friends yet. He'll be the most hunted man in the world when the news breaks. Everyone will want him, dead or alive. But we're getting him first."

"I can't go hunting after Markus Bolt."

"You're not. Your assignment is to watch his daughter Amanda."

"You think he'll head to her?"

"Either Amanda or her mother. They're his only family. It's a possibility."

Sam shook his head. "There's no way he'll come back to America. No reason to risk it."

"Traitors don't often make great decisions. Maybe he regrets what he did. Maybe he just wants to see his family again." Woodruff shrugged. "I knew him slightly. He did like to talk about his kids, the three times I met with him."

So this was a surveillance job, where it was rather

unlikely that the main target would show up. "It doesn't seem like she would be interested in seeing him."

"We don't believe that she's been in contact with him since he defected thirteen years ago. We just need you to watch her. We are trying to minimize the number of people involved. We want this chance to find him and question him ourselves, without the world knowing. So very few Americans know this news, fewer than ten right now, including you. Section K will handle Bolt."

"Define *handle*."

"Capture him and debrief him."

"Not kill him? He wrecked so many lives." Bolt had exposed a large number of intel assets to the Russians when he defected, both American and allied, and several of them had vanished or died. Others had their intel careers destroyed.

"We want him alive, if possible." Woodruff fell silent as footsteps approached—a neighbor of Sam's, walking her dog.

"Hey, Sam," the woman said.

"Hey, Melissa," Sam said. She had her flashlight and she cast her light up on Sam and Woodruff, at their legs.

"You doing good?" she asked as her dog strained to keep walking and she slowed.

"Just fine," Sam said. Woodruff said nothing. The neighbor kept going and Woodruff waited until she was another block away before speaking.

"Suburbia," he asked. "How do you stand it?"

"Where is Amanda Bolt?"

"Miami. She went through some bad times as a kid after her father defected. She lives with a boyfriend, she is part owner of a small business with him. We've not kept steady eyes on her for years. Never thought there was a need."

"And I do what?"

He handed Sam an envelope, the same one Sam had noticed him holding at the game. "Details inside. Right now, you're a babysitter. You don't approach her. You don't talk to her unless she talks to you. You absolutely don't tell her that her father's dropped out of sight and could be on his way back from Russia for a cozy family reunion."

"And if he shows up?"

"I don't think she'll welcome him, but obviously our psychologists have profiled her and seeing him, unexpectedly, would be such a profound shock that she might well talk to him. Amanda was just a kid when she had to deal with the fallout of his crimes, so she might want an explanation. She might want to hear his rationale before she rejects him."

"And if he shows up?" Sam asked again.

"Contact us and take him into custody."

"Custody. I don't see a badge or pair of handcuffs in my kit."

"You're worried about law and order now?"

"I'm worried about consequences once he gets a lawyer."

"Sam." Woodruff flexed a very small smile. "Markus shows up, you grab him, you give him to Section K. He will vanish. It won't be a news story. The Russians will never be sure that we have him or we don't. This will make them very nervous. Let them sweat the way we did when he defected. He'll be kept in some dark hole, our country's latest and greatest secret. He's close to the ruling circle in Russia. He might be able to give us quite a bit of information."

"You almost sound excited."

"I lost friends because of that guy. Exposed, caught, murdered. He gutted a dozen operations at the CIA."

"So if he shows up to see Amanda, I detain him."

"You call me, we'll extract him, and then you come home."

"And what about Amanda?"

"What about her?"

"Say her father makes contact with her. She knows he's in America. Suddenly he disappears again? What's to keep her from going to the press or her elected representative or the police?"

"Then maybe you should make sure he doesn't reach her. Catch him on his approach to her. Watch her, but also watch who approaches her. He might have help. He might try and reach out to her himself, but that means him getting close and you need to grab him first. Assuming he has any interest in her at all. You may just be sitting in Miami for a few days until his body turns up elsewhere because the Russians eliminated him first."

Sam glanced up at the moon, peering down from above the trees. "Why would he do this now? Why give up a comfortable life in Russia with his billionaire buddies?"

"Maybe life wasn't comfortable. Maybe he pissed off his hosts and he had to run. Maybe he had unfinished business here. Considering he's a traitorous piece of garbage, does it matter?"

"Worst case: what am I supposed to do, gun down her father in front of her if he resists?"

He snorted. "If that happens, we'll deal with it. You seem very concerned about her."

"She was a child who had to carry the sins of her father. People are cruel." And that was all Sam was willing to say to this man.

"No one crueler than her father. Read the file. Then

get on a flight tomorrow morning to Miami. Isn't one of your bars there?"

"You know about the bars?"

Woodruff smiled. "I like a nice drink after work." He turned away and vanished into the night.

Sam stood for a moment. Then he checked his mailbox, using his phone as a flashlight. Water bill, a real estate agent's promo piece, a fund-raiser envelope for the Lakehaven school system, a direct mail postcard from a local orthodontist. Sam had made a normal life here. He did the occasional job for Section K, but mostly he ran his bars. It was a good life, and while he wanted Markus Bolt caught and tried for his crimes, he didn't want to be playing guard dog for Bolt's daughter for however long it might take.

Maybe there's another reason they asked you to stop a traitor, he thought. He pushed the idea away. After so many years, it sometimes still felt like he was being tested, measured.

Because of Lucy.

A car drove past him and stopped a block away at his house. In the porchlight, he saw his son get out of the car, say thanks to Matt, and go inside the house.

Matt turned around and drove off once Daniel was inside the house. Sam waved, but in the darkness, he didn't see him.

It was always hard to leave Daniel, he thought. Harder for something like this. Leave on a business trip and come back with blood on your hands. Hey, son, I have to go see how my bar in Miami is doing. And also maybe kill a traitor. Woodruff might have made noises about detaining Bolt, but the message was clear to Sam: Kill Bolt if he had to. He could not be allowed to escape.

Sam Capra headed back toward his house from the mailboxes, not seeing the figure deep in the shadows, the person watching his movements from the darkness of the wooded greenbelt, watching him hurry toward the most important person in his life.

4

"GREAT GAME," SAM SAID AS he came into the kitchen. Daniel was sitting at his usual spot at the kitchen table, his school tablet hooked up to a keyboard, working on an assignment. Lakehaven had a very strong school district academically, and there was a lot of homework and special projects assigned. During basketball season, it was a challenge for Daniel to stay ahead.

"Thanks," Daniel said, not looking up.

"Seriously, I'm proud of you. How you've applied yourself to improving your shooting and your defense."

"Thanks," Daniel said again.

"How was RJ's?" That was the name of the burger place the basketball team favored.

"Fine," he said. Still not looking up.

We're deep in monosyllabic land, Sam thought.

Sam set the envelope Woodruff had given him down on the table across from his son. "Are you mad at me?"

"No."

"That's really great, because I wanted to apologize to you for how I acted at the game."

Daniel didn't look up.

"I'm sorry. I got... I got an upsetting message right at the end there, and I shouldn't have checked my phone, I should've focused on you."

"It was my big moment, Dad, and you didn't care." His voice was soft.

"I do care. I care so much. And I'm really sorry. You've played so well, Daniel, and win or lose, I'm proud of you but...you were amazing tonight."

For a moment Daniel looked up at him and broke into a smile. Sam felt the punch in his heart. Everything he'd been through with Lucy, her crimes, her betrayal, from it he had Daniel, and Daniel was worth all the pain in the world.

"Are you going to be mad at me if I tell you I'm having to go out of town and it might be for several days?"

The smile faded. "Is that what your message was about?"

"Yes. There's a problem at one of the bars, I've got to deal with it myself."

"Can I stay here alone?"

"You cannot."

"I'm old enough."

"You're not staying here alone. I'm not comfortable with that."

"You just said all the nice stuff before you dropped this on me."

"All of it's true."

"Do I have to go stay at Nana and Papa's?"

"No. Since Papa's recovering from surgery, I think they've got their hands full." Sam's father, Alex, had begun to slip into dementia last year, and he'd just put his arm through a glass pane in the back door, necessitating surgery to repair a damaged tendon. Sam's mom, Simone, was a retired doctor and preferred to monitor and control every aspect of her husband's treatment. Sam and Daniel saw them often, as they only lived fifteen minutes away, but it was increasingly fraught, with his father's confusion and his mother's insistence that he wasn't getting worse. "I'm going to ask Leonie to stay with you."

"Or I could come with you. Where are you going?"

"You can't miss school. I'm going to Miami." There was no point in lying to him about his destination. He owned a bar in Miami, so it was a logical cover.

"What's the problem with the bar there?"

This was the first time Daniel had asked about his reason for travel. Normally when Sam went to visit his bars (or had a clandestine op to conduct, using his bar ownership as his cover), Daniel shrugged it off. "It's losing a lot of money and I need to figure out why."

The lie was easy to tell. But it was still a lie.

"Leonie's not my nanny anymore, Dad," Daniel said. "She has a life of her own."

"I know. Did she tell you to say that?"

"No." Daniel gave him a look of disbelief, the kind only a teenager could muster.

"Do you have a preference? Leonie or stay with a friend?"

Daniel surrendered. "Leonie."

"I'll call her and ask. If it's a friend, who?"

"Not sure. You can't just dump me on people with such short notice, Dad."

"I am not dumping you." Sam struggled not to sound argumentative. His brain was full of the details required to hunt down a trained operative, a traitor, like Markus Bolt, and he was debating housing logistics with a middle schooler. "I'm doing my best to be sure you're taken care of when I have to be gone."

"Or you could just get a normal dad job. Sell the bars and be at home."

This was a new kind of suggestion. Daniel was full of surprises tonight. "What is a normal dad job that I am suited for, Daniel?" He was curious.

"You could sell insurance or work as a consultant or . . . I don't know. Matt works at some kind of marketing firm, I think."

A shift in the air thrummed between them. The teenager not wanting to admit that he didn't want his dad to leave, to be gone so much, and the longing for the more normal life Daniel saw with his friends and their parents around him.

"I could try those jobs, but I'm not sure I'd be good at them. I like my job because I'm good at it. Do you not want me to go?" That would be a new intel community excuse to make to someone like Woodruff. *Sorry, my kid doesn't want me to find your traitor for you.*

"You're here but . . . you're not here. Like at the game tonight."

Sam took a deep breath. *Sorry, I saw a known assassin enter the gym, knew he was there for me, and was trying to watch him so no one else was endangered. So you were safe.*

Those were words he could never say. "I'm sorry," Sam said.

"I know it's just you doing it all for us," Daniel said. "You're doing your best but I wish you didn't travel so much." Now he looked at Sam, and his face was so much like Lucy's, it made Sam's heart hurt. Daniel was thirteen now. In five years, he'd be gone off to college. Maybe he'd come home during the summers, maybe not. Maybe he'd get a job postgraduation in Austin, maybe not. Time ticked past, and if you stood there, you wasted it. Sam felt sometimes he had wasted so much.

"I'll try to do better. But this trip, it's not a problem I can foist off on someone else or say no to."

"And when I'm older, I'll understand. Got it."

There was something else at play here, something else that had the usually steady Daniel riled. "Is everything else okay? School all right?"

"Yes, fine."

"Is it about a girl?"

"Wow, Dad. Really, everything is fine." He stomped upstairs.

A real talent, that, being able to zero in on what his son's issue was and offer brilliant paternal advice. The little boy who used to run to him when he came through the front door, the stink of his dirty work done in Finland or South Africa or Brazil washed off him, and the warm embrace of his child that pushed back every bad memory, every regret. *Daddy, Daddy, guess what I did while you were gone?* The little boy wasn't running to him now; he was running from him.

Sam called Leonie, who had for years been the closest maternal figure Daniel knew. Her staying with Daniel had enabled Sam to do his intelligence work for years, without worry, until Daniel got old enough to start asking questions about Dad's travel and times away.

But then Leonie, nanny, had met Matt, the other single father in the neighborhood, and that was that.

He hoped Leonie could keep Daniel. She was part of the shield he'd carefully built around his son. He needed Daniel . . . not to ask questions.

5

Moscow

K<small>IRILL HAD BROUGHT FLOWERS FOR</small> Mama—red carnations for patriotism—and her favorite honey cake because he could tell that her depression was returning when he talked to her on the phone a few days ago. He'd been busy on an assignment in Japan, the hit had gone well and cleanly, and when he called her again, and she didn't answer her phone, he could imagine her sprawled on the coach, too blue to move. He was a good son; he knew how to cheer her up. Carnations, cake, a pot of tea, and her relief at his safe return.

But...there was a guard he didn't recognize at the gate, and as he drove up the long drive to the estate house, there were several cars he didn't recognize parked in front. And a government van.

Carrying the flowers and the honey cake box, he ran up the steps. The front door was locked. A sinking feeling nestled in his stomach. He rang the doorbell.

Neither Mama nor Markus answered the door. It was an older man, stern-faced. It took Kirill a couple of moments to recognize him.

Duderov. The special assistant to President Morozov.

The younger agents, like Kirill, who were more connected to Western culture, called him the "Dude." But not to his face.

"What is it?" Kirill said. "What's happened? Is my mother all right?" A cold dread seized his guts. If Markus had hurt her...

The Dude's voice was low. "Come inside, Kirill Denisovich. Are you alone? No girlfriend waiting in the car?" The Dude looked past his shoulder.

"I'm alone," Kirill said. He stepped into the home and moved past Duderov. "Where is my mother?"

"She's fine. She's in her room, resting."

Kirill walked into the den. He saw a man and a woman, both senior operations agents he knew, searching through the bookshelves. Mama was very neat, orderly, and now the books spilled out over the floor. A stack of framed photos that normally shared the shelves with the books were stacked on a chair, taken from their frames. The television had been taken down from its mount on the wall and another woman was removing the back cover, searching for something. They all glanced at him as he stood next to Duderov, staring.

"Where is Markus?" Kirill asked.

"Let's talk. Before you see your mother."

He's dead, Kirill thought. *The old American bastard is dead and Mama will be a wreck. But why are they searching the house?*

The Dude steered Kirill into his old bedroom.

"What's happened?" Kirill said. Bracing himself.

"Your stepfather has vanished. Either someone has taken him or"—here the Dude cleared his throat—"he has left Russia."

Kirill stared. Then he laughed, a short, sudden

guffaw. "Where would he go? The rest of the world is closed to him."

"We don't know. Why would he leave our loving embrace?"

Kirill turned to walk out, to go find Mama, and Duderov put a hand on his arm. Kirill looked at it. And then looked back at the Dude. He released Kirill's arm, but like it was his idea.

"Your mother says she knows nothing, and I want to believe her. She said he said he was going to Sochi for a fishing trip with Illya Markarkin. He packed light. There is no trace that he boarded a flight to Sochi. She called Markarkin and it was a surprise to him that she thought Markus was there."

"Then someone grabbed him. The Americans have wanted their revenge for years."

"And he's been here for years, and they've let him be because it would be a huge incident to attack or kidnap him on Russian soil. So why would they now?"

"You think...he left Russia? Why? He's a dead man walking to the Americans." *That means he's left my mother, too. The bastard. The unforgivable bastard. How dare he hurt Mama.*

"I thought you might know his motivations."

Kirill was careful to keep his face expressionless. "Markus and I are not particularly close."

"Even though you were instructed to improve your relationship."

"He married my mother when I was fifteen. Our... relationship was established then. It has not varied much. We are polite to each other. For my mother's sake."

"I need your help, Kirill."

Kirill waited.

"We have kept his disappearance top secret. No press. No announcement even to the close circle around

Morozov. The West doesn't know. The people in this house know and fewer than five others."

"Why stay silent? Alert the Americans; they'll be glad to kill him." He kept his voice low, should Mama emerge from her room or wherever in the house they were keeping her.

"I thought you were smarter than this. They won't kill him. They'll capture him, question him, get him to talk about his years deep in the Russian elite. It would be a disaster for us." The Dude cleared his throat. "He's a traitor. It's a taint in the brain if you ask me. He will betray us as surely as he betrayed them."

Kirill nodded. "As he has betrayed my mother." A cold anger surged in him. *I was right. I was always right about him.*

"I want you to find him. Bring him back to us."

Kirill shook his head.

"You're his stepson. You can reason with him."

"Send someone else and send them to kill him before he can talk."

"If you persuade him to return, fine. If you cannot, then you must eliminate him." Duderov smiled.

Kirill kept his face impassive and chose his words with care. "He is my stepfather and I wouldn't hurt my mother that way."

"You could free Sonia Timofeyevna of him. Or return him to her. You would be a hero, Kirill Denisovich."

Kirill had never wanted a job less. They could not ask this of him, he thought, but of course they would. "Let me see my mother."

The Dude smiled. "Of course." He led Kirill to his mother's bedroom, as if he were a guest in his own mother's home.

Two men were slowly dismantling chairs and furniture, looking for hidden compartments. Looking for some trace where Markus had gone.

Mama was sitting on the bed amid the destruction, clutching an old, faded shirt of Markus's, looking lost. She looked up at her son and a wave of humiliation passed over her face. "He's gone. Or he was taken. Maybe they took him. The damned Americans. They took him." It was a refuge for an abandoned wife.

"Please," Kirill said to the searchers, and at the Dude's nod, they walked out and shut the door behind them. The Dude, of course, stayed.

"They are looking for some sign that he had plans to leave. Help to leave, or information to buy his life. A flash drive, a phone, a bank account number. It's ridiculous. He was taken. I told Mikhail"—she gestured at the Dude—"that he *must* have been taken."

"We have to consider all possibilities, Sonia Timofeyevna," the Dude said in a soothing voice.

Kirill sat next to her, put his arm around her. "Mama." He kissed her forehead. "They will find him."

"Kirill will find him," the Dude said quietly, and Kirill pretended not to hear him.

"He told me he was going fishing in Sochi. With Illya Markarkin. He's done that before, they're good friends."

"I will speak to Markarkin, see what he knows," Kirill said. He had to promise some action to Mama.

"Where else would he have gone? Perhaps...it must be another woman." Mama steeled her voice. "I would not be happy but perhaps I could forgive that, after some time." She jabbed a finger at Duderov. "If my house has been torn up over some whore of his, I will need a new house. As nice as this one, Mikhail."

Kirill glanced at Duderov. "I don't think it's that, Mama," Kirill said. "Tell me what he's done in recent days. Did you notice anything?" He wished Duderov would leave, but then he decided the searchers had probably planted a bug in here for Duderov as soon as they began their work.

"Our lives have been quiet. He wasn't feeling good. His stomach was upset. He took it easy. He read, he watched TV. He didn't have briefings in the past couple of weeks." Sonia Timofeyevna patted Kirill's hand. "You know, he still got briefings. Where the intel czars and czarinas tell him what they've learned about the Americans, and he interprets it and gives them his analysis of what it might mean. He's very valuable to them. To Bobo. He didn't have a briefing last week, but he met with Bobo for lunch."

Bobo was Yuri Boborin—Markus's handler, responsible for his happiness as a defector. Kirill would speak to him.

"You said he didn't feel well."

"Vomiting, stomach pain. Very pale, sweaty. I thought it was a virus, so I made him chicken soup with potatoes and noodles. Like I make for you, sweetie, when you're sick." She touched Kirill's cheek.

"But then he felt better?"

"He saw his doctor."

"Who is…" the Dude said.

"Dr. Rudenko."

The Dude went to the door, opened it a crack, spoke to one of his underlings in a soft whisper, and then shut the door. Mama watched the Dude and waited for him to resume paying attention to her, and then spoke. "He said he had to get away. So he would go to the Black Sea and fish with Illya Markarkin." She grabbed Kirill's hand. "Is he dead? Did Bobo kill him?"

"Markus might…have left the country."

She laughed again at this. "No one likes him outside Russia. Where would he go?"

"America," the Dude said. "Maybe he defected back to America."

Mama stared, then collapsed into tears. "No, no. Markus! Are you saying I will never see him again?"

She sobbed, and Kirill stroked her hair and murmured reassurances to her. The Dude walked out. He returned with a stern-faced woman with a medical bag. She examined Sonia Timofeyevna, took her temperature and blood pressure, and gave her a sedative shot. Mama protested, saying she wanted to talk to Bobo, find out why Markus had left.

"I'll stay with her," the woman told Kirill. He kissed his mother's forehead and walked outside with the Dude. He felt dizzy, and angry, and he needed to hit something. Or someone.

"Where is Boborin?" Kirill asked. He made sure his voice didn't shake with rage.

"He's at the headquarters."

"Does he know Markus is missing?"

"Yes."

Because now Kirill had started to think through the ramifications, not only to his family, but to his nation. This was about Mama, but it was bigger than Mama. If Markus decided to run—how much damage could he do to Russia? He had been a pet, paraded around, debriefed, asked for his insights and analysis into the Western intel agencies.

Markus knew much of what Russia knew. Worse, he knew what Russia didn't know. The pet could have turned on its master.

"Sir! Sir!" One of the searchers came rushing down the stairs. "I found this, well-hidden in the guest bedroom, under a floorboard." She held aloft a phone. "A burner phone, I think. It has only called one number. In America."

The Dude seized it from her and looked at the code. "That's an area code for Miami. He's been in contact with someone there."

"His daughter, Amanda. Or his ex-wife, Karen," Kirill said. "They both live in Miami, last Markus told me."

The Dude, already pale, got paler. "But better them than the CIA."

"We don't know who the family is talking to, though," Kirill said.

The Dude resumed his look of barely contained misery.

"I want to talk to Bobo," Kirill said. "Now."

6

Austin

DURING HER YEARS CARING FOR Daniel, Leonie had never quite fit in with the other Lakehaven nannies. She was a bit older than the usual Lakehaven *au pair*, she had gone to art school, and for an unpleasant stretch of time she had been the chief identity forger for a global criminal syndicate. (That wasn't a detail she ever shared with the other nannies.) Sam had extricated her from that life. Leonie, hurting from her own losses, had found solace in being a surrogate mom to Daniel, a child she adored.

Then she'd met Matt the Divorced Dad when his son, James, and Daniel were in elementary school together, and they'd married, and moved into a house five minutes away.

Sam called her cell and it went to voice mail; he called Matt's next and Matt answered.

"Hey, buddy! How's the game star?" Matt loved sports.

"He's fine, Matt, thanks."

"That last shot…" And Matt made a noise like a chef's kiss.

"Thanks, Matt. Is Leonie there?"

"Nope. She's out getting her evening walk with our neighbor."

"I hate to ask, but I've had an emergency come up and I've got to go to Miami. Could the game star stay with y'all or Leonie stay over here for a few days?"

"I'll check with her. Let me have her call you back."

"How's she feeling?"

"Baby kicking up a storm yesterday."

"Oh, that's great, Matt."

"What's in Miami?" Matt asked, and as Sam turned, Daniel was standing in front of him, having just come downstairs.

"Just an issue with my bar there that needs some attention."

"Global entertainment empire. I love it." Matt often said things like this and it made Sam sometimes wonder what quiet, thoughtful Leonie saw in Matt's gabby loudness. *Opposites attract*, he thought. Plus, he was in no position to question her choices. He had made the worst possible choices in his relationships.

"I don't know about empire. More like scattered holdings."

"I saw Annie cozying up to you. You know she's divorced?"

"We were just talking."

"Now that I'm off the market"—Matt laughed—"I think you're the next HSD."

"The what?"

"Hot Single Dad. I am reliably informed that is the term." Matt laughed again.

Sam rolled his eyes. "And I am reliably informed I am not that. Anyway, I don't have time to date." He couldn't. He and Lucy had shared a life because they were both in the CIA during the marriage. He now worked for the most secret, discreet team in American intel. Sam couldn't imagine being married to someone and concealing that aspect of his life. He hadn't tried to have another relationship in the past few years. He and Leonie had slept together once—twelve years ago—but that had been fueled by desperation and fear and loneliness. (And Matt didn't know this.) They weren't a good match as a couple and had never tried to make that work. He was sometimes aware that the moms in his son's class eyed him and thought of him for their single sisters, or friends, or coworkers, and he had gently rebuffed the attempts to connect him with Ellen's cousin or Diana's college roommate.

He'd made his choice about his life and who he let into it. Even though Daniel sometimes wondered aloud why Dad didn't date.

"All right. I'll text Leonie and she'll text you back," Matt said.

"Thanks." He hung up.

"Trying to dump me somewhere?" Daniel said. He went to the fridge, pulled out a bottled orange juice, popped the top, and drank.

"Leonie, as we discussed."

"And if she says no, then I can stay here alone, right?"

"I said no."

"Dad. Leonie is five minutes away. I'm not the kid who's going to have friends over and get drunk or high. I can get my meals from a delivery service or I can make a sandwich."

"I don't know how long I might be gone and I'm not comfortable leaving you here." What if he died on a mission like this? He tried to imagine Seaforth, someone with a Federal Intelligence Analysis Office card, coming to the front door and Daniel, all alone, answering it and them saying: *I'm so very sorry, Daniel, but your father...*

"It'd be fine, Dad. I promise."

His doorbell rang. He answered. Leonie, seven months pregnant, frowning at him.

"What's the problem?" Leonie came in from the porch, her hand resting on her prominent baby bump. She smiled at Daniel. "Hey, I heard you were the superstar tonight."

"Matt's my fan club president," Daniel said. "Tell Dad I'll be fine here alone."

"He'll be fine here alone," Leonie said. "Not really, but he asked me to tell you that."

Daniel rolled his eyes.

"How are you feeling?" Sam asked.

"Fine. Energetic. I went for a walk with a friend and we were coming up on your house when Matt texted so I sent her on her way."

"You want some water?"

She shook her head. "Daniel, go upstairs and let me see what I can work out with your dad."

Daniel started to speak and then thought better of it. He went up the stairs.

Sam waited until he heard the soft closing of Daniel's bedroom door. "Can he stay with y'all for a few?"

"Is this about a job for Section K?" Leonie, having once been a part of that world, was his only friend who knew of his secret work.

Reflexively Sam glanced up the stairs. No sign of Daniel.

"Obviously," Leonie said. "For how long?"

"A few days."

"Dangerous?"

"Possibly."

"Have you considered . . . not doing this to him?"

"Leonie. It's a yes-or-no question. Can you stay here with him, or can he stay with you and Matt?"

She ran a hand along her belly bump. "He can stay with us, I think."

Something in her tone caught his ear—a hesitancy. "I'm sorry if Daniel is a distraction. I can make other arrangements."

"Matt and James love having Daniel around." She took a deep breath. "You know Matt's ex, she's had a lot of problems staying sober, and the court's not letting James see her until she gets back in a program, and James is just having a rough time." She sighed. "And he's about to become a big brother, and it's a lot. But maybe having a friend like Daniel around will help."

"Well, I appreciate it more than I can say." He realized this was likely the last time he could ask her for help; once the baby arrived, Leonie couldn't come and be a de facto parent to Daniel when he needed her to. She had a new family, full of their own problems and issues and joys. Matt's jollity was maybe a cover for what he was dealing with as a dad.

"You being able to help makes me able to do this job," he said quietly. "Thank you."

"Yeah, and because of that, I should say no, but I'd rather watch over Daniel than have someone else do it. You're leaving tomorrow?"

"Yes."

"I'll take good care of him. You take good care of you." She paused like she wanted to say more. He waited. But she just shook her head slightly.

Leonie hugged Sam and left. He went upstairs, knocked on Daniel's door. Daniel was lying across his bed, reading a book for English. "You'll stay at Leonie's. You'll have fun with James."

"Fine," Daniel said, not looking at him.

He was mad. So be it. Sam went back downstairs, sat down at the table, and opened the envelope—the homework Woodruff had given him. Inside was a thick folder full of printed reports.

7

––⦿⦿⦿––

I⟊ HAD BEEN A WHILE since Sam had had to read a paper file—most of the profiles he received were digitized and set to self-delete if he didn't trash them. Section K had never sent a paper file to him, much less one delivered by a killer rather than a courier.

But then, this was Markus Bolt. The most special case imaginable.

He opened the folder. Inside was a printed copy of the highlights of Bolt's CIA service file.

Markus Bolt. Now in his mid-fifties. Born in Omaha, raised there and in Los Angeles after his father relocated right before Bolt started high school. He had the spy's advantage of an unremarkable face, one that might be hard to remember. He had joined the CIA straight out of college, where he had triple-majored in history, political science, and Russian—an ideal background for recruitment by the CIA. He joined the agency, and they funded his master's degree in history and his further fluency in Russian. He went to Russia as a field officer, posing as a scientific liaison, covering himself in intelligence glory for ten years until he was badly hurt in a car accident in Moscow. Suspicion was that the Russians knew he was a dangerous spy and staged the accident to get him out of the country. He returned to the US, where he was in charge of running informant rings inside Russia—men and women who would share the secrets not only of the Russian government but also of the billionaire oligarchs who'd so neatly taken over the country with their investments and their bodyguards and their funneling of fortunes around the world. They were now far closer to the levers of power than the sad, unappreciated bureaucrat who needed money or pride, but Markus Bolt worked them all. A maestro of the opposition to Russia's plans.

Until he didn't.

Suddenly, without apparent warning or suspicion, he fled his Washington home, leaving behind his wife and two teenage children. They thought he was going to London for a meeting. He went to Miami instead, where no one was looking for him, and flew from there to London and then to Moscow, where he proclaimed his loyalty to the Russian government, derided the governments of NATO, and gave the Russians a list of operatives from multiple intelligence services working on cases against the Russian leadership—American, British, Canadian, French, German, and more. Names he'd adroitly pulled from access to other intelligence agencies.

People he betrayed without another thought.

He appeared in photographs three more times after his defection: once at Red Square, standing near the Russian president, Morozov; once on a billionaire's yacht sunning in the Caspian Sea; and once on television after his oldest child had committed suicide, in a taped statement, angrily claiming that his son had been killed by the Americans in revenge. Otherwise, he was a ghost—not seen on the streets of Moscow. Not seen in public. It was too big a risk—intel agencies could put a price on his head and send in a killer to finish him. He was a prize to the Russians, and they didn't want to lose him.

The report mentioned he'd married again, to a Russian

woman. Sonia Timofeyevna Antonova, a former Miss Russia (there were photos of her in the evening gown competition), and also the widow of a suspected SRV bureaucrat. He was known to be a friend to the billionaire clique. But Bolt wasn't an ideological trophy the way a traitor like Donald McLean had been. He'd sold out for money, not ideals.

He had not been seen in public in nearly four years.

Sam paged through the rest. There were psychological evaluations, performance reviews (ironically stellar), interviews with his colleagues in the aftermath of the defection where his every move, his every e-mail, his every sneeze had been analyzed.

He had financial problems, the most typical reason for betrayal. People sold out their country for shockingly little. Bolt had argued that his innovative approaches were like running a nimble startup company inside the Agency; he should have been paid more. His wife had a gambling problem—Sam read a statement from her bookie. Bolt himself had expensive tastes—he'd grown up with money and had never readjusted to a more modest government salary.

He had emotional problems. He often spoke to his wife of feeling unappreciated for his talents, for being forced to report to those he considered his intellectual inferiors.

He had ideological problems. Some of his later-revealed communications with Russian assets hinted at too much interest in their personal life, too much admiration for the vast profiteering that the oligarchs indulged in, for their grossly indulgent lifestyles. (Sam decided the author of this part of the file was kind of a prude.)

So many problems, Sam thought, but so few warning signs. It was almost as if Bolt's successes had blinded his colleagues to his shortcomings and his risks. But espionage and intelligence were run by humans: flawed humans who didn't want to think the worst of a colleague who had done so much to protect the West.

He'd gotten away with it until he didn't.

Sam found a handwritten page, unsigned, written in a neat cursive.

The top of the page read: *Markus Bolt—His Traitor's Dance*.

Sam knew the term—a traitor's dance referred to the series of steps taken by a betrayer to cover their tracks, make their escape, and land where they believed they would be safe.

Bolt had not simply run to Russia. He had stolen data from the Agency databases that included information on overseas informants and operatives from the US, the UK, and other allied countries. He had gone home to pack, had argued with his wife, and supposedly left for the airport to go to London. Instead, he went to Miami, where he remained for a day, and then departed Miami for London, under an alias and using a Belgian passport. He boarded a flight to Moscow, called a contact he had at the SVR, and officially defected. He was hidden in the house of one of the billionaires in the unofficial court of elites surrounding the Russian president. The Russians denied that they had him for two weeks, long enough for them to act against those on Bolt's list.

Sam put the paper down.

Why go to Miami first? What was there? It was his wife's hometown, but they weren't living there. Or was it just a dodge, him trying to get lost before he used his fake passport?

Sam's first overseas assignment with the Agency's Special Projects division had been, with Lucy, to London. His focus was on the criminal syndicates whose connections with enemy governments and terrorist groups could pose a threat to American national security. His cover was working for a consulting company that provided an economic front. He had heard stories about men and women in the UK burned by Bolt's defection. Careers ruined, families torn apart, two UK agents who were targeted and killed, their murderers never caught. It could never be laid on the Russian government. But people were dead, lives ruined, families cracked.

All because of this one man.

Markus Bolt would be the most hunted person on the planet if it became widely known that he had left Russia.

Why would he? He had nothing to gain here and everything to lose.

Sam dug into the next section of the file. The Bolt family.

He stared at their pictures for a long time.

The family of a traitor. It was a very limited club. His breath suddenly felt tight in his chest. He glanced up toward the second floor.

He knew what that was like. Except Lucy's treason had never gone public, never reflected on him or Daniel. So, he thought, he didn't know. Not the humiliation of it. But the sheer shock of the betrayal. That he knew.

Wife, Karen; son, Allan; daughter, Amanda. Karen Bolt also worked for the government, at the Pentagon. She was a former military officer who had gone the consulting route after leaving the Army. Patriotic, tough, intelligent. It seemed from her interviews that she could not believe that Markus had not only defected but also spied, and she had never suspected that there was a hint of impropriety. She admitted to the gambling problem; Markus had paid off her debts, but he'd told her he'd gotten loans from friends, and the idea of having to pay people back meant she'd gotten the problem under control. She had a warm, expressive smile in the included photo, one presumably taken before the betrayal.

They always assume the spouse knows. They have to. Lucy's treason should have ended his career; it was only by clearing his own name that he'd had a hope to stay in intel work. But there were still people he had known back then who would never trust him. Not because he didn't know, but because . . . she had so thoroughly fooled him. It spoke to poor judgment on his part, in their minds. It was part of the reason why he worked for Seaforth, along with the other quirky rejects and dropouts from the "regular" intelligence community who ended up in Section K.

They were the leftovers.

Allan Bolt, the son. He was the oldest. Fifteen when his father jumped. He looked like a bright, sensitive kid—there were a range of school photos of him, from first grade through college. He had taken his father's defection very, very hard. He had been bullied in school—beyond psychological intimidation—and physically attacked. The Bolts had had to move from DC to Florida, trying to avoid the press, who fortunately lost interest in them fairly quickly.

Allan had killed himself three years ago, walking into the waters off Islamorada in the Keys. He'd started up a restaurant supply business that was struggling. He'd told his mother that people didn't want to hire him, given his father's actions, and so he'd had to be self-employed and he didn't have a talent for it. He was close to bankruptcy. He'd left a note for his mom and his sister, placed under a stone, next to his car keys and his wallet. A security guard had found the items the next morning. Allan had never married, no kids. His body was not recovered. A copy of the note was attached to a picture of Allan, smiling tentatively, as though he'd forgotten how to smile.

It read, "I suppose I should blame Dad for the life I've had, the never-ending shame of it. But maybe I could have been stronger. I think he was weak, and I got that from him. Why aren't I stronger? I love you, Mom and Amanda. Dad—you won't care but I have nothing to say to you. Nothing." He was twenty-five. An online article reporting on his death called him Markus Bolt's final victim.

Sam couldn't read that and not feel a wrenching surge of emotion. Reading Allan's note made him feel sick.

Never, Daniel. You can never know.

The next section of papers. Amanda, the younger child. Seaforth had nicknamed this kind of targeted surveillance "birdwatching" so Amanda Bolt was his "bird," so to speak. She had been twelve when her father fled to Russia. A government psychologist had talked to her, and she had not known of her father's activities or understood them. She asked when her father would be coming back, expressed fear for her brother and her mother. Later reports—the Agency had clearly helped the family in their relocation, trying to shield them— showed that Amanda had grown into an angry, bitter young woman. There had been an issue with drinking, with drugs, a report from an FBI agent that indicated Amanda's mother had sought treatment for her. She had finished college, worked for a while as a music teacher at a small, prestigious private school in Coral Gables, but had resigned her post. She had started a courier business with a boyfriend named Roberto Mendez.

The file included a list of her known associates, with printouts of social media posts where they discussed weekend plans or work-related activities: the boyfriend Roberto, two close female friends she'd known since high school, an ex she remained friends with.

She had an apartment in Miami. Whoever had

created this file had thoughtfully included an aerial map that would be useful to him in figuring out how to surveil her residence.

The final section of the report was titled: *Phenomenon Known as "The Bolties."*

Bolties?

He read the analysis:

After Bolt's defection, online commentators, bloggers, and conspiracy theorists began analyzing and offering various takes on Markus Bolt's guilt, why he had done it, and what he would do now. It was as if a group of online amateur detectives applied themselves to the case. Communities began to sprout up on various social media platforms or websites where every aspect of the Bolt case was discussed.

Some commentators began to refer to themselves as "Bolties," indicating their obsession with the case, and the man. (Generally, they are careful not to imply endorsement of Bolt's actions, just their fascination with the case.) A variety of theories, from plausible to ludicrous, were offered to explain the defection and the resulting damage. Theories ranged from Bolt being offered millions to defect (likeliest, yet unproven) to being under the control of alien forces who had negotiated a separate peace with the Russian government.

There was more, but he didn't read it. He would have time to finish it on the flight.

He went back and reread Allan's suicide note. He closed his eyes and started planning out options on how to get close enough to Amanda Bolt to protect her and yet not give away that he was her birdwatcher.

*   *   *

Daniel stared at the ceiling. It was so unfair. He was thirteen now, he was self-reliant (well, as long as Dad filled the fridge with food), and he could be trusted. He was a good kid, and he kind of relished the idea of staying alone at home. It would be a thing to brag about to his friends. *Oh, yeah, Dad's on a business trip, I'm here on my own. I can handle it.* He thought he might be able to talk Leonie into letting him stay at least one night at home on his own. Leonie was family; she would trust him more than Dad would.

His phone beeped. An incoming text. A number he didn't recognize.

The text read: Hello, Daniel.

Some scammer, he thought, but then how did they know his name?

Then the next: Did you know your dad has so many secrets? So many. Maybe I'll tell you one. The big one.

He stared at the screen, then furiously texted: Who is this?

Ask him about your mom. Ask him the hard questions. Bye

Daniel texted back: Who is this? I'm deleting the message.

You can't delete your curiosity, though, can you? Bye, Daniel, take care, don't be scared of the truth.

Daniel read the words. He closed the text window. On his bureau there was a picture of his parents, shortly after they married. It was one of the few pictures of his mom that he had; she had been camera shy, Dad said. They looked so happy, so full of promise, her leaning into Dad's broad shoulder, her arms around his neck as if she were clinging to him like he was her last hope.

Also on his bureau was the one picture of him and his mom together, her holding him the day he was born.

Sometimes he wondered about it. Why were there not more?

He looked again at his phone. It had to be a prank. Someone being sick. In a rush of bravery, he tapped the phone number to call it; got a *this number is not in service* message. He ended the call.

But. *Don't be scared of the truth.* What truth? Mom had died from an undiagnosed heart condition. It had been sudden and awful, and she was gone before Daniel could remember her. They went to her grave on her birthday and the anniversary of the day she died, and Dad didn't say much and Daniel would leave the fresh flowers by her headstone. And then they would leave, and Daniel would wonder what his mother had been like, how sad had she been to know she was dying. Dad just never talked about her, unless Daniel asked.

Don't be scared of the truth.

He pushed the phone away as if it were radioactive.

"Dad?" Daniel, standing on the stairs.

Sam closed the file. "Yeah?"

Daniel didn't answer immediately, and Sam glanced up at him. Daniel, biting his lip, a nervous habit.

"Can we talk about Mom when you get back?"

Sam, having just read about the destruction of a family because of treason, took a deep breath. "What about her?"

"I just want to talk about her. Just . . . generally."

"Um, okay. All right."

"I wondered about something, though."

"What?"

"Why is there only the one picture of her holding me as a baby?"

"What?"

"I just . . . there are no pictures of her and me like there are of you and her, and I wondered why. Pictures of me, and pictures of her, but not pictures of me with her."

"What has brought this up?"

"I just...I just wondered."

The day had come. Finally. Right when he had to leave. The day there would be more questions. He had managed to deal with them before, lying to his own son because he had no choice, because the truth was more than a boy should bear.

What happened to my mom?

She died of an undiagnosed heart condition.

What really happened to my mom?

She's not dead. She's in a coma.

Why don't I have family on her side?

She had no family I wanted you to know.

What are you going to go do in Miami, Dad?

Hunt a traitor. It's funny because I'm the husband of a traitor. It's a lovely symmetry, isn't it?

"Sure," Sam said. "Sure, buddy, let's talk about your mom when I get back."

8

Moscow

Yuri Boborin sat at a desk in the headquarters, playing solitaire on his assistant's desk with a 32-card Russian deck. He was a short man, thick in the waist, with a still full head of hair going silver.

Kirill came in and sat across from him. He'd asked to speak to him alone. The small crowd that had been in Bobo's offices—two assistants and an armed guard, perhaps there to watch Bobo or protect Bobo—had stepped out into the hallway. The operations center, down the hall, was fully staffed all hours, every day, and the Dude had arranged for Kirill to use an entrance and go to the office without being seen. Markus's disappearance was going to remain a closely guarded secret as long as they could keep it.

Bobo didn't look directly at him. He was one of the most powerful men in Russia, and now he looked like he awaited the fall of the sword.

"A card game? Now?" Kirill asked. "During this crisis?"

"I have not slept in two days, Kirill Denisovich. Ten minutes of this clears my mind. How was Japan?"

"It's done. I'm not here to talk about Japan."

"How is your sweet mother?"

"Angry at you for losing Markus."

Now he looked up, blinked watery eyes.

Yuri Boborin was a senior SVR director who had been in charge of Markus since his arrival in Russia. He had set up Markus to be an honored guest, arranged his housing, introduced him to the elites (who were all eager to meet their pet traitor), and had introduced him to Mama (regrettably while still married to Papa, although the marriage had not lasted long once Markus exerted his charms). Kirill had never forgiven him that one.

Kirill sat down on the edge of the desk. "Mama said he's been sick. Is it serious?"

"I have spoken to his doctor. He is in good health."

"Have you seen records? Tests?"

"Yes, of course. It's hurtful, Kirill. I have been his friend and ally here."

"How surprising a traitor could betray you."

"Don't mock me. Getting Markus to defect was my greatest triumph." He cleared his throat. "But after the dog has won the prize, it still has to be fed, groomed, and taken outside. Markus turned into a job."

"What will it be like for you if your dog has slipped his leash, Bobo?"

Bobo moved a card, frowned. "You see, there is not just my leash. The yard has fences."

"And he's gone through a fence. With a burner phone he never should have been able to acquire, calling home to Florida. He's your responsibility."

"We did not expressly forbid him contact with his family. He's his own man."

"Whose travel is monitored. Whose movements are tracked. Who is kept out of the public eye."

"For his own protection." Bobo played another card.

"You know, we thought of killing him after he came here. In case he was here to spy on us. We voted on it. We decided better to keep him alive; it would be a bad message to anyone else who might spy for us. Instead he became our show dog—as if to prove how good we treat those who help us."

"Could the Americans have gotten to him here? He is supposed to have a bodyguard."

"He and your mother complained. Constantly, in the past few months. The bodyguard annoyed them, whoever I assigned. One talked too much about her personal life. One wanted to ask too much about Markus's work in America. One talked too much about the TV shows he likes." Bobo shrugged. "Markus said enough of the people he hung around with had protection, so he didn't need it. And that was true. Let the billionaires watch over him."

The past few months. Maybe Markus had wanted to slip the leash for a while. Kirill knew if Markus didn't want a bodyguard watching him, Markus could easily sway Mama to his side and make her think ditching security was her idea.

"And you gave in?"

"I dialed the protection detail back, appropriately, and it was approved."

"And so, no one was watching him as closely as they should."

"What was there to watch? Where was he to go? Where would he go now? He's hated outside of Russia."

"He betrayed America; he could betray us."

"Do you think the Americans would believe a word out of his mouth? Kirill, you know he would be killed on sight. They wouldn't negotiate with him. They aren't going to capture him and put him in their Colorado Supermax with his fellow traitors. He would be facing a death penalty."

"They would deal with him if he spied on us. If he had the information to buy his life."

"He didn't spy on us. It would have been suicide." Bobo cleared his throat, ran a hand through his gray hair. "Maybe he went off and killed himself. I should be so lucky. You can give the eulogy."

"Bobo. You ought to be organizing the search for him and you're here playing solitaire. What has happened?"

Bobo took a deep breath. "The powers that be have told me to sit down. I cannot be leading anything because, you see, he is not missing. He has not left the safety of our embrace. It is like when there was no crime in the Soviet Union. He cannot be a problem if there is no problem."

"You know for certain he's running back to the Americans?"

"No. He might have an easier time with the Germans or the French or the Poles. They could shield him from both sides. But they might just turn him over immediately. There would be points for that."

"So, not really a choice. I need something more than Miami to start my search."

"Kirill." Bobo gave a sigh. "They'll retire me over this. If you go after him, and you don't bring him back or kill him, they'll end your career, too." He coughed. "Just stay away from it."

"My mother needs him. It sickens me, but she does. I can find him and get him back here quietly. Now. Do any enemy intel services know yet?"

"I think not. We have detected no chatter, no unusual communications that say that they do. Of course, we cannot be certain."

"Would he go to his family in Miami?"

"Well." Bobo started counting off on his fingers. "His ex-wife tried to kill him, so not her."

"What?"

"Ah. Not widely known. She confronted him right before his traitor's dance, before he left DC for Miami. She demanded a divorce and he told her no, which was his ego talking, as he was literally abandoning her in that moment, but he still told her no."

"He's such an ass."

"I guess he said it to allay suspicion, and she tried to stab him. He took the knife from her and she calmed down and he left. Of course, this could be a lie he made up. But why? He gains nothing from it."

"Why did she want the divorce? I mean, there are so many reasons I can imagine."

"She always claimed she didn't know he was working for us. Perhaps she knew and she was trying to protect herself and her children."

So, he would not turn to the ex-wife, Karen. "His son is dead. What about the daughter? Amanda?"

"I believe he was closer to Allan than Amanda. But I did once find, in his apartment, a set of letters that he wrote to her and of course we could not allow him to send. Handwritten ones. I don't know what he was thinking, like he was going to mail them through Russian Post and we wouldn't know. Or he wrote them because he needed to say them but not send them."

"His apartment?"

"He had an apartment near the headquarters, for when he needed to be close."

Mama had never mentioned an apartment. "Was it for other women? Just tell me."

"No. He just wanted a place to be alone. We monitored it, of course. We've searched it. Nothing there."

Markus was a Russian doll with secrets inside secrets. "Do you have them? The letters?"

"Yes." He got up, went into his spacious office, opened

a safe. He brought back a small pack of letters. "He didn't write them all at once. When the mood took him, I suppose, maybe when he was missing Amanda."

"I'll need these. Did he write to his son?"

Bobo handed him the unsent letters. "A few. They're there as well."

Now to the hardest question he'd ever asked in his line of work. "Is there any information he could have gotten that he could barter to the Americans for amnesty?"

Bobo played his cards. He finally noticed the red eight of hearts he could move.

"He needs some gift to give them. What could he know?" Kirill asked.

Bobo shrugged. "He was everyone's pet. The court"— it was a nickname for the elite billionaire circle around Morozov, much like the aristocracy that orbited the czars—"well, they all wanted to know him, be around him. We have so few defectors now; it used to maybe be about ideology. Our workers' paradise. I'm old enough to remember how right we thought we were. Our defectors could tell themselves that. Now it's always about money and power and their own bitterness. But still—a traitor is a flawed person. I had to watch him, monitor him, use him, but I never trusted him." He cleared his throat. "We pulled him in when there was something we wanted his take on. If the American intel services would react in a certain way to a certain action. A poisoning of a dissident in Paris. Exposing one of their agents here instead of feeding them misinformation. So he could tell the Americans something of operations we considered and executed. It's all old news. But if Markus put his mind to it, it could do a great deal of damage. We kept him sequestered for much of the first year here, but there was too much pressure from the court—they liked showing him off. They liked him. He was often at the vacation houses of the inner circle. He was at their parties. There, he could have gathered information that could hurt them. If you hurt them, you hurt Morozov, you hurt Russia."

"Hurting them personally is not the same as hurting Russia."

"They *are* Russia. They control everything. They have the generals in their pockets, because they're always scared if the people turn against them, the military will follow. They remember Romania in 1989. If the elites knew he vanished, they'd be terrified of what he might know about them. It will be a humiliation of Russia."

"And a humiliation of my mother. It might even reflect upon me," Kirill said. The elites would ask both him and his mother, *How could you have not known? How could you have not spotted he might be planning a run?* His own career could be at stake, and he was not going to let Markus win. Never, ever.

"I'm going to find him and bring him back. But I don't think he'd approach his family. He needs to approach someone who can protect him and cut a deal with him."

Bobo abandoned his cards and went to a conference room.

"They made me put a presentation together for you. And for who I'll have to apologize to if this all goes badly." His voice shook. "I don't know what they'll do to me."

Bobo had been one of his father's closest friends. The anger Kirill felt toward Markus boiled up again. He was a destroyer.

Find and kill him. Never mind orders. Don't bring him back. Say he resisted and you had no choice. Save your mother from this monster, save Bobo.

Kirill sat down.

"So, we have to understand why he's done this because

his reasoning will influence the choices he's making now. So he's either gone back for an emotional reason, such as his family, or he knows something he wants the Americans to know."

"What might he know? Were we going to launch the nukes tomorrow?"

"Of course not, Kirill Denisovich. So one of two things happened: The first is that he learned something so compelling that he decided to take it back to the Americans regardless of consequences—something that would make him act in a way he could tell himself was heroic." Bobo twisted the last word.

"That seems unlikely."

"Yet possible. It could also be something so powerful that he felt it could buy him a ticket and some level of forgiveness back home. Or worse, he has been a double agent this entire time, never a true traitor, and he finally found what he was looking for here. The reason he abandoned his family, his life."

The thought made Kirill cold. No. They could not have all been fooled. That wasn't a possibility.

"The other likely option is that something has happened not here but in America. With his family, or someone he is close to. Someone who needs him."

"He abandoned Amanda and Karen. Why would he go back? He doesn't care about them." It was strange to talk about Markus's family like he knew them. He imagined he shared a loathing for him with them, and little else.

"You're not a father, Kirill. Or a husband."

"He never once indicated to me that he had regrets for leaving them. You said Amanda hates him, Karen tried to stab him. Why would he go back?"

Bobo clicked a button on his laptop, and an audio recording started playing.

BOBO's voice (in English): How are you doing? I'm very sorry about Allan.

MARKUS's voice: He killed himself. I never thought...

BOBO: No one ever does.

MARKUS: I don't need your fake sympathy.

BOBO: I am genuinely sorry, Markus. I am.

MARKUS: I ruined their lives.

BOBO: No. They went on.

MARKUS: Clearly he did not. That he thought this was an option...

BOBO: You cannot know what was in his mind. In his life.

MARKUS: His life has been a train wreck.

BOBO: How do you know?

MARKUS: I've kept tabs on my kids.

BOBO: I told you to make the break complete. It was the only way to move forward. And how does it look for you to have any contact with anyone in America? It looks bad, for me and for you.

MARKUS: They're my children. I said I kept tabs, not that I was in touch with them.

BOBO: Really do you think they feel the same way toward you? They hate you. We know this.

MARKUS: I know they're angry with me but they're still my children.

BOBO: No, Markus, they are not. They don't consider you their father anymore. I got their debriefings from the CIA.

MARKUS: You have someone inside who could do that? Watching them?

BOBO: I have intel resources watching them. Checking on them. There were a couple of people inside American intel who threatened them. Who thought you would return if their lives were at stake. They lost their jobs for suggesting violence against them.

MARKUS: Who?

BOBO: It doesn't matter. They're there and you're here. Always.

MARKUS: One of them could have hurt my son.

BOBO: He killed himself, Markus, and I'm sorry, but that's all the story there. Killing your kids would gain those people no advantage.

MARKUS: Except to make me pay.

BOBO: It's not like you were going to ever see them again.

MARKUS: You've never been cruel to me, Bobo.

BOBO: And I'm not now. I am so sorry.

MARKUS: I can't even comfort Karen or Amanda.

[Several moments of silence.]

MARKUS: Did one of these people who hate me hurt my son?

BOBO: No.

The recording ended. Bobo shrugged at Kirill. "So, he knew we had a resource inside American intel who could update us on his family."

"Do you still have the asset? Can they tell us what's going on?"

Bobo didn't answer the first question. "The phone called someone in South Florida. I think you should start by putting eyes on the daughter and the mother."

Bobo had an asset inside American intel. Would he risk exposing that person to help Markus? Did Markus know who it was and that's who he would run to?

Markus doing so risked blowing the asset's cover. Maybe Markus didn't care. The asset might handle Markus by getting rid of him. No one wanted to be a traitor's friend.

"The only emotional trigger could be his family? No one else?"

"No one else."

"I want all his files, Bobo, all of them, from past to present. Encode them but I'm taking them with me."

"I don't think that's—"

"I'm not discussing, I'm telling you. Or you get someone else to clean up your mess. Someone you don't trust as much to keep his mouth shut as me."

"All right, Kiryushenka," Bobo said, using a pet form of his name. "I'll give you the files."

"All of them, Bobo."

He nodded.

"Your asset. Are you going to tell me who that is?"

"No."

"Does Markus know?"

"He did not know when he was in America. I don't know if he has learned."

"Would this be his ticket to bargain, the name of this asset?"

"He could just give it to them if he knew it. He wouldn't have to return to America and risk his neck."

They stared at each other. "Maybe you should pull your asset."

"That's not possible."

"Who is it, Bobo?"

"I can't tell you. I don't have the clearance to tell you."

"I don't care."

"If you're captured, I can't have you giving the name."

"I won't be captured."

"Please. You aren't going to kill yourself. Maybe people would have done that for communism, to spit in the face of the capitalists. Now we are the capitalists. You're not going to die for a bunch of billionaires."

"Russia is still my country," Kirill said. "And I'm not going to die." He stood. "I would need clearance to leave, to use an assumed name. Are you giving that to me?"

"No one is to know. We don't want a record of you on a commercial flight. I'll make a phone call, get a private jet loaned to you. Illya Markarkin owes us a favor, I'll tell him to fly you to Miami."

"I need a contact there. Cash, a place to stay, a weapon. A place to bring my stepfather once I've found him." If he called him his stepfather, it would sound better, Kirill thought.

"Do you know how many Russians there are in South Florida? Not a problem."

"Not a loudmouthed rich guy. Not one who will create a problem for me."

"Yes, Kiryushenka."

Don't call me that, he thought. *Papa called me that.* But then he could see the tremble in Bobo's hands, and he realized how frightened his old family friend was, and what was at stake for him. He could be accused of treason, of failing in his duties to Mother Russia. At the very least he would lose his vaunted position here.

Markus running was just so…inconsiderate. And Kirill was going to make him pay.

PART TWO

9

Austin

GOOD-BYE WAS FASTER THAN SAM wanted it to be. The basketball team had early morning practice, and he drove Daniel to the gym on his way to the airport. He had a strange feeling now every time he went on a mission—what would his son think if he didn't come back? What story would his superiors spin? Bar owner killed in mugging. Bar owner found dead. Bar owner vanishes, possibly kidnapped.

Daniel would never know the truth about both his parents. He was good at his job and he'd always come home.

"Okay, have a good day. Mind Leonie."

"We'll talk about my mom when you get back?"

"Of course."

"Okay, Dad, I love you."

"Love you, too." He wanted to give Daniel a hug, but the other players were ambling into the gym. Instead, Daniel got out and retrieved his gym bag and backpack from the back of the SUV and went into the gym without a backward glance at his father. Sam felt empty. The

questions he had never wanted to answer were beginning to be raised.

He drove to Austin-Bergstrom International Airport,
using his hands-free phone to call Leonie on the way.

"Hey," she said.

"Hey. Daniel surprised me by asking questions about
his mother last night."

"Why would she come up now?"

"I don't know. He hasn't mentioned her in a while.
The last time was when he asked me what music she
liked."

"Okay," Leonie said. "He may not ask me anything
since I never knew her." Sam had told Daniel that he'd
found Leonie through a nanny service—another lie.
But you didn't tell your son that you'd rescued his nanny
from a criminal syndicate. "Sam, you knew this day
would come."

"Yes." Sam could only hope that the CIA had covered
its tracks carefully. They had managed to erase Lucy's
identity as a former CIA agent from the public record.
So he had to trust that the cover story invented for her
would hold.

"If he does ask, just stall him until I'm back."

"You know I'll take good care of him while you're
gone. But this is the last time, at least for a while,
what with the baby coming. You need to find another
resource."

"I know. I am forever grateful to you."

"I know. I am grateful to you, too. Keeping me in his
life."

"You're family."

"Okay, enough," she said. "Do not make the pregnant
woman cry."

"Okay. Thanks."

"I'll call you if there's a problem. Sam?"

"Yeah?"

"Daniel loves you. You're his whole world. Don't ever forget that."

"I won't."

She told him good-bye and hung up.

He parked in the long-term airport lot, with the other dads and moms who were traveling on their normal parent jobs that Daniel wished Sam had. Took a deep breath. Looked at himself in the mirror and said, *Go do your job, do it right, get home to your son.*

10

⚬⚬⚬⚬

Moscow

THE PRIVATE JET BELONGED TO an oligarch named Illya Markarkin, the friend who Bolt had told Mama was hosting him for a Black Sea fishing trip.

There was no fishing trip. So Illya didn't want to be suspected of helping Bolt and was desperate to cooperate and clear his name. Illya kept insisting loudly to Bobo, to the Dude, that he knew nothing of Bolt's escape.

Illya was providing free and private transportation to Kirill. Bobo provided Kirill a new passport in the name of Kirill Borisovich Markarkin, allowing him to pass as a relative of Illya's. He and Bobo met the plane at Vnukovo Airport outside Moscow, driven there in a government limo.

Bobo watched the Markarkin limousine arrive and said: "Illya is an old friend of the president. He and his staffer only know we need to get you into Florida, under an assumed name. They say they were already planning to fly there today because Illya got a Russian girl named Maria pregnant in Sunny Isles." Kirill knew that was an enclave between Miami and Fort Lauderdale where many wealthy Russians had bought condos and retail spaces. "And Maria is waiting to have her baby on American soil."

"If Markus knew of this planned trip, then that would have given him cover," Kirill said. "No one would have been looking for him if they thought he was off on Illya's fishing boat and meanwhile Illya is in Miami. Do they know who I really am?"

"Illya knows you are Markus's stepson, of course, and he knows you now work for me. I do not think he has shared that information with his assistant."

Kirill watched the assistant get out of the car. A woman in her mid-to-late thirties, in a well-cut gray suit, no-nonsense as she talked to the pilot, standing at the stairs to the plane, checking off items on a tablet computer. Illya Markarkin stood close to the limo, talking on the phone, a panicked look on his face. The woman glanced at Bobo's limo, parked thirty feet away.

"Is his assistant another mistress?" Kirill asked.

"I do not think so. She might be the one keeping Illya's businesses afloat. Very smart, very capable. He found her in London. She's a tough one. Her name is Valeria."

"Illya and this Valeria will likely notice I'm traveling on a passport with Illya's surname when we arrive."

"They will say you are his cousin, if asked. Mother Russia asks this favor of them. They'll be quiet. If they speak of this, we have told them that neither Maria nor her baby will be allowed in Russia, ever." He cleared his throat.

"You're charming, Bobo. What a pleasant flight it will be."

"Illya is scared of being seen as too close to Markus, and his assistant will comply. And one of his planes will be standing by to whisk you and Markus home when you find him."

"Dead or alive?"

"Preferably alive." He patted Kirill's arm. "They'll leave you alone. Read your files. Stick to our plan. Find him, bring him home. To your mother, and to me. That's a good boy."

11

Austin

AFTER PRACTICE, DANIEL PICKED UP his backpack and headed for class. First period was math, which he didn't much like, and he got through the fifty minutes without thinking too much about his dad and the weird text from last night. About Dad and his secrets, and about a particularly big one.

He focused on the math; it was a good distraction.

Second period was choir. His favorite. Everyone had to take choir, orchestra, or band in sixth grade, and he'd taken choir because learning an instrument didn't appeal to him, and he'd thought he could just do choir the one year, but he'd really liked the director and he sang well and now as a seventh grader he was in the varsity boys choir with mostly eighth graders, who were actually pretty nice to him, maybe because he was on the basketball team.

He dropped off his backpack and went to the cubby that held his choral notebook. Mrs. Stauffer, the choir director, was calling the boys into the rehearsal hall. He grabbed his black binder with his music and took his seat. The room was big, and lots of trophies from many years of choral competitions were on shelves along the walls—Lakehaven Middle School had a strong reputation. Mrs. Stauffer made her choristers work.

"All right, boys, we're not sounding strong on this river piece"—many of the songs for middle school boys' choirs seemed to center on logging or seafaring or other preindustrial pursuits—"so let's start at the beginning, tenors."

Daniel opened his black binder and saw a note on a new piece of paper hole-punched in with the music, and he read the carefully printed words:

> Your mother's grave is empty. She left a message for you.

Daniel Capra stared at the words. What was this? He closed the binder before his two friends he sat between, James (basketball player, tenor, son of Matt, stepson of Leonie) and Wiley (cool geek, also a tenor), noticed it. He closed it with a slam. Loudly. He could hear the sound of his own breathing.

"Are you okay?" James asked. The other boys started singing the part, Mrs. Stauffer calling out where they needed to focus.

Daniel nodded. And didn't look at James. He reopened the binder, careful to slip his thumb in and open it so that the back of the terrible page showed. He followed along with the music, barely singing, wondering who could have done this. First the text last night. Then this.

Lakehaven schools did not tolerate bullying, although it still happened, and no one had ever teased him about having lost his mother. No one ever brought it up to him. It wasn't the kind of weapon that a kid chose to use, at least so far as he knew. His stomach felt sick, and he didn't sing well during the period, and James, who viewed singing the same as a sport in that it was a team effort, gave him a startled look.

"Are you okay, D?" James asked.

"Fine," Daniel said. They left, but when the other boys tucked their black binders back into their slots, he instead slid his into his backpack.

He got through the next two periods—French, which Lakehaven ISD started offering in middle school, and science—and then it was time for lunch. Normally he sat with James and Wiley and other kids from the boys and girls basketball teams. Instead, he took the binder and sat outside the cafeteria, in a hallway, and when the sixth and eighth graders (who had the lunch periods before and after his) had gone into their classrooms, he opened the binder again and reread the note left for him.

Your mother's grave is empty. She left a message for you.

What did that even mean? That she was buried somewhere else? Why would someone even say this to him? And what message? A letter? It was cruel. It was sick.

His face suddenly felt hot. Dad, keeping secrets. Not ever volunteering to talk about his mother. And this, after last night's texts. Who could have left it? He tried to order his thoughts. It had to be a kid. Some stranger couldn't have come into the school and left it. And his slot was marked with a number, not his name. *They would have to know his number.* It had to be someone in choir, but he was on good terms with every boy, wasn't he? Did someone dislike him secretly, or hold a grudge? And how did a kid block a text number?

He felt mad now. He just wanted to go and shoot baskets and dribble the ball until his hands hurt.

"Are you all right?" a woman's voice said.

Daniel glanced up. It was a woman, in her thirties,

one he recognized as one of the school counselors, but he didn't really know her. He remembered her name was Ms. Dorridge. She gave him an uncertain smile.

"Yes, ma'am," he said. "I'm fine."

"You're Daniel Capra, right?"

"Yes," he said. He stood up.

"Not hungry?"

"No." But he realized how odd this looked; he couldn't claim he was out here studying, as he had no books open, and he could have studied inside the cafeteria if he wanted.

"Need an alone moment?" she asked.

"Yeah, I guess I did." She was a counselor, he thought. He could show this to her. But then it would turn into a thing, he thought, her trying to figure out who was sending this message to him, and for sure she'd call Dad. He didn't want that. Not right now. Not with Dad and his secrets.

But this was the kind of thing they told you to talk to counselors about. Not to carry it around.

"Is something going on that you'd like to discuss?" she asked.

After a moment he shook his head. He thought Ms. Dorridge would press him about it, but she said, "Okay, Daniel. If you change your mind, you know where to find me or Mrs. Kaplan."

He opened his mouth—but what did you say? She glanced at the choir binder. "I had to sing a solo once. It was nerve-racking. I prefer duets."

He forced himself to smile. "It's not that. The eighth graders get all the solos anyway."

"Okay, Daniel," she said. "Maybe go inside and get some lunch before the period's done."

He nodded and she stood watching him as he went

back in. He grabbed a chicken sandwich, fries, and a juice and sat down across from James.

James said, "Are you okay?"

"Why is everyone asking me that?"

"Because you're acting weird," James said. "And you sang like crap in choir today."

"Thanks, and it's nothing."

"It's your sudden fame," James said. "You get the winning shot, the adoration, the screaming fans. It's overwhelmed you."

"The only screaming fan was your dad," Daniel said. "He doesn't count."

"Yeah, he screamed for you more than for me," James said. But not with anger in his tone.

Not even Dad went nuts at the games. That would have been nice. If Dad had let his cool crack, just once, and had screamed and cheered for him instead of sitting there in his iciness.

"We got the history project to work on," James said. He hated history and always wanted Daniel to be on his project team, because Daniel would do the work. "Can I come over after school and work on it?" Meaning, Daniel knew, if James could come over and watch Daniel work on it.

"I'm staying with y'all. My dad is on another business trip."

"Oh," James said. "Leonie didn't say anything to me. Are we sharing a room? They're turning the guest room into the nursery."

"I guess. Is that okay?"

"Sure." Normally James would be excited to have him sleeping over. "Cool with me."

Something was off. Daniel could feel it. He waited for James to say something more. He didn't.

"Have you ever heard anyone say anything about my mom?" Daniel asked.

James looked back down at his empty plate and then at Daniel. "Your mom. What do you mean?"

"Just, anything about her."

"I don't see why someone would bring up *your* mom."

Daniel realized he should have stayed quiet. James's mom had a drug or drinking problem—James never talked about it—but she wasn't allowed to see James right now. He hoped no one had teased James about this, but Daniel figured most people didn't even know.

"Or," Daniel said, "maybe they've asked why I don't have a mom?"

"Oh. No. Not that I remember. Why?"

Daniel was scared and his brain felt full of worms, crawling around in his head saying, *Your mother's grave is empty*. He could show James the note. He was his friend. He started to reach for the binder.

And then he stopped.

Because what if it wasn't a joke?

Because he'd just realized it could mean more than his mother was buried somewhere else.

It could mean she was still alive.

But that would mean his father had told him a tremendous, unforgivable lie. That couldn't be so. His dad wouldn't do that to him. Daniel's throat closed up and he thought he would choke as he stared down at the remains of his lunch.

Would he?

Did you know your dad has so many secrets? So many. Maybe I'll tell you one. The big one.

"Daniel?" James asked.

"Nothing," Daniel said. "Never mind."

12

⎯⎯⎯⎯⎯⎯⎯⎯⎯⎯

En route to Miami

THE PRIVATE JET TOOK OFF into the thin clouds above Moscow. Illya Markarkin sank into one of the leather chairs, drinking a large vodka brought to him by the flight attendant, a young man. He closed his eyes, and when Kirill attempted to ask Illya a question, Illya raised a silencing hand.

The attractive assistant had been on her phone, in the private room at the rear of the plane. She emerged and sat across from Kirill. He studied her. She was maybe ten years older than he was, blond hair, minimal jewelry, an air of competent authority. If she was Illya's mistress—not uncommon among the oligarchs—then she was a subtler one than some of the others he'd seen.

"Kirill," he said to her with a nod.

"Of course, Kirill Borisovich Markarkin. A cousin, I believe," she said. There was for a moment a wry tone in her voice.

Kirill cleared his throat and wondered again if she knew why he was really here. Would Illya have told her? Probably not, but some assistants seemed to know all.

"And you?" he asked.

"Valeria Garrison."

"An English surname."

"My husband was English." Her accent wasn't English; he guessed she might be from Eastern Europe.

"Was?"

"I am a widow."

"I'm sorry for your loss. And you work for ..." He gestured toward Illya, slumped, with eyes closed.

She nodded. "Yes, I am his executive assistant. Oh, and please, call me Val; everyone does. That was my husband's nickname for me."

"Does Illya require a lot of assisting?"

"I am sitting right here, I can hear you," Illya said. He downed the rest of the vodka. Val watched her boss in silence and then put her gaze back to Kirill for a moment before returning to her work on a thin laptop she'd pulled from a side pocket in her chair. Kirill had his own iPad—with details on Markus, but encoded so only Kirill's thumbprint would open it—and he started to read through Bobo's notes about Illya.

Illya and Markus had been friends since Markus defected. He wondered if Illya regretted that now. He noticed that the unsent letters Markus wrote to his daughter were included in the list of files. He'd save those for last.

"Val," Illya said. "I want you to find out something for me. Find out what men in Miami have been seen around with Maria. This baby probably isn't even mine."

Her voice was patient. "You know there is no one else. And there was already a test. It's yours," Val said, not looking up from her tablet. "Sir," she added, since Kirill was there.

"Tests can be faked," Illya said. "Maria just wants my money."

Kirill pressed the intercom to the cockpit. "Please tell me when we're clear of Russian airspace," he said to the pilot, who acknowledged his request.

He said nothing else and Illya Markarkin stared at him, confused. Val glanced at Illya, as if wondering why he would want to know.

Time passed. Illya gestured at the flight attendant to refill his vodka glass twice more. Kirill saw Val stare hard at Illya both times, and Illya ignored her.

Illya said: "Don't give me that look. I am paying a great deal of money for her to have the baby in America, for citizenship. She doesn't even care about the baby being Russian. It's just her ticket to stay in America as long as she likes."

"That is the vodka talking," Val said, and Kirill didn't think she sounded like an assistant, but more a chiding daughter.

"You," Illya said to Kirill. "You have a girlfriend? My advice, don't have one. They are nothing but trouble."

Kirill said, "I do not have time for a relationship."

"Relationship. She's nothing but a leech. Like your stepfather."

The silence that fell was awkward. Val seemed to be making a point of not looking at Kirill. For a while there were only the sounds of the engines and Illya slurping another glass of vodka.

"We are no longer in Russian airspace," the pilot announced over the intercom.

Slowly Kirill got up from his seat and put aside the encoded tablet that held Bobo's files he'd been reading. Illya looked into his glass, as though he couldn't be bothered.

Kirill took the glass from his hand. "We have many hours until we reach Florida, Illya Petrovich. And I'm already weary of your whining. You got the young woman pregnant, face the consequences. Be there for her. Be a father. Be a good one, because the baby is your best chance of having done something right and decent. It's a fresh start. Secondly, as my name is Kirill Markarkin while I am on this trip, I do not have a stepfather that you need to mention and you will not make that mistake again. You will not drink more vodka during this flight. Or while you are in Florida. And you will keep your mouth shut."

"This is my plane," Illya began, and then Kirill seized his neck, in a special way, and Illya stopped speaking and his mouth seemed to freeze.

Val stood. But she didn't interfere.

"I don't care. You are going to apologize to your assistant right now for both embarrassing her with your actions and for acting like a drunken idiot. Then you are going to write a nice note, to give to Maria, apologizing for any unkindness you have shown to her because I'm guessing this isn't the first time you've spoken harshly about her." Maybe he'd have him write a note to Markus, too.

"I will have you killed for this," Illya gasped, paling.

"No, you won't." Kirill released Illya, who collapsed back in the chair. "Sober up and then we'll have a chat, just you and I."

When Illya had his breath back, he said, "I'm sorry, Val, I'm sorry. The vodka." He looked at the floor.

"Perhaps some tea instead." She gestured at the flight attendant, who nodded and hurried to brew a pot.

"I should go lie down," Illya said.

"Yes. You're exhausted," Val said. "I'll have the tea brought to you."

"Thank you, Val." He stood, wavering, sudden shame on his face. He took a bottled water from the bar and started gulping it and vanished into the plane's bedroom. Val sat back down and returned to her notes.

"See. Isn't that nice?" Kirill sat. "Now, I have some work to do, that is incredibly important to every prominent family in Russia, so I would appreciate no more arguing, only harmony." He started scanning the tablet. "Perhaps you can think of baby names. Maria may not have selected one yet?"

Val didn't speak. The flight attendant poured tea for them all and took a cup into Illya's room. He quickly retreated back to his station and slipped in earphones. Kirill read through the files until he felt the weight of Val's gaze on him.

"You were considering interfering when I grabbed him," he said, not looking at her.

"He's my boss."

"You're not his bodyguard."

She said nothing for a long moment, and he said, "Oh, are you?" Interesting.

Val ignored the question and said, "He's a complete mess."

"I could tell."

"He loves Maria, and he has no confidence she loves him as deeply. His own father was not kind and Illya is anxious about fatherhood."

"Don't defend him."

"I'm not. I know him well. He's afraid she'll stay in America and find a younger man. I know the difficult, troubled man Illya can be...and I know the kind man he could be."

Kirill had not expected such brutal honesty from an oligarch's underling. He thought, *We're having a moment.* Then he pushed the thought away. He had a job to do, nothing more.

"Why do you need us to sneak into the United States?"

He had not expected such a bald question. But Illya had mentioned his stepfather. Maybe she knew. "I have a problem to solve there. Nothing more."

She studied his expression. "Whatever you're doing," she said, "don't get caught. Illya has enough headaches."

"You actually like him."

"I understand him. And I've had worse bosses." She put her gaze back to the laptop.

A couple of hours passed in silence. Illya came out of the small bedroom, looking ashamed, and got another bottle of water.

"Feeling better?" Kirill asked.

Illya nodded.

"I'd like to talk to you in private. Now."

"Yes, of course." And Kirill knew that Val could hear the fear in her boss's voice and would wonder what it meant.

The two men went into the bedroom.

Val slipped wireless earbuds into her ears. On her laptop, she activated the bug in the bedroom. She settled back to listen to the conversation.

She needed to know what Kirill knew.

Kirill shut the door behind him. "I need to know what you know about Markus, if you're sober enough to talk now."

"I am. I am sorry. Please do not tell Maria how...I behaved."

"Let us focus on Markus."

Illya nodded.

"He cultivated a friendship with you?"

"We...we had mutual interests. Fishing. Books—I like reading English and American novels. But really, everyone in Morozov's circle wanted to be his friend."

"What did you do before Morozov was president?"

"I ran a private intelligence and security firm, full of ex-KGB intel officers. I had worked with Morozov in the KGB back in the old days. We worked in Austria together. Then came home. Morozov stayed working in the government and I set up shop in Saint Petersburg. Then he gave me a company to run."

The president, now many years in office, had been generous to his friends, turning over newly private companies to their control. "What'd he give you?"

"I was lucky. Timber company. A billion a year, it makes. Renewable, we won't run out of trees in Russia. There's less fighting than among the energy oligarchs," Illya said. "I owe him everything so I certainly wouldn't help Markus Bolt defect back to the United States." He spat into a tissue. "You must believe me. I'll help you however I can." His hand, holding the tissue, shook slightly.

"But you and Markus were friends."

"Yes," Illya said. "But always a challenge. He needed to be admired. He needed our applause, I think, to salve his conscience that he was a traitor. And he could be very funny. You would not think that a traitor could be funny. He told me about the idiots at the CIA. People he fooled, for so long. People who should have seen through him and didn't."

"So you don't think he'll run to his old intelligence comrades?"

"He has no friends left there."

Except Bobo has someone inside American intel, Kirill thought. And if Markus knows that, he might well run to that person.

"Unless Bolt wants to make a deal," Illya said, as though just considering the idea.

"He would have to have something very valuable to offer in trade for his life."

Illya cleared his throat and ran a hand through his thinning hair. "He was briefed. On CIA activities and his opinion was asked, so he could tell them what we know about them. He knows much of what Russia knows. And he could talk about the ruling class. The divisions, the rivalries, the alliances. He could cause trouble in Morozov's circle. He might know where we've hidden money, what...overseas involvement we have."

In other words, which criminal syndicates in the West you're backing, Kirill thought. Sometimes he looked at Russia and hated what he saw. The fleeting chance his nation had had, long ago, coming out of the collapse of the Soviet Union, to join the brotherhood of democracies, and they had not. They had not grabbed their chance and they'd slipped back into authoritarianism. So instead of an incompetent crowd who sneered at money, they traded it for a crowd obsessed with money. Two far pendulum swings.

"Or...he..."

"What, Illya?"

"You have to kill Markus if you find him." Illya lowered his voice to a whisper. "Immediately. Don't try to reason with him. Don't argue or talk. Just kill him."

"Why?"

"You must keep it to yourself. It being known would put you and your mother in great danger. There will be a purge over this, and you and she are the ones likely to be hurt."

Kirill felt cold. "What has Markus done?"

"They will say you and your mama must have known. Maybe even helped him."

"What?"

"He..." Illya cleared his throat. "Markus has information on our president. And our money."

"What do you mean, our money?"

"The money of all the elites around the president."

Kirill said nothing, waiting, feeling ice creep along his skin.

"Morozov has little money of his own in the West. This is so the US, the West, they cannot put holds on his accounts or control how he moves money around the world. None of it is in his name. But he can access *our* money. Those of his friends he has raised up. That's the price. We are his economic armor." Illya cleared his throat again, seemed to labor to speak for a moment, as if the words were thorns in his throat. "There are shell companies, hiding billions in dollars."

"How many billions?"

"Forty, fifty." As if a ten-billion-dollar difference could be a rounding error. "I don't know exactly. I... I handle a lot of the shell companies. Running timber, I'm less visible than the friends of his who have banks or energy or technology companies. The West does not pay attention to me. Timber is boring, yes? No one cares." He sat down on the edge of the small bed. "I have a list. A chart. Of how all the companies connect, how the money is moved. It's complicated, arcane, to keep the Westerners from imposing sanctions on us, or damaging our economy. Markus has it, I think. He knows the structure. This is why he ran. He had a ticket to buy his way home."

Kirill felt cold. "How?"

"Two weeks ago, he was down at my estate in Sochi for a fishing trip. We like to fish. Just him and me and not so much the drinking. With the other oligarchs in the court, it's always the drinking so much vodka, the parties, the girls brought in. Fine when I was younger, but now I prefer the quiet. So did Markus. I thought we were friends. But then I caught him coming out of my office. He said he was looking for a pen. I believed him but it nagged at me, why was he in my study, and after I heard he was missing, I had my computer guy check and a file had been copied to an external flash drive. It was this map of all the companies, of where all the money is."

"You think this financial map is his ticket home? The Americans will still put him in prison."

"He has it," Illya said. "I'm sure of it. If it's not his ticket home, it's his ticket out of Russia. He could threaten to hand it over if we come after him."

"Does Morozov know?"

"My God, no. Of course not."

"Does your assistant know?"

"No. Leave Val out of this. No one knows. Except my computer guy, and I pay him well not to talk. I told him he would be blamed for the security breach." Illya shook his head. "If anyone knew, I wouldn't be allowed to be on this plane flying to America. I would be ruined, Morozov would strip me of everything I own." His voice wavered.

"Move the money, then, into new safe accounts."

"I cannot…without revealing to them all that I had the financial map. And I don't control the individual accounts, I just know the connections, the flow. I'm dead if I tell them. Please. You have to find him and kill him outright."

Kirill considered. If he broke this news, it would surely not stay contained in the elite circle. And he could not risk anything that put his mother under suspicion.

"Do…do you think Bolt's still an American agent? Like his defection was a long game?" That was a terrifying thought. Surely that possibility had been considered; if there had been a hint of it, Bolt would have been dead years ago. And what would that mean to his mother—if she was suspected of knowing this, or worse, *not* knowing. Failure to detect his spying would be as unforgivable as knowing about it. His own career would be destroyed as well. You didn't know your stepfather, who betrayed America, was betraying us? You suspected nothing? You saw nothing?

There was no forgiveness in failure to see betrayal.

Illya ran a hand through his hair. "No. I think he decided he had to get back and he had to get them something that would give him a chance at leverage. And he'd watched me enough to know I had the information. He's still a spy. He wants *something* back in America. It is insanity for him to return."

"He wants to see his daughter?"

"Amanda, I know he was fond of her. He told me once he thought of bringing Amanda with him when he came to Russia...but he didn't. And his son, Allan..."

"His son died. Why are you telling me this?" Kirill could, after all, report this immediately to Bobo.

"Because Sonia Timofeyevna was assigned to watch over him. If he was able to acquire intel and she didn't know...she has failed the president."

Kirill's worst nightmare. He tried to laugh it off. "Mama? Spy on Markus? You have to be kidding. She..."

He stopped because of the look on Illya's face. "You are not kidding."

"She was to watch Markus. I know you think your mother is a scatterbrained person, Kirill, just a pretty face perhaps, but she is deeply loyal to Russia. And after your father's sad death...she was asked by Duderov and Bobo to watch Markus because he liked her so well. To be part of his life since your father was gone. No one fully trusts a traitor."

And yet the circle had trusted him just enough, in their homes and in their drinking parties, and now might pay a price.

Kirill felt a thickness in his throat. Had the destruction of his family been a kind of game, a psy op exercise against a traitor? His father was dead from grief and depression, his mother then available...for a job. To share a bed with a traitor, to watch him, report if he stepped out of line, and if she had failed...then she would pay a price.

This job wasn't about hating Markus; this was now about saving his mother.

Kirill sat next to Illya on the bed. He had been filled with righteous energy and purpose to find Markus, a man he loathed, and now he felt shaky.

The letters. The letters he'd written to his daughter. Bobo had put those on his iPad; he needed to read them. An answer might be there.

He could not fail. He could not.

13

Miami

IT WAS RARE THAT SAM saw a dead woman. But then there she was, walking through the airport as he exited the secure area behind her, heading for ground transportation and baggage claim. She was a ghost, whispered about in the dark world of crime that he was forced to inhabit at times, a name that had supposedly died years ago. And yet here she was.

He nearly froze. He had no weapon at hand, but he was sure she did, and if she spotted him, she might well shoot him dead right here in Miami International, witnesses be damned.

He could not forget the face, the confident walk, the steady gaze assessing all around her for both danger and opportunity. They knew each other.

Marianne.

A legend in certain circles that dealt in death and retribution. A German woman with an erased past. A top hit woman, known for her mentorship of pairs—there were *always* two with her—of young apprentice killers she'd recruit, train, and then send out into the world.

Marianne was supposed to be dead.

He'd read an intel report that indicated a woman and her two male companions had been killed in a house near New York City, and evidence on the scene indicated that it was the famous Marianne and her two latest apprentices. She was dressed in a stylish white suit and now she was flanked by a tall male who looked like he'd played American football and a shorter, athletic woman with reddish-blond hair. He turned away as Marianne cast her gaze across the crowd, toward him. He took ten steps and then turned back. She wasn't looking at him; she kept walking.

There were any number of people in Miami who might be the target of a contract killer. But Sam arriving to look for Markus Bolt and Marianne and her two trainee-killers at the airport the same morning—no. It could not be coincidence. Maybe the Russians really wanted to keep this quiet, and rather than sending their own operatives—and risking diplomatic sanction—they had sent a contract professional.

She knew and worked with Russians.

Follow her, and perhaps be made—he was sure she would remember his face—or let her walk out and alert Woodruff that she was in town, possibly tied to the hunt for Bolt.

He followed the trio at a respectful distance, pulling his dark navy baseball cap lower on his head, hanging back and to Marianne's left.

With earpiece in place, he activated his phone. Woodruff answered immediately. "Yes?"

"I just arrived in Miami. In the airport I just spotted a woman I believe to be a hired killer known as Marianne. German national but could be traveling under any passport. She has two associates with her. I'm following."

"Marianne was reported dead years ago."

"Well, her step is really spry for a dead woman." Marianne and her partners were exiting the airport and too much of the crowd between them had veered off to the baggage claim carousels. Sam parallel tracked them as they walked along the access road, hanging back, watching them through the windows. "I'm guessing she's here to target Bolt. The Russians know he could come here for Amanda."

"The Russians," Woodruff said, "already have hundreds of citizens in the Miami area that could be their eyes and ears."

"And they could immediately report a Markus Bolt sighting to Marianne for cleanup." Now Marianne and her companions were getting into a large car that had picked them up. She wouldn't be renting her own transportation—she would have a handler here, arriving first, who would take care of those logistical needs. You would not see Marianne's face on the security cameras at the car rental place or checking into a hotel.

"It means that the Russians might not be risking their own agents here on American soil. They want Bolt put down and vanished, then they control the story. Marianne could do that."

"You're certain it's her."

"Yes."

"In normal circumstances I'd alert the FBI to the presence of a foreign contract killer on American soil," Woodruff said. "But I can't do that now. You'll have to take care of her if she becomes a problem."

Three against one. He felt sweat, then a flutter in his guts. "Marianne might set up surveillance on Amanda same as me. If she spots me, she'll try to eliminate me as competition."

"She might be working for a South Florida Russian. Someone who gets rid of this problem would gain quite

a bit of status and favor with Morozov and his crew."
Woodruff paused. "You have permission to kill her and
her team if needed."

"That carries its own problems. She's trained a couple
of dozen contract killers through her program and her
protégés are fiercely loyal to her even once they leave her
nest."

"And if she's laid low for a while, those would have
been the people protecting her," Woodruff said. "She
could call in a lot of help."

"I'm already outnumbered," Sam said. This felt like
losing before he started.

"We can't add more people and keep this quiet,"
Woodruff said. "You're resourceful, figure it out."

"If she puts Amanda under surveillance..."

"If she's working with the Russian locals, they may
have their own leads. They know more than we do."

This was bad, Sam thought. The worst possible start.
I need to get to Amanda. Now.

He saw his ride arriving at the curb, in a familiar blue
SUV with a vanity license plate: BKSRCK. The window
went down. A former librarian peered out at him.

"I just spotted three contract killers," he said.

"Then you better hurry into the car, asshole," Paige
said.

14

KIRILL RETURNED TO HIS SEAT, leaving Illya moping in the bedroom. Val was still in her seat, laptop open, earbuds in. She gave him a neutral glance and then returned her attention to her work.

He opened the letters file on his iPad and started scanning through the unsent letters.

Phrases and complaints jumped out at him. Bolt's letters to Amanda tended to be shorter than Kirill had expected, and sometimes ended oddly, as if he hadn't known how to say another good-bye.

Did your mother tell you she tried to kill me? Do you wish she had succeeded? I tried to protect her and she went crazy. This is why I worry about you. The effect your mother could have on you.

There are people who wish me ill and might take it out on you. They already did on Allan. I want you to be careful in trusting people.

There's so much about my old life you don't know. And I don't know how to tell you.

There's one thing I wish I had told you before I left. Especially since Allan is gone. I still cannot tell you now. Because I'm not sure how you would react.

The Russians treat me well, but it's hard to make a friend and feel you can trust them. I have only myself to blame for that. No one will ever fully trust me again. The price I pay. I would trust you, though, if you were here.

I thought of bringing you with me. I did. You could have had a good life here; they would have made you into a little Russian princess. But I knew I could not make that choice for you.

I know you are back in Miami. I want you to be careful. I have a friend who might be able to help you.

I married again. I've never discussed this with you because you are my family and cannot be replaced. I think you would like her. She's kind, very pretty, and she puts up with me. I do well with patient people. And no, I didn't know her before I came to Russia, she wasn't part of that decision. She has a son around Allan's age. A good kid, smart. He doesn't like me so much, and I understand...he blames me for something not my fault. And he doesn't understand what his mom sees in me. There's a lot of good in me, if someone takes the time to look.

Kirill leaned back in the chair. *A lot of good.* The narcissism. The self-regard. There was no *How are you doing, Amanda?* in the letters. No real sign of interest in his daughter's life. No concern for the wreckage he'd left behind, just a litany of his own problems and issues, as if his abandoned daughter was just a sounding board. Perhaps he didn't ask because he never intended to mail them. Maybe the letters were a kind of journal in disguise. But there wasn't good in Markus Bolt, not to Kirill. He was glad Markus didn't mention him again.

Those were the letters to Amanda. And as Bobo had mentioned, there were a few written to Allan, before and after his disappearance.

> There is something I need to tell you. Your sister won't understand. It's why your mother tried to hurt me.

> The fishing here is very good but different from the Keys. I miss you, when it was just you and I out on the boat. And we could talk. You were the only person I could trust, with my fears and my hopes. I miss you so much.

> I felt you understood me when no one else did. I know it has been hard for you. I know you need money. I want to find a way to help you.

> I have one last secret. I have to find a way to tell you.

And what was that, Markus? The identity of Bobo's asset in the CIA? Did you tell Allan your secret somehow?

Did you get your son killed?

Kirill looked up at Val. She had shut her laptop, closed her eyes, and seemed to be dozing. Kirill got up and went back to the room where Illya lay on the bed. He could see the man was trembling.

"I want you to feel relieved that you told me the truth. I'll help you and we'll get the financial map back."

"Thank you," Illya said.

"Is there a phone on this plane?" Kirill asked.

"Yes."

"I'm calling my mother."

"I would be very careful what you say. Others might be listening to your mama's phone calls. In case Markus calls her."

You have to find him, Mama's words, the pressure of her grip on his arm. More than a woman worried about her husband. Why hadn't she told Kirill of her assignment? Had she even had a choice?

"There's a phone there you can use." Illya got up and stopped at the door. "Kirill Denisovich, find him. Kill him. If you want out of working in intel after this, I'll take good care of you. Give you a job in timber. It's nice and quiet in timber. Or if you don't like working in an office, you can run my security detail. Val runs it as well right now but it might be too much for her."

"Go," Kirill said.

Illya closed the door behind him.

Kirill picked up the phone, dialed home. The Dude answered.

"Duderov. Let me speak to my mother."

"Have you found him?"

Interesting, the Dude pretending he didn't know that Kirill wasn't yet in America. The distancing, already beginning in case he failed. "I'm en route still. Please put her on."

Silence.

"I am not asking again," Kirill said. "Put her on now."

He could hear the phone being handed over. "Yes, Kiryushenka?" Mama said.

"I want to know that you're okay," he said.

"Of course. Just anxious for you to find Markus. And bring him home to me."

"Do you really love him?"

"What a question. He's my husband."

"Answer me."

Five long seconds of silence. "Of course I love him."

"It wasn't just that you were assigned to watch him?"

Mama paused, lowered her voice. "I agreed to watch him. To protect him. Because I cared."

"Did he talk much about his son?"

"No. It was painful. The not knowing. If Allan had killed himself or if the Americans had killed him, you know, for revenge."

"Where will he go? To Amanda?"

"I told you, I don't know."

"He must be taking them something to barter with." This was a test, to see if she knew about the financial map that Illya had mentioned. But the Dude was probably standing right next to her and maybe she couldn't speak freely.

"He would not have brought any such leverage home." This was for the listeners, if there were any. Mama knew nothing and she wanted that established. "Because if he had, I would have found it, and I would have turned him in." For a moment she didn't sound like the shy wife, living in her famous husband's shadow.

"I know you would, Mama."

"But he must not have. He loves Russia. He gave up everything for it." Playing into the official story now, the one where he did not betray his hosts.

Kirill thought about the warmth in the letters to Allan, never to be mailed. "Mama, tell me about Allan."

"What about him?"

"It must have been hard to lose his son." Kirill thought then he should have talked more with Markus when Allan died. He had just thought that it must have been an unwelcome hell to be Markus's son. He had simply said *I'm sorry for your loss* to Markus and avoided him in his grief. He remembered Mama had cried for a boy she never knew.

"He never accepted he was dead. For a while he talked about Allan like he was dead and then he talked about his son like he was still alive."

"Odd," Kirill said. The root of his latest treachery needed to lie in his American past, for all their sakes. "Allan's body was never found. Maybe Markus knows where he is."

"I don't think Allan has been in hiding all these years. Plus, Allan was ashamed of Markus. I know that much. He got a letter from him before."

"A letter. From Allan."

"Yes. I made a copy of it and gave it to Duderov. So, you know, we could help Markus."

"Of course, Mama. What did the letter say?"

"That Allan was ashamed of his father, that he never wanted to see him again. That he couldn't have a decent career, that he was only seen as a traitor's son. That he had ruined Allan's life. Markus let me read it. It was sad. And it was just a letter. Too short to be encoded, and nothing hidden on the paper."

"Can you take a photo of this letter and send it to me?"

"After I told Bobo it had arrived," she said, "Bobo took it and analyzed it and made sure nothing was hidden in it, no microfilm, no codes, no messages. He made a copy and gave the original back to Markus, who burned it. It hurt him too much to keep it."

"Were there any other letters from his family?"

"No," she said.

"How did Allan's letter even reach him?" he said. Had Allan just mailed it? Surely the Americans wouldn't allow that? Would they?

"It was brought to him. By an American woman who was in Russia. A friend of Allan's, I think."

"What was her name?"

"I don't know. But Markus knew her. We were out walking in Gorky Park. He had a security detail, of course; we were afraid back then that the Americans would send someone to kill him although it would have been an outrage on Russian soil. He saw her—I saw him see her, if that makes sense."

"You mean he recognized her."

"Yes. She was sitting on a park bench, reading a paperback book, eating an ice cream. He sat next to her. They sat next to each other, for maybe one minute. Exchanged whispers. It made me nervous; I took a picture on my phone. She got up without looking at him and she left the book behind. He retrieved the book. Slipped it into his pocket in his coat. And joined us at the ice cream wagon, where I was treating the detail to cones. The letter was inside the book."

"He knew she would be there?"

"We walked there often. But he must have known he was being watched by Americans and they would try to make contact with him there."

"He never said who she was?"

"No. I assume she was just a friend acting as a courier." She sighed. "She was young, pretty, rather petite. And pregnant."

"Pregnant?"

"Yes. Just starting to show. But I could tell. I suppose a pregnant woman would not raise suspicion as quickly."

"Did Markus write Allan back?"

"He did. The next day I had to go to the best stationery store in Moscow for him. He couldn't mail it. He wrote the letter and sealed it. He wrote *For my son* on it. I didn't open it. He had sealed it so I could not, with these golden sticky seals all along the edge of the envelope. And I felt . . . I shouldn't. It wasn't about Russia versus America, but it was between father and son. I took his answer back to the park the next day. The pregnant woman was there, same bench, reading a different book. I sat next to her. She didn't look up from the book. She said, *He'll never see his son again, but Allan will be all right.* Her Russian had an American accent. I got up and left the letter behind. I walked away, and when I turned back, she was gone."

"Mama, why didn't you ever tell me this?" Kirill wasn't saying that for the listeners.

"It was between him and his son," she repeated. "I told Bobo afterwards."

"And you don't know what was in the letter to Allan?"

"No. Markus said he tried to apologize again and tell him something helpful."

Something helpful? What advice could a traitor father give to a devastated son? *Work hard, marry for love, don't betray your country like I did?* "Mama, I really need to know. This is no time for secrets. Did you read it?"

"No. I swear. Maybe I should have; Bobo was angry with me for not telling him until a few days later. But I thought of the pain of his kids. And Markus told me and Bobo all he wrote back was an apology."

Perhaps Markus's one communication back to the United States after his betrayal.

Bringing him a message, a great risk, from Allan. Why had the Americans bothered? Why give the traitor the comfort even of harsh words from his child? Unless she wasn't American intel, but truly just a friend of Allan's. Maybe that was how Markus recognized her. And when she'd gotten up and left behind her book, he'd figured out this was an amateur's version of a message drop.

"Did Markus hear from Allan again?"

"Not that I know of."

"Did you see the woman again?"

"No, I didn't."

Kirill was unsure what to think. "Would you know her if you saw her again?"

"Yes. Oh, and I know her name, because Markus said it. It was Lucy."

15

Austin

Your mother's grave is empty.

Daniel knew the way to the cemetery where his mom was buried. He and Dad didn't go often, but they went on his mother's birthday and the anniversary of her death and Daniel would solemnly leave the flowers that his father gave him. It occurred to him that he had never seen Dad leave a bouquet—he always let Daniel do it.

Your mother's grave is empty.

When he and James got home after playing pickup basketball after school, Leonie was sitting on the couch, her hands folded on her belly bump, watching a documentary about a famous artist on a streaming service. She was really into art. Which made sense, as she was now the art teacher at the school he attended. That was a little weird, the nanny who had been his virtual mom growing up now being a teacher there, but it also meant he saw her in the hallways and he was always (usually) glad to see her. He didn't take art this quarter, but she was still careful not to treat him differently from any other student when she saw him. At school he was careful to call her Mrs. Sullivan, not Leonie.

"There's snacks out, boys," Leonie said from the couch. "Eat them before I do. We're having pizza for dinner."

James grabbed a bag of potato chips and stomped upstairs to shower and start his homework.

Daniel put down his backpack and thought of showing Leonie the text message. It seemed dumb when it was most likely a mean kid trying to prank him. But people didn't really ask him about his mom's death. If someone asked where his mom was, he said she was dead, and if they kept asking (adults never did), he would say she died suddenly of an undiagnosed heart condition.

"Could we go to the cemetery?" he asked. "To my mom's grave?" he added unnecessarily. He thought his voice sounded awkward.

Leonie looked up at him, but he noticed she didn't seem surprised. "Sure. But why?"

"I just would like to go."

Leonie kept looking at him. "You don't normally go except on her birthday, and the other day."

What did you call it? Her deathday? "I know. But..."

"But what?" She patted the seat next to her on the couch. "Talk to me."

He sat next to her. "I'm old enough to know more."

She gave him a speculative glance. "I don't know what you mean by more." She took his hand. "I know it's unfair. I know you wish you had a mom."

"I have you." He couldn't look her in the face, though, when he said that. He wasn't her kid; she had a stepdaughter and stepson and she was about to have her own baby. She didn't need him anymore. Everything was going to change and it scared him. But he couldn't say that.

"Yes, sweetie, you do, now and forever. You know I'm always here for you."

"You're gonna be a great mom," he said, still looking down.

She squeezed his hand and now he looked at her face and saw an unexpected sadness. He knew she'd had a baby before she was his nanny, one that had died very young, and so she'd been a mom once before. A terrific one, he was sure.

"Thanks." She squeezed his hand. "You understand nothing changes between you and me. I'm here for you, forever. Always. We're a team."

"Can we go to her grave just because I want to?"

"Sure."

16

LEONIE DROVE DANIEL. IT WAS a beautiful day in Lake-haven, the sun bright in a cloudless sky. They parked near the grave on a road that wound through the cemetery. She'd stopped at the grocery and bought him a bouquet of mixed flowers, just like his dad would whenever they visited.

As they walked toward his mom's grave, he noticed another car parking, down from theirs, a woman walking to another grave, her hands clasped. He wondered suddenly if there had been many people at his mom's funeral. Didn't she have friends from high school or college? None of them had ever reached out to him. *I knew your mom. I loved your mom.* None of his father's few friends seemed to have known his mom. Even Leonie said she hadn't known her personally.

It was like his mother had existed long enough to marry Dad and have Daniel, and then she was gone, truly gone, with no shred of memory living in other people.

He stopped at her grave. The tombstone read "LUCY COLLINS CAPRA," with her dates underneath. No "BELOVED WIFE" or "LOVING MOTHER" or any of the other things one might say. His father would have picked out the tombstone. Dad could have said something more.

He laid down the flowers. *Your mom's grave is empty.* He put his hand on the grass. How could you know if there was a coffin under the green? It was crazy to take that message seriously, but he also could feel there was something like a wall around his mother's story, the way his father's eyes went distant whenever he had to talk about Mom, the way Dad didn't seem to share many memories of Mom—at Christmas, or Thanksgiving. The way his own grandparents, his dad's parents, had said, "We didn't know her that well," like it was a fast, short, tragic marriage.

He knelt down on the grass. And thought about the problem. If you sank a long metal pole, you'd hit the coffin, right? You'd feel the resistance. You'd need a pole six feet long. Were people buried six feet down? Or was that not true anymore? And what if there was a coffin? Was it empty? He tried to imagine driving a pole into the ground, awaiting the resistance of his own mother's casket.

This was crazy.

Why would anyone lie about his mother to him? No one had a reason he could think of.

So maybe it wasn't a lie.

"Daniel. What are you thinking?" Leonie asked.

Leonie knew him too well, reading the confusion on his face.

He wanted to show her the message. More than anything. But if he did, she would tell Dad and that would be the end of it.

And he wanted to know.

He wondered how to get into the cemetery later. There would have to be a way. And to get a pole.

"Daniel, look at me. Are you all right?"

"Yeah, I'm fine." He stood. He glanced over at the woman standing at a grave, now glancing at him and

Leonie. Older, sunglasses, in jeans and a dark shirt. She looked away when Daniel looked at her. She hadn't brought flowers like Daniel had. She turned and headed to her car.

Leonie was watching him, as though trying to measure his thoughts. "Daniel?"

"I'm ready to go," he told her.

17

⟨⟨⟨⟨⟩⟩⟩⟩

Miami

Amanda Bolt lived in an older apartment complex close to the Coconut Grove neighborhood. Paige drove past it three times, letting Sam look at the property from different angles—its exits, entrances, neighbors, and approaches. He had to consider it enemy territory.

No immediate sign of Marianne and her team. They were killers, not agents or special operations; he considered and decided it was unlikely they would mount a sustained surveillance operation where they might be noticed or observed. It was more likely that she would be watched by a local Russian recruited by the SVR, and Marianne and company would be summoned quickly if Bolt showed up. That way Russian hands could be kept clean.

There wasn't an easy way for him to monitor Amanda's comings and goings and not be noticed. He needed a roost if he was going to be a watchful hawk.

"Do they have vacancies?"

"When I called, the manager said they had two apartments available, year leases only. Amanda's in apartment

212. I broke into their office network from the parking lot and found the empty units are one next to hers, hallelujah, and one further down the hall with a good view of the parking lot. I wasn't sure which you would prefer, if either."

"Both. Call them back and lease them."

"It's a year lease, Sam."

"Doesn't matter. Section K is paying."

"Both of them, won't that be suspicious? Under what names?"

"Sam Chevalier and his brother, Danny. Two brothers leasing won't be weird."

"They'll do a background and employment check. I can't conjure you up out of thin air."

"I've had to use the aliases before here in Miami. I'll give you their fake socials and bank info. Sam and his brother, Danny, are on the bar payroll. As of right now. You'll find they have a credit and employment history."

Paige laughed. "You never fail to charm. All right."

"Obviously I'm Sam Chevalier. We'll say Danny's out of the country; that's why I'm leasing it for him." Daniel was named for Sam's brother.

"I better not get arrested for fraud," she said.

"You won't. We'll even prepay the year."

Paige pulled in and they went into the manager's office. Sam got a quick tour of both apartments, which were clean, small, and well maintained. He produced a credit card in the name of Sam Chevalier, an employment history as an assistant manager of multiple bars who was taking a new job at Amado, a bar he owned in Miami (where Paige was already the manager), and offered to prepay the first six months' rent. That softened the manager when he asked about renting an apartment for his brother as well, unseen. An hour later Sam had two rented apartments.

Surveillance sometimes started with paperwork.

Sam asked Paige to call a furniture rental store and get the basics for a stay: bed, couch, tables, and chairs. He took the keys and went up to the apartment next to Amanda's. He went inside. He listened at the wall; heard nothing. Each apartment had assigned parking and he walked down to the other apartment he'd rented, which had a view of the parking lot, and looked out at the two spots marked with Amanda and Roberto's number 212—they were both empty.

Amanda and the boyfriend weren't home.

Paige came up to the apartment. "So right next door, that's sweet."

"It's actually a little too close for comfort. They'll notice me. She could hear me if I can hear her."

"The furniture will be here tomorrow morning, first appointment I can get. You're sleeping on the floor here. Unless you want to camp in the apartment above the bar." Every bar he owned had a residence attached, which served as a safe house if Sam or another Section K operative needed a base or needed to move a person out of danger.

"No, I'll stay here."

"I'll scrounge you up a sleeping bag and a towel and some soap," Paige said.

"Great work today, thanks."

"So. She's Markus Bolt's kid?"

"Yeah."

"I'd almost forgotten about him," Paige said. "A lot of other crises since he took off."

Sam said nothing.

Paige crossed her arms. "You look thin. You need to eat."

"I'm fine."

"How's your boy?" Paige knew very little of his personal life, but she knew he had a son.

"He's okay. Growing. He's gonna be taller than me, I think."

"Let's get you fed, equipped, and set for your incredibly exciting waiting game," Paige said.

They drove back to Amado, a smaller high-end bar on the Miracle Mile, and he went up to the safe house above it. He got the surveillance equipment he needed: miniature cameras, smaller than what was available on the commercial market. Microphones, digital recorders, listening devices.

He and Paige ate a fast, late lunch of burgers and Parmesan fries and then he drove back to his new apartment. He walked down toward his door, noticing a sallow young man standing in front of Amanda's apartment.

Maybe this was the Russians making their move. Watching her to see if their pet traitor showed up.

18

London, en route to Miami

THE MARKARKIN JET REFUELED IN London and they all stayed on the plane. When they took off again, Illya retired to the bedroom with a fresh cup of tea. He looked worn, and Kirill wondered if he could keep quiet. He seemed to feel relief that he had told Kirill about the financial info that Bolt might use to buy his life, as if it were now Kirill's problem to solve.

Kirill sat down across from Val. She seemed to live on her laptop, but she had taken a break to open a thick book, written in English.

He let five minutes pass in silence. "How long have you worked for him?" Kirill asked.

She made a point of finishing the passage she was reading, inserting a bookmark, and closing the book. "Two years. Since my husband died. My husband was one of his London bankers."

"How did he die?"

"Traffic accident in London." Her voice wavered, ever so slightly. "A hit-and-run."

"I'm sorry for your loss."

"Philip and I had gotten to be friends with Illya, and he offered me a job. I didn't have much to keep me in London, and it was a good offer, and...I didn't want to stay in the apartment. Too many memories. It was a fresh start for me to work for Illya. As he jokes, he's in Moscow half the time, London half, Miami half."

"He also offered me a job," Kirill said.

"Doing what?"

"Security."

"It would be a good position. Illya's not really a target for anyone."

So far, Kirill thought. "He said you handle security now." He remembered her standing when he manhandled Illya.

"Only coordinating schedules with his team and making sure they adhere to the contract," she said.

"He didn't bring security with him." *Unless*, he thought, *that's you*.

"He has a guard detail in Miami that walks around with him. When he's not there, they guard Maria."

"Illya knows a lot of the Russian community in Miami?" Kirill asked. It was vast, thousands upon thousands, some of whom still returned regularly to Russia, others who meant to stay and make a home in the United States.

"He and Maria know all the influential ones. And the ones who wish to be. Mostly he knows the older crowd, she knows the younger."

That might be a valuable resource of information. Surely Bolt would avoid Russians. But maybe someone would be willing to help him, for a price.

"I suspect you know them all, too," Kirill said. He could guess that Val had made Illya's business her business.

Val shrugged. "I wonder...what you are doing in Miami. Pretending to be a distant cousin."

He didn't answer.

Val didn't press with a follow-up question. She closed her eyes, her book in her lap. She seemed to fall asleep in her seat. Kirill stayed quiet.

He read, reviewing the files on his tablet, hoping for another insight.

So. There had been at least one contact made between Markus and America, with this young woman named Lucy as the cutout. Surely the Americans knew about it. The Lucy woman was either CIA or a Bolt family friend, helping get a message to him. But if she was CIA, she would have tried to kill him, yes? Except it would have been a suicide mission and she appeared to be pregnant.

Unless none of it was truly about Allan. Maybe the message from him wasn't from him. Maybe it contained a code, or a phrase that communicated something else to Markus, and his response wasn't really for Allan's eyes, but for someone else's.

The CIA's perhaps. And why were they talking to their traitor? Not that they would have believed him anyway. A wilderness of mirrors, where nothing made sense.

Yet it had happened. The plainest explanation was that this woman was a friend of Allan's, willing to do a favor. Maybe a girlfriend, pregnant with his child. That would explain a lot.

And what was so important, so vital, that Allan would send his pregnant girlfriend to Russia to confront his father? Because even the passing of a message, done this way, was a confrontation of sorts. An accounting. A chance for a son to give voice to his anger.

So his son had something to say to him, and Markus had sent back some kind of apology, reasoning, explanation. He found a mention of the interaction in the files he'd missed before, thirteen years ago, based on Mama's report to Bobo. The woman had entered Russia on an American passport; her name was Lucy Carrier. She had spent four days in Russia, arriving in Moscow from a connecting flight in London, staying at the Four Seasons. She was not known to be a CIA asset. She was a Miami-based real estate agent; there were printouts of her smiling face, taken from the firm's website. It was suspected that she was a personal friend of Allan Bolt, given they both lived in South Florida, and she had never returned to Russia. So, not of great interest. Just a friend doing a favor. There was no record or report that she was romantically involved with Allan Bolt.

He went to the real estate firm's website. It was still running, but Lucy Carrier was no longer listed as an employee. He searched for her name. A number of Lucy Carriers appeared, but when he tightened the search to Florida and paged down, he found no mention of her. None. He searched Florida birth records for that year; no mention of a child born to a woman with her name. Mama had been sure she was pregnant. It could have been a fake bump, or Mama was mistaken.

He considered. Maybe Lucy Carrier hadn't needed to exist for long. A throwaway identity. Which meant she was CIA or some other American agency.

Bobo's intelligence analysts didn't offer a determination on who Lucy Carrier was...but Markus had recognized her. He knew her. Why hadn't this been investigated more?

He called Bobo.

"Lucy Carrier," Kirill said.

"Ah. The mystery."

"What can you tell me about her beyond what's in the file?"

"At first we thought she was a CIA contact. But if she was, she would have been someone he knew."

"Is this someone he might turn to in Miami? Even though she appears to have vanished?"

"Possibly," Bobo said after a moment. "Assuming she was a family friend and not intel."

"But you never confirmed that?"

"We had some Russian citizens who live in Miami ask around—we kept a bit of an eye on Allan in those years. A friend of Allan's said she was another friend of Allan's. That was our confirmation."

"So, pregnant, she came to Moscow to do a favor for Allan. Was the baby Allan's?"

"I don't know. According to the reports from the local Russians, she was married to a guy in Miami named Terrill Carrier. We didn't...we didn't push this after Allan died. You know how depressed Markus was."

"Yes. I remember."

"There was no more contact. There was no more son."

"Did Mama tell you what was in his letter?"

"She said she didn't open it, given how securely he had sealed it. She was afraid to—this Lucy might have told Markus she was spying on him."

Something helpful, Mama had said. Markus tried to tell his abandoned son something helpful. But no one, except Markus, knew what that was.

He kept reading through the file, trying to decide on a plan. His initial thought had been to watch Bolt's wife or daughter—although it didn't seem likely he would approach his family, who hated him and might still blame him for Allan's death.

He looked at Val. She still appeared to be asleep. He

got up and went into the large lavatory. On his own phone, he called Bobo back. "What support do I have amongst the locals?"

There were thousands of Russians living in South Florida: real estate investors, wealthy businesspeople who had second homes there, rich couples who were paying hundreds of thousands of dollars for so-called birth packages, which enabled them to birth their children in America, assuring US citizenship and a lifetime of easy movement between the two countries.

"Obviously we're not telling people that Bolt may have headed home. I'm not about to gossip with a bunch of Russians drinking on South Beach that our most famous defector has fled there."

"Bobo, isn't there anyone who could help me? Anyone you trust?"

"I need you to be a lone wolf. Find him, sedate him, put him back on Illya's plane. If anyone in the Russian community knows, they'll talk, and we cannot have that, Kirill."

Kirill took a deep breath. "Did he make friends among any of them now living in Miami, when they were back in Russia? I know you keep tight watch over every Russian living in America. So they won't be turned against us."

"The Americans can't give them as much as we do. They're wealthy because of Morozov. They're loyal."

"There's always someone who feels wronged. Someone who is mad." Or someone already in the pay of Americans.

"I'll see. But the point, I remind you, is to handle this quietly. I prefer no one even know you are there."

Kirill opened the lavatory door and peered out. Val hadn't moved. Maybe he should just use the resources at hand. A woman who was organized, spoke Russian, but was not Russian. Who might be, even though it was an unpleasant thought, expendable. He closed the door again. "I'll figure it out."

"If you can't get him back on the Markarkin plane, kill him and dump the body in the Atlantic or the Everglades. Just make him vanish. And then come home."

"My mother doesn't want him dead, Bobo."

"She may change her mind on that front. I'm counting on you. Do your duty. Remember your father."

"What in hell is that supposed to mean?"

For a moment Bobo was silent. "He...he took your mother from your father. You ought to hate him. It's fine to hate him now."

"I don't need you to tell me how to feel," Kirill said.

"I wasn't," Bobo said.

"Illya has an assistant. Valeria Garrison. What do you know about her?"

"Just a moment..." He could hear Bobo shuffling files. "Yes. The British woman."

"Not originally."

A slight pause as he scanned the inevitable file on her. "She's originally from Romania, emigrated to London about fifteen years ago. She was married to a UK banker, Philip Garrison, who worked for Illya and some other friends of the president. He was killed, leaving a pub in Richmond. He was drunk and he staggered out into the street apparently. The driver didn't stop. The case remains open."

"How was this banker useful?"

"He set up a number of...less-visible accounts under shell companies so Illya and others could access cash in the West, for real estate and investment."

"We didn't kill him?"

"We did not. Why are you asking about her?"

"I was just curious. Unusual to have a British woman

working for someone like Illya in such a trusted position." So she knew people in the broader Russian financial network beyond Illya Markarkin. And Markus was paving his road home with secret financial information.

"Ah, I think Illya liked·her and her husband. I hear she's very efficient."

"And she's not his mistress?"

"Not to our knowledge. But I don't need you comforting a widow. Stay focused."

"And she was fully vetted?"

"Yes. No ties to UK intelligence or law enforcement. Again, why the questions?" Bobo sounded impatient.

"Again, just curiosity."

"I'll tell your mom you'll be home soon. With her husband."

Kirill hung up and returned to his seat. Val snored, very slightly. He sat in silence for several long minutes. The plane hit some turbulence and shook sharply. Val sat up quickly, her hand going to her hip, closing on nothing. She blinked at him. The jet settled back into calm.

"You had a nap," he said.

"I guess I did." She got up and fished a moist wipe out of her purse, dabbed at her face.

"What are Illya's plans in Miami? Does he have actual business to conduct?" Kirill asked.

She shook her head. "Mending fences with Maria mostly. The whole point of the flight was to get you where you need to be, as the president wishes."

"So you don't need to be...assisting him."

She glanced at him. "Well, he's not generally capable of making his own dinner reservations, but my duties should be relatively light."

"Perhaps then you can assist me."

Her gaze narrowed. "Assist you."

"I may need to…navigate the Russian community there. And to get back quickly to this jet, and have it ready to depart on very short notice. May I count on you?"

"Whoever you are, you have Illya pissing his pants, so I don't really have a choice, do I?"

"Of course you do, Val. But it will help Illya if you help me."

Val got up and fished a bottle of vodka from the bar refrigerator; the flight attendant had excused himself to the cockpit. She poured them each a small, neat glass. Kirill accepted his, knowing he would take the barest sip. She leaned back in her chair. "What are you really doing in Miami?"

"Protecting Russia. Protecting Illya. If this goes badly, he'll be dead or broke."

He expected her to react with shock or disbelief but she remained calm, studying him. Val said, "I would be out of a job if either of those things happened."

He nodded.

"I have to find someone here," he said. "And bring him home to Russia."

"Who?"

"That doesn't matter right now. I have a couple of leads. I think having a woman with me might open some doors."

She let her question go. "You mean make you look less like a guy who is going to pull a gun out and kill someone."

"Do I look like that?" He shifted slightly in his seat.

"A little bit, Kirill. But then I watch a lot of bad action movies."

He laughed. "Then you can help me soften my image. I need someone who can navigate the community here, introduce me if needed, help me find things. You have an organized mind."

"Illya will have to say yes. I can't just ignore my responsibilities to him."

"Illya will make this a priority."

She leveled her gaze at him. Ten minutes ago he'd wondered if he'd have to eliminate her if she knew too much and now he wondered what it would be like to kiss her. He pushed the thought away.

"All right," Val said. "I'll help you."

19

***

Austin

LEONIE AND MATT SERVED UP pizza for dinner. James had a big math test to study for, so Daniel asked—so he wouldn't disturb his friend's studying—if he could do some of his schoolwork at his house, since it was just a five-minute walk. Matt and Leonie exchanged a glance and Leonie said, "Sure."

Daniel walked home, the light from his phone aimed at the sidewalk. His house was dark; he'd forgotten to leave on any lights. He came in by keying in a code on the garage pad and turned on the downstairs lights. It was usually just him and Dad at the dinner table; Dad didn't make time for girlfriends, and he didn't have so many friends in Austin. Dad worked a lot.

Daniel went up to his room. The rest of the house was spare in its decoration, but Daniel's room was like a nest of sorts. Posters of his favorite basketball players, framed tickets from when his dad had taken him back to New Orleans (where they had lived before Austin) and they'd gone to a Saints game, pictures of him and his dad on trips: Kauai, Montreal, London. His room had always been his sanctuary. On the bureau was just the one picture of him and his mom, her holding him the day he was born, and she didn't look happy. She looked confused. Maybe being a mother had overwhelmed her, what with her underlying health issues. He had the picture, framed, on his bureau.

He sat on his bed and stared at the picture for a while. He could see some of his mom in him; he had his dad's eyes, but his mom's mouth and nose.

That echo in his face was all that was left of her; he was all that was left of her.

It made him feel like he owed her something. He had never gotten to do anything for her.

Your mother's grave is empty.

He'd told Leonie a fib; his last class had a substitute teacher, and she'd given them study hall and so he'd cranked out his homework already.

Daniel opened his laptop and started his research. He learned most burials now were four feet down, and there would likely be a concrete shell over the casket. So he could test it with a shorter pole maybe? But that would tell him nothing if he hit the shell. He couldn't dig to uncover the casket and get through the concrete.

There had to be an easier way.

He realized, reading about funerals, that there would be paperwork tied to it—signed forms, contracts, bills, and such. He knew nothing about paperwork except it was something adults dealt with, like when Dad had to sign permission forms. His dad would have paid for his mom's funeral so there would be records.

He went up to his father's office. Dad worked for himself, owning his bars, so he had an office at home, for when he wasn't at one of the properties. The older Daniel had gotten, the less traveling Dad had done, as though Dad had realized that Daniel wouldn't be at home forever. Daniel was glad. But he also thought of the time Dad had come back from a tour of his European bars with a broken arm and a black eye. Someone had tried to mug him in Amsterdam, Dad had said, and he should have just given up his wallet, but he didn't and the guys beat him up and left him lying in the street. That had scared Daniel badly, but he didn't want to say that to Dad.

The office door had a special lock—an entry pad, like the garage—but Daniel knew the combination. He'd seen Dad enter the six numbers, which seemed random to him. Daniel asked him why he locked the doors when he was away, like Daniel had any interest in his work, and Dad said, "Burglars," which seemed an odd answer. But then Dad said, "There's nothing interesting in here," and Daniel wasn't very curious.

He punched in the numbers: 4-6-9-3-3-2.

He'd been in the office before when it wasn't locked up, of course, so seeing it was nothing new.

The walls were covered with pictures of Dad's bars—their signs, or photos of people enjoying themselves inside. Dad was in a few of the photos. Sometimes he smiled. He looked very much the host, especially in the bars in New York, Sydney, Paris, and Tokyo, where he wore a suit. People looked happy in the bars. Daniel had been to his father's bars in Austin and New Orleans but none of the others. They weren't a chain; each bar had its own name, its own identity, its own style. *Can't I go on a trip with you?* he'd asked. *No*, Dad had said, almost abruptly. *No*, he'd said again, softer and quieter. *Bars aren't places for kids. It would bore you.* And that had been the end of the conversation.

It was a little weird, though, that the bars weren't a chain. Restaurants had chains. And why didn't Dad own a bunch of bars, say, here in Texas? To own one bar in New York, one in Los Angeles, one in Sydney...it wasn't very *efficient*, was it? It was a sudden realization.

His father's office had a closet. There were some file cabinets in there. He'd never looked in them. He tried one; it was locked. He went to the desk and found a small key that looked like it might match.

He tried it.

The file cabinet opened. It wasn't very full. There were folders, with his dad's tight, neat handwriting, with tabs for mortgage and life insurance and other things adults worried about.

There wasn't a folder marked "FUNERAL" or "LUCY." But then he saw one labeled "LAKEHAVEN CEMETERY."

Daniel pulled the folder out. He sat on the floor. There wasn't much. Dad had bought the plot around the time they moved from New Orleans to Austin nine years ago. Mom had originally been buried in New Orleans, he knew.

Because of the note, he was thinking of the casket, where it was.

There was only the plot purchase.

That paperwork to move and rebury a casket wasn't here. Wouldn't Dad have to have paid to move the coffin? Why hadn't he?

He was a kid, and he realized he didn't know exactly how such things worked, but there would have to be a fee or a charge for reburying the casket, right? Digging up a coffin and moving it to another state wasn't free. He looked closely again at the receipt. It wasn't made out to Sam Capra. It was made out to some company name he'd never heard of, Collins-Capra Property LLC.

Collins, his mother's maiden name.

So if this company bought the plot, who had paid to have his mother reburied? He looked through the rest of the files and didn't find anything relating to the reburial.

He took the file and put it into his backpack. He could look at it more later, when James was asleep.

He went to Dad's computer. He had never done this before; tried to access Dad's computer. The screen woke when he moved the mouse and it asked, of course, for a password. He knew a couple of the passwords that his father used on online shopping accounts. He tried to use those; neither worked. Neither did the obvious variants. He sighed.

He looked again at the text he'd gotten, talking about his father's secrets. Maybe there was a faster way. He texted the number:

I got your note in my choir binder. Who are you?

He waited; no response for five minutes. Then:

I think you deserve the truth, Daniel. That's all. I don't want to hurt you. But this was the best way I could get your attention and maybe get you to listen while your dad was going to be away.

And then, in the next text, a picture of his dad and his mom. Younger, smiling brightly, in jackets, with Big Ben behind them. A photo of the two of them in London. Mom was pregnant. With him. He'd not seen this picture before.

Whoever this was—they had this photo. A family photo. They knew Dad was gone. And Daniel was alone in this house. A sudden wave of fear washed over him. He closed his father's office door, heard the locks reengage. He ran down the stairs. He left on the kitchen lights and went out to the garage.

No one there, no one waiting. He keyed in the access code and lowered the garage door.

He walked along the darkened street. The night was quiet.

He noticed a car, parked along the road, in front of

the entrance to the neighborhood pool, not by a house. He tensed but kept walking.

As he got to the car, he heard the soft hum of the window lowering.

"Daniel," a voice said from the darkness. He lifted his phone and aimed the light.

Sitting in the driver's seat was a woman. The woman from the cemetery today, who had watched him. He could see the shape of another person on the passenger side, but he couldn't make out details.

"Who are you?" Daniel asked.

"A friend."

"I don't know you. Are you sending me those texts and notes?"

"I mean you no harm."

"Who are you?"

"Tomorrow, after school, come home. I mean your real house, not your former nanny's. We can sit outside and we can talk. Or we can meet in a public place, like a library or a coffee shop. I want you to feel safe and to know I only want to talk to you."

"I could call the police on you."

"I don't think you will. I know what happened with your mom."

"Who are you?" He looked at the woman's face. "I'm not going to meet with some stranger."

"I knew your mom. And I've not had the courage to come talk to you. But things have changed. You deserve to know about your mom."

"Daniel?" He could hear Matt's voice calling to him from the yard, two houses down. "Is that you?"

The car pulled forward, leaving Daniel behind. He watched it drive away. He kept walking along the sidewalk, then up through the yard where Matt stood. "I was about to walk down to the house and check on you," Matt said. "You all right, buddy?"

"Yes, I'm fine," Daniel said. His voice sounded weirdly normal. He felt dizzy.

"Who was in that car talking to you?"

He nearly told Matt the truth. But if he did, it would be A Thing, and he wanted to know what this woman would say.

So he lied. "Oh, a friend from math class. He told his mom to pull over because he wanted to ask me something about the homework."

"Oh. All right."

"I need to go finish my homework," he said.

Matt followed him into the house but did a quick detour down the hall toward his home office.

Daniel dropped the backpack on the floor.

Leonie was sitting in the den, watching another show on a streaming service, as he walked in.

Daniel collapsed on the couch next to her. He wanted to put his head in her lap, the way he had when he was little, but she had the baby bump and he was too old for comforting.

"Everything okay?" She paused her show.

He could tell her everything. He should. But she would tell Dad. Dad, and Leonie, would put a stop to all this.

"It's just unfair," he said. The words surprised him. "Unfair." His face felt hot. He'd never talked about this before. He'd kept it inside. "That I don't have a mom."

"Baby, I know. I know." Leonie hadn't called him baby in a long time. He was going to be taller than her soon and she wasn't his mom, but she was the closest thing he'd ever had to one. She put her arm around his shoulders.

"I can't really miss her when I didn't know her," Daniel said.

"You miss the idea of her," Leonie said quietly.

He nodded, miserable. "I feel bad feeling that way. Like having Dad isn't enough. I mean, I'm okay but I just wish I could have known her."

Leonie squeezed his shoulder. "I didn't know her. But I know . . . she loved you. That she tried to protect you . . ."

From what? Leonie seemed to have run out of words. He wanted to ask but he didn't.

"Protect you . . . and take care of you."

"Did Dad love her?" This was the boldest question of all.

Leonie blinked at him. "Of course he did. Why . . . why would you ask that?"

"Are you lying to me?" he asked suddenly.

"No," she said. "I didn't know your mom. I met your dad after she had died, when he needed a nanny. You know that."

He said nothing and she said, "Why would you ask if he loved her?"

He felt his mouth tremble. "Because he never says anything good about her. He never mentions that he loved her. He doesn't tell me about their happy times or fun they had . . . or anything."

"I think . . . I think her death was very hard on him. And you know he doesn't share his feelings easily."

"Bull," he said. "Every day he tells me he loves me, so I'll know it. He shares his feelings. Just not about her." Daniel turned his face away. The question rose to his lips and he couldn't keep it in. "Is she buried here? For real?"

Leonie turned his head to face her. She had paled. "What . . . what makes you ask that?"

"Is she?" Now he stared at her, raised his jaw a little in defiance.

"Of course she is." Leonie's voice was sudden steel. "Why on earth would you even think otherwise?"

He'd hit a nerve, and he was already regretting this. Leonie had the look on her face that an adult got when a kid had pushed a boundary too far. He didn't know what to say.

"Because...what would even make you think this?" She stared at him. "Did someone suggest such a thing to you?"

And then he knew, in the way that a kid knows, that there was a sliver of truth she was hiding in her rising outrage. It was like seeing a beacon through a dense fog. "You sure seem upset."

"You can't say this insanity to your dad. You just cannot." She crossed her arms, then suddenly uncrossed them and grabbed his hand. "Where do you think she is if she's not buried here? I'm just curious to hear your theory."

"I don't know. I don't know."

"What made you think this?" she pressed. "Is that why you wanted to go to the grave today? Someone gave you this idea, Daniel, and I want to know who."

He said nothing. He turned away. She touched his shoulder then she got up.

"What's going on?" Matt asked, coming back down the hall. "Y'all okay?"

"Yes," Daniel said before Leonie could answer. "I've just had a real long day."

Great, he thought. *You upset your pregnant nanny and she'll tell Dad this, and now that's it's all said aloud, it sounds crazy.*

20

⚬⚬⚬⚬

Miami

SAM APPROACHED THE MAN KNOCKING on Amanda's door—who stood between him and his own apartment.

Sam thought, *He's expecting her to be home in the middle of the workday, so what's her work schedule? Or does this guy not know it, or is he just testing the waters?*

The pale young man knocked again. He glanced at Sam as Sam headed his way. He had pale gray eyes, dark hair. His gaze, resting on Sam, was unsettling. He didn't look like a threat, but he also didn't look like you'd want him to pet your dog.

Sam considered. Could be a guy knocking on doors for a political cause or for door-to-door sales, but he wasn't wearing a credentials lanyard or a shirt with a logo and he didn't have a petition pad. Also, he was biting his lip; his posture showed his anxiety.

Maybe he worked for Marianne and her protégés.

Sam took all that reading in less than five seconds.

"Hello," the young man said. His mouth worked in an approximation of a smile, but it was more like a twitch. He found smile mode and then stayed there.

Sam said, "Hey," as he walked around the guy and slid his key into his lock.

"You haven't seen your neighbor, have you?" the young man asked. His voice was low, reedy.

Maybe this guy was with Bolt. Maybe a minion sent here to scope out the lay of the land. Like Bolt could have minions. All sorts of bad guys had. God only knew how much money the Russians had paid Bolt over the years. He'd been a spymaster. He knew how to recruit, how to funnel money, how to delegate.

Sam faced an instant choice. If this guy was just a friend of hers, it was fine to admit to not knowing Amanda. If this guy was a scout for Bolt, then any new person in his daughter's vicinity would be suspicious. Bolt would know from the lack of media coverage that so far the Russians had been silent about his escape, or departure, and Bolt could not be certain the Americans knew yet about his possible return. If he'd hired helpers in paving the way back to Amanda—this guy could be one.

Just here to scope the territory around Amanda, same as Sam.

"Uh, no, sorry, I haven't seen them today," Sam said. "Are you a friend of theirs?"

"Yes," he said after a moment. "I went to school with Amanda. We're old friends. And you are?"

"Sam Chevalier. Just a neighbor."

"I thought she'd be here. It's her day off." He almost sounded offended.

"Did you want to leave a message?"

The pale gray eyes narrowed. The mouth moved again slightly. "No, thank you. I don't think I've seen you around before."

"I keep odd hours. I work at a nightclub." True, but skimming the truth.

"Ah. Nice to meet you." But he didn't budge.

Sam quickly entered his apartment and closed the door behind him so that the guy couldn't see it was empty so far of furniture.

Sam stood on the other side of the door. He heard the guy knock again on Amanda's door. "Amanda. Please. I only want to be of help." Still no answer. Sam, watching through the door's peephole, couldn't see him, but the knocking stopped. He was leaving.

Amanda wasn't here. Or at least she wasn't answering the door for this guy.

He might not have much time before she was back.

Quickly Sam laid out the surveillance tools on the floor, organizing them. This was the most delicate part of the operation, and not one he'd known he could immediately implement. She might be home and simply not answering her door. It would be better to know. Her car wasn't here—her file told him she drove a BMW and her parking place was empty when he'd checked earlier.

But he wondered if the odd gray-eyed guy would be watching her front door from a distance—it faced the pool, and the street, and so did, by extension, Sam's.

Sam listened at their shared wall. No sound. This could be his chance. He packed the surveillance gear carefully into a backpack, arranged in the order he'd need to retrieve it. Microphones, two tiny cameras. Minimal kit. If Markus Bolt showed up, he'd no doubt search her apartment for bugs, but if Sam heard him inside the apartment, this was over.

This was a risk. He hadn't established their daily pattern through surveillance. But if he could monitor them and Bolt contacted her, this would be much easier, and he'd be home to Daniel sooner. The other risk was that she, and her apartment, was already being watched—by

Marianne's team, by the Russians, by the gray-eyed man. Him breaking into the apartment would be an immediate flag for action by any hostile party.

He listened at the wall once more. Silence.

He stepped out of the apartment. He risked knocking at the door, already deciding he was just the new neighbor saying hi. No answer.

There was a piece of paper wedged into the doorjamb, folded, marked "AMANDA." He glanced around and pulled it free.

In a neat, spidery handwriting, he read:

The past doesn't have to be what you thought it was. Please listen to me. I can help you in a way no one else can or will. Please take my call, Mandy. Or let us get together and talk.

The past? What did that mean? And "Mandy" seemed to imply familiarity; the file hadn't noted she went by a nickname.

Sam knelt before the door and put the note down on their welcome mat. The lock was not a complicated one; he slid his Japanese lock picks into place, worked the first lock in under a minute. Section K training made him fast at this. He pushed open the door, listened to the silence within.

He stepped inside and closed the door behind him, leaving the note behind on the mat. More silence. He relocked the door.

Had anyone watching seen him? He'd probably know soon enough.

The apartment was a mirror image of his own in terms of layout. He moved first to the kitchen. There was some room between the top of the cabinets and the ceiling, presumably for decorative items, and he slipped a tiny audio bug there. Then he moved to the den. Another bug slipped on the underside of the coffee table. Another one on the underside of a crowded bookshelf. Sam paused for a moment to study the shelves—you could learn about a person from what they read. Lots of worn paperbacks—fantasy, romance, and a few memoirs. None of the books about her father. No books on politics or Russia or espionage. She wanted none of that, and he could not blame her.

He went into the bedroom. The bed was unmade, laundry scattered across the floor. But just on the left side. The right side was tidy. The laundry was female clothing, so he guessed it was Amanda's and that her boyfriend, Roberto, was the neat freak. He carefully put a bug on the underside of the bed frame. He didn't relish listening to pillow talk—or whatever else they might do. He made a silent promise to Amanda to delete the recordings and images once her father was found, hopefully elsewhere. There was no call for Woodruff or Section K to keep them.

The cameras now. Sam went back to the den and hid a tiny one along the frame of a mirror above the fireplace. He stepped back and could see it only because he was looking for it. He went into the bedroom and placed one above the sliding glass door that led to the balcony.

He heard a key slide and rattle in the front door lock.

Someone was arriving home.

Immediately he stepped out onto the balcony that fronted both the den and the bedroom. He jumped from Amanda's railing to his own balcony and slid open the sliding glass door that led into his own den. He closed it behind him and opened the laptop he'd left on the floor.

He activated the feed, his system finding the bugs and making a wireless connection. He wished he'd had time to test the placements, but he'd have to wait until the target apartment was empty again.

"...I'm going to kill that little freak," he heard a deep, masculine voice say.

"No, you're not." A female voice. He guessed it was Amanda Bolt.

"I want him to leave you the hell alone."

They'd found the note, he guessed.

"If I talk to him...maybe he will leave me alone."

The wireless camera feed kicked in and windows appeared on his screen.

Amanda Bolt and her boyfriend, Roberto—he'd seen their photos in the file—were in the apartment's den. He slipped in an earpiece so they wouldn't hear an echo of their own voices through the thin apartment walls.

Amanda looked older than in her photos. Dark hair, cropped around her shoulders, eyeglasses, dressed in a polo shirt with a courier company logo on the right side and faded jeans. A little wreath of a rose tattoo around her forearm. Her arms were crossed, so he could see it clearly.

Roberto was a wiry guy, tall, wearing jeans and the same courier service polo shirt, someone who clearly spent some time in a gym. Dark hair, a goatee, an expensive watch on the wrist.

Amanda was pacing the floor, clearly upset, and Roberto kept trying to comfort her with an embrace. He was holding the note.

"He needs to be taught a lesson," Roberto said. "He'll bother you until you give in. I'm not having it."

"You can't go beat him up. I don't think he's well."

"I don't want him bothering us."

"If I talk to him a little bit, or listen to what he has to say no matter how crazy, maybe he'll leave me alone."

"But you don't have to give that to him just because he asks. You don't ever have to talk to those people."

She stared at the floor. "He's crazy. This is all he cares about." She headed toward the kitchen, stepping out of sight of the den camera. Roberto kept talking to her and Sam could hear the opening and closing of a refrigerator door. "But so what if he does?"

"Because bringing up all that stuff with your dad again, he could go to the press. That could mean journalists poking around us. Conspiracy theorists. You don't need that attention, babe. We don't need to be under a microscope."

"I'm sorry my sordid past may affect the business." Her voice was sharp.

Why, Sam wondered, was Roberto concerned about attention? Something else at play here.

"I didn't mean it that way." Apology in his tone.

"Sure you did. You act worried all the time. I thought we were doing well."

"We are . . . I just want to do better. A lot better. I want to take good care of you, Amanda. Give you all the good things you deserve."

"I just want to be happy," she said simply. "And I don't want you constantly worrying about money or the business."

"If you won't let me beat him up, then we need another option to keep him away," Roberto said.

Amanda came back into the camera's view. She was holding a large glass, full of red wine. She sipped it. Her voice trembled. "One life to live and this—this is how he spends his days. I'll never understand the fascination."

"He's garbage and yet they admire him," Roberto said.

Amanda took a long sip of her wine. "I don't want to go meet with him. I don't even want to know what his latest theory is and why he can't just tell it to me on the phone if he needs to tell me. I just want him to leave us alone."

"Then you won't meet with him. Let's think on what to do. You sit. I'll make dinner tonight." Roberto kissed the top of her head, and then stepped out of frame, heading into the kitchen.

Amanda sat down on the sofa, drank her wine, turned on the television news.

The nerdy-looking interloper was somehow trying to set up a meeting with her. So it had to be about more than relaying some information, and it must have to do with her father. Sam needed to know what.

He checked the news feeds. Still no word leaking from Russia that Markus Bolt had gone missing. He set news alerts to chime on his phone if keywords like #MarkusBolt or #traitor started appearing in news feeds.

He watched the camera feed. Amanda got up after several minutes and went into the bedroom. Sam activated the camera there. He saw her close the bedroom door. She knelt by the little cabinet next to one side of the bed and she pulled a drawer entirely free of the cabinet.

Amanda was positioned between him and whatever she was doing or looking at—Sam couldn't see. She remained in place, as though reading something; he saw a slight movement of her elbow. Then she stopped and reached for the drawer and slid it back into place.

She got to her feet. A lock of her dark hair had fallen into her face and she eased it back. She looked ready to cry. She blew out air from her lungs, took a deep breath, looked up at the ceiling as if to compose herself.

Then she went back into the den.

So who was the pale man, and how was he a threat,

and how did he tie to Amanda and the Bolt family? And what was in that bedside table?

"Hey," Ricardo said. "You want to go down to the pool? It might help you relax."

Sam was suddenly glad he'd packed a swimsuit. Then his phone rang. He glanced at the screen. Leonie.

21

Hey," Sam said.

"Daniel's asking about Lucy," Leonie said. "Why you don't talk about her much. I told him it was painful."

"Thank you."

"And we went to her grave."

"What?"

"He wanted to go. I bought some flowers for him to lay on her grave."

Sam forced himself to take a deep breath. This could be handled. "All right. It's just normal curiosity."

"Something triggered this," Leonie said. "And I'm wondering if it's me."

"What do you mean?"

"I'm . . . I don't want this to sound wrong. Or entitled. But I'm the closest thing to a mom he's had. And I'm about to have a baby, and I think he thinks I won't have any more time for him. I think that's what's driving this."

Sam closed his eyes. "You're right. I should have foreseen this as a possibility and taken precautions."

"Sam, he's not an operation. He's a kid."

"I'll talk to him. Can you put him on?"

"He's at your house right now, getting some stuff he needs."

"Will you have him call me when he's back?"

"Do you have time for him?"

Did he have time for him. He knew Leonie didn't mean the question to be a blow, but it landed all the same. "Of course."

"I ask," Leonie said, "because being mentally distracted when you're on a mission could be fatal." Her voice had fallen to a whisper so her husband and stepchildren wouldn't hear. "You have to be at the top of your game."

"Then why did you tell me this?" he said.

"Because I do need to know how you want me to handle it."

Handle it. He'd had no choice about the lies he'd told to his son. Only when he had rescued the infant Daniel had he had time to think: *Oh, the lies I will have to tell him.* By then the fiction created by the Agency about Lucy's "death" had been set in irreversible motion.

"Sam?" Leonie asked.

He needed to be down at that pool, eavesdropping, hearing what was happening in Amanda's life. Nothing he could say would stem Daniel's curiosity. "I'll text him later and set up a time to talk."

"Okay. I'm sorry about this. I don't want to give you a distraction, but I figured he'll call you and I didn't want it to be a surprise."

"Thanks, Leonie." He said his good-bye and hung up. He went to his bag, changed into a T-shirt and a swimsuit, grabbed a tablet. He could talk to Daniel later; the sooner he found out what was happening around Amanda, maybe the sooner he would catch her father and get home to see his son.

22

Even though it was a lovely, warm Miami night, the apartment pool wasn't busy. Two women sitting in the shallow end, on the steps, sipping from plastic cups. Another couple on lounge chairs, drying from a swim, talking quietly. And at a table, Roberto and Amanda. He'd doffed his shirt to show tattoos of vines and crosses winding up both muscular arms. Amanda had a thick book open but wasn't reading it, listening to what Roberto was saying.

Sam picked a lounge chair between the couple and Roberto and Amanda, not far from the shallow end. He would not initiate conversation. He would wait to be spoken to. It wasn't a huge complex and he assumed that many of the tenants knew each other; although it seemed to him that people were more disinterested in their neighbors than ever. He tapped the reading app on his tablet and opened a novel he'd bought but hadn't started. He kept his eyes on the screen.

No one was paying attention to Sam. The couple were talking, holding hands, laughing softly. The two women in the shallows were also talking softly and then he saw one of them giving him a speculative look. He put his attention to the screen. Roberto walked past him and stepped into the water, saying hi to the two women, who said hi back, and then he glided into the deeper part of the pool. Sam glanced over at Amanda—she had her book open, her hand on the page, but was staring at some point past the book, lost in thought.

He felt the weight of a stare on him. Roberto, having swum to the other side of the pool, was watching him. Sam put his gaze back to the tablet.

A minute or two of quiet passed. Sam read the same paragraph in the book three times.

"Hey," a woman's voice said.

Sam didn't look up.

"Hey. Excuse me. Blond guy."

Sam, fitting that description, glanced up. One of the women on the pool steps was smiling at him. "Would you be a total sweetheart and bring us that wine bottle in the cooler?" She pointed over to a lounge chair next to his and he noticed a rosé wine bottle sticking out of a cheap plastic cooler.

The two women were both smiling at him. He got up, brought the cooler to the pool's edge.

"Thanks," the first woman said. "I'm Tara and this is Lily."

"Hi. I'm Sam."

"Did you just move in?" This was Lily, the other woman.

"Yeah." He saw Roberto taking in the conversation.

"New to Miami?" Tara asked.

"No. I own a bar here."

"Oh, so bringing drinks to ladies is *exactly* your skill set." Tara gave him a mischievous smile.

"Yeah," he said with a laugh.

"What bar do you own?" Lily asked.

"This one," he said, pointing at his shirt. *Amado*, in faded blue cursive writing, with a stylized heart positioned above the name.

"Oh, awesome!" Tara said. "On the Miracle Mile . . . I think I've driven past it."

"Well, next time stop in instead of driving by." He gave his best host smile.

"Isn't the evening your busy time?" Tara asked. "Shouldn't you be . . . shaking a shaker?" She had a sly smile.

Sam kept his return smile measured. "Perk of being the owner. I've got a great team running it. I'll probably swing by there later."

"Well, maybe we will, too," Tara said.

"It's a work night," Lily said. "I've got an eight a.m. meeting tomorrow. Can't we go Friday?"

"Killjoy," Tara said. "Do you have drink specials?" At least, he thought, she was dialing down the flirtiness.

"Yes, but not later."

"Not even if you're a friend of the owner?" And the flirtiness was back.

"Stop that," Lily said. "Tara is incorrigible."

"Well, we'll see," Sam said. "Ask for me if you decide to go and I'm not already behind the bar."

"I will," Tara said. Her smile was bright and full of promise.

"Enjoy your swim," Sam said. He had decided it was best he not appear too eager to engage or to fit in. At any moment Amanda might learn her traitorous father was on the loose, and she might be very suspicious of any new acquaintances who were making an undue effort to slide into her life.

He retook his seat. He looked up and saw Amanda watching him. *We have so much in common*, Sam thought. *The stain of treason, the weight of guilt over what a loved one did. You just don't know it. If I do my job right, your father will never even get close to you. You'll never know he was back. And you'll never know I kept him from you.* He glanced away lest his emotion play out on his face.

"You're my new neighbor, right?" Amanda said. He saw Roberto immediately start swimming back toward the shallow end of the pool.

He doesn't like her talking to another guy, even casually, he thought.

"I'm in 211," he said. "Are you next door?"

She nodded. "I'm Amanda in 212, that's my boyfriend, Roberto." Roberto climbed out of the pool, grabbed a towel, offered his dripping hand to shake. Sam took it without hesitation.

"Nice to meet y'all," Sam said. "I'm Sam Chevalier."

"I'm sorry, I don't think we've ever been to your bar," Amanda said. "Sorry, I was eavesdropping."

Don't apologize, he thought. *I'm doing the same to you.* "Come by sometime," Sam said. "If I'm not behind the bar, I'll likely be in the back."

Roberto toweled off. "Tough business, owning a bar. My folks were restauranteurs."

"Yeah, it's a lot of work."

"What did you do before the bar?" Roberto asked.

It seemed a sudden, awkward question. "I've been owning bars for quite a long while." He didn't explain the plural and he saw Tara paying attention to his answer. "Once it gets in your blood."

"Well, that's great," Roberto said. He gave Sam a smile that wasn't particularly warm.

And Sam decided to play a card. Maybe too early, but he wanted to act. Not wait.

"Oh, there was a guy looking for you this afternoon. Knocking at your door when I was coming back to my place. He asked me if I had seen anyone at your apartment today and I had to tell him I hadn't. He was kind of ... persistent about it."

"Oh, I'll bet he was," Roberto said. His voice hardened. "Mind telling me what he looked like?"

Sam described the visitor. Pale, gray-eyed, intense.

Amanda and Roberto looked at each other, Amanda frowning.

"Is there a problem?" Sam asked. *And, oh, can I be of help? See me as an ally.*

"That guy has been bothering Amanda," Roberto said.

"I'm sorry," Sam said.

"Not your fault. Thanks for telling us." Roberto nodded. It was a *Hey, you're a good guy* nod.

"I can chase him off if he comes around again," Sam said. "What's his name?"

"We can handle it," Amanda said. Roberto started to say something and stopped.

Momentary silence, grown awkward.

"Sure," Sam said. "Well, nice to meet you all. Come by Amado sometime if you like."

"Well, *I* will if they won't," Tara said, downing the last of her rosé. Sam nodded and went back to his apartment. He changed into clothes suitable for the bar—a tropical-weight dark shirt, linen slacks, and dress shoes. He packed a small bag for his intended activities later in the night and headed back downstairs. He did mean to go to the bar, to brief Paige on how she could help him tomorrow, but as he approached the parking lot, Amanda stepped out from the pool entrance.

"Hey, Sam."

"Hey," he said.

"Don't take this the wrong way . . . Tara . . . she's kind of a mess right now. Her boyfriend dumped her, and Roberto and I gave her a job a few months ago. She's kind of bouncing around and . . . I wouldn't want her to be taken advantage of."

She cared about her friend, that was sweet, Sam thought. "Sure. I understand."

"I mean I just armed you with information that she's vulnerable and I'll guess we'll see what kind of guy you are." She gave him a bold look.

"Wow. Blunt," Sam said. "I appreciate you're looking out for your friend."

"I appreciate you appreciating that." Her gaze was direct. "Also, that guy that showed up...he's not a stalker, he's just kind of a well-intentioned pest. He's an old friend but we're not really friends anymore. But it would be best if you would let me know if he shows up again rather than tell Roberto. Just tell me."

"So there's not a fight." Sam nodded. "I don't think this guy would last long against Roberto." But that guy also looked like he might fight very, very dirty.

"I don't want to see Gandy beaten up."

"His name is Gandy?"

"It's his last name, that's just what people call him."

"Well, I'll let you know if I see him again."

"Thank you."

"You and Roberto come by Amado if you like, the drinks are on me. So you know I'm a well-intentioned guy."

That got a slight smile from her. "We tend to have early mornings at our business, so maybe some other time."

"What do y'all do?"

"We own a local courier service. If you ever have courier needs, call us. Fast-n-Friendly."

"I'll remember."

"Well, it was nice to meet you, Sam."

He was so tempted to take a shortcut. He could say: *I'm here to protect you. Here to help you. We think there's a threat against you from Russia.* Not even mention her dad. *Come stay at my place above the bar, you'll be safe there.* But he couldn't. There was no threat, other than her dad, and being so direct would open a thousand questions. And that wasn't his assignment. So he just said, "Nice to meet you, too."

Amanda nodded and Sam went to his car. Scanning the lot, looking for a threat. Like Marianne and her murderous prodigies. Or the pale-eyed Gandy, lurking.

Nothing. A quiet night in Miami. It would be a long night for him. He pushed away Leonie's worries about Daniel; his son would be fine, he was just a kid with questions. He needed to put a protective net around Amanda Bolt, and surveilling the apartment was just the beginning.

But he needed the night to go deeper into darkness.

23

IN MIAMI, A CUSTOMS AGENT came aboard the plane and checked and stamped their passports. The new fake passport for Kirill Borisovich Markarkin passed inspection—just another wealthy Russian coming to South Florida. Kirill noticed Val's passport was still a UK issue.

That business concluded, a hired car, owned by a local Russian business, awaited them. Kirill helped the driver load the bags into the trunk and then shut the trunk door.

"Get back in the car, please," Kirill said to the driver in Russian, who obeyed after a nod from Val.

"We're not going to Sunny Isles with you," he said to Illya.

"Val?" Illya glanced at his assistant.

"Kirill needs my help. I've acquired a car for him and I'll go with him in case I'm useful. I've made dinner reservations for you and Maria at that Italian place you like. Pavel will drive you. I've set aside an empty condo in your building for Kirill to stay, and I'll stay in my usual one. But he has work to do this evening. Go enjoy your evening with Maria."

Illya crossed the asphalt and grabbed the lapel of Kirill's jacket. It surprised Kirill and he didn't fight back.

"You are not involving my assistant in this."

"We have a common need to see this done quickly and efficiently, yes? She's helping me."

"Illya, it's fine. I can help him navigate Miami so he can do what he needs to do. And then get back home."

"Bolt is dangerous, and you are not dragging my assistant into this."

And there it was, the name said aloud, and Illya turned away and let go of Kirill. Illya leaned on the back of the car. Kirill glanced at Val; her face was expressionless.

"I'll keep her safe," Kirill said. "Val is doing a brave service to Mother Russia. Be proud of her."

Illya's mouth worked as if he didn't know what to say. "Be careful," he finally said.

"I'll take good care of her," Kirill said.

Illya went and hugged Val, who appeared surprised by this display of emotion, and then he got in his limo.

"I borrowed a car from a friend of Illya's so there would not be a rental record. It's a spare Mercedes of his," Val said as they headed through the airport. When they walked back outside, the humidity hit Kirill again like a fist. He followed Val as she checked her phone and walked to a Mercedes sedan, parked on the top floor in a short-term lot. Val knelt and pried loose a key in a magnetic holder on the underside.

"Thank you." This was why he needed her; she was helping him cover his tracks. "What Illya said . . ."

"This trip is about Markus Bolt. Did the Americans snatch him and bring him here? Or is someone here threatening him, and you're supposed to protect him and deal with it?"

He made his choice to tell her. Bobo could be mad at him later. "No. We think Markus ran here."

"Ran. He left Russia? Voluntarily?"

"Yes, apparently."

"Why?"

"We don't know." He paused. "I don't know. It's suicide if the Americans catch him."

"And you're here to bring him back. His own stepson." She cleared her throat. "He mentioned you to me the last time he visited Illya. Showed me a photo of the two of you, with your mother. I remembered you. Is your mother all right?"

He appreciated the question. "Yes. I am hopeful he will listen to me, to reason, and come home if he's here."

"But you're more than his stepson," she said very quietly. "Hence the new passport. Hence the cover story. The Americans cannot know you are in Miami."

He nodded.

"I will never tell, Kirill. Never. He's made trouble for Illya in doing this?"

"Yes." He did not want to tell her about the financial map. She did not need to know that, and it could endanger her.

They got in the car, Val taking the driver's seat. She started the engine to power up the air-conditioning. "Where to?"

Kirill had weighed it. There were three options. One, Bolt might go directly to his family, most likely his daughter, Amanda. That was a highly risky approach. *Hello, darling, I'm home from my treason, how has your life been?* Two, Bolt might approach one of his former CIA colleagues here in Miami to broker a surrender—there were several. Three, Bolt might look for Lucy, an apparent family friend who might help broker a deal with his family—or maybe the CIA if she still had any ties to them.

"Kirill? Where are we going?" Val asked again.

He decided. "I need to find a real estate agent named

Lucy Carrier. She used to work at this office." And he showed her the address on his tablet, from the file.

Val stared at the picture of Lucy Carrier for several long seconds. As if memorizing it. "Very well," she said. "Let's go."

24

THE REAL ESTATE OFFICE THAT had once employed Lucy Carrier was a small one, close to Coral Gables. When Kirill and Val stepped inside, an older, heavyset man was walking toward the door as they entered. He appeared to be the only employee still in the office.

"Sorry, y'all, I'm just closing up. Tell me what you're looking for and I'll get on it in the mornin'." His Southern accent seemed exaggerated, like it was a sales tool.

"Hello. I am looking for information on Lucy Carrier. She was an agent here, many years ago."

The practiced smile, for one moment, wavered. "Why on earth would you be interested in her?"

"Are you Mr. Carrier?" Kirill asked. The report said Lucy Carrier had been married to a Terrell Carrier, owner of the firm.

"I am," he said. "Terrell Carrier."

"So you were married to Lucy."

"Briefly," he said. His mouth thinned, but the smile stayed on, as if through force of habit. "Very briefly. It didn't work out." He flexed an awkward smile at Val, who smiled back. "What do y'all folks want with Lucy?"

"Perhaps you know where she is working now, sir?" Val asked.

"I don't. She wasn't a very good real estate agent, to be sure. I think she must've left the business."

"Ah. She was busy with her trips to Russia."

"Russia? I can't imagine why she'd go there. But doesn't matter, she hasn't worked here in years."

"Perhaps you could call Lucy for me."

"I'm sure I couldn't. I don't have her number."

"We really do need to find her. I would so appreciate if you would give us an answer." Something cold now in Kirill's voice, because he felt sure this man was lying to them.

The two men stared at each other.

"I don't want any trouble," Terrell Carrier said. His voice trembled.

Kirill had a Glock under his jacket, but he didn't want to use it, and then Val said brightly, "Perhaps you know a friend of Lucy's? Someone who might put us in touch with her."

"Why are you looking for her?"

Val smiled. "She helped a friend of ours who had moved back to Russia from Miami. Sadly, he passed away. And he left her a remembrance. We don't mean her any harm, we're just looking to give it to her."

"What remembrance?"

"It's some money he left her."

"A Russian guy left Lucy money." Terrell Carrier's voice was flat.

"You sound surprised."

"I didn't think she really had a friend in Russia. I guess I was wrong."

"How long were you married?" Val asked. Kirill was silent, letting her do the talking.

Carrier tensed, slightly. "Not long. Less than a year. We weren't a good match."

"I'm sorry it didn't work. But you have on a wedding ring."

"Yes. I remarried. I'm sorry I can't help you."

"If…if, though," Val said, "you had to find Lucy yourself, where would you go? Who would you ask? And we'll leave you alone."

"A guy named Hollister. Greg Hollister. He was a friend of Lucy's. He might know. I don't have any way to contact him, though. None of this is my problem. I'm not involved."

"Greg Hollister," Kirill said, as if tasting the name. Surely when they left, Terrell would call and inform this Hollister someone was looking for Lucy. Kirill thought he should kill him. But he also didn't want to leave a trail of bodies in Miami.

It was a strange thing, to decide whether or not to kill a man while he stood there blinking at you.

"Thank you for your help," Val said suddenly. She took Kirill by the arm. Kirill looked at Val as if she'd lost his mind. Carrier followed them to the door and locked it behind them as they left.

"Let's go," Val said.

"Why…why did you…" Kirill started

"You can't kill him."

"I wasn't going to kill him," he lied.

Val said, "You thought about it because you want to be sure that he doesn't call Hollister and warn him."

Is she particularly smart at reading situations or am I showing my emotions? He had to do better. "I'm sure he will if he knows how to reach him after all these years."

"Not yet. He's stood at the glass door since we walked out, watching us, and he doesn't have his phone. Allow me. Stay here, you scare him. We need him to not be scared."

Val went back up to the door and said something that Kirill couldn't hear. But he stayed put, something in his instinct telling him to let Val try whatever she wanted to try. Val spoke again, and after a moment, Carrier let Val inside the office. Twenty minutes passed. The humidity chased Kirill back into the car, but he couldn't turn on the air-conditioning without the keys. Then he saw in the rearview mirror that she had exited the office with Carrier and the real estate agent shook her hand at the door, Val laughing, and then the man shut the door.

Kirill stared as Val sauntered toward him.

"Oh, sorry, should have given you the keys." She started the engine and he leaned, grateful, into the blast of cold air.

"It's handled," she said.

"What... what did you do?"

"I bought a house from him." Val lowered the visor, checked her reflection in the mirror, snapped it closed.

He wasn't sure he'd heard her correctly. "You did what?"

"Well, actually, one of Illya's shell companies bought it, and I acted as his agent. I asked our new friend Terrell what house was his hardest to sell, one in the expensive range, and he showed me a truly hideous mansion in Coral Gables. Bad layout, bad decor, also there was a murder there, a man killed his wife and his own mother and then committed suicide."

"Horrible," Kirill said. Staring at her.

"So, it's been on the market for months and he can't get anyone to touch it. I told him if he forgot about your visit and didn't call Greg Hollister that I would buy the house."

"How much?"

"Three million dollars. Of course, the sale is contingent on Terrell keeping his mouth shut. But I wired the money to him, in a holding account. It's through a shell company not tied to Illya." She gave him a bright smile. "I got the feeling Terrell is not close or very friendly with this Hollister. Maybe there's a history there."

Kirill stared. "And the real estate man believes you?"

"Oh, of course. And I'll keep my end of the bargain."

"That's . . . that's a very large bribe."

"Well, you get what you want, and Illya can sell it to some other new money Russian who doesn't know better." She paused. "The house is empty. I thought you might find that useful."

Kirill risked a smile. This was a woman. The thought of kissing her occurred to him again and he pushed it away, afraid she'd see the thought in his face. "Possibly very useful, Val. Thank you." He gave her a broad smile.

"It's nothing," Val said and this staggered Kirill a bit. "It's much better than killing him, isn't it?"

"Yes. Yes. It is. Thank you."

"Do you have to kill people often?" she asked.

He shook his head. "No."

She looked up into his face and flicked a small smile. "Good. And you don't have to today."

"I need to find out who Greg Hollister is and if he can point me to this Lucy Carrier."

"I don't think the house sale will be enough to keep Terrell from going to the police if you kill this Hollister."

"I'm not . . . I'm not here to kill anyone." Well, one person, but he'd prefer not to.

"Is she your only lead? She and this Hollister man?"

He thought of the report, of the data that Bobo's team had gathered. "There are people here, on the Internet, who admire Markus. Who think that he is somehow a hero. It's very strange. They've never met him."

"But these people . . . you think he would reach out to them?"

"Possibly. But who knows if he would trust them?"

"Can we eat? I'm starving. And tired—my body thinks it's past midnight. I bought a house; you can buy me dinner."

He had no time. Not for what might look or sound... like a date. Markus had to be found. If he didn't find him in the first twenty-four hours, he might not find him at all.

"You can take a break to eat, yes?"

"I shouldn't." Then he thought of something. Markus had left a burner phone behind. "Do you have an American phone?"

"I do," she said. She dug in her purse and handed him an iPhone, tapping in her access code. He went, without asking permission, to her call history. "There's only a couple of numbers here."

"Mostly I call Maria," she said, "and reassure her that Illya loves her."

"There's a number Markus called repeatedly here. A burner phone, we think. Maybe it was Lucy or this Hollister. If I call it from your phone, that will tell them who's calling. They could trace your number."

She took back the phone, fiddled with the screen. "There. Now the number is shielded. Illya had me add that app to all our phones. For security."

He wondered what Illya had been up to, to need that capability. Probably talking to his bankers, his money launderers. Kirill tried calling the burner number he'd memorized, which had been a South Florida lifeline to Markus.

No answer, no voice mail. Just ringing. He let it ring twenty times then ended the call. He felt angry now. He'd tried to reach out to Markus's contact here—whoever that was—and they would know a call was placed.

"Let's eat," he said, changing his mind. He had to have food.

She nodded. "All right. And while we do, we can find out who Greg Hollister is first, before rushing in." She started to drive; he called Bobo.

"Yes?" Bobo said, sounding exhausted.

"Do you know the name Greg Hollister?"

A hesitation. "I'll see if we have a file on him."

"He is connected to Lucy Carrier, according to her ex-husband. I've tried to call the burner phone number, nothing. Can we not track that phone?"

"I think the phone has been deactivated," Bobo said. "No activity on it for days now."

"I'm going to eat, and in that time can you find out about Hollister?"

"Yes."

"How is my mother?"

"She's actually here at the office."

"She should be home in bed."

"I told her that. Here."

Mama's voice. "Have you found him yet?"

"No, I just got here, Mama. Did he ever mention a person named Greg Hollister?"

"No. I don't recognize that name."

"Maybe he's one of the people he betrayed? Or worked with?"

"Those people were all dead to him once he came to Russia," Mama said.

"Think. Think."

"I don't need you to tell me to think," Mama said. "I think all the time. I don't know the name."

"All right, Mama. Thank you."

"Don't kill him," she said suddenly. "Can you do that for me? Don't kill him."

Silence in the car, Val not looking at him. She could hear Mama's voice on his phone. "I'll do my best," he said in a strained voice.

"That's not enough. Promise me."

"I have to go, Mama. I'm sorry. I'll talk to you soon." He ended the call. He wished Val hadn't heard that.

"Kirill," Val said softly. "You're a good son." She gave him a glance and then put her gaze back on the road.

He didn't know what to say. This just wasn't like his other missions. She drove to the restaurant, and he was grateful for her silence.

25

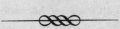

Sam drove to Amado on the Miracle Mile. He went in through the back entrance. The bar itself looked like a slice of retro Miami, with Art Deco styling in the interior, serving up a curated list of classic cocktails. The crowd tended to be well behaved and well dressed, younger, professional types. The draw was an easy ambiance, drinks, and light appetizers.

Paige was behind the bar, talking to one of the bartenders, and she nodded at Sam as he came in. Stairs at the very back led to an apartment above the bar, insulated against the sound, a safe house where normally Sam would stay if he was in Miami on bar or Section K business.

He activated the feeds to the cameras in Amanda's apartment on a large screen mounted on the wall. Amanda lounged on the couch; Roberto lay on the bed with his laptop. They were having a quiet evening at home.

Paige came in, arms crossed. She watched Amanda on the screen.

"Well, this is creepy," she said.

"I made contact with her," Sam said. "We met poolside."

"I thought you were just going to watch them."

"I'm accelerating the schedule."

"All right, Speedy, what do you need?"

"There's a guy who's been coming around looking for her. I think we kept assuming Bolt would make his own approach. But Bolt's got to have resources from his time in Russia, from having billionaire buddies. He could hire people to make an approach to her. She says his last name is Gandy. She said he used to be a friend, and he alluded to their past in the note he left her. Are you still hacked into the apartment rental office computer?"

Paige nodded. "I've got a back door open into their network for now."

"See if there's security camera footage of him in the parking lot. He was there around three this afternoon."

Paige shrugged, went to the safe house's computer. Tapped on the keyboard, accessed the digital security feed. Checked the time span. "Is this him?" she asked, putting the feed up on the big computer next to the images of Amanda watching TV in her home. He saw the man walking toward a truck, getting in.

"Yes. Can you get the license plate?"

"I think so." She froze and then magnified the image. It was a Georgia plate.

She did a search through Section K access of a state database. "The car is owned by Dennis Gandy of Atlanta. Do you want me to do a workup on him?"

"Yes, please." He needed a moment to gather his thoughts. "I want to know if Dennis Gandy has any ties to Bolt or ties to Russia."

"Are you okay?" Paige glanced at him.

"Sure, why?"

"You just seem preoccupied."

Sam sat down. "Do you think I'm a good father?" His voice was low and quiet.

Paige studied his face. "Despite your numerous other failings, I would imagine you are."

"Does a good father stay in this line of work?"

"If we told all parents they couldn't fight the bad guys, or they should feel guilty, then we wouldn't have many ... people fighting the bad guys," she said.

"I feel like he's just been through so much."

"But he doesn't even remember it." Paige knew the history of his marriage; he'd told her one night, just the two of them in the bar. It was classified information and it was a mistake. He shouldn't have done it. But he didn't have many friends who he could confide in. Paige was like a big sister, easy to talk to, and he trusted her.

"I told him she was dead. She's not."

"But the Agency made that decision and you had to go along with it. It's not like you tried to lie to him."

"I could have stood up for him. I could have argued it was unfair to him. Or his best interests. But this way..."

"Don't blame yourself."

"And if she ever wakes up? What do I tell him?"

"Has anyone given you reason to believe that could happen?"

"No." But he hadn't talked to Lucy's doctors in a while. They were no longer married, thanks to a private hearing with a judge kept out of the public record, and the physicians didn't have to tell him anything about her condition. She was in a secure facility in Virginia, a place where the intel community's permanently disabled, whether for physical or mental reasons, were kept. Where there wouldn't be questions. Where there weren't often visitors, certainly not where a thirteen-year-old boy could go visit a mother he didn't remember, a mother who had perhaps loved him just a little bit but had loved money more and let him get close to very bad people to be used as a pawn.

She didn't deserve him.

He'd never let her near Daniel again.

"I used to have a live camera feed I could access," he said. "They set it up for me. Because even though I divorced her afterwards, I just... I wanted to see her."

"To see if she would recover?"

"If she recovered, she would have faced serious charges. She wasn't going to waltz back into our lives. But I stopped using the feed as Daniel got older. I was afraid he'd catch me watching it. And I'd have to confess to the terrible, great lie I'd told him. The greatest lie a parent could tell a child."

"You weren't in a good place when you made that decision."

"Still my choice. I could have told him..."

"Told him what? He wasn't old enough to understand. And he started to think of Leonie as his mom."

"Which she isn't."

"She isn't, but he understands now."

"Lucy has a grave in Austin. I told Daniel I had Lucy's remains moved there when we moved there so we could visit her. I just piled onto the lie. He asked Leonie to take him there today. He never does that."

"You fleshed out the story you had to tell to protect him." Paige crossed her arms.

"You really aren't going to let me doubt my choices, are you?"

Paige stood up. "I know what you've done. I know what you've sacrificed for this country. I know you've made bad choices and good choices, and no, Sam, I don't think you should really beat yourself up right now. You asked if you were a good father. A good father asks himself the hard questions but also does the best he can. None of us are perfect."

"Perfect? I was an easy mark. I loved her. Or I loved

the person she pretended to be, the person I told myself she was. With all my heart, and I didn't even truly know her. I'm amazed anyone let me stay working in intel."

"She fooled a lot of people who weren't even emotionally involved with her." Paige came over and gave him a sisterly hug. He hugged her back. She let him go and patted his head and went back to the laptop.

"So did Markus Bolt. I feel for his daughter. I'm sure she thought they knew him, too."

"I would imagine," Paige said, "that it's a very particular kind of pain."

He nodded.

"So let's protect Amanda and keep him from her." She patted his shoulder. "Dennis Gandy. Let's find out who he is." She went back to her computer.

Sam went downstairs to check on the bar. And yes, Tara from the apartment pool sat at the bar, with a glass of red wine. She saw him and gave him a smile.

Well, he thought. She could be an interesting source of information on Amanda Bolt. He got himself a glass of club soda. The stool next to her was empty, and he sat down. "Where's Lily?"

"Like she said, a work night," Tara said. "Lily is deeply responsible." She made a slight frown, then laughed. "I actually have been here before. With my ex."

"Well, I'm glad you're back."

"So, you've owned this bar for a while?"

"Yes, a few years."

"But you just moved to Miami?"

"I actually own a number of bars. I just wanted to be in Miami because I'll probably expand here."

"A man with ambitions."

"Usually tempered by reality. What do you do?" This was weird, he thought, talking with an attractive, funny woman who showed interest in him, no Daniel around.

Not a date. He was on a mission and she was a potential information source. But it was nice to talk. Just for a minute.

"You mean aside from drinking rosé at the pool and nagging Lily? I just started working for Roberto and Amanda at their courier service. I just help keep things running. It's boring."

"I would imagine courier services are fast-paced."

"It can't compete with owning bars, Sam. You're like the coolest guy the moment you share your job."

He laughed. "Well, thanks, but you know self-employment is not always so glamorous."

"True. Same with Roberto and Amanda. Let me know if you hear arguing through the walls." Tara took a big gulp of her Malbec.

"Oh, really?" It was always good to find a gossip in Sam's line of work.

"The drama with those two is constant." She did a slightly dramatic eye roll.

He thought, *My hidden cameras haven't shown me much of that.* "How so?"

"They work together. They live together. It's a little too joined at the hip to be healthy. Roberto's a possessive guy. He doesn't seem to like Amanda going off anywhere without him."

"You don't mean like he would threaten her?"

"Just don't show interest in her. He gets antsy."

"Um, well, she seems really nice, but I'm not interested in her."

She gave him a speculative glance. "You married? Girlfriend?"

"No and no," he said. He always avoided details. He had never been particularly good at dating. His parents moved constantly with their relief work, always taking him and his brother to some new corner of the globe; he'd only stayed in one place for long when he went to Harvard. There he had felt academically inadequate and socially awkward, and immersed himself in his studies; then he believed that Danny had been killed in Afghanistan, and Sam made joining the CIA his goal. He'd been hired straight out of college, met Lucy there, married her quickly, blinded and giddy with the thought that a girl like her could love him. And he'd hardly dated since. It now seemed rude not to ask Tara's status, but he didn't want to lead her along if she was interested in him; he wasn't staying. *Just in town long enough to find the traitor, ma'am.* "You?"

"Not married, thankfully. I dodged a bullet there." And she smiled not at him but at her wineglass.

"So, as a neighbor, is there anything I should know about Roberto and Amanda—I mean, he's not violent, right?"

"Like he would hurt her? No. I don't think so."

"What about this guy who's been coming around, this Gandy dude. What's his deal?"

She ran a finger along the stem of her wineglass. "This is awkward because we don't talk about it much, but do you know who Amanda is?"

"Should I? Was she on a reality show or something?"

"Her father was a CIA guy who defected to Russia years ago. Markus Bolt. You remember him?"

"Vaguely. Yeah. It was in the news."

"Yes. Left Amanda and his family behind."

"Oh, that's awful."

Tara leaned closer. "It really messed her up. I think it made her look for guys that wouldn't leave her but for the wrong reasons. So it's been a string of control freaks, guys who hover, guys who don't want her out on her own, ever. Because she thinks it means they won't leave her." Tara smiled, pleased with her amateur psychology.

"That...doesn't sound healthy."

"No." She said this in a sad tone. "But she's just so unaware about herself."

"How long have your known them?"

"Not long. A few months. I moved here after my breakup with my boyfriend. Which I'm over."

"Oh. She made it sound like you might be a bit vulnerable right now."

Tara's mouth narrowed. "Oh, did she? How nice of her to watch out for me."

"I think she meant well."

"She can try to solve my problems rather than her own."

"You mean her problems beyond having a traitor for a dad and a possessive boyfriend? So who's this guy bothering her? Gandy? I just got a weird vibe when I talked to him."

"He started showing up about five days ago. I got the impression maybe he's an old boyfriend. Someone from her past."

"She knew him?"

"She said they used to be friends. Not sure why they fell out."

"Well, I'll keep my eyes peeled for that Gandy dude."

"The one time I talked to him, when I was down at the pool the other night and he stopped by looking for her, I saw he had a gun. Under his jacket."

"Like what, he's a cop?" Sam had not realized that he was armed when they spoke. Either he hadn't been then, or Sam had gotten sloppy.

"No," she said. "I don't think he's a cop. I think Roberto and Amanda are into some weird trouble. I think it has to do with her dad. Because she's happy to talk about anything except her dad, and she won't talk about this, either." She finished her wine. "Tomorrow's a busy day." She placed a credit card down on the bar.

"The wine's on me," he said. "Thanks for the welcome to the neighborhood."

"Thanks," she said, collecting her card. "Maybe I'll get Roberto and Amanda to come here tomorrow night with me, if you'll be here."

"I have nowhere else to be," he said with a smile.

His phone chimed. Daniel. But the phone didn't display his name, just a specific tune played.

She watched him tense at the tone. "Someone important calling," she said. "Sure you don't have a girlfriend?"

"My mom," he said.

"Aw, that's sweet. You heading home?"

"No, I've got some work to do before closing."

"It's a nice bar and it was nice to meet you," she said.

The phone stopped chiming.

"Nice to meet you, too, Tara."

"See you back at Melrose Place," she said.

He didn't get the reference, the name of the complex was Perry Palms. A side effect of a nomadic childhood spent overseas, often without television. But he smiled instead.

The night was winding down, fewer than eight customers remaining. The assistant manager on duty nodded at him as he went back up to the safe house.

Tomorrow Roberto and Amanda would be at work. He had to take a precaution tonight in case Bolt contacted her through her work.

Gandy, armed, showing up more than once at Amanda's apartment.

Marianne, arriving in Miami with her assistant assassins.

Amanda's boyfriend being shady and controlling, which could make his job harder.

He didn't need these complications.

He already had one big complication. Because Daniel was calling, instead of texting, his vastly preferred way to contact Sam. He went upstairs. He called his son back.

26

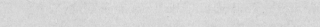

Daniel answered on the second ring. "Hey, Dad."

"You called?" Sam said. "Everything okay?"

"Yes," he said in an uncertain voice.

"How was school?"

"School's okay. I have some questions about Mom."

Sam decided not to mention Leonie's warning call; Daniel might stop talking to her.

"Um, okay." Sam sat down on the couch. Paige got up from the laptop and excused herself. "What's brought this on?"

Silence. Then Daniel said, "I'm old enough to ask."

"You are."

"Um. Okay. Where was Mom buried in New Orleans?"

Sam made his voice steady. "She wasn't. She was cremated in New York. So her remains were in an urn. Not in a cemetery."

"You buried the urn?" Daniel sounded confused.

"When we settled in Austin, I knew you would want a place to visit her. That was a suggestion that the grief counselors made for me. That she have a special resting place, not just be on the shelf. So I bought the plot and the headstone."

"Oh. And she's there?"

He tried not to hesitate. "Yes."

"Um. Okay. Why didn't you tell me she was cremated?"

"I...it wasn't the kind of thing I would just tell you when you were younger, but now you know. What does it matter?" And the moment he said it, Sam said, "I'm sorry. It does matter to you. I see that."

"It's okay," Daniel said. "Did a lot of people know this?"

"Know...that she was cremated? I don't think anyone outside of the family knows. It's no one's business and not the kind of thing I talk about generally."

"When she got sick...this heart condition...?"

"It was just unlucky. Just undiagnosed."

"Like she just died? In front of you?"

"No. She collapsed. She was taken to a hospital. She died there."

"Where? Which hospital?"

"New York. The hospital was St. James's." The CIA had created a paper trail there for Lucy Capra's "passing." It was the same hospital Lucy had been rushed to under her fake name before she was transferred, under that name, to a private hospital and listed as deceased. But this was the conversation he wished he'd had with Daniel face to face.

"You were living in New York?" Daniel asked.

"Yes, then."

Daniel wasn't saying anything more. The silence between them thickened. Then Daniel said: "Did you live in London?"

He knows more than I've told him. How? "Briefly. We were both assigned there by our company; we weren't there for very long at all."

"You never told me you lived in London."

"It just never came up." There was no way he could know. It had been part of the CIA whitewashing of the Capra family history. "Mom and I lived in London for

a while. Not for long. For our jobs. You...she got pregnant with you in London. That's all. How did you know
we'd lived there?"

"What jobs?"

"The kind you get right out of college. Working for a
consulting firm. We both hated it."

"Is that where you met?"

No. We met in CIA training. "Yes," he said.

"You told me once you met in New York."

"Well, it was all at the same company," Sam said.
"Do you think I'm lying to you?" Now he was on the
offensive.

"Oh. You never mentioned London."

"You never asked," Sam said, but he regretted it
instantly. "I just...it's hard for me to talk about. Still.
What made you ask about London?"

"I found a picture of you and Mom there. Big Ben
behind you."

Sam couldn't remember such a picture being taken,
but it was possible. No story could be completely airtight.
"Um, all right. Where did you find it?"

"Um...In a book I guess you had with you then. Like
it was a bookmark."

"Oh. All right." His mind raced. All of his belongings
in London had been seized by the CIA when they took
him into custody, when they believed that Lucy was a
traitor and that he was aware of her treason. Any book
would have been torn apart looking for patterns sugges-
tive of encoding for messages she might have sent to Russia. He had nothing left from then. How would a picture
have come into play? Sometimes his father and he traded
books, and they might have had a photo of him and Lucy
in London. *Maybe.*

"Was it Nana or Papa who gave you the picture?"
Those were Daniel's nicknames for Sam's mom and

dad. His father's mind was slipping...it was part of the reason they'd come to Austin to retire. They had friends there from their relief worker days, a support system.

"It was just in the book, Dad. Don't make a federal case out of it."

But he felt it was something more. Daniel did not normally lie to him. And he felt he was being told a lie. "Fine. Was there anything else? How was school?" Like now, now, they could have a normal conversation. Something had to have happened to spur on these questions.

"It was okay. I didn't have a great practice today. We have a tournament Saturday."

"I'll still be here probably." He felt a bright, hot hatred for Markus Bolt. And anger at himself. "I'll try to get home as soon as I can."

"You got your stuff to do," Daniel said. "It's all right." Sam could hear the quiet click of the boy swallowing. "I'm sorry I upset you."

"I'm sorry, Daniel. I'm sorry. I'm sorry." He felt bile crawl in his throat, tears hot in his eyes. "I love you. We'll...we'll have a long talk when I am home."

"I love you, too, Dad," Daniel said. "Good night."

"Good night," Sam said. He hung up. He immediately called his mom.

"Hi, Sam," she said.

"Listen, Mom, this will sound weird, but I need to know. Did you have a picture of me and Lucy in London?"

"Yes," she said, slowly. "I believe so. In front of Big Ben?"

"Yes," Sam said.

"Yes. Lucy sent it to us, along with some others."

"Oh. Okay. Thanks. Daniel found it in a book. Dad must have left it there in one he borrowed from me. Daniel just had questions."

"Is he okay?"

"Yes. Just . . . he didn't realize we had lived in London. He's reaching this age of curiosity and he wants details."

"I guess that's natural. Do you want me to go over and see him? Or maybe have him over? See if I can see what's bugging him?" Mom was a doctor, so she enjoyed fixing people.

"No," he said slowly. He was worried Daniel would ask questions his mother, who knew nothing of his service with Section K, couldn't answer. Which might raise more questions. "I'll talk to him when I get home."

"I love you, Sam, and you're a good father," Mom said. Sam told her he loved her, too, thanked her, and ended the call. It was a lot of new questions at once. But he could handle Daniel.

He hoped.

27

THEY WENT TO A SEAFOOD restaurant that Val knew, good food, quiet, and they got a large booth in the back corner. The maitre d' recognized Val and called her by name and asked after Maria. It made Kirill nervous; there were other Russians here. But maybe that wasn't bad—maybe he blended in. Just another young ambitious guy no one knew.

Val opened up her laptop and started searching. She stopped only when their shrimp appetizer arrived and she devoured hers. It made Kirill smile. She had an intensity about her that he admired. He felt she was the kind of person who would not shy away from a challenge.

"There are three Greg Hollisters I can find in the area. One of them is seventy, retired, and worked in computer engineering in Seattle for many years. One is fourteen, and I think from these Faceplace postings, he's the older Greg's grandson and namesake and the reason his grandfather retired here. One moved here from Dallas just last year and is in his twenties."

"So none of those."

"Likely not."

"So it was a fake name," Val said.

"We need to talk to him again. Apply a little pressure. But if we go to his house, there's a wife to deal with. I don't want witnesses. I mean, people who know I talked to him."

"If I can get him to the house I've bought, we can talk in private," Val said. "But you can't...do more."

"He gave us a fake name. He's probably warned the guy."

"Perhaps. Maybe he didn't know it was a fake name. What if he can lead us to your stepfather?"

Kirill tensed.

"No one can hear us, no one's paying attention. This is Miami."

He looked out across the room. "Why did you bring me here?"

"The food's good."

"But I see two sons of elites here."

"You know them, but they don't know you."

He was silent.

"I want to ask what you do back in Russia, but I don't want to know."

"Let's not talk about me. I'm classified."

Val laughed.

"Tell me about your time in England," he said. He was curious about her husband. He wondered what kind of man she liked.

Her face grew somber. "It's not interesting."

"You're not from England originally?"

"I emigrated there from Romania after school. Got a job working for a temp agency. So then I worked for a small technology consulting firm and one of our clients was a bank. I met my husband there. He worked in the international division." She sipped at her water. "We married. I was happy. After he died, Illya had been one of his main clients, and he offered me a job in Moscow. I liked Illya and I needed a change. So." She shrugged. "It's not a particularly interesting story."

"You said it was an accident."

"Yes. A hit-and-run. The driver was never caught, though."

"I'm sorry," he said. Then he said quietly, "Forgive me, Val, but was there any suspicion of foul play?"

She stared at him. "Why would you ask that?"

"Because an international banker with ties to Russia could be a target. Forgive my bluntness. Surely this occurred to you." He thought of Illya's financial map that he claimed Bolt had stolen. Maybe Val knew about it; knew the threat it could be.

"It occurred to me."

"What was his name?"

"Philip."

"Did Philip talk much about his business?"

"Not a lot." She put her gaze to her plate. "I did sometimes meet his clients. Illya had a girlfriend then in London so he came there often. He liked to take us out to dinner. Sometimes he'd drink too much vodka. He'd talk about living some of the places where he'd had Philip hide money." She shrugged. "I don't think Philip broke laws, but I think he was finding loopholes for Illya to hide money in the West. Even in America. Some states are easier than others to park money under shell companies."

He wondered if he should trust her. He wanted to. It was an odd thing.

"What was Philip like?"

"Kind. Smart, ambitious, thoughtful. He loved to bring me little gifts." She smiled at her memory. "My friends were surprised I fell for him. He was not the handsomest man. But I thought he had a sweet face, and he made me laugh, and I loved his smile. He was one of the good ones."

Not like me, Kirill thought. *I'm one of the bad ones.* Of course she would be drawn to a steady, reliable man. Not the kind who went to foreign capitals to kill or steal or spy. That would not be a match for Val.

"Those girls are watching you," Val said. He glanced over at the large table across from them. He'd heard Russian being spoken there when they entered the restaurant and walked past. Two of the young women were glancing their way. They were lovely, dark-haired, dressed in the Miami style of wispy skirts and lots of jewelry. "Their fathers are both real estate investors from St. Petersburg; they secretly own a company that is inside another company and buys up American houses in residential neighborhoods. I met them at a party of Maria's last year."

"You have a good memory."

"They were little snots to Maria, and I keep a mental list of people who are…little snots. Right now, they're outraged," Val said, with a small laugh. "I'm ten years older than you, they're wondering why we're having dinner."

And why couldn't he have a dinner date with a woman a few years older than him. Not even a date. Just dinner. She was just helping him. He cleared his throat. "They don't know who I am."

"No, but they know you're Russian."

"Bobo said…" And then he realized she wouldn't know who Bobo was. Better to go back to his original subject. He made a point to stare for a moment at the girls, and then turn his full smile toward Val.

"You're bad," she said. Shaking her head.

"I know I am. I'm going to ask you a couple of questions, and giving me true answers will not be disloyal to Illya. He is in serious trouble with Bolt on the run. I'm trying to help him. I like Illya, too. He trusted me with some important information that could help me find

Bolt, but I have to find Bolt before he can use this information and hurt Illya."

"Is this about hidden money? Or shell companies? You can tell me."

Kirill decided. Desperate times meant desperate measures. She knew more of Illya's secrets than he'd first realized. But of course Illya trusted someone this capable. He told her quickly, about Illya's financial map and that Bolt had apparently taken it, possibly as a bargaining chip. Her only reaction was to tighten her mouth and then close her eyes.

"Is this the kind of network Philip could have helped him build from London?"

"Yes," she said. "Once he laughed about how hard it was to make up company names that didn't sound too random and still sounded vaguely corporate. I asked, how many did he have to come up with? He said… thousands." She closed her eyes. "Oh, Illya."

"What if we warn the elites…have them move their money?"

"Much of it is interconnected, the companies nested in each other. Moving such large funds all at once would attract notice and it would take time to establish the new shells. There would be a panic. But I don't know a great deal of detail about the setup."

"Did Illya tell you that this network existed?"

"No. But I'm not surprised."

"But…you bought a house using it today."

"I know about most of the shell companies he holds, not other people's."

"How many shell companies does he have?"

She hesitated. "Dozens."

"Okay. You have access to at least one."

"I have access to about five," she said. "All in the West. Why?"

"Just good to know." Their dinners arrived. Kirill looked up only when he was halfway done. "Sorry. I should be a better conversationalist."

"You're hungry, and anxious. It's fine." She set down her fork. "I guess you'll have to kill him if he won't come along peacefully."

"Who?"

"Your stepfather."

He took a sip of water. "I'm not discussing with you what I'll do or won't do. It's best you do not know."

"It's not hard to figure out now what your orders are. And that you're maybe one of a few, or the only one looking for him. You're the knife in the dark. If he won't come back. If the Americans are closing in and you can't get him back to Russia."

"I'm not commenting on that, Val."

"Your own stepfather. They could send another operative. They sent you. It's cruel to do this to you, Kirill."

"Val...you do not know the whole story. The hope is I can talk to him. Reason with him. Obviously."

"What's your relationship with him like?"

Kirill could not have imagined that he would be discussing this with her when he'd boarded Illya's plane. But here he was. "Not always warm. I thought he genuinely loved my mom, but now..." He cleared his throat, took another sip of water. "My father...my father killed himself after Bolt came to Russia. My parents' marriage was in trouble when Bolt entered the picture. He was besotted with my mother. She's very pretty." He always hated explaining this, although he was proud of Mama. "She's a former Miss Russia. You know, like...the beauty pageant. She was in the top fifteen at Miss Universe. My father was one of her bodyguards—he was an internal security agent. They fell in love and she married Papa after her year as Miss Russia was over."

"Ah. Son of a beauty queen. So that's why you're so handsome." Her smile was wry.

Kirill froze. He didn't know what to say. Any other woman, any other bar, he might have given her that slightly crooked smile that seemed to work so well, fall into flirtation. He couldn't with Val. He felt his cheeks redden. "People have always underestimated Mama. That she is just a pretty face. But Bolt...he tricked her. He made her love him. He was this celebrity in Russia, the man all the powerful people wanted to meet, to see. And he fell for Mama. And Papa was devastated, and he was kept from seeing Mama because...Morozov and all the circle wanted Bolt to be happy. To share everything he knew. And Papa killed himself." He took a deep breath. "I found him."

Val was silent for several seconds. Then she took his hand. He was so surprised, he nearly pulled it away.

"You don't talk about this much, do you?" It surprised him again; her sharing an observation instead of offering sympathy.

Now he looked at her. "I do not."

She squeezed his hand and then let it go. "Thank you for telling me. I'm sorry."

"I have said too much."

"No. I can help you, Kirill. Let's think."

Like he was a child who couldn't puzzle this out. He pulled his hand back. "I don't need help. I can't involve you further."

"I am already involved and don't be mad because you showed me this side of you."

He stared then looked away.

"You think he could have turned to this Lucy, who came to see him in Russia. She was not someone he betrayed when he came over, yes?"

"Yes. As far as I know."

"So she is still here, or she is somewhere else, and the man who sent her to use a cover of being Terrell Carrier's wife is someone that Bolt might turn to for help."

"He called someone in South Florida. It could be this Lucy. She's the only person who's made contact with him, the only American we know of, since his defection."

"So her...or his family."

"I have no other lead at the moment. And that just seems obvious, to watch them; he'll expect that. I don't think he would go to them. If his son hadn't killed himself...then maybe. But Karen and Amanda blamed Markus, in the press reports after Allan died. I think they would slam a door in his face and call the FBI. But this woman, he may think she can help him. So find her, maybe I find him."

"You might make your mother a widow again," she said. "Are you ready for that?"

He said nothing.

"But you'll avenge your dad, so there's that."

"Val...you make it sound like a Greek tragedy."

"It is, Kirill. Maybe you should just go home and let this unfold. I can have Illya's plane ready in an hour. Just go home."

"And just let him redefect and make a mockery of us."

"Who cares? Then don't go home. Stay here with the thousands of other Russians."

It was like she had seen through him. His desire to be free from the life he'd chosen out of duty. He swallowed. "I cannot. If you knew me better, you would understand. I can't come home without him. I can't face my mother or..."

"Or the men who sent you. Well, they chose their knife well."

"You think I'm a monster."

"No. I think they set you up so you'll do whatever it

takes. If we can find him...you can get your life back on your terms, Kirill."

"You don't know me. Why would you help me?"

"Because it will help Illya. He helped me in my darkest hour. I guess I'm paying it forward."

How would he look at Mama if he had to kill Markus? He would figure out a way. He would solve that problem when he came to it. First he had to find Bolt. Because Mama, and he knew this about her, would likely say that if he didn't bring Bolt home in some form, dead or alive, that he had failed her and Russia.

He took a deep breath. Normally on his jobs he was calm. Never nervous, because his work was dangerous, and if he messed up, he could face death or years in a foreign prison.

"Let me make a suggestion. We know Terrell lied to us or was lied to himself. I think he's lying. So we talk to him again, but maybe let me talk first."

Kirill, after a moment, nodded.

"You're the lone wolf. Trust me."

He nodded again.

Val picked up her phone, found the newest contact in it. Made the call. "Terrell. Hello, it's Valeria Garrison. I'm sorry it's late, but can you meet me at the house? If you want this deal to go through, I think we should talk. And I don't want to trouble your wife, your family, by coming by."

Kirill could hear the man's voice.

"Yes, I know it's late. But it's important. Thank you."

She set down the phone. "He'll meet us there."

28

THE COURIER SERVICE'S OFFICE WAS in a strip mall lot, not far from the Miami Airport. Sam drove past the building twice. He expected that it would have security cameras in the lot, and possibly inside the building. It sat at one end of the center, next to a nail salon. Also closed. None of the businesses here were open late.

He drove into the lot and, with one hand on his Section K phone, thumbed an app that used a signal jammer to identify and send a stronger signal using the same radio frequency as the lot's wireless cameras. The cameras, inside and out, would cease to function as long as the app issued the radio frequency.

He only had a few minutes. He went to the lot behind the building, where a half-dozen courier vans were parked. He picked the locks on the back door—it took him four minutes. He entered and a soft chime started from an alarm pad. He broke open the cover and connected a thumb drive into the service port. The alarm stopped, believing that a service code had been entered.

He used his small flashlight and searched the office. A floor dedicated for processing packages that were delivered here and not directly picked up. More desks and cubicles, with computers one could use to track the delivery vehicles and route them to minimize time. A larger enclosed office with "R. Mendez" on the door. Roberto. And the cubicle closest to his office had a picture on the desk of Roberto and Amanda, in swimsuits, standing on a beach, a glorious sunset behind them. This was her desk, her computer.

Sam felt a sudden sharp ache in his chest, his guts. He and Lucy had worked together. He was a field operative based in London; she worked as a network administrator for the CIA front company that they used as a base. His parents had worked together as well, nomads across the world (his mother a doctor, his father an accountant) for an Episcopal relief agency. They had warned him, kindly, that working with your spouse could create new pressures, new challenges, but also new joy and new opportunity. Mom and Dad said it had deepened their relationship.

Lucy had turned traitor and bombed their office, killing their coworkers and leaving Sam framed for her crime.

The spy who couldn't see what was in front of him, someone had told him.

Working together, that hadn't worked out so well.

He let the beam of the flashlight play along the picture. Roberto was smiling broadly, but Amanda looked more reserved. She didn't look unhappy, but she looked like maybe someone had just told her to smile and she didn't want to. He searched quickly through her desk. Pens, legal pads, cords for her laptop, a candy bar, a picture frame turned facedown. He turned it over. A photo of Amanda, with a young man who bore a strong resemblance to Markus Bolt, and an older woman with her arm around their shoulders, standing in the middle. Mrs. Bolt. Their mother.

A picture she kept, but didn't have to see constantly.

Only when she wanted. It was how he kept pictures of Lucy, or his brother.

He turned his attention back to his work. With the cubicle arrangement, there was no obvious place to hide a camera. He hated open floor plans because it oddly made it harder to spy on people. He considered option two. He slid a Section K–issued flash drive into the laptop's port. Within ten minutes he'd broken her password (a regrettable *Roberto4evah*) and installed two phantom programs on her laptop. Her monitor's camera, or her own laptop's camera, would activate but not display the green light that would tell her the camera and microphone were active. He would be able to enter a code on his own computer and send it to hers, and he could watch her at work. This would have been easier if she'd had an office phone to bug, but according to her background file, she had a mobile phone, one she likely used for work, and it wasn't here. The hidden camera program was set to expire in two weeks, and he could remotely delete it as well if he didn't need it. It would be tedious to watch her at work, but if her father showed up, he'd know. The second program would send him a record of all her e-mails, messages, and texts sent to this computer, in case her father reached out to her electronically.

He stood up.

Sam did a fast search of Roberto's office. It was very tidy and neat, like Roberto's side of the bedroom. His desk was neat; one of the drawers was locked.

He used his lock picks and got inside.

A gun. A Beretta, loaded. A bag with about five thousand in cash in it. And a piece of paper, with words printed on it, in a range of fonts. Like an old-style ransom note, when the words were clipped out of magazines and glued together.

It read, "Bring her to me or I'll tell the world." The top of the paper had been torn, like it had been taped to a door or wall and ripped down from it.

Bring her to me. A gun, and a cache of money. A down payment? Money for them to run? They weren't running, though; they were having a quiet night at home.

Time to go.

He found a spot for the tiny camera in Roberto's office, above the doorjamb. It was a risk but he took it. There wasn't a laptop here for him to bug; Roberto must have taken it home.

What did this threat mean? And how odd it was—made to look like an old ransom note, when it wasn't. An extra touch that could speak to a disturbed mind or someone who imagined himself adding a bit of style to a threat.

But he assumed *she* was Amanda, and Roberto had a secret someone was going to tell.

He guessed Gandy's threats were escalating.

Sam hurried to the back door, removed the alarm reader, and relocked the doors. Back in his car, he drove out of the lot and cut off the interference signal for the wireless cameras. Any surveillance job like this was a risk. He stopped at a grocery store and bought some more essentials—he didn't want to stock up because he didn't want to be here long. He checked the news for a hopeful headline where Markus Bolt had been captured in Europe or it was announced he had left Russia. Neither.

He drove back to the bar, thinking.

Someone had threatened Roberto to hand over Amanda. Maybe not a middleman. Maybe Bolt himself.

Roberto hadn't. Was he refusing to? Sam had hoped if Amanda was in danger, Roberto would be his ally to protect his girlfriend.

Was the money in the drawer a bribe to go along with the threat? Or was Roberto keeping cash to go on the run? What was the threat of exposure? Was something more than deliveries going on in this office?

There was a danger to Amanda, and Roberto knew about it. Might be time for Sam to find his pressure point.

29

THE BAR HAD A SECOND life—a crowd of ten had arrived and taken over a back table, a genial group sharing bottles of wine, apparently celebrating a business win. Sam smiled and nodded at them. He wondered, sometimes, what it would be like to have a big set of friends. He hadn't really had that before. People you could talk to openly, share your wins, share your triumphs. *Yes, I stole the financial transfers information from the military attaché of a troubled Middle Eastern government so we could pressure him into spying for us. Yay me, I destroyed the research being done into a viral agent being developed in an abandoned government lab in Macedonia by a crazy extremist. Yes, I had a heartfelt face-to-face with a hired killer dispatched to murder a military officer, paid him more, and sent him back to kill his client. Here's to me.*

He walked upstairs to the office.

Paige was at the desk, laptop open.

Paige said, "Here's my initial workup on Dennis Gandy." She pulled up Gandy's Georgia driver's license on the screen and a set of browser windows. "He lives in Atlanta, works for a small web design firm as a developer. No criminal record."

"He sounds boring."

"I found a dirty little secret, though. Please applaud.

Under the name SensibleGenius, he also runs one of the largest 'Boltie' discussion groups on the Internet."

Sam remembered the term from his file. "Boltie. As in he's a Markus Bolt conspiracy theorist." No wonder Amanda didn't want to talk to him.

"Yes. He never posts under his own name; few of them do. I just broke into his Internet provider's logs—thanks to that Section K hacker tool kit you gave me last time you were here—and looked at his recent activity, and found he'd been posting to this crazy Boltie discussion site. I've been reading this stuff like it's for my book club."

"How crazy is it?"

"Gandy mostly doesn't wade into the arguments among them as to why Bolt committed treason or if he's guilty; he runs the site. But these theories—have you done a deep dive into them?"

"Not really. It seemed kind of fringe."

"Well, I've made a list of the Bolties' greatest hits. Theory number one, that Markus Bolt had to flee because he had proof that there were secret Russian agents at the highest levels of our government, including a former vice president. Second, that Markus Bolt stole personal information on the CIA leadership and members of Congress and has been blackmailing them from Russia ever since—sort of a transplanted puppet master."

"That one is possible and frightening."

"Yet delusional! Third, that Markus Bolt stole millions from the CIA to redistribute to the poor and this is why they framed him for treason. Or he stole it for some other reason."

"I don't suppose that he simply sold out his country for money and to boost his ego is ever on the list?"

"Oh, for sure, any logical reason gets mentioned and then explained away." Paige shrugged, flipping through the browser windows. "These guys are real petty bitches.

Very sure of themselves and very dismissive of their crit-
ics. I'd probably like them in real life."

"How many people are in these groups?"

"Dozens, all with too much spare time. Some of the
postings are thoughtful, lots are just . . . crazy."

"And Bolt goes missing, and now this clown is showing up at Amanda's doorstep." Sam started to pace the
floor. "Would Bolt reach out to his, um, fan club?"

"Seems risky. Why would he trust these people to
be quiet? Their currency is having what they believe is
insider knowledge. Bolt talking to them would be an
accomplishment they'd need to trumpet."

"He could say he was able to prove one of their theories if they help him but stay quiet at first."

"You're one of these theorists, you get an e-mail from
the guy you're obsessed with, you stay quiet? I think
most of these folks would immediately post that they got
an e-mail from someone purporting to be Bolt. Then it
would be analyzed for its wording, its authenticity, etc."

"Show me Gandy's postings, please," he asked.

Paige brought up a browser window with many tabs,
and she clicked through them. Sam read them. "There's
no mention here that Bolt has disappeared from Russia."

"No, that news hasn't broken. It would light them all
up, I'm sure."

"What do they think?"

"It varies. Some think, yes, he's a traitor. Others think
he was framed, no way to prove his innocence, and that
he had no choice to stay alive but to flee to Russia. Those
tend to be the most 'out there.' They're always trying to
figure out who the *real* traitor is." Paige shook her head.
"I mean . . . the guy ran. He didn't try and defend himself. They tend to skip over the logical parts."

Sam read through Dennis Gandy's postings hiding
behind the name SensibleGenius. He tended to be on the

edgier side, arguing that Bolt exposed corruption in the CIA and therefore could not have betrayed his country. Or that Bolt and another agent were blamed for stealing millions from a CIA account when it was done by someone else, and Bolt had to run for his life.

It seemed an odd theory. "What's the name of this other agent?"

"He doesn't say." She shrugged. "Gandy has theories; he has no proof."

"Do we have a track on where Gandy is staying?"

"No. He has used his credit card here, for buying gas north of town and for restaurants, but so far not for lodging."

"Let's see where he bought." Paige brought up the map, keyed with red dots where he'd used his credit card. It was a neat circle near a residential neighborhood. He might be near there.

"He might be staying with a friend. Or he used a credit card not in his name, or paid cash."

"How many rentals in that area?"

"A few dozen right now."

"He's here for a reason. He's trying to talk to Amanda; she wants nothing to do with him. He might be the one trying to threaten Roberto to get to Amanda. This feels right. Like maybe this guy, of all the Bolties, could keep his mouth shut long enough."

"Helping Bolt would also be a crime. He may not want to own it right now," Paige said.

"I'm going to go back to the apartment. I think he'll show up again. If he does, I'm grabbing him."

"And you'll avoid being arrested for kidnapping just how?"

"Find something on him that will shut him up. If he's the one who threatened extortion or he's aiding a traitor, I'll have leverage."

30

***

Austin

JAMES WAS STILL STUDYING IN his room, on his bed, when Daniel came back.

Daniel put down his backpack. He sat down at James's desk (rarely used).

He looked at his friend. His friend looked back at him. "What?" James said.

"I need to tell you something, but you can't tell your dad or Leonie."

This got James's interest. He sat up.

"You promise?"

"Yes," James said after a moment.

"At lunch—when I asked you about my mom, and you thought I was being all weird, it was because someone left a note in my choir binder. About her."

"What did it say?"

He didn't want to say anything about empty graves to James. "That she'd left a message for me. Like, before she died."

James just stared at him.

"And I think I know who might have left it, but I'm wondering how they could have gotten into the school."

"You mean like it wasn't another kid."

"Yeah."

"Why would a kid leave you a note like that?"

"I don't think a kid did," Daniel said. "But I want to know who did it."

"How would you know?"

"There are security cameras. Feeds. We ought to be able to see who goes down the hall to the choir room and who doesn't belong."

James frowned. "How would we get the video? Or are you saying you want to show this to Mr. Ramsey and have him look at the video?"

"No. Because he'll tell my dad. I don't want my dad to know."

"Why not? Your dad is cool."

"Not really. And he gets tense whenever my mom is mentioned. He thinks he hides it from me. He doesn't." Now for the hard part. "You work as a student aide in the office. You know where the video controls are."

"I don't know how to run that." His eyes widened.

"We just have to swipe the video recording for yesterday and today. We won't watch them there, where we might get caught."

"Just seeing the hallway isn't going to be enough. I don't think there's a camera where the choir binders are."

"I mean, someone who isn't supposed to be on school grounds getting access to the building...they did it somehow. Or they got someone to do it for them."

"Why do you need to know? It's a prank."

"Maybe. But if someone left this kind of note for you, wouldn't you want to know?"

"Yeah," James said after a moment. "But you're asking me to steal school property."

"I'll steal it," Daniel said. "I'm not asking you to do that. But I do need your help."

"How? The office is locked up if no one's there."

"Do you have a key?"

"No. I know where they're kept," James said after a moment.

"I have an idea," Daniel said.

31

***

Miami

It had gone bad very quickly.

Terrell arrived to open the house, smiling, uncertain. "Where's your friend?"

"In the backyard," she said. She waited until they were inside. She followed. "I asked him to wait out there. So we could talk."

Terrell was sweating slightly. "I hope you're not reconsidering the purchase. Since you hadn't even seen the house. I have Russian clients like that; they trust me that the property will be suitable."

"The house is fine. My boss is always looking for a good investment. I just want to know..."

And then Kirill entering behind them, through the unlocked front door. "The backyard needs a mowing," he said.

Terrell's pasted smile wavered a bit. "I'll get that taken care of, gratis, of course."

"I'm so glad we've met you, Terrell," Val said. "You are so accommodating. But we really do need to have a serious conversation."

Terrell swallowed. "I really can't stay long, happy to leave you the keys so you can settle in or explore..."

Val took the keys from his hand. "There is no man named Greg Hollister that matches your story. You lied to us, Terrell."

"I didn't! I didn't!"

"Where is your ex-wife?" Kirill asked again softly. "Lucy Carrier."

Terrell paled.

"Terrell," Val said softly. "Look at me. It's important we know. We don't mean her harm. But we have to find her. She could be in danger."

"She was never my wife," Terrell said, his voice a bleat. "Please." He took a deep breath. "She said...she said she needed to use my name. For travel. Just once."

"How did she even know you?" Val asked.

"We went to school together. In Arizona. She paid me just to borrow my name. And she sent business my way. Russians, with money. She showed up here. Pregnant. I heard from some friends at school that she'd married some guy and moved to London. She told me she was CIA and she needed this cover for a trip. She put a hundred thousand for me in an account overseas. It took me five years to work up the nerve to touch the money or move it. I had to do it slowly. Some of my Russian clients helped me." *See*, his face seemed to say, *I'm just like you.*

Val and Kirill glanced at each other.

"Please don't kill me. Please don't."

"We won't," Val said. "I promise you."

"I don't work for the CIA. I'm just a real estate guy."

"Didn't you think that the CIA could create an identity for her if needed?" Kirill asked.

"Yes. But she said it was so secret, it was easier to do it this way. And I wasn't going to argue with the money. So I put her on the website as a real estate agent, told the office I'd married a college friend, she was going to work from home, not be in the office. It was only for two months. Then I told them all the marriage was annulled, a mistake, she'd gone back to Arizona. No more Lucy Carrier. I needed the money. And I wanted to help my friend." He looked like he might cry. "I never talked to Lucy again. I saw in the alumni newsletter she died of a heart problem. I don't think that's true. I think she died of something else because she was clearly involved in dangerous stuff. But I've kept my mouth shut. I'm really good at keeping my mouth shut. Please. Please." He coughed. "I have a lot of Russian clients now. I can be trusted."

"I know you can, Terrell," Val said. She kept her voice reassuring.

"Did she give you a name of someone to contact if something went wrong?" Kirill asked.

"No."

"Did anyone ever come to check up on you or her identity? Inquiring about her?" Val asked.

"Just once. One time. That was it. A guy who said he was Greg Hollister." A pause. "I didn't know his name then."

"Then? But you do now?" Val glanced at Kirill.

He nodded frantically. "He told me his name was Greg Hollister. That he knew Lucy. His real name is Grayson Cortez. I know it because…I saw an article about him. At the Miami paper's website. I saw his picture. He wrote a book about working in intelligence. Now he works for some think tank. He was the guy who came and told me that it was time to say that Lucy and I had broken up. That she didn't need the cover anymore." He swallowed. "I swear, that's all I know. Can I go now?"

"Just a moment." Kirill pulled Val to the other side of

the large living room. "So the CIA sent her to Markus," he said in hushed Russian.

"The CIA doesn't need the help of a real estate agent to create a cover. This smells like maybe she acted on her own, paid off this guy, and later on the CIA found out about it and cleaned it up."

"That's a fair point," Kirill said. "I think we have to kill him." He measured her with a stare.

"Kirill, we need to let him go," Val whispered, still speaking Russian.

Kirill barely shook his head.

"If you kill him, he'll go missing. The police will be looking at all his recent clients. That includes us. We've bought his silence. And this house."

"You don't know how this works. He's a loose end."

"The time you take disposing of his body could be spent finding your stepfather. You know I'm right. Killing him is a complicating factor. I promise you, I can keep him quiet."

Kirill took a deep breath and turned and walked back to Terrell, switching back to English. "Has anyone else approached you about Lucy Carrier? In the past few days?"

"No. No."

"Don't lie to me. I'll know if you lie to me."

"It was just the one time. To help her. To help the country."

"You never talked to her again?"

"No. Never heard from her. I don't know that she was actually pregnant, man. It could have been a fake baby bump." He wiped at his eyes. "She didn't really die of a heart condition, did she? Unless the pregnancy brought that on. I thought I was doing a good thing."

And making a profit, Kirill thought, but he said nothing.

Val touched his shoulder and smiled. "It's all right, Terrell. If you say nothing, you'll get a lot more business. Including this commission. Just keep quiet as you've done."

He nodded emphatically. "I just want to sell real estate," he said. His voice shook slightly. "I don't want anything else. Nothing else is my business."

"You said you recognized this Grayson Cortez as the man who visited you. You didn't ever reach out to him, ask about Lucy? Ask for more money for your silence?"

"No. No, never." Terrell's eyes widened in shock.

"And no one ever came looking for Lucy before us?"

"No, sir, no. I swear."

"All right. What's your wife's name?"

Terrell blinked hard again. "What? Uh, Julie."

"Okay, well, if you talk about this, I'll have to hurt Julie. And it might not be me, in case I get arrested or killed or I go home, but it will be someone here who owes me and does what I say. Not to mention the tax issues you'll have from that bribe you took. Probably would destroy your business, your marriage."

"Yes, sir, yes, sir, I won't say anything, sir."

"Go home," Val said. "Leave the keys. Enjoy your evening."

Terrell got up and bolted out of the house.

Kirill gave a sigh. "He could run straight to the police."

"He won't. Thank you," Val said, "for not killing him."

"I don't know why I'm listening to you."

"Because you know I'm right. You said get in, get out, with as little fuss as possible. He's small fish, he doesn't matter. This Grayson Cortez, he matters." She searched on her phone. "Tax records for the county. He owns property here. The house isn't terribly far. Shall we pay him a visit?"

*   *   *

The Cortez house was large, in an older neighborhood not far from Coral Gables, and several cars were parked in front of it. Kirill parked their car, two houses down.

Val lowered her window. They could hear laughter, an off-tune rendition of "Happy Birthday" being sung from the backyard.

"We're not going to talk to him tonight," she said quietly.

He nodded. "He's retired. He might well be alone at home all day. Tomorrow."

They drove to Sunny Isles. Val directed him to a modern tower of condominiums, one of several along the beach. "This one is Illya's."

"The whole building?"

"Yes. He co-owns it with another oligarch, under a shell company. I mean elite. They don't like the O-word." She said this last part in English, and Kirill flicked a smile. She directed him to a numbered slot in the parking garage.

"They own it in a shell company inside another shell company. The condo unit you're in is furnished—Illya has put guests up there before. His penthouse is just one floor up, in case he needs you."

"I don't work for Illya," he said.

"Well. Okay. In case you need him, then," Val amended and Kirill laughed. He felt exhausted, jet-lagged, but the adrenaline of the hunt, his need to capture Markus and make him pay for what he'd done to his family, felt like a burning inside him.

"And where are you?" he asked.

"Down the hall from you," she said quietly. Looking at him.

For an odd moment it felt like it was a date ending,

and he was nervous about whether or not he could attempt a kiss.

She cleared her throat. "Do you think you'll need me tomorrow?"

"Perhaps I should go see this Cortez alone."

"I think I quite smoothed your path with our friend Terrell. You got what you wanted with minimum impact. Maybe I can help with Cortez as well. Fewer ripples work in your favor. Perhaps I should talk to him alone."

"It's a different thing to threaten a small businessman compared to someone ex-intel, who might call the FBI after getting a visit from foreign intelligence."

"Then let me talk to him. I'll use my best British accent. Say I'm a student of intel, read his book, wanted to talk to him. Fangirl, appeal to his ego. You stay out of it."

Exhaustion washed over Kirill like a wave. "If Cortez is helping Markus, he's not hiding him at his house. Not with all those people there tonight."

"*Why* is Bolt here? Do you know? You probably can't tell me."

"I don't know," Kirill said. He got out of the car. She followed him. They walked toward the elevator. Another car accelerated past them and parked crookedly in front of them, and vomited out a foursome of drunk Russians, two young men, two young women, driven by a uniformed driver who looked embarrassed. The four could barely stand and they reached the elevator before Kirill and Val did.

"Oh, hey, I know you," one of the guys said after jabbing the button to summon the elevator. "You're Illya Markarkin's secretary."

"Yes," Val said. "Hello. How are you all this evening?"

"You tell that Markarkin bastard that he owes me an apology. Calling my father to make sure I paid the mortgage on my condo. I was a little bit late but I'm always good for it."

"Mr. Markarkin doesn't own the building and he doesn't make those phone calls."

"Oh. Do you, bitch? Is it you?" And the guy lurched toward her and Kirill stepped in and knocked him to the ground with a single punch. The three others stared and then one of the women launched herself at Kirill, who stopped her with a hand covering her face and shoved her back.

"You do not speak to Mr. Markarkin's staff that way. Or to anyone else here," Kirill said.

"You can't do this. Do you know who my father is?" the guy on the ground yelled.

Kirill slightly tilted his head. "In fact, I do, Vasili Vasilievich. But here's the thing. You don't know who I am."

The elevator arrived and the door slid open and Kirill gestured to Val to enter. She did and he followed. The foursome stared at them, the young drunk still lying on the concrete, dazed.

"We'll send it back down for you," Kirill said as the door slid closed. He could see Val's tension ease slightly.

"No ripples, I thought," Val said. "They'll talk about you being here."

"They won't know who I am," he said.

"Vasili's father is a powerful man."

"Who should be ashamed of his son's behavior toward you."

"And he won't be. Please don't punch anyone else on my behalf here on the property. You won't be coming back here but I have to."

Kirill frowned. He had thought she would be thankful, perhaps see him as her rescuer. That wasn't how her mind worked. "I'm sorry," he said.

The doors slid open. The hallway was broad, nicely carpeted. Val led him toward a door on the left. "Ocean view," she said, handing him a keycard. "I had our concierge stock the kitchen with basics for you but let me know if you need anything else."

He paused. He thought about asking her inside for vodka, see what happened. She intrigued him. But he was exhausted, he needed to be sharp, and she was already enough of a complication.

"Thank you," he said. "For everything today." He was not used to having a helper, not used to thanking someone.

"I'm happy to help you tomorrow."

"Let me think on it. I don't want to put you in danger."

She nodded. "I'm safe with you. Good night, Kirill." She gave him a long look and a smile, then turned and walked down to a door three units away from his and entered with her own passkey. He watched her.

Idiot, he told himself. *She was waiting for you to kiss her.* He went inside the condo. The kitchen light was on. The condo was large, expansive, beautifully furnished. He did a sweep to make sure he was alone, then poured a glass of cold water from the tap and drank it down. The couple hours of sleep he'd gotten on the plane weren't going to be enough. He felt weary to his bones, and the hunt was just starting. It was the middle of the night in Moscow, and he needed to talk to Bobo but instead he dropped his bag in the bedroom. The balcony faced the ocean and he went out to watch the moonlight on the water. He stood in the dark quiet, the ocean breeze against his face.

Mama would like it here. A sunny, warm place surrounded by fellow Russians. Why couldn't he bring her here after he dealt with Markus? A fresh start. She could not come under her own name, of course; the Americans knew she was married to Markus and probably wouldn't let her in the country, but if Kirill could be reinvented as a Markarkin cousin, so could she.

No. She would never leave Russia; he knew this. So he would not leave, either.

He went back to the bedroom, got undressed, took a long shower to wipe the grime of the day off him. He collapsed in the bed after making sure his Glock was in reach. He worried that, with so much on his mind, he would not sleep, further reducing his efficiency.

He heard a soft knock on the door.

He answered it, with a sheet wrapped around him.

Val. In a robe. "I can't sleep," she said.

"Neither can I."

"May I come in?" she asked.

He nodded.

She stepped inside and he closed the door. Her kiss against his mouth was soft but insistent. She moved to the bedroom with him. She pulled the curtains, although the room looked out over the ocean.

"I don't usually..." he started.

"I can tell. You're sweet, Kirill."

He didn't want to say he was bad at relationships. Not now. They kissed again and he eased her onto the bed, her hands exploring him. His exhaustion vanished, for a while.

Later he felt utterly spent. Her head was on his shoulder, her finger touching his jaw. He looked down at her and smiled. Sleep claimed him and his last thought was of Val's enigmatic smile, watching him.

32

SAM DROVE PAST THE APARTMENT parking lot, looking for surveillance. A sign that Marianne and her squad were nearby, watching Amanda, waiting for their target to arrive.

No sign. No suspiciously parked cars along the road. He turned into the lot, drove slowly. No one in a car. He parked.

It was almost troubling that there was no sign of them. They were taking a different approach. Maybe a more effective one than his.

He walked up to his apartment. He wondered which one was Tara's. She could be a useful source of information but she could also be an obstacle. Ask too many questions about Amanda and she'd get suspicious as to his intent. A few people were sitting by the pool, talking quietly. They turned to watch him walk—the new tenant heading to his place. He let himself into his apartment. He'd left lights on and made a quick check that no one had been inside. He got a glass of water, drank it down.

He'd done everything by the book.

Bugged the apartment. Bugged the workplace. Made an unexpected contact with the target. Identified a likely primary threat.

So if all went to plan, he'd know the minute that Bolt

showed up at his daughter's workplace or reached out to her.

He'd also know if the FBI showed up to talk to Amanda, and he had to leave Miami before he got caught carrying out an illegal intel operation on American soil.

He just had to wait.

And he was bad at waiting, especially with rogue factors like Gandy and Marianne in play.

He'd carried out the orders, the protocols. But this Gandy guy—this Gandy guy was the unexpected connection to Bolt. There was no evidence that Gandy and Bolt had ever been in touch. No reason to think that Bolt would favor a "Boltie," an odd hanger-on, someone who strangely admired him for his nerve and his notoriety and could overlook that pesky treason Bolt had committed.

But what other friend would a traitor have who might help?

He sent Woodruff an encrypted report.

Woodruff called him five minutes later. "Tell me about this Dennis Gandy. If he's helping Bolt, and you have to kill Bolt, you may have to kill him."

"I'm not killing some idiot who's mesmerized by Bolt." If Bolt was in with Gandy, then he'd have to get Bolt away. Make him vanish and then Gandy could not prove anything. He could rave that Bolt had come back to America. Gandy was a conspiracy theorist. And while like-minded people on the Internet might believe him, the powers that mattered wouldn't.

Woodruff just ignored his answer. "It would help to know this Gandy's weaknesses. Is he in debt? Does he need a job? Anti-government type who didn't pay his taxes?"

"We've found the basics out about him. He may be trying to blackmail Amanda's boyfriend, Roberto Mendez."

"We'll dig into Gandy and Mendez. I'll call you when I know more." Woodruff hung up.

Sam leaned against the wall and watched the monitor. Amanda was restless, watching a movie on her couch, something on a streaming service. Roberto kissed her on the cheek; she didn't move.

Had they had an argument? It seemed like there was tension between them. He rewound the tapes from when he'd been at the bar. Looked for a sign of disagreement. Nothing new. The tension must still be centered on Gandy.

Roberto went into their bedroom and went to sleep.

It had been a very long day. Watching Amanda watch a movie was boring. Sam dozed off in front of the monitors.

Sam woke with a start, confused, wondering why he wasn't home. Then he remembered, his brain crowded with thoughts of his son and his questions. He got up and checked the camera feeds, only turning on the bedroom camera when he could hear the soft snoring of Roberto. It was 2:00 a.m. He'd slept for a couple of hours.

Amanda still wasn't in bed. He checked the other camera feed—she was still sitting on the couch, her laptop open. She'd stopped watching the streaming service and was on the Web.

He could see, from the angle, that she had a browser window open. And she was doing an Internet search on...her father.

Sam felt a sharp thorn of panic in his chest. Was she searching for her father's name online because he'd been in touch with her and Sam had somehow missed that?

Roberto stumbled out from the bedroom. "Babe? It's late. Are you all right?"

"Yes," Amanda said.

"What are you doing?"

"Nothing." Then she paused and said, "I'm scared of Dennis. I think he's crazy."

"I won't let him bother you. I promise." Then he cleared his throat. "Amanda, could he know anything about our private lives? Or our work?"

The threatening note, Sam thought.

"What do you mean?"

"I mean, could he somehow spy on us?"

"Oh, come on. It's not genetic."

"Amanda..."

"Please. I just want him to stop trying to talk to me."

"I'll get him to stop. I'll find a way."

"You can't hurt him."

"I won't need to."

After a moment Amanda closed the laptop and stumbled to Roberto, who embraced her in a hug. They went into the bedroom and collapsed onto the bed. Amanda was making soft crying noises, Roberto making whispers of reassurance.

Sam closed the screen for the bedroom camera.

His phone chimed. Paige. He answered.

"Were you awake?" she said. She knew he often slept little while on an assignment. Neither did she.

"Yes. And I think I want to go on the offensive. I want to find Gandy. I don't want to wait for him to come back here, Bolt in tow. I need to capture Bolt before he reaches Amanda. Before this escalates and before Marianne and her team or the Russians can find him." *And let me get home to Daniel*, he thought.

"You just don't want to sit in that apartment. Waiting."

He was silent for a moment. "My son is asking questions I'm not ready for. I thought I was ready. I thought... I had it handled. But he has his own mind. I need to be there for him right now. But...this. This is huge and I can't walk away from it."

"Catching a traitor isn't going to fix how you feel about your wife."

Typical Paige, cutting to the chase. "I don't know what you mean."

"Whatever. That you didn't see her for what she was. That's been the thorn in your brain for a long time, Sam, and your son is either going to help you finally pull it out or push it in deeper. Look at Amanda and her brother and her mom. None of them knew Bolt. None of them, and they were together as a family a lot longer than you were married to Lucy."

Sam was silent.

"You have nothing to prove."

"Okay. I have nothing to prove. I still want to find Gandy. If Bolt's with him, I can...solve this."

"Kill him?"

"Turn him over to my boss. And then forget I ever saw him." He sighed. "Can we not talk about Lucy anymore?"

"I don't know what all you've been through. I don't know how you've handled it. But you're a good father. I know Daniel has to be a great kid."

"That's a nice vote of confidence," he said. "Thanks." But he wasn't at all sure how true any of it was.

He told Paige good night. He ended the call and activated the bedroom bug. He heard the sounds of soft snoring, so he turned on the camera. Amanda lay on the bed, Roberto asleep next to her. She was curled under the sheets, holding her pillow. Awake. Restless. Afraid.

He looked at her and he thought, *This is what the truth did to her, knowing the awfulness of her father. I can't let Daniel know. I can't ever let Daniel know.*

PART THREE

33

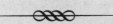

Austin

THE LIE BEFORE BEDTIME LAST night had been easy. "Coach wants us at practice fifteen minutes early," Daniel said. "Do you mind?"

Matt glanced up. "Is everything okay?"

"Sure, yeah. It's just for a meeting, I think."

"All right. I was going to stay and watch practice," Matt said. He liked to do this before going to work some days.

"Not tomorrow, Dad," James said. "Just not a good day for it."

"Is something going on?" Leonie asked.

"No," Daniel and James said together.

"All right, I'll take them and then will come home for a bit." Leonie, as art teacher, didn't have to be there quite that early.

"Thanks, Leonie," James said.

Now Leonie let them out by the gym door, then circled the lot.

"Ramsey goes into his office, checks e-mail, then he

leaves the main office and locks it back up because no one else is there," Daniel said. "So I need you to distract him."

James nodded, looking sickly.

"You are such a do-gooder," Daniel said.

"That's not the insult you think it is."

The two boys went into the gym. They were early, no other players there yet, no sign of Coach Ramsey—who was the school assistant principal and had made a deal when he took the job that he could keep coaching basketball, which was a passion of his. Daniel and James were already in practice gear and watching from the gym door's window when Daniel saw Mr. Ramsey pull in and park. James grabbed a basketball. James tucked his phone in his waistband, in the small of his back. Daniel followed as James headed for the main entrance—the main administration office was just to the entrance's left. Daniel stood back in the dark and saw Mr. Ramsey unlock the office door and step inside. If he locked it back up after him, this wouldn't work.

He didn't.

"Oh, God," James said. "Here we go."

James walked into the offices. "Coach?" he called. On just the other side of the counter were two of the assistant principal offices, one with the light on. Ramsey was at his desk, looking at something on his computer.

James stood in the doorway, blocking as much of it as he could. Ramsey had his eyes on his screen, probably checking his e-mails, making sure no irritated parent had blasted him with a complaint or an issue overnight.

"Good morning, Coach," James said.

"Hey, what's up?"

"Can I talk to you privately?" And James shut the office door. *Hurry, Daniel*, he thought.

* * *

Daniel ran through the unlocked office door, past Ramsey's closed door, and past the closed doors of other offices. He had maybe a couple of minutes, depending on how long James could delay their coach. He opened the drawer at a desk that James said an administrator sometimes forgot to lock and found a ring of keys. One was red (James had told him they were color coded) and he hurried to the room where the security videos were. It was locked. He tried the key.

It worked.

His heart felt like it was nearly in his mouth. He went to a stack of labeled discs and the one on the top was two days ago. It couldn't be this easy.

But it was.

He stuck the disc in the back of his basketball shorts, pulled his practice T-shirt over it to hide it. He shut the door, relocked it. He put the keys back in the lax administrator's drawer. He was going to have to get past the closed Ramsey door and out without being caught.

He was just past Ramsey's door when Ms. Dorridge—the counselor who had talked to him yesterday—came into the office.

"Hey, Daniel," she said, obviously surprised to see him. "You're not supposed to be in here."

"Oh, I'm just getting Coach Ramsey... Practice is starting and we need him in the gym."

She looked at him, suspicious but not wanting to be.

He knocked on the door, heard Ramsey say, "Come in," and opened it. James turned to him, all frowns.

"Coach? Just checking on if we can start practice?"

"Sure, Daniel, we'll be there in a second," Ramsey said. James didn't turn to look at him.

"Okay." He closed the door and smiled at Ms. Dorridge. "Have a good day," he said to her.

"You, too, Daniel," she said. "I'm always here for you."

Did counselors say this every time they talked with a kid? Or was she just kind of needy, like please please please come to me with your problems?

"I'm really fine," he said.

"You just seemed upset yesterday."

"I'm okay." Daniel gave her his best good-student smile. "Thanks." He hurried past her, back out into the main hallway—and nearly straight into Leonie.

"Hey," she said. "What are you doing out here? I thought you had a meeting."

She hadn't driven home; she had a couple of books in her hand.

"We did," he said. "It was in Coach Ramsey's office." He needed to get her out of here before Ramsey and James came out and she asked more questions. "Did you forget something?"

"Oh, yeah, I meant to bring these books home from the art room and figured I'd do it now because I keep forgetting. You all right?"

He must have had an invisible sign on his chest that read "Ask me if I'm all right," visible only to adults. "Yes, I'm fine," he said. "I'll see you later." He went past her; she watched him for a moment, then she walked on and out of the building. He went into the gym, slipped the stolen disc into his bag, and started shooting baskets with his teammates. Two minutes later James came in with Coach Ramsey. James didn't look at him, just joined the practice.

"Hey," he said to James, who nodded, looking relieved that the ordeal was over.

After practice, Daniel showered and got dressed for school. He wouldn't be able to talk to James until choir.

James fell into step next to him as they headed toward their classes. "Did you get it?"

"Yes."

"I didn't think you'd actually be able to get it." His voice sounded drained, distant. "Oh, man, we're gonna get expelled."

"No. They'll just think they misplaced it." He decided not to mention the close calls with Ms. Dorridge and Leonie. James seemed kind of freaked as it was.

"What if there's a camera in the office that caught you?" James said suddenly.

"There's not, they're filming where the kids are," Daniel said, uncertain, but keeping his tone confident. That was a problem for tomorrow. "What did you say to Coach?"

"I was first going to ask for more playing time, but that seemed like a yes or no and wouldn't give you time to get the recording. So I did this long thing about school pressure and my dad always riding me to play harder, score more"—for a moment his voice wavered—"and he said he'd talk to my dad. Which is not what I wanted."

"Oh, man, James, I'm sorry."

"It's okay. You got what you needed?" His voice trembled a little.

"I think." He'd have to wait until he was home to watch it. His school laptop didn't have a disc drive in it and he'd need uninterrupted time to go through the disc. "Thanks, James. I appreciate it."

"You have to find a way to put it back when you're done," James said.

"I thought maybe you could do that. Tomorrow during your office aide period."

James sighed. "Okay, fine. Fine." They broke apart to go to their different classes. Just get through the day,

Daniel thought. Just get through today. He could go and watch the video, maybe fast-forward through it, before the woman came over to talk to him.

And if it was her on the video, then he'd have some leverage against her.

34

Miami

SAM WAS UP EARLY THE next morning. He watched Roberto and Amanda get ready for work—and noticed a strain between them. They weren't talking. He waited for them to leave and then rewound last night's video until it became clear they'd had an argument before bedtime, while he was bugging their office. Maybe that was why Amanda had been sleepless and Roberto had apologized while asking her to come back to bed.

He played it back:

Roberto: I'm busting my ass to take good care of you and you treat me like this.

Amanda: I'm not treating you any way. You're being hopeless.

Roberto: Are you cheating on me or not?

Amanda: This is ridiculous. We work together. We live together. We're joined at the hip. When, exactly, am I supposed to have time or space to cheat on you?

Roberto: That wasn't an answer. Why do you have two phones? Why?

Amanda: Because I want to.

Two phones. One Roberto didn't know about until now.
Who was she in touch with? Her dad? What secret was
Amanda keeping?

Amanda: My mom sent it to me.
Roberto: Your mom. Do I look stupid?
Amanda: Yes. Yes, you do, and you're not stupid so
please can't you trust me?
Roberto: Why is your mom sending you a secret
phone?
Amanda: It's not a secret. It's a phone she wants to
contact me and only me on. She's worried her other
phone is compromised.
Roberto: Why?
Amanda: Please don't make me say this.
Roberto: Tell me.
Amanda: She thinks people are watching her.
Maybe the CIA, maybe the Russians, sent by Dad.

(Here her voice wavered.)

Roberto: Why would anyone spy on her?
Amanda: Because she's how she is.
Roberto (sounding resigned): You're paranoid.
You're both paranoid.
Amanda: Maybe, but I'm not cheating on you. So
will you please stop this?
Roberto: Show me the phone. Show me the calls.

She did. He studied the screen.

Amanda: It's just one number. See? Please don't
make me call it. It's just Mom, and if she knows that
you know about the phone, she'll tell me to destroy it
and she'll send another.

Roberto: What, she thinks I'm with the CIA now? Is she crazy?
Amanda: A little. Watch.

Sam watched her tap the screen, hold the phone slightly away from her head so Roberto could hear.

Voice on phone: Yes?
Amanda: Mom. I'm just checking on you.
Karen Bolt: I thought…I thought he was here. Last night. But it was just a dream. I thought he was standing by my bed.
Amanda: Mom, he's not there. You know that.
Karen Bolt: Someone's been watching me. I can feel it. I know it.
Amanda: No one is interested in us, Mom, not about that, not anymore.

Then she said something Sam couldn't quite hear, put the phone to her ear, and moved away from Roberto.
Then she hung up.

Roberto: All right. All right. I'm sorry.
Amanda (sarcastically): Thanks for being so trusting of me, I really appreciate it. You've made me feel special.
Roberto: Amanda, listen—
Amanda: I don't want to talk any more right now.

She sat on the couch and opened a laptop.
Roberto stared at her and then went into the bedroom and slammed the door.
Amanda put the phone on the coffee table.

Sam stopped the video. He checked the current feed; the phone was no longer on the coffee table. Maybe that was what she'd hidden in the bedside table when he'd watched her on video before? It seemed a likely guess.

He jumped from his balcony to theirs. Picked the lock on the door, went inside. He checked the bedside table; yes, the phone was there.

This was a wrinkle. Could it be Bolt heightening Karen Bolt's suspicions? *I thought he was standing by my bed.* Knowing Bolt was on the loose, her words chilled him. Maybe Bolt was considering an approach to his wife, not his daughter.

He felt a surge of sympathy for Mrs. Bolt. He knew what it was to be in her shoes. Spouse of a traitor. *Why didn't you know? How could you not know? Weren't you suspicious? You were in on it with him/her, weren't you? You had to be. Didn't you wonder where the extra money came from? Did you not know your own husband, your own wife?* And it didn't help that so many spouses did know, did suspect. Because there was unexplained money, or unexplained trips, or a simmering anger or frustration that made someone ripe for betrayal.

None of that had been apparent with Bolt.

He did another quick search of the apartment. He found a box beneath the bed, on Roberto's side. Full of cash. Another collection of cash tied to Roberto. It was odd, and Sam didn't like odd. Why was he keeping cash around like this? Was someone paying him off, or did he anticipate a need to have ready money? For himself, or to pay off someone else? He put the box back, left again via the balcony, and returned to his apartment.

He checked the briefing file on Bolt. Mrs. Bolt lived near Miami. She had a home willed to her by a close friend who had passed. She worked part-time at a high-end resort on Biscayne Bay as a receptionist and guest relations person. A quiet life. She had resumed her maiden name of Karen English.

He called Woodruff. "Who is watching the former Mrs. Bolt?"

"Why?"

Sam explained about the conversation.

"He won't approach his ex."

"You seem very confident."

"We are, trust us. He won't go near Karen. Anything else to report?"

Sam considered. Maybe Marianne and team were watching Karen, and that was making her suspicious. "No. Have you got more on Gandy?"

"Yes. It just came in. We've got a skeleton crew to stay under the radar." He sounded defensive. "You were right to push him to our attention. He's not from Atlanta. He grew up in McLean."

McLean, close to the CIA headquarters.

"His parents were both Agency. His mother worked in IT support. She died a few years back from cancer. Dad…his dad killed himself, a few months after Bolt defected. He was accused of embezzling two hundred thousand in Agency funds. The Gandys lived six houses down from the Bolts. Dennis and Amanda Bolt went to elementary school together."

"Was there any connection to Bolt?"

"They didn't work together—Bill Gandy worked in finance, but his work didn't overlap with Bolt's. Other than being neighbors and being friendly because their kids were in school together, not a tie. He was interviewed when Bolt defected—he didn't know anything, there was nothing to tie their activities together."

"Karen Bolt had a gambling problem, right? That

was part of Markus's motivation to spy, to pay off her debts. And he has a neighbor who steals money?"

"But nothing to tie them," Woodruff said, with infinite patience.

"How old was Dennis when this happened?"

"Twelve. Same as Amanda."

"Bolt defects," Sam said slowly. "Weeks later Gandy's dad steals Agency funds and kills himself when he's caught. Now Gandy's son is stalking Bolt's daughter."

"Dennis Gandy is just a weird guy."

"Why is he so sure Bolt is innocent?"

"He's a childhood friend. He can claim to have known Bolt. That would give him huge credibility with that conspiracy crowd. To them, he's an insider," Woodruff said. "It's just a way to get attention. Maybe insisting Bolt is innocent is a way to insist his dad is innocent."

"He doesn't write this Boltie stuff under his own name, though."

"Attention is still attention," Woodruff said.

"Let's say Bolt reads this stuff the Bolties post. He might be like us and able to figure out that the site's moderator is the kid that used to live down the street. Maybe he's been in touch with Dennis, maybe told him things that made him feel better about his father. Dennis could approach Amanda maybe without raising red flags. C'mon, I need to find this guy." It was an angle they hadn't considered, a childhood friend of Amanda's assisting the fugitive.

"What has Amanda said about him?"

"She thinks he's crazy and not someone she still considers a friend."

"Yeah, the challenge is Dennis burned his bridges with Amanda a year ago, when he got deeper into this conspiracy stuff. We found some of his old blog entries. He brags that he knew the Bolt family and was their neighbor, but then that boasting falls off fairly rapidly. We got his cell records. He called her phone a couple of times a year ago—she sent him a text saying she had no interest in talking to him about her dad. No contact since."

"Does he ever write about his dad?"

"No, not directly. He has talked about his belief that there was a traitor inside the CIA, someone other than Bolt or his father, and this mythical boogeyman framed them both."

"You said no connection, there it is," Sam said.

"But it's not real, Sam. It's not. It's in his head."

In his head, behind those empty eyes. Sam took a deep breath. "Where's he staying?"

"No use of his credit card at a hotel or hostel or through a lodging service. He's at a friend's or using another payment method."

"Search his social network. Who does he know in Miami? He's not from here; it can't be a long list. I'll get Paige on it, too."

"I should have thought of this. We thought he would beeline to his family. Because the Russians could leak this news at any time."

"Also—what can we find out on Amanda's boyfriend? He got a threatening note about turning Amanda over to someone, and he's got wads of cash stashed at both his office and his apartment."

"Mendez has no criminal record," Woodruff said. "He's clean. But he's not your focus, Bolt is." He paused.

"I know," Sam said. "Trust me, I know."

"We need to make Bolt disappear. Call me when you've found him or have actionable data." He hung up.

Sam texted Paige with the added details on Dennis Gandy. She answered she'd start digging into his social media for clues. He activated the camera feeds he'd set up at the courier office; both worked, but neither Roberto nor Amanda was at their desk—they hadn't had time to reach the office yet.

He showered quickly and made coffee and toast.

35

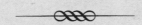

His phone buzzed with a text from Daniel:

Did my mother have any family at all? Any? Couldn't we check through one of those genetic testing sites? Love you.

The words were a knife in his heart and the last two gave it a twist.

He blinked himself awake, got up, remembered he hadn't bothered with a coffeemaker. This wasn't home. He texted him back: We can certainly consider that if you like. What do you hope to gain from finding someone?

Someone who knew her.

I knew your mom better than anybody.

But you don't like her, Daniel texted.

That's not true, Sam texted, biting his lip. I loved her.

I don't know, Dad. I'm not sure you do.

Sam sat down on the floor.

He called his son. Daniel let the phone ring four times before he answered, probably shocked that his father had abandoned the preferred texting for an actual live conversation.

"Hey, Dad." Daniel sounded slightly abashed. "I'm in the hallway. Going to class."

"You don't know how I loved her."

"It doesn't seem like you do."

"I will always love her because I had you with her."

"That's not loving her, that's loving me."

The next lie was so hard to tell, but he'd thought about it before if he needed to use it. "We'd been through some stuff before she got sick. I don't know that we would have stayed married much longer."

He could hear the buzz of student voices in the hallway. "You've never said that to me before. You were going to divorce her?"

"It would have been mutual. Our lives were going in different directions."

"And you didn't leave her only because she got sick?"

Sam felt like something broke in time. Like his life had accelerated into a dreaded moment. "I wouldn't leave her in a time of need. It's hard to explain." That at least was a truth.

"Did she leave a message for me? Something you haven't shared with me? Like a letter?"

"No. Of course not." The thought was horrifying. Lucy actually speaking, in any way, to his child now. No. *No.*

"You haven't lied to me about any of this, have you?"

"Of course not." Because Sam could say nothing else. Because if he did, if he told the truth his son deserved, it would destroy everything. He closed his eyes. He was an operative, trained to listen for those intonations of voice that betrayed hidden intent, or concealment of information.

Using what the intel masters taught you. On your own child. His shame burned hot in his chest. He forced his voice toward steadiness. "Daniel. Has someone said something to you that made you ask me that?"

"No. No." Daniel said, too quickly. "I don't know what to think. I want you to come home."

"I can't right now."

"It's just a bar, Dad."

Just a bar. If he only knew. "Daniel. I know it seems

like what I do isn't important. I know. But it is. This is how I...take care of us. I'll be home as soon as I can. Please, we'll talk about this when I get home."

"All right. Bye, Dad." And he hung up.

Wow, the drama. The teenage years were here. Plus—he was right, and Sam was wrong, and that was the worst. He took a deep breath. Amanda and Roberto were gone and he'd activate the cameras in the office by the time they reached their jobs.

The phone buzzed, and Sam hoped that Daniel was calling him back, but it wasn't the special ring he had set up for Daniel. It was Paige.

"I found a possibility. Dennis Gandy and Amanda Bolt don't have any mutual friends on social media. I think Amanda may have just...stepped away from people in her past after her father defected. But Gandy's got a friend in Miami, on Faceplace. I just sent you a screen capture."

Sam opened the laptop, accessed the encoded message.

A picture of Dennis Gandy, standing in a backyard with a guy his age, with thick dark hair and a broad smile. "Friends since first grade!" the caption read.

"The friend is named Carlos Cortez. The picture is three years old. Carlos has a page, as well. He works in international banking. It looks like from the pictures he posts on social media that he travels frequently to South America," Paige said.

"So Carlos might be gone from his house for an extended period and Gandy could hide someone there," Sam said.

"I have an address for Carlos. But what are you going to do? Go and break in? What are you going to say if he calls the police and you get caught?"

"I won't get caught." He was already deciding what he'd need to investigate.

Maybe he was about to be lucky. Maybe Markus Bolt was sitting in a dark den in that house, watching the news to see if his name came up, if anyone was hunting for him, if Dennis Gandy could somehow get a message to his daughter.

He clicked on Carlos Cortez's page. Saw a posting of Carlos with an older man, with a mustache and a broad grin.

That face. Sam stared at that face and his heart, his stomach clenched.

36

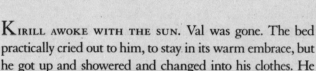

KIRILL AWOKE WITH THE SUN. Val was gone. The bed practically cried out to him, to stay in its warm embrace, but he got up and showered and changed into his clothes. He donned what he thought would work in Miami—light gray pants and a loose shirt Mama had packed for him, a green one with parrots on it. He couldn't decide if he looked like he belonged in Miami or looked like a foolish tourist.

A gentle knock on the door. He took his gun with him, checked the peephole. Val, dressed and showered, with a tray of food. He opened the door.

"I brought you breakfast," she said. She was in a light linen suit and looked impeccable. The parrot shirt would not work in her company, he thought, then he remembered he didn't have to bring her along.

"Thank you." *Do I kiss her?* He felt awkward as a schoolboy.

She walked in: teapot, toast, a scrambled egg. "You didn't eat regularly yesterday; you need strength."

I need you, he thought, the thirst for her unbidden. He pushed it away and sat down at the table. "This is kind of you, thank you."

"It doesn't need to be uncomfortable this morning," she said. Her smile was slight. "All is well."

He nodded, a little embarrassed. She was a widow

nearly ten years older than him. Maybe she had no desire
to have a relationship. Maybe he was just her bit of fun. He
felt a little drunk smiling at her.

"I had a thought on today," she said. "You said Bolt's
daughter is here."

"Yes."

"But you don't think he'll approach her."

"I think she would report him."

"But...she's the best reason for him to have returned
to America. We don't know why. It has to be her. Perhaps she's ill. Or she reached out to him."

The burner phone, Kirill thought. The one no one
answered. "You think Grayson Cortez is a dead end?"

"I think Cortez is not a daughter," she said quietly.
She stole a piece of his toast and munched.

He finished eating. "I have to report in," he said. *And
change my shirt*, he thought.

"I like the shirt," she said, as if reading his mind. She
poured herself a cup of strong tea from the pot.

He went to the coffee table and opened his laptop. He
wrote up a fast report, encoded it, and sent it to Duderov
and Bobo. He didn't feel like crafting separate, politi-
cally aware reports to each of them. He took his laptop
and went to the bedroom, opened his suitcase, and found
a dark, dressy polo shirt, navy with soft silver piping on
the collar and the sleeves. Mama had bought it for him.
He put that on instead.

His laptop chirped, twice, and he saw Bobo and Duderov both on screen, waiting for him, trying to contact
him for a meeting. He activated an encoding link so
their conversation could not be heard or watched.

"Both of you at once," Kirill said. "Lucky me."

"Your report..." Duderov said. "We have an update
for you. The play is the daughter."

"She'll turn him in."

"Kirill," Duderov said. "Bolt has an illness. It's terminal."

"Why did you not tell me this before?"

"We only discovered it. He'd paid off his doctor to conceal test results to us. Paid him off significantly, with money he took from an account we didn't know about. I think Illya might have set it up for him."

Kirill got up and shut the bedroom door; he could see Val in the kitchen, washing off his dirty plate and putting it in the dishwasher. He didn't want Val to hear about anything involving Illya. She was loyal to her boss and he respected that.

He sat back down. "Details," he said. He read through the medical file they'd just sent him.

"The doctor broke quickly once we told him Bolt had left Russia. Bolt paid him nearly a million in US dollars to keep the diagnosis quiet. We think he wants to see Amanda before he dies," Bobo said.

"Don't waste your time on Cortez. Steer clear of him," the Dude added.

It was an odd phrasing. Almost like a warning. "All right. So what do you want me to do?"

"Watch Amanda, see if he approaches her."

"That's an idiotic idea to just sit and wait," Kirill said. "At least for someone with my skills. Send over a surveillance team; surely you can trust five more people to keep this quiet."

"You're the fastest route to finding him."

Bolt had taken the financial network information to buy a way back into American graces (at least in some form). Why did he need that if he needed Amanda? To get the cooperation of the American government. To get them to give him treatment, if Amanda agreed. He couldn't take her back to Russia and she probably wouldn't go there willingly on her own. Would she help him live to face justice?

"I could kidnap her," Kirill said.

"No. Approach her differently."

"Do you think she'll even talk to a Russian?" Kirill asked. "She'll suspect me instantly of being tied to her father."

"Then don't be a Russian."

"What about a Brit?" He thought of Val. She'd lived in London a long time. Her accent was softer than his.

"Fine. You have documentation?"

"Yes." He had a British passport in his bag, along with four other nationalities. It was sometimes useful not to be Russian. Let them think he meant to use a British ID. He meant to send Val to talk to Amanda.

"How long does he have?"

"He likely dies within a year," said Bobo. He and Duderov both stared at him from the screen. Now they were a united front. A reason for Bolt's return, other than treason, made their lives easier.

"Why did he just not ask if she would come to Russia?"

"He must have known she would say no."

"All right. So I watch her?"

"Or talk to her. Tell her you have information on her father."

"Why would she care?"

"Make it interesting. That he wants to send her money."

"All right. What about Cortez?" Something made him ask. Instinct.

"No," they said, nearly together. Bobo cleared his throat. "He has ties to American intelligence."

"Yes. And Cortez is the kind of person who he'd make a deal with. He needs to have a face-to-face with someone to negotiate his return. Cortez feels likely. He's here, he's in physical proximity to Amanda," Kirill said.

"I am telling you to stay clear of him," Bobo said. "He'd immediately report you to authorities. It's too big a risk."

"All right," Kirill said after a moment. He had to wrap his head around Bolt being terminally ill. "My mother . . . does she know about his illness?"

"We confirmed with her that he was seeing Dr. Rudenko. She confirmed that but did not know he'd seen a specialist. He had concealed his condition from her as well."

Oh, Mama. "How is she?"

"About as well as an abandoned wife can feel," Duderov said.

"I'd like to speak to her."

"Perhaps later," Bobo said. "She is still being debriefed, given this new information."

Debriefed. Kirill didn't like the sound of that. It sounded like detained.

"She doesn't know anything."

"She was supposed to watch him and she either let her emotions sway her or she became complacent."

Mama was in trouble. He felt a surge of fury. "I am risking my life here to do as you ask and you're not going to bully my mother. Or turn her into the scapegoat for your failures."

"She was closest to him and yet she knew none of this, she says," Bobo said.

"I will get back on Illya's plane and come home if you treat her poorly," Kirill said. "You were in charge of him officially. She was his wife and you asked her to spy on him. Markus is garbage but Mama loves him, and you had no right to put her in that position."

"Let's calm down, Kirill. The one at fault here is Markus. When he's dealt with, we can all have a calm discussion," Duderov said, the silky voice of reason.

He nearly told them about the financial network. But that would just panic them, and it would be death for Illya, and maybe Val. Oligarchs who had crossed the president had ended up dead before, poisoned, or shot, like journalists.

"Fine," Kirill said. "I'll work the Amanda Bolt angle."

"Hurry. We cannot keep this news quiet forever," Duderov said. "I'll expect a report tonight."

"I'm sure Bobo will prepare one for you," Kirill said sharply. Duderov blinked off the connection and Kirill regretted his words—the Dude held Mama's immediate future in his hands.

"You could handle that better," Bobo said. "Don't worry about Sonia, I'll help her. You have Amanda's address in the file."

"This Lucy Carrier. She wasn't a helper to Markus? A fellow turncoat?"

"No. She might have been a girlfriend."

"I didn't think he cheated on his American wife."

"He hadn't, so he said. But he could have lied to us. But again, I want you avoiding the American intel connections. Report back this evening." Bobo terminated the encoded call.

Kirill closed the laptop. He went back out to the kitchen. Val was finishing her tea.

"What is Illya doing today?" Kirill asked.

"Spending time with Maria," she said. "He's agitated. He woke me up with an early phone call to tell me he didn't sleep well. I have told him to calm down."

"I want the jet ready to go, fueled, crew on standby."

She nodded. "I assumed as much and made arrangements."

"Thank you. I need your help today."

She nodded after a moment. "All right."

"How is your British accent? Can you pass?"

37

Sam steadied his breath. On his Section K phone, he looked in the online property tax records and found an address for Grayson Cortez near Coral Gables.

He drove there. He concentrated on the feel of the wheel in his hand, pushing the memories away, trying to keep his mind clear. He stopped at a light and closed his eyes.

The dark of the prison cell. The sudden light. The smiling face, infinitely patient, saying, *You just have to tell us the truth about your wife. She's abandoned you. You don't need to keep protecting her.*

The blare of a horn. Sam jerked back to now, waved politely at the driver behind him, went through the green.

All you have to do is tell us what you know. The cloth pulled over his face, the slosh of the water. *Please, please, I don't know anything*, Sam had said.

I don't believe you, the voice said. *You're a good guy, Sam, why are you lying to me? Why are you choosing violence?*

Please. No. Please.

It's my job, Sam. I study traitors. So I can understand them. And I don't understand why you're making me do this.

And then the men tilting him back, the water starting its slow, inexorable trickle that felt like death.

He kept driving. *You have arrived at your destination*, his phone informed him. He stopped the car.

The house was immaculate.

The cold of the cell. The stone against his face. The guards taking him out into the empty prison yard for a walk for ten minutes... he was the only prisoner, he realized. The empty sky, the cloud-pale sun. Not even knowing which country he was in. The walls with the tiny, barred windows.

He stared at the broad windows of the house. He got out of the car.

He walked toward the front door.

The prison door opened; he had nothing but the clothes on his back. His companion was a guard he hadn't seen before and a man who told him he could go back to America... under the watchful eye of the Agency. No apology. No news of his wife.

No smiling interrogator with his gentle voice.

He walked up to the front door and rang the doorbell.

After a few moments a man in his sixties answered. He was tall, solidly built, jet-black hair with gray streaking it. His face was slightly asymmetrical, as though his left orbital or cheek had been broken and not healed quite properly. There was a scar.

Sam stared at him. "Hello, Mr. Cortez."

Grayson Cortez wasn't smiling now. "Sam Capra."

"You remember me."

Sam powered a fist into the man's chest. He careened back and fell, scrabbling backward. Sam stepped into the home's foyer and slammed the door shut with his foot.

Cortez said, "Listen, I was just doing my job..."

Sam yanked him to his feet again, just to shove him into his own den. He went over a coffee table and onto the couch. Sam, one-handed, picked him up and pushed him over the edge of the couch so Cortez's head was close to the floor, his feet in the air.

"I could put the towel on you. Pour water on it so it feels like you're drowning. And ask you all my questions in a soft, gentle voice." Sam's voice trembled. "But I won't. Right now, I'm just doing my job."

"Your job?"

"You told me once that you study traitors. I need help understanding one."

"Your wife?"

"Markus Bolt."

Sam expected shock on his face. Instead Cortez's stare remained steady. "What do you care about Markus Bolt?"

"I just want to talk to you about him."

"The last time I saw you, you left me this." He pointed at the little scar.

"Did I? I don't remember landing a punch after the Tasering and the beating."

"And they let you out," he said.

"I was innocent."

"Yes," Cortez said. "You were. And I was wrong. I'm sorry, Sam. I am truly sorry." He took a deep breath and closed his eyes, as though bracing for a blow.

Sam took a deep breath and let go of him. He pulled Cortez up to a sitting position on the coach.

"The worst part of what you did to me was that you smiled through it," Sam said.

"I have to play a part," Cortez said. "That's my mask." He took a deep breath. "I just made some coffee. Do you want some?"

Sam, after a moment, nodded. He followed Cortez into the kitchen.

There were already two cups out on the counter. Cortez pulled the coffee decanter from the brewer; Sam braced himself in case the man decided to fling it at him, but he didn't; he just poured cups.

But two cups. "Were you expecting someone?"

"No. A neighbor sometimes comes over for coffee. He's retired, too, but he texted me that he's going to a morning event at his granddaughter's school. Cream? Sugar?"

"Black is fine. Thank you."

Cortez handed him the mug. His gaze met Sam's. "Markus Bolt. Let's talk."

Cortez had three grown children and he was very proud of them. The wall in the living room was full of photos of his two daughters and his son—the one Sam had found on social media. Sports, academic fairs, graduations, awards. Sam studied the pictures. He did not put up pictures of Daniel, not like this. He should do this. But Daniel would probably roll his eyes. *Don't ask him*, Sam thought. *Just do it. Put up the pictures.* Had he been taking enough pictures? Not to put in frames. They all lived on his phone. His chest felt tighter looking at these pictures than it had when Cortez searched him.

Sam noticed no pictures of a wife.

Cortez gestured to the couch and Sam sat and Cortez took a chair across from him. "Is your wife still alive?" Cortez asked.

"She died of an undiagnosed heart ailment."

"That's the official story. I know she took a bullet at Yankee Stadium. I got to read the file."

Sam kept his face expressionless.

"I'm sorry I never got to talk to her. She fascinated me." Cortez paused, sipped his coffee. "There really are so few female traitors acting independently of their husbands. Usually, it's the husband waltzing toward treason, and he makes his wife his dance partner."

A case study. "I can't discuss her."

"They put you under a gag order."

Sam nodded. "I divorced her. She's not my responsibility anymore."

"So who decides that she still lives?"

"The Agency, I guess."

"Do they think she's going to wake up one day?"

"Stranger things have happened. And maybe they want to have her come back so they can interview her. Maybe they'll ask you to be on the team."

"I still consult for them, but mostly I'm retired. I doubt there's much of her brain worth picking."

Sam stiffened but tried not to show it. Cortez noticed. "You still have feelings for her?" Like it would make an interesting addendum to a paper.

"We had a son together."

"Who she endangered, if I recall."

"His name is Daniel." Why was he telling this man this? Because he'd read the files, he knew.

"He must be . . ."

"Thirteen."

"And the world doesn't know his mother was a traitor, so Daniel doesn't know. Does he?" Cortez almost leaned forward, sitting on the edge of his seat, his fascination drawing him forward. "A most unusual dynamic."

"I didn't know. There are other spouses of traitors who didn't know."

"Well, often because the betrayal was driven by anger or ideology. Your wife, and Markus Bolt, were both corrupted by a criminal syndicate."

"Bolt? He just defected to Russia."

"What *is* Russia's leadership? Oligarch billionaires, many of whom have ties to organized crime."

"But my wife didn't betray us for Russia."

"She did it for a vicious criminal syndicate...intent on creating chaos in politics and economies that they could leverage for their own gain."

"That criminal syndicate"—Sam realized he knew something Cortez didn't—"was brought together by the CIA originally."

Cortez froze.

"Oh," Sam said, almost innocently, tired of the lecturing tone from Cortez, "did you not know that?"

For a few moments Cortez said nothing, and Sam could hear the slow tick of a clock on the wall. "Regardless of whoever formed them, Lucy Collins Capra betrayed her nation, her agency, and her family. Other agents were pulled into her orbit. We had not really seen a traitor like her before."

"How close were you to Bolt?"

"What's your sudden interest, and why are you in Miami again?"

Sam chose his words carefully. "I thought...I thought of approaching his family. Because I'm going to have to tell my son the truth about his mother. I wondered how the Bolt family had handled it."

Cortez stared at him. The silence grew.

"I knew them before, of course. We lived a few houses away. My kids were in school with Amanda and Allan."

Same as Dennis Gandy. An odd web of neighbors... who just happened to work in intelligence.

"I was working for a different agency, but that was during a period where cross-functionality was encouraged. I was one of Bolt's trainers. I did a psychological assessment on him that obviously was flawed." Cortez sipped his coffee. "Later, as neighbors and elementary school dads, we became friends. Or closer acquaintances—I'm not sure Markus has ever had a friend." He cleared his throat. "He did more damage to us than your wife did. She hurt us. But he *exposed* us. As not being disciplined enough, as not being careful enough, of employing weaklings."

"Did you talk to him much in his last days?"

"I was part of his traitor's dance: his escape route. He wanted to meet with me. He was running agents in Eastern Europe. Gathering information on money laundering or arms deals being brokered by the Russian elite and their intel agencies. He had a concern about one of his agents and wanted to talk with me."

"He had a concern about an agent he planned on exposing to the Russians? Why even bother?"

Cortez didn't answer. "He wanted to position that agent as the betrayer. Not himself, I think, and he also…he came to my house. We talked in my study. I left him alone for a few moments and we believe he stole an encrypted list off my laptop. It had the name of my agents on it. Three of them ended up dead a week after Bolt jumped." He closed his eyes for a moment.

"They didn't toss you from intelligence work at that point?" Sam asked bluntly.

"We believe they already had the names of the agents. His theft from me just detailed how they were paid, what leverage we had on them. It made them easier to corner and kill all at once." He sipped his coffee again. "I shouldn't be telling you any of this, but hey, you're Lucy Capra's husband, you're a bigger screwup than I'll ever be."

"And you're retired now?"

"I retired soon after. I got a think tank position and came home."

Sam raised an eyebrow. "But that was before Lucy. You interrogated me."

"I consult from time to time. They brought me in to talk to you. I wrote up a report. I did write a final report saying I felt you were telling the truth, that you didn't know. For what that's worth. It was my job to break you if you knew. Not to establish your innocence. I am sorry."

"Thank you."

"It's the only reason I'm talking to you about this."

"He came here to Miami before he left for Russia. Why?" It bothered him that Miami was Cortez's hometown as well. It seemed an odd coincidence. And now back here again.

"Why are we back on Bolt? What's your interest? You said you were doing your job."

"It's my turn to ask and your turn to answer."

"All right," Cortez said. "I said he thought he might be being watched and going to Miami was a way to throw them off his trail. If he couldn't get to Moscow, he could get to Cuba eventually, and they'd get him to the Russians."

"So he runs to Miami, with its large Russian population. Did he have a friend here? Someone who could hide him? Help him to Moscow?"

"You're after accomplices now?" Cortez stared at him. "Years later?"

"It's more curiosity."

"We don't know who helped him here," Cortez said slowly. "No one. But likely a Russian did. Gave him money, got him on a flight."

"Wait, a private jet?"

"No. He flew commercial to London, then to Moscow."

Sam decided to abandon subterfuge.

"So who's Dennis Gandy?"

Cortez blinked.

"Do you know the name?"

"Yes. He's friends with my son. Or they were when they were younger."

"Dennis's parents were your neighbors and his father also worked in intel."

"Yes. Bill Gandy. He killed himself." He shook his head sadly. "Dennis is an odd duck. I'm not sure why Carlos has stayed friends with him."

"Dennis has been pestering Amanda Bolt. Coming around her apartment, looking for her."

"And how do you know that?"

"Because I've been keeping an eye on her."

Sam saw movement coming from the hallway. A woman, stepping out from the shadows. He recognized her immediately from the file. Karen English Bolt, Markus's American wife. Her hair was dark, shot with gray, pulled back into a bun. She wore jeans and a navy sweatshirt, red-framed eyeglasses that in the light Sam could see were smudged with fingerprints. Dark circles beneath her eyes. Dried paint on the sweatshirt.

And she held a gun.

"Karen," Cortez said. "Karen, put that down."

The gun was leveled at Sam. "What do you mean, keeping an eye on her?" Her voice shook.

"Hi, Karen," Sam said. "I'm Sam. You really don't want to shoot me. I'm happy to talk to you about this if you'll put down the gun."

"Why are you watching my daughter? Who sent you?" She raised the gun. She was out of his reach, and there was no cover to be had in the living room.

"Why are you here, Karen?" Sam asked. Two cups. The story about a neighbor was a lie.

"I am asking the questions."

"Did you interrogate her, too, after Bolt defected? Is this old school week at your house?"

Cortez shook his head. "We're old friends. She came to see me this morning because she thinks someone's watching her."

Sam thought of the conversation between Amanda and Ricardo; Amanda had said the same thing.

"Why are you surveilling my daughter?" Karen asked again. "Answer me." The gun, still locked on Sam.

"I was sent to protect her," Sam said. "From her father. He fled Russia. Under cloak. We think he might approach her."

Silence. Karen and Cortez looked at each other, shock in their faces. "How? How could he have gotten out?" Cortez said.

"Because he's Markus Bolt. I think he must have had help. And I think Dennis Gandy is helping him. Dennis has been reaching out to Amanda, in person, electronically, and I think he's trying to get her to engage with him so he can take her to Bolt. He's tried to get Roberto to help him bring her to either him or Dennis." He glanced at Cortez. "I found pics of your son and Gandy together at your son's house on social media. That's why I came to see you. In case you knew about this."

"I didn't," Cortez said. He stared at Karen. "Karen, I swear to you, I didn't."

"I believe you, Grayson." Karen gestured at Sam with the gun toward an easy chair in the corner. "You, sit down. Hands on head."

"Karen, Sam was a Special Projects operative. He may still be. I would stay well back of him," Cortez said.

"I'm not armed," Sam said.

"You don't need to be," Karen said. "I worked intel, too. I can imagine what you're capable of. Who are you working for?"

"Section K. I'm a fixer. All I'm doing is protecting Amanda if her father approaches her. And detaining him."

"Was someone sent to watch me?"

"They didn't think he would approach you."

"Well, I did try to kill him when he left me," Karen said. "But I've thought someone has been watching me." Her voice grew more ragged.

Sam knew she thought this; but he wasn't about to admit that he'd bugged her daughter's apartment and workplace. "How so?"

"Could feel it. Could sense it. Every now and then one of those people who are obsessed with Markus's story come sniffing around my life when I just want to be left alone. They drove Allan crazy." Her voice wobbled.

"I'm sorry," Sam said. "The Russians are hunting him, too. They've hired contract killers. They've no doubt got their own people. They're trying to keep it quiet to grab him back or eliminate him. I suspect it's them watching you, trying to cover every base. I urge you to keep it quiet as well."

"Markus would never in a million years come see me," Karen said.

"Even so, we wanted to protect you." He wasn't sure why he'd decided to be frank; maybe it was because he could see in Karen Bolt the doubt and fear and anger he'd felt in the wake of Lucy. They weren't so different, he and Karen. She had been told terrible lies by her husband and comforting lies, he was sure, by the Agency after Bolt's defection.

"Fixer." Her mouth shifted slightly. "Were you supposed to catch Markus?"

"Preferably before he reached Amanda. We didn't want her to know he was loose. We didn't want to put her through that."

"Grayson," she said. "Go check my car. See if there's a tracker on it."

"They can just trace your phone," Sam said helpfully.

"Karen, put up the gun, please. We're all on the same team," Grayson Cortez said.

She eased on the safety and put it in the back of her jeans. She stood behind the couch. "Grayson, go do as I asked, please."

Grayson Cortez glanced at them both and then went out to the driveway.

Karen Bolt looked at him. Her mouth trembled. "It would have broken a lesser person," she said. "Having your husband betray your marriage, your children, your country. Then losing a child to suicide. I said it would not break me. I made that a promise to myself."

"You're clearly a strong woman."

"Don't patronize me."

"I don't intend to," Sam said. He cleared his throat. "The Russians don't know we know he's running. Section K wants to question him and keep him detained, so the Russians don't know if he's alive or dead. But not running free. Not hurting you or Amanda. Or turning either of you into a target for the Russians."

"What is Section K?"

"We clean up messes like Markus. We don't exist in any official report. I'm trusting you by even saying its name." He thought, perhaps, she had not been trusted in the past.

"Do you have permission to kill him?" She'd seemed fatigued but now her eyes were bright.

"Yes. If he's a threat to Amanda, or you, or anyone. But my bosses want him alive."

"I'm the wrong lure. Markus won't come near me." She gave him a sad little smile. "What a small, exclusive club it is that you and I belong to. I heard Grayson talking about your son. And your wife."

Sam said nothing to this.

"I wonder if they knew each other," she said. Her voice was like a knife. She might look worn down, but she wasn't. She had tried to kill a traitor. Paint-spackled sweatshirt and uncertain smile be damned, she was dangerous.

"They did not," Sam said quickly.

"Hmmm. I mean, they could have worked together. Been aware of each other."

"There would be no point."

"Because according to Cortez, she worked for criminals, and he worked for Russia. Like that couldn't intersect."

"Why did you try to kill him? It's not in the news accounts. They covered for you."

"If I had, maybe our lives would have been different. His treason would have come out; I don't think any American jury would have convicted me. It would have been justifiable homicide."

"So he got away from you, and you didn't call the police."

"I thought he was just leaving me. I didn't know he was betraying the country. I should have tried harder." She leaned forward on the couch. "It was stupid. He was packing his bag. A work trip to London, he said. We had argued...I knew he had a secret, I thought it was an affair. He said he'd made some deals to pay off my gambling." She stopped for a moment. "But that was bull. He did it for his own gratification, to show he was smarter. Blaming me, or my debts, was just a way to justify it to himself. We argued about him leaving. He said something about he'd move to Europe and take the kids with him, because my gambling meant I was unfit. It was something in how he said it. I got a knife from the kitchen and told him he'd never separate me from my children. He laughed. I tried to stab him and he took the knife from me."

"Why did you think he was leaving you?" He thought this was so critical, to know this. Before Grayson Cortez returned. It was a weird, sudden vibe between them. The unexpected surge of connection. He realized Woodruff had been wrong to put surveillance on the family. He should have just been honest with them.

"I thought he was having an affair. I was certain of it."

"With who?" Sam asked.

"I didn't know. I knew he was being secretive. That he'd lied to me about a couple of trips, and he tried to make me think it was work, but I felt certain it wasn't. It should be so easy for a spy to cheat on a spouse. He had a whole infrastructure behind him to help deceive me."

"What made you think it was an affair?"

"I followed him one night. He had a meeting with one of his Ivans, as he called them. He had informants here and overseas. His Russian informants—usually I suspected they were a bureaucrat based in DC or New York, or perhaps one of the Russian elite who was out of favor with the rest or needed a chance to do business in the West and not be monitored so closely. Often they want something for their children, admission to a Western university or unfrozen bank accounts or some such."

"And he could arrange that?"

"He could help. You know, that's why he left. He was taking bribes from them, on what intel he didn't share with the Agency. He knew a lot of their secrets and he'd taken money to keep it quiet. His reports kept getting vaguer and less interesting because he was stripping all the good stuff out and parking money in overseas accounts."

"So you followed him."

"I thought…some of his informants were women. Wives or girlfriends of the Russian elite. And maybe he'd gotten too close to one. I just wanted to know. If I was going to leave him, I could hardly argue in a divorce court about his activities. Everything would have been classified. My gambling would have been his winning card. I needed something to counter it."

"So you followed him," Sam said again.

"Yes. He went to a hotel in Alexandria. I had to be careful following him. He sat alone, at a table. I stood back, at the edge of the lobby, behind a column, with his back to me. Another man joined him, an older man, short, a bit heavy. I thought, okay, Markus is just chatting with one of his Ivans, but it's right here in public so this can't be an actual informant. This is someone he can meet with in public. They talked for ten minutes and then the man left. But then I saw, on the opposite side of the bar, this young woman. Early twenties, pretty. Hair pulled back, an Arizona Cardinals cap on, in a coat. She got up and left and went to the elevator. She took the elevator to the tenth floor. Markus stayed put."

Arizona, Sam thought. Lucy was from Arizona. She had a couple of Cardinals caps. Just coincidence. Lots of women from Arizona. "What date was this?"

She told him. It was during the time he and Lucy were still here in Virginia, soon to depart for London.

Would two people who turned traitor be working together? It had never been suggested to him that Bolt and Lucy were connected.

"Then he got up, about ten minutes later. He also went to the elevator. Up to the tenth floor. The elevator came back down. I took it up." Her voice trembled slightly. Then she stopped. And she stared at him, her eyes lit in a weird kind of triumph.

"And?"

"And I'll tell you the rest when you have me and my daughter somewhere safe. When you've found Markus. When you've captured him or...ended him."

"Forget playing waiting games. Just answer me. Was it my wife there with your husband?"

She nodded and then Cortez reentered. He was holding a small tracking device. "Under your car, near the left rear bumper."

The silence between Sam and Karen stretched out. "You know my request," she said.

Sam slid out his phone. He called Woodruff. Without preamble he said: "I'm with Karen Bolt. She's asked me to protect her and her daughter."

"You idiot. You weren't supposed to chat with them."

"The situation changed," Sam said. "Talking with the family is the only viable option."

"Where are you?"

"At Grayson Cortez's house. Do you know who he is?"

"Yes. You were going to sit quietly and watch Amanda."

"Field work is fluid," Sam said. "I built a bond with Mrs. Bolt."

"I bet you did."

Karen leaned toward Sam's phone. "We're under your protection now, Section K boss guy, and Sam and I are going to go get my daughter. Right. Now."

38

VAL PARKED IN THE LOT, luckily finding a spot close to the front door. Kirill said, "I want you to leave your phone on in your purse, so I can hear. I'll mute my side."

"That doesn't make me comfortable. Amanda could notice. I'd have to leave the purse open."

Kirill took a deep breath. "I just don't like the idea of sending you into trouble."

"Why do you think Amanda and her boyfriend are dangerous?"

"Not dangerous, but she could get violent if you mention her dad."

"Why do you think that?"

"We've kept a distant eye on Amanda and Allan. Just to be able to tell Markus how they were doing. People used to approach her about her dad and she would get very upset."

"That's sad," Val said.

"Yes, it is." Kirill nodded. "It would be ideal if we could get her into the car."

"She's not going to get into a car with you," Val said. "Ideally she'll follow us in her car. I could maybe ride with her."

"This seems like something she won't fall for," Kirill said. "She's probably smarter than that real estate agent."

"We could tell her that her stepbrother is waiting outside to meet her."

"I doubt that would interest her," Kirill said. He hadn't really thought of Amanda being his stepsister. She had just been a name that Markus rarely mentioned.

"I'll figure out something." Val got out of the car and walked, without looking, back toward the delivery service's office.

There was a young woman sitting at a front counter. Her name tag said Tara. She glanced up with a bright smile. "Hi, may I help you?"

"Why, yes," Val said, in her poshest British accent, the one she used to use to make her husband laugh. "I'd like to see Amanda Bolt, please. It's about a business offer."

"You want... to buy our business?" Amanda repeated. She stared at the woman standing at the front desk, next to a confused-looking Tara.

The Englishwoman nodded. "Well, I represent a potential buyer. A holding company that owns several businesses locally. My name is Valeria Garrison." She offered her hand to shake, and Amanda shook it. Tara stared, and then took a step back.

"Um, I'm not sure we're for sale."

"And I apologize, I know this must seem odd, but my client didn't give me much advance warning of their interest in your firm. Normally I'd call for an appointment."

"And who's your client?"

"Could we discuss this somewhere more privately?" Val smiled brightly. "With you and Roberto?"

"Roberto's in a call with our biggest client right now," Amanda said. "Let's you and I talk. Tara, when Roberto comes out of his call, will you ask him to join us?" Tara nodded and hurried off. Amanda thought that she could quickly assess whether this woman was some kind of crackpot and get her out or if the offer was legitimate. She felt a surge of excitement course through her. Maybe this could be serious money. Roberto was so worried and anxious all the time...which she didn't understand, as the business was doing well. This could be the answer.

She walked Valeria Garrison to an empty conference room, asked her if she wanted anything to drink, which Valeria declined. Valeria sat at the table and Amanda shut the door. Val glanced at the projections and notes written on a whiteboard in colored markers. She kept her hands under the table, her purse close to her chair. She'd unzipped it so she could access what she needed, but the phone was turned off. She didn't want Kirill to hear what she was going to say to Amanda Bolt.

Amanda sat and said, "I'm curious as to why our company."

"Please, call me Val. You've had strong growth. Of the regional delivery companies, our client feels you have a most promising future."

"We're private. How would your client know about our growth?"

"There are indicators. The increase in your delivery vans, that you've been regularly hiring and posting job notices. Of course, we'd want to know more details about revenue, sales, expenses, and so forth."

"You'd have to talk to Roberto about that. He handles the big picture stuff, I'm more the firefighter on day-to-day concerns."

Val broadened her smile. "You keep the ship running."

Amanda nodded slightly. "Sort of. How much were you thinking of offering for the company?"

"We'd have to do an assessment, obviously, and would

want to review your assets and cash flow. But a firm like this, usually we'd start with an offer of a few million."

Million. Amanda's breath caught in her throat. Was this for real? She should know how much the business was worth, but Roberto liked to keep the figures close to his chest. "Okay, well, I'd have to talk with Roberto."

Val took a deep breath and kept her smile in place. "Amanda. I want you to understand something before we proceed. I represent a Russian buyer. I need to know that you'll be okay with that."

Ten seconds of silence. "Why wouldn't I be?"

"I know your...history," Val said. "You might have certain negative feelings toward Russians. Entirely understandable."

"My history, as you put it, does not affect my business decisions."

"The client has a personal connection to your father."

Seconds ticked by. Amanda said, "What do you mean?"

"He knows him. Your father has no interest in the transaction. But I'm just being up front with you. I thought you would respect that."

"Who is this Russian?"

"His name is Illya Markarkin."

"And does he want to buy the business because I own it? Like a favor to my father somehow? I don't need money that badly."

"No, I think it's actually to make your father suffer."

"Suffer?" Now Amanda's voice rose slightly.

"You'll never willingly speak to your father again, I assume."

Her face had colored. "You assume correctly."

"But my client will speak to you. Regularly. And he'll rub that in the face of your father. That he speaks to you and your father cannot."

"You want me to sell this company," she said, "to irritate my father."

"No, I want you to sell it because it makes business sense. Irritating your father is just a side benefit to my client."

Amanda laughed. "This is all quite bizarre."

"I won't waste your time further if you're not interested in the actual deal. But as soon as you dig into my history, you're going to find Illya Markarkin and it's not hard to figure out that he knows your father. All the Russian elite do."

"Do you know my father?"

"I've met him a couple of times."

"What did you think of him?"

"Why would my opinion matter?"

"I haven't seen or contacted him since I was a kid. What is he like now?" She paused. "I cannot imagine he is happy."

Val took a deep breath, as if organizing her thoughts. "He's very quiet and polite. He enjoys the attention the Russians give him. He's a narcissist of the first order. There is nothing he would not do to advance his own interests."

"He married again. Have you met his wife?"

"I have not." *His stepson is just outside*, Val thought. *But you won't see him, either.*

"I saw a picture of her. She's gorgeous. A former Miss Russia."

"Yes. That's true."

"So this Markarkin buys the company. Does he want us to still work here?"

Val took a deep breath. "Well, Mr. Markarkin won't want to run it himself. I'm sure he'd consider keeping you and Roberto on."

"Or just me," she said.

Interesting, Val thought. "No room for the boyfriend."

"He won't want to work for someone else. It's just his style."

"But you would work for your father's enemy?"

"For a few million? Sure."

She could be leveraged, Val thought. "Would you like to speak to Mr. Markarkin? Perhaps alone? Without Roberto?"

She would always think that Amanda was starting to nod her head and then the door opened. Roberto came in. "Who the hell are you?" he demanded.

"My name is Valeria Garrison. I represent a potential—"

"Yeah, Tara told me. We're not for sale. Good-bye."

"Roberto—" Amanda started.

"We are not for sale. Leave, please."

"Is this not an equal partnership?" Val asked politely.

"No, it's not," Roberto said. "I own sixty percent, she owns forty."

"You could sell your share then," Val said to Amanda, unruffled. "Our offer to you still stands. My client would be an excellent partner to you."

"She can't sell without my approval," Roberto said. His voice rose, grew ragged.

"Amanda," Val said calmly, staring back at Roberto, unblinking, "do you want to sell? Do you want out?"

Amanda made a noise in her throat. Roberto looked ill. Pale, and sweating. "You can sell, too, Roberto," she said. "Surely a generous offer should be considered fully, by both parties."

"I want you to leave right now," he said, his voice soft and broken.

"Or what? Will you call the police?"

Roberto stared at her. He took a step back.

"I thought not." Val put her gaze back to Amanda's shocked face; Amanda kept glancing between her and Roberto. "I'm offering you an escape route," Val said.

Amanda stared at her. "What . . . what do you mean?"

"Get out, get out right now," Roberto said. He stood over Val, as if ready to yank her out of her seat.

"You're in danger," Val said to Amanda.

"Shut up and get out," Roberto said, grabbing at her arm.

It happened very quickly. Val spun out of his grasp, throwing him off balance. She pulled something from her jacket's sleeve. A syringe. The needle was in Roberto's neck before he regained his footing. He tried to slap at it but she'd thumbed down the plunger. Roberto dropped like a sack.

"Roberto!" Amanda cried out and then she saw the gun Val had drawn from her purse. "What have you done . . . what is this?" She sounded horrified. But she didn't run. She knelt next to Roberto, which fit the psychological profile Val had of her.

"Amanda. Look at me."

Amanda looked at her. Val said, "I am not a danger to you. I am here to help you. This is me getting you to safety."

"Safety? You hurt Roberto . . ."

"He won't sell to anyone because he's cleaning a load of dirty money through here," Val said. "I'm going to give you the benefit of the doubt that you didn't know this. He's put you in great danger. And criminal liability."

"You're lying, he didn't, he wouldn't . . ."

"Is he scared all the time and you don't know why?"

Amanda didn't answer, which was an answer in itself.

"I've been investigating a longtime network of financial laundering operations. The courier service is one of them. I'm going to show you some interesting financial documents. Once you see them, I feel you'll be much more inclined to be free of your boyfriend."

Amanda touched Roberto. He was out, moaning softly.

"I didn't give him much," Val said. "He'll only be out for a few. The problem is, you and I have to get out of here without being seen, because there are Russians watching your front door. And I don't want them to see us leaving."

39

⸙

Kirill waited. He didn't like this. Of course it was a heavy lie to tell, to offer money for a business and be believed, and perhaps the negotiations had taken a serious turn. He glanced at his phone. He'd give her a few more minutes before presenting himself as Val's partner in business, and getting a chance to read the room.

Amanda appeared again in the doorway. A laptop in her hands.

"Follow me," Amanda said.

Val stepped out into the hallway and Amanda closed the door behind her. "He'll be okay?"

"Yes. He'll be awake within ten minutes."

Amanda hurried toward the rear area of the building. Packages were being routed, scanned, and gathered for loading. Val followed her. Amanda stopped where a few keys hung and grabbed one. "We have a driver out sick today. Roberto covered for him this morning."

They went out the back, Val tensing in case Kirill had decided to monitor this side of the building or if he had help he hadn't told her about. Her hand went into her purse and closed around the loaded Glock at the bottom.

Amanda went to a van, opened it, and Val got in on the other side.

"I cannot believe I am doing this," Amanda said. "This ends everything, doesn't it? My relationship. My work."

"The Russian watching us is in a gray sedan, parked up near the front. So let's exit on the far side; he won't see us."

"Where am I going to?" Amanda said.

Val opened her phone, pressed an app that was labeled for horoscopes. It instead asked for her fingerprint and then opened into a hidden phone app. She dialed a number. "Terrell? Valeria. As one of your very best customers, I need your help. It's an emergency."

Kirill finally got out of the car. Something had gone wrong. Or Val was being stonewalled, and they needed to consider a different approach. He texted Val, in English: I'm coming in.

No answer.

He went to the front door, stepped inside. No sign of Val waiting in the reception area. A young woman at the counter, in a shirt with the courier company's logo, glanced up at him. She had on a name tag: Tara.

"Hello, Tara," Kirill said, trying to minimize his accent. "My colleague is here to meet with the owners."

"Oh, yeah. Um, okay. If you'll follow me?" He followed her along a twist of hallways and she knocked on a conference door. No answer. She opened up the door. No one was sitting at the table. Kirill looked over her head.

"Oh. They were in here," she said.

Kirill pushed past her. He could see a man sitting against the wall, blinking, on the other side of the table. He slowly got to his feet.

No, Kirill thought. No. She couldn't.

"Roberto, are you okay?" Tara asked.

"Fine," he said hoarsely.

"Where is Amanda and that English lady? This is her business partner."

Roberto stared at him. "Who the hell are you? Tara, get out. Go!"

Tara scrambled out and shut the door behind her.

"Who are you?" Roberto repeated. "Are you with Dennis?"

"What happened here? Where is Val?"

"That bitch of yours jabbed me with a needle and knocked me out. Is Dennis behind this?"

Kirill felt ice creep into his chest. "She did what?"

"Oh, don't act all innocent. You listen to me. You have messed with the wrong courier company. We are going to destroy you. Tell Dennis…"

Kirill's hand lashed out, caught Roberto by the throat. "I don't know this Dennis and I don't care. Where are they?"

"I don't…"

"They didn't come out the front." He squeezed. Hard.

Roberto's eyes widened. "Then…the back…the delivery vehicles…"

Kirill shoved him away and headed for the back of the building. He scanned the package sorting area, the open bay door, the vans and trucks parked behind. He went out the back.

No sign of Val or Amanda Bolt.

He went back to the conference room. Roberto was on a phone, speaking rapid Spanish into it. Kirill picked up enough to say, "Someone making an offer on the business…I think they know…I need you to send someone…" He stopped when he saw Kirill.

"I want to make something very clear to you," Kirill said. "I want to know where Amanda and the English-woman are." He didn't know what name Val had given them, and now he realized why she hadn't wanted her phone on for him to listen. Who was she? What was her agenda? She had gotten to Amanda Bolt neatly and quickly and spirited her away, and now she held all the cards if Amanda was why Markus had come home.

She had played him. He had to stay calm to undo the damage.

Before anyone knew.

"I don't know, you say this English bitch is with you, she took Amanda." This man was in a panic about the offer on his business and why he wouldn't take it. There must be something rotten about the business that Amanda didn't know, Kirill surmised. Kirill knew the Russian elite, and money laundering was a way of life. So it was his first guess. "How much are you cleaning each month? This is a small operation but you could lie about volume. It's not like it's inventory that stays here."

Roberto didn't answer but his mouth twitched. Kirill thought he'd nailed the problem.

"Do you have a way to track the vans?"

"We just use the driver's phones." He pushed past Kirill and ran to his office. He stared at the desk. "My laptop is gone." A rising panic crept into his voice. "No, no, no..."

"If you hear from Amanda or...the Englishwoman, you call this number." He wrote it down on a sticky note from a pad resting at the center of the table, next to some pens. It was a Miami number, owned by Bobo, and the calls could be routed to him.

"Please, just give Amanda back to me. What do you want?"

"The Englishwoman will not harm Amanda. She's in no danger." He hoped that was true. "Call me when you hear from them, and I can help you." He turned and left. Illya. She must be doing this for Illya. He had told her to bring Amanda to him, perhaps with the idea that if he had Amanda, he could get Bolt to come talk to him. Please let it be that simple.

Which meant Illya had a way to get in touch with Bolt.

He got out to his car and tried Val's number again. Nothing.

He tried Illya's number. A young woman answered in Russian.

"I need to speak to Illya."

"He's asleep right now," she said. He guessed this was the long-suffering Maria.

"Wake him up. This is . . . his cousin, Kirill."

"I won't wake him up and he doesn't have a cousin Kirill that I know."

"Put him on the phone right now."

"I don't know you," she said again, and hung up.

Where would she go? he wondered. Would she take Amanda to Illya's building? Possibly. Maybe this was all okay, and she would call or text him in a minute to say, *I have Amanda, all is well.*

Or maybe she had fooled him. She could be pursuing her own payday, her own agenda.

In which case she had played him and played Illya. Who was she?

She wants what Bolt has, he thought, *the financial network map.* She could sell that to the highest bidder. She could give it to any government she worked for.

His heart turned in his chest. He got in the car. This was his greatest failure and he had only himself to blame. He'd wanted a helper, he'd wanted to feel like someone was on his side, and he'd chosen badly. He hadn't thought with his brain. He'd given in to the pressure of trying to bring Bolt back for his mother and his masters while knowing he would likely have to kill his own stepfather.

He took a deep breath. He could deal. He just had to find Val before she reached out to Bolt.

He headed back to Illya's condo building.

No. Wait.

That house she bought from Terrell Carrier. Would they go there? No one else around, no one to see.

He turned the car around and headed toward the house.

He didn't notice the SUV turning into the office lot behind him.

40

---⁜⁜⁜---

Austin

As soon as he was back at Matt and Leonie's after school, Daniel took the disc and ran to his house. James didn't want to see what was on the video, and they'd decided the less he knew the better.

Daniel let himself into his house. He walked through the empty rooms, expecting the woman from the car to lurch out of the shadows and grab him. But nothing like that happened. He went to the back door. Through the glass he could see the woman from the car—from the cemetery—on the deck, sitting quietly, as promised. A small briefcase sat by her.

He had to decide. He couldn't keep her waiting. He put the disc on the table and stepped out onto the deck. He shut the door behind him. She was in her sixties, graying hair cut short, wearing jeans and a blue sweater. She looked like an unthreatening grandmother.

She smiled, but it was measured, not warm, as if she knew false enthusiasm would send him running. "Hello, Daniel. I'm glad you came."

He said nothing. He thought he should offer her a

glass of water or something to drink, like Dad did when they had a visitor, but this was too weird.

"Do you know who I am, Daniel?" the woman said. "Have you ever seen a picture of me?"

Daniel stared at her. "No."

"I've had to wait to approach you until your father left. Because he doesn't quite approve of me."

"I could just text my dad that a strange woman is trying to get me alone at my house."

"You could. I won't stop you. It's your choice. I'm here to help you, not hurt you."

"Help me how?" He sat down on a chair across from her.

She stared at him for a moment, then blinked. "I'm sorry. I just...of course I've *seen* you. But to be this close—there's so much of your mother's face in yours." Her voice caught. "More than I thought when I saw you last night."

He pushed down the emotional surge he felt. "Help me how?" he repeated.

"By giving you answers. Ones I think you've never been given because you didn't know the questions to ask."

He blinked; he wasn't sure what that was supposed to mean. "You followed me and Leonie to the cemetery."

"Well, I'd been to your mother's grave before. I didn't leave flowers because I didn't want to raise your father's suspicions."

"What's your name?"

"Clarice. Does that name mean anything to you?"

"No."

For a moment the smile wavered, as if touched by pain, but then she blinked twice and the smile was back, reset. "I don't suppose that it would. That he would tell you."

"Tell me?" Daniel echoed.

"You never knew your mother. I knew her well. Better than anyone else did, including your father."

"How did you know her?"

"I'm her aunt. That makes me your great-aunt."

"She was an orphan," he said slowly.

"Orphans still have aunts. Lucky ones, that is. Her parents—your grandparents—died when she was twelve. Do you even know their names?"

"Robert and Barbara Collins." Dad had told him that, once, when he'd asked. *Did she have brothers or sisters?* Daniel asked. *No. Other family? No,* Dad said. *No.*

But here was an aunt. Dad had lied to him.

"But he didn't tell you I existed," Clarice said.

"No."

"You only think of the Capras as your family. You have another."

"Are you the one sending me the text messages? Putting the note in my folder?"

"We just wanted to get your attention."

"Well, you did, it freaked me out."

"I'm sorry. But please understand. I couldn't just walk up to you and tell you all this and have you believe it." She steadied her gaze. "And I wanted to see what you would do. If you immediately told your father about the text or the note, you wouldn't be very open to what we had to say. That you kept it quiet...made me feel I could try and reach out to you."

"How do you know I didn't tell him?"

"Because he wouldn't have left you. Or he would have taken you with him. Or he would have called me and told me to stay away."

"What's this message my mom left for me?"

"We'll get to that. I just...let's just talk first."

"I think you should leave. I don't know you and I

don't...I don't believe you. My dad wouldn't lie. My dad—"

"Your dad loves you. I'm not here to tell you your daddy doesn't love you; of course he does. But shutting us out..."

"Who is *us*?"

"Me. And you have an uncle, too. He's kept you from us."

"Why didn't you write or call me before?"

"Because he told me I couldn't. He's your father, so we respected that."

Daniel frowned. "Why would he not want you in my life?" *Well, she's the type of person who spied on us, so she's kind of creepy, that might be answer number one.*

"I wish I knew. He just wanted to be sure I wasn't."

"I don't believe that."

"I brought you something." She patted the briefcase. It was old and worn, like something from a movie back before people had backpacks or cell phones. "It was her father's, but you could tell your dad you found it at Goodwill and thought it was 'retro cool.' That way you would have something she treasured and he wouldn't know. It would be our secret."

A secret. From Dad. He had not had one of those before, at least nothing important. Dad pretty much knew everything. But it appeared Dad had several secrets. He glanced at the briefcase. "What's in it? Or do you think I'm going to carry that around at school?"

"Pictures. Of her. One of you together that she sent to me. I want you to have them."

"Is this the message she left for me?"

"No. Just photos you should have. You deserve to have. Do you have a lot of pictures of her?"

"One. Just one. I'm a baby and she's holding me."

A stricken look crossed her face. "Is your father in the picture?"

How did she know? "No. Just us."

"Are there any pictures of the three of you together?"

"No," he said after a moment.

"I thought so," she said, and there was a strange triumph in her voice.

"Why are you doing this?"

"Because you're worth it. Because you're old enough to know more." She took a deep breath. "Look at the pictures. You may have questions for me, and I'll be happy to answer them. On the back of the first stack of pictures, the ones with the blue rubber band, the first ten have a number on the back. In order that's my real phone number. You can reach me there." Clarice stood up. "I would give you a hug, but I don't think you're a big hugger, from what I understand. I think it must go back to the unfortunate start you had in life. Losing your mother. And just never getting to learn about her."

"If you're trying to make me think that my dad is bad, you're not going to be able to do that. I know him, you don't."

"Have you ever felt he was holding back, talking about your mom?"

Daniel kept his mouth shut. But he thought, *Yes. Always.*

"I thought as much. There's a lot you don't know. A lot that happened around the time you were born. But I'm not going to tell it to you until you ask to know. I don't want to rush you or pressure you. Look at the pictures. Your uncle and I would be happy to talk to you again. Answer your questions."

"Why do this now? Just because you're too scared to come talk to me when my dad's here?"

"No. Because I'm dying, sweet boy," Clarice said. "And this is my last chance to talk to you. Your mom never got the chance."

"Dying?" he whispered.

Clarice got up without answering him, and she walked out the backyard gate. He was frozen, watching her as she shut the heavy gate behind her.

There hadn't been a car parked in front of the house, he suddenly realized. He ran to the gate. She walked down the street and turned right onto another street.

She was staying somewhere here in the neighborhood. So she could watch him and Dad.

He didn't chase her. He wanted to think. He took the briefcase inside the house. He set it down next to the disc.

That first. He put the disc in the player. It started up with a time stamp of 12:00 a.m. that morning he'd gotten the note. He found the footage for the choir hallway. Empty, with just a single light on. He fast-forwarded through the night hours. Nothing. He cranked it up to speed. At 6:21, the video went to static. Like it was damaged. It was like that for three long minutes. Then back into focus.

A blip.

Or someone knew there was a camera there and took some kind of precaution. Did that seem like Clarice? Someone who could plant a note and also wipe out camera feeds? Maybe she was some kind of computer techie person; he didn't ask her what she did for a job. Maybe it was just a glitch. He checked the feeds from around the school. It happened on all of them. A system-wide problem.

He forwarded on as the picture came back into normal focus.

The video just showed the choir director walking toward the choir hall, then students as first period started. He watched it, at high speed, as the first two periods went and came and then finally Daniel saw himself, walking along the hallway, toward the unexpected.

Daniel ejected the disc and put it back in its case. Someone had taken precautions not to be caught. Not to leave evidence.

He opened Clarice's briefcase. He suddenly remembered last year, reading mythology in English, and the story of Pandora's box. He wondered what he would find, what trouble it could bring.

The photos were loosely organized by time. The ones on top were a pinched-face couple, holding a baby. He looked at the back: Bob and Barb, with baby Lucy.

His mother, as a baby.

More photos of Lucy Collins, as a child, as a preteen, as a teenager. He carefully studied each one. Lucy at the piano, looking resentful about practicing. Lucy with her parents. Lucy without her parents, the smile gone from her face in most of the photos, or very faint. A girl who had lost everything. She was pretty. She didn't look happy. Daniel had lost her but he still had his dad. A world without Dad was beyond comprehension. What had his mother gone through, losing both her parents?

There were some photos of her with friends, and she stood slightly away, slightly off, as if not wanting human contact. A few pictures with her and a younger Clarice. She was pale in those photos, the weight of losing her parents clear. He found it hard to breathe. His mother had always been dead to him, and here was proof she'd had a whole life before him, before Dad, her own dreams and hopes and fears.

Clarice was his aunt. What would be the motivation of faking or altering these old pictures?

He suddenly needed Dad. He started to call him, then stopped. What would he say? *My aunt you didn't want me to know about visited me. I'm looking at a bunch of photos of my mom. It's like I'm learning about her without you to guide me and that can't be right, Dad. It shouldn't be this way.*

Dad would yell at him for meeting Clarice. He would freak out. He would fly home and ground Daniel for the rest of his natural life.

She left a message for you. What did that even mean? Would Dad even let him see such a message? Did Dad know about this?

Daniel put his phone back in his pocket. Less temptation.

There was a last stack of photos, bound with a blue rubber band. These, all of Mom with Dad. It was only thirteen years ago but Dad looked so much younger, more like a kid than like Dad. This was a smaller grouping of photos. Pictures of the two of them, Dad's arm around Mom—Daniel had never got to call her Mom but it seemed wrong to think of her as Lucy or the more formal "Mother" or the more distant "my mother"—and she was smiling, just a bit more. A picture of them at a pub, with beers in front of them; a picture of them in front of the US Capitol; a picture of them on what looked like a hike in the woods; a picture of them obviously in London, with Big Ben behind them—the same photo that had been texted to him; a picture of them walking in a park; a few of his mother, alone, and in the last one, she had her hand on her stomach, the heavy swell of pregnancy, a sad, gentle smile on her face.

Me, Daniel thought. *When she was expecting me.*

One more picture: Mom, again noticeably pregnant. On the back was written, "Don't worry Aunt C if you don't hear from me for a while. A lot going on but all is well. Look how far along I am." His mother's handwriting. This photo must have been treasured by Clarice, but she was giving it to him. He stared at the picture.

Daniel was not a kid who cried easily. He tended to hold in his anger and his grief but this, moment after moment after moment of seeing his mom vibrant and alive, cut him open and the tears welled up and burst past his defenses. He pushed the photo away, doubled over, sobbing, fighting for control. He cried hard for five minutes and then got ahold of his emotions. He went to the entry hall half-bath and splashed cold water on his face.

He heard someone try the front door. Then the doorbell rang. He dried off his face and ran back to the kitchen table. He shoved the photos and the security disc back in the briefcase. He went to the door and opened it.

Leonie. "Hey," she said. "You all right?"

"Yes. I just came over to get a book." He was careful to keep his voice from shaking.

"And to have a little space?"

He nodded after a moment. She glanced around, as though looking for a lit cigarette or opened beer can.

"Are you okay?" he asked. She was about as pregnant now as Mom in the picture. He realized he was staring at her.

"Sure. I'm more worried about you."

"I'm fine."

"I think you're upset."

He shrugged. "I'm honestly fine."

"Everything okay with you and James?"

"We're fine."

"Because I'm detecting some tension." Now Leonie sounded like a mom.

"Not from me. But if there was some, he's your stepson. You should take his side. It will matter more to him. Dad and I could move away next month and maybe you'd never see me again." The words fell out in a rush.

Her eyes widened. "Daniel. I will always be a part of your life. Always. I mean—as long as you want me in it. You know I love you."

He wanted to say it back and he couldn't. Not right now. "Okay," he said, knowing it sounded weak.

The house was silent, her watching him.

"Why don't you find your book and come back with me?" She was wary now, suspicious of his being here alone. She glanced at the briefcase. "What's that?"

He grabbed it. "My retro-cool book bag." He wouldn't be able to look at the pictures at Matt and Leonie's house. But he didn't want to leave the pictures behind.

He walked with her back to her house. He glanced down the street where Clarice had walked and turned. "Do people ever rent out houses here? Like, you know, for short times? Like vacations?"

"Yeah, but it's frowned upon. Why?"

He tried to remember what kind of car Clarice had spoken to him from in the darkness. He had been so surprised by her words that it hadn't registered with him. "I just wondered."

Leonie stopped him. "What's going on with you?"

They were standing on the street, him holding an old weird briefcase his unknown aunt had just given him, his father not telling him the truth about his mother's family, the proof of it in his hands.

"Nothing," he said. He looked into the face of the woman who had raised him, and he smiled, like nothing was wrong. "Really, I'm fine, don't worry about me. I just have a lot of homework."

41

<hr />

Miami

SHE KNOWS ME AS HER new neighbor," Sam said as he parked in front of the courier service. "So she may react to seeing us together."

"If her father showed up, what were you gonna do? Kill him in front of her?"

"No."

"Fixer," Karen said. "I know what that can mean." She sounded nervous; Amanda had not been answering her cell phone. But that could mean she was in a meeting or on a delivery run if a driver was out sick.

"I could wait in the car," he said. "You could just go in and get her."

"Maybe we should preserve your cover. Would you be home during the day?"

"Maybe. She believes I own a bar here."

"So I arrived at her apartment, distraught, knocked on your door to see if you knew where she was, and you offered to drive me to her office," Karen said. "There. That way you can still keep an eye on her.

"Sam," she said.

"Yes?"

"My girl is all I have." Karen Bolt stared ahead, through the windshield, not at him. "Since I lost my boy. I cannot lose her. I need you to understand that."

"I understand." He understood all too well.

"So I need you to protect my girl. I know you must be good. They wouldn't have sent you otherwise. I need to know she'll be okay."

"I will protect her," he said quietly.

"Markus took everything from me. *Everything.* My sense of who I was, who he was. My marriage. My children's sense of who they were and what their world was. The lives we had in McLean." Her voice grew unsteady. "The way the world looked at me. What people thought of me." Now he could hear the suppressed sob in her tone. "You get that. You get that in a way most people don't. They say they understand. They do not."

He didn't say anything; he just stared at her.

"She'll want to go home. We need to take her to Grayson's."

"How close are y'all? Can Cortez be trusted?"

"I know you have good reason to not like him, but I trust him completely."

They got out of the SUV. They walked to the front door. Sam held it for Karen and she ducked in and Sam followed. He saw Tara sitting at the front desk, looking worried. Her gaze widened when she saw him.

"Sam. Hey. How can I help you?" but she didn't seem that interested in helping. She seemed exhausted.

"Tara, hi. This is Amanda's mom. She wanted to see Amanda if she's available."

"Um. She is not. She left with a woman who was trying to make an offer to buy the company and all hell broke loose. Amanda left, and then a Russian guy came..."

"Russian guy?" Sam said. "Describe him."

"Uh, mid-twenties. Dark hair, dark eyes, athletic looking, cute. He said he was the woman's business partner. I didn't get their names. He and Roberto argued and I think it was a surprise to both of them that English lady and Amanda took off. I don't think she was actually English, though. I think her accent was fake." She spat out the last word.

"Describe her."

"Um, late thirties. Blond hair. She moved with confidence. Like a dancer."

"But you don't think she was English."

"Just a feeling."

"I don't understand," Karen said. "You're saying my daughter left with this fake Englishwoman without telling anyone she was leaving?" Panic dawned in her eyes.

"That would be it," Tara said. "Hi, I'm Tara. I also am a neighbor of Amanda's and Sam's."

Karen didn't say hi back. "And the Russian and Roberto?"

"They both left. Separately. I think I'm supposed to close up. It's like totally dramatic and everyone's freaked out."

"Can you show us Amanda's desk?" Sam couldn't let on that he already knew where it was.

Tara nodded and led them back into the hallways, to Amanda's cubicle. Her work laptop was still there, connected to the monitor. Sam disconnected it.

"You can't take that——" Tara started and Sam handed it to Karen.

"I'm not, her mother is."

He crossed from the cubicle to Roberto's office. That laptop was gone.

"Sam, what is happening? Do you know?" Karen asked.

"No," he said. "Tara, if you hear from either of them, please have them call me. Tell them Karen's with me."

"Um, all right. Are you going to be at your bar later tonight? I could use a drink after today."

"Not sure." He put on his host smile. "But we'll talk later. Thanks."

"It was nice to meet you..." Tara started to say to Karen, but the older woman was already heading down the hallway. Sam followed her, with a shrug of apology to Tara.

Karen waited until they were back in the car. "Has my daughter been kidnapped? The Russians have her, don't they? Are they trying to use her to get Markus to surrender to them?"

"Possibly." He hoped not. He had failed in his job if they had Amanda. Woodruff would explode.

Sam pulled a laptop from his bag. He fired up the camera feed from the hidden cameras he'd put in Roberto's office and on Amanda's computer.

"What are you doing?"

"I had them under surveillance. Don't yell at me."

She didn't.

He rewound the recording from the current time stamp. He saw, from the angle of her monitor, Amanda walking past the cubicle with a woman. But he could only see the backs of their heads.

He paused, reran it. No more detail.

He checked the audio download of Amanda's computer's microphone to see if he could hear their voices or what they were saying. It was indistinct, but he heard a British accent saying, "And how long have you had the business?"

But the voice, the lowness of it, was oddly familiar.

He accelerated the video feed, Karen watching over his shoulder.

He stopped when he saw Tara—well, guessing it was her—walking with a tall man who met the description of the Russian. Again, the back of the head. He forwarded it. The Russian, heading out. Now he saw his face, captured in a freeze of the cubicle's entrance.

He didn't know him. He knew the faces of a number of Russian operatives, but he'd worried it might be Marianne's male trainee he'd spotted at the airport. This wasn't that guy. He screen-captured the face and sent it to Woodruff, requesting an ID. He wasn't optimistic; he was young, and probably new.

"So one Russian took her and the other came looking for them?"

"Amanda and the woman didn't leave from the front. They must have decided to take one of the delivery vans. Which could mean Amanda went willingly. If a meeting with her father was offered, would she go?"

"No," Karen said immediately. "She blames him for Allan's suicide, for everything that's gone wrong in her life. She has always told me she loathes him."

Sam thought, *Would you talk to Lucy? If the doctors called and said, "Hey, she woke up and she's coherent, she could understand you and she has some things to say to you," would you talk to her?* He wasn't sure. He thought not. What could she possibly say?

"That girl. What's her name? Tara?" Karen said.

"Yes."

"She's leaving. I guess she's not locking up tonight." Karen pointed. Sam saw Tara hurrying to her car, roaring out of the lot.

"She's just a friend of your daughter's; she's fine."

"Right now I don't trust anyone. Maybe Amanda's gone home. We should try there."

* * *

They drove back to the apartment complex, delayed by a car accident on a main road between the office and the apartments. Sam tensed. Anyone could be watching here—Marianne and her assassins, Bolt himself. Karen could be a target. She didn't seem to care; she got out of the car. Sam followed.

"Her car's not here," Karen said.

"The delivery van's not here, either. She's not here."

"I need to know, Sam, that she's okay. And I need to know what Roberto knows." She got out of the car. "Maybe if Traitor X is watching, he'll come over to say hi."

"Traitor X."

"Short for traitorous ex-husband."

They could hear the raised voices as they approached the two apartments at the end of the hall. Roberto, screaming in anger. Karen tried the door. Locked. She pulled keys from her purse and fit one in.

"Don't tell Roberto my daughter gave me a key." She opened the door. Sam pushed past her, going in first.

"You can't tell!" Roberto was yelling. "You can't."

Tara stood in the apartment's living room, arms crossed. Roberto yelling at her, spit flicking off his lip.

"Tell what?" Karen asked.

"Get the hell out of here! She's not here!" Roberto yelled.

"She lives here, and I have a key, and I want to know why the hell these Russians are hovering around your office."

"Karen, she's not here. I don't know where she is," Roberto said.

"What are you not supposed to tell, Tara?" Sam asked easily.

Tara looked helplessly at Roberto. "This is none of my business, really, so I should go."

Sam blocked her way. "What do you know, Tara?"

"Nothing. Please let me pass." She glanced at Roberto. "Should I even show up for work tomorrow?"

He nodded. "She'll be back by then."

Tara pushed past Sam. He said, "I'll be at the bar later." She nodded and he let her go.

"Roberto," Karen said. "Sam is a friend, and you can tell him what you tell me."

"What do you mean, a friend?"

"He's helping me."

"What, keep an eye on your daughter? That's sick, Karen, even for you."

"Who are these people?"

"I never saw them before in my life. Ever."

"Why did you react violently to them offering to buy?"

"Because I don't want to sell, asshole."

"Where is my daughter, Roberto?" Karen asked gently.

"I don't know."

"But you're not calling the police, are you? I mean, you were basically told she might be kidnapped, and you haven't called the police."

The silence in the room grew thick. Roberto finally said, "I'm sure she's fine. She's mad at me; she went to cool off."

"You don't want attention at the couriers."

"Why are you here and speaking to me?" Roberto said. "I don't know you."

"I'm only asking this out of concern for Amanda and where she is and who has her. Give me your laptop."

"What? No. Get the hell out of here." Now he leveled a stare at Sam. "You're messing with the wrong guy."

"I somehow doubt that."

"You have no idea," Roberto said. "Now get the hell out."

Sam looked at him for a moment. Then he slammed his fist into Roberto's chest. Roberto wasn't braced for it and he dropped his phone and gasped and then Sam hit him hard again in the throat. Roberto went down; Karen knelt beside him.

Sam picked up the phone. Looked at recent calls. One number, multiple times. He committed it to memory and showed the phone screen to Roberto.

"Who are you calling again and again? Is that the Russian?"

Roberto, unable to speak, gasped and shook his head.

Sam thumbed the number. It dialed again.

Answered on the third ring. "I told you I don't have her."

Sam knew the voice. Dennis Gandy.

He looked at Karen.

"Hi, Dennis," Sam said.

"Who is this?" Dennis's whispery voice grew louder.

"If you have Amanda, you need to let her go right now. Otherwise I will rain down so much pain. If you're helping...someone get to her, you'll be going to prison for the rest of your life."

"It sounds like it's up to me to save Amanda," he said. Then Gandy ended the call.

Roberto looked up at him. "Please...please just leave us alone."

"Why is Dennis Gandy the guy you're calling when she goes missing?"

"I thought...he was behind it."

"Did he leave that note demanding you turn her over to him?"

Karen gave Sam a startled look.

"Yes," Roberto said. "But he says he doesn't have her. But he must have sent that woman and the Russian dude."

"What did he threaten to tell her about you? What does he have on you?"

"I don't know, I swear. No. He didn't send the woman. That's why he's upset."

"Wait, Dennis Gandy like from when the kids were young?" Karen asked.

Roberto shook his head. "Just let me handle this. Karen, if you want her back, don't call the police. I am begging you."

Karen started arguing with him and Sam steered her out of the apartment, ignoring her protests. He unlocked his apartment and went in, and she followed. He opened his laptop and activated the monitor feeds.

"We can see what he does and says when we're not there. He may reveal more."

"You weren't kidding about surveillance." Her voice was cold.

"This was all to protect your daughter."

"Which you have failed to do."

"We'll find her." They watched on a camera as Roberto paced the floor, in a clear panic, and was texting on his phone.

"I suppose you didn't bug his phone."

"No. Never had a chance where he wouldn't know."

Karen sat on the couch. "Markus has her. It has to be it. That woman has taken her to her father."

"We've tried to keep this a controlled environment," Sam said. "That's fallen apart. Hell is starting to break loose. You were military; you know what that's like in the field. Not every moment is predictable."

"My operations never went this far south."

"Well, I'm improvising under a lot of constraints. Sorry."

"My daughter's life is at stake. She's finally got her act

together. What happens if she sees her dad again? All that could be undone."

"I'll do my best to find her. I promise you that. I think I know where Gandy might be staying. I can go there now."

"Not without me."

"It could be dangerous."

"This is my daughter."

"Karen. Did you get along with Dennis Gandy when you all lived in McLean?"

"No," she said after a moment. "He was a creepy little bastard, and I did not like him. Why is he even in Amanda's life again?"

"Then he may not open up if you're there. Let me talk to him."

She took a deep breath. "I'll wait in the car, then."

He thought of arguing with her, but he considered if it was Daniel in danger, he couldn't have sat in a house.

"Fine. Let's go." He powered down the laptop. They left. He saw Tara, pacing by the pool, talking on the phone, speaking in a low urgent whisper.

He gestured at Karen to wait and he stepped over to her. "What doesn't he want you telling?"

Tara turned off her phone. The flirty smile was gone. Now there was steel in her stare. "None of this concerns you. I'd get out of Miami if I were you. I'm not sure you realize the hornet's nest that's been kicked over."

"What?"

"Don't show back up at the office. I'd tell Mommy over there to not call the police; we'll find Amanda. We'll take care of it."

"Who's we?"

"You don't want to know," she said, and turned and walked away.

Nothing here was as it seemed, he thought. But Roberto's problems were secondary to finding Amanda.

He went back to Karen. "We can try chasing whoever took Amanda or go after the leverage we need to get her back. Everyone wants Markus. I have a thought on where Gandy might be and that means it's where Markus might be. But it's between you and me, we don't include Cortez. You in?"

Karen nodded. "Where?"

42

SAM SAID, "HIS SON CARLOS'S house."

"Why not? He could probably give us a key."

"Let's say we tell him. Cortez insists on coming with us; it's his son's house. If his son is sheltering Gandy, and Gandy's turned this into Bolt's safe house, he'll want to protect his son. Hiding a traitor—it's a crime. Maybe Carlos Cortez gets hit as being an accessory. And what's the damage to Cortez's reputation if his son's involved?"

"Grayson Cortez has been my friend for thirty years." Her voice was steady. "Carlos is a good guy."

"And Carlos is, according to his social media page, out of town quite a lot," Sam said. "Gandy's been off the credit card radar and so he's staying somewhere. If he's helping Markus, he's hiding him, and an absent friend's house might be the best bet. We need Markus to trade for Amanda, I'm thinking."

Karen weighed his words.

Sam said, "Look, I'm driving to Carlos's now. I'm not telling Grayson. If you want to call him, I won't stop you, but if Dennis has Markus, then I don't want Grayson hovering, worrying about how his son's implicated." He paused. "It might get ugly."

Karen said nothing for a long ten seconds. Then she said: "Let's go."

*   *   *

Carlos Cortez's house sat on a quiet street in an older residential neighborhood. There was no car in the driveway—Carlos Cortez and/or Dennis Gandy wasn't home. Sam made three orbits of the neighborhood, watching an elderly woman walk a pair of poodles and making sure she had proceeded past the house. The streets here tended to be straight, not offering places to park out of sight, but he parked in front of a house three houses down with a For Sale sign in front—he thought it would be less likely to draw attention from a curious neighbor.

"Markus could be inside there." Karen's voice trembled, very slightly.

Yes, Sam thought, that was the other possibility. There were five:

1. No one was home, and Gandy had never stayed here. He was off the grid somewhere else.
2. No one was home, but Gandy was staying here.
3. Gandy was here.
4. Markus was here.
5. Amanda was here, because the Englishwoman who had taken her was somehow tied to Gandy or Markus.

All the windows had curtains or blinds drawn.

He pulled his field case from the backseat. Karen watched as he opened the case. Lock picks, another surveillance remote camera, audio bugs that were minuscule and easy to hide, zip ties to bind a captive.

And a gun.

If Bolt was inside...he could end this. One shot and done. Bolt was a bad guy who had, without question of guilt, betrayed his nation and committed treason. And if Sam found him in there, he could end the traitor's dance, pull the car up to the driveway, and get the body into the trunk.

And what would Karen do? Or say? She'd be an accomplice. He thought she would be just fine.

But it was still her choice. He met her gaze.

"You do," she said, "what you have to do."

And if Amanda was here…was he supposed to kill Bolt in front of his own daughter?

"I don't want Amanda to see what I might have to do," he said.

"You do what you must," she said. "I'll deal with Amanda."

He loaded the gun. But he would not kill Bolt, especially if Amanda was inside. The man had too much to tell, to share.

He also took three pairs of restraints and gags. He put this all in a small string bag that he slipped over his shoulder, except for the gun, wedged in the small of his back, a knife strapped to his ankle, and the lock picks in his front pocket. He wore dark slacks and a gray shirt. He got out of the car, took a few of the For Sale flyers, rolled them up into a cylinder. He could say he was going to leave the flyers at front doors if challenged by a neighbor. He had sunglasses and a dark cap, trying not to look conspicuous or noticeable.

Karen watched him in silence.

"Stay here, sit in the driver's seat, keep the engine running," he said. "If you hear gunshots, leave and go to Cortez's house. If anyone other than me comes out that front door, go. If Amanda's inside, I'll send her out and you take her to my bar." He gave her the address for Amado. "Ask for Paige. There's an upstairs apartment where you all can stay and be safe."

She nodded. "Please be careful. If Amanda's in there…"

"I'll keep her safe," he promised.

*   *   *

Sam hurried across the lawns and reached the house. He'd decided not to knock or ring the doorbell but to go in the back, since no car was in the driveway. The backyard fence gate was locked and so he just went over it, bracing himself for a dog to rush him, but there was none. He knelt in the shade and listened to the silence inside the house. He moved slowly to the back door. The yard needed a mow; there were beer bottles on the patio table. Two of them.

He considered. Would Markus Bolt have been sitting out on a patio, relaxing? Probably not. He'd stay inside, away from neighbors' eyes. This might be a dead end.

He listened at the door. No sound inside—no soft-voiced hum of television. He tried the door.

Unlocked. That raised the odds that someone was home.

He opened the door slowly.

It was a breakfast nook, next to a kitchen. Empty, lights off. He slid in and shut the door behind him. Listened. Heard nothing. Maybe Gandy was careless about locks, although that didn't seem a likely stance for someone so deep into conspiracies, who might see enemies in the pantry or at the grocery or on the other side of a social media interaction.

He pulled his gun. Put a suppressor on it. Moved out of the kitchen, treading silently, into a dining room. He could see the front door, on the left, and he guessed the other side of the house must be a hallway leading to bedrooms. If Bolt was here . . . he'd be there.

But the house sounded empty.

He moved across the dining room. Stopped where the wall stopped, opening into a small den. Bookshelves without many books, but lots of framed photos.

The floor was tile, with colorful rugs scattered. No floorboards to creak. He listened.

And he heard it, the slightest exhale, one powered by adrenaline. Other side of the wall.

Then behind him. Quiet voice, German-inflected. "Drop your weapon, *bitte.*"

He glanced over his shoulder at her. Marianne.

"I'm placing my weapon on the floor," he said in German. He did so. The young soldierly man he'd seen walking with her at the airport came around the corner, kicked Sam's gun away. Didn't touch it. Didn't want, Sam realized, his prints on it.

"Hello, Sam," Marianne said.

"I heard you were dead," he said in English. "I'm delighted you're still among the living." If she was true to form, there was another hireling here in the house; she always worked with two at a time. Being Marianne-trained was a point of honor in the dark art of assassination; and apparently she got a percentage from her protégés for some period after they left the nest.

"Thank you, Sam. So generous. Where is your friend?"

"We parted ways years ago." He did not intend to discuss Mila with her. "I assume you're here for the same reason I'm here."

"Why are you here?" Marianne asked.

He didn't answer—they stared at each other. She said in German, "Start breaking his fingers on his right hand if he doesn't answer."

The man stepped toward Sam, and Sam said in German, "This is Carlos Cortez's house. He hasn't checked in when he was supposed to."

"This man is a CIA asset?"

"Yes," Sam lied with ease.

"Do I look," Marianne said, "like I've had a recent IQ drop?"

"You look lovely and intelligent as always," Sam said, and Marianne shook her head.

"Can we not have an adult conversation? You are looking for Markus Bolt."

They'd followed the same track he had, by different means. Gandy to Bolt. Which meant they didn't have a more substantive lead, or at least her client, whoever that was, didn't. "Bolt's still in Russia," Sam said. "They caught him. Did you not hear?"

Her face was impassive. "My client would have told me."

"Maybe your client doesn't know."

"Maybe my client would like to purchase the name of your information source in Russia who knows so much. You're going to tell me how much the American government knows about Bolt's return and where he is." Marianne glanced at the protégé.

He reached for Sam, for his hand, and Sam moved faster than the young soldier had expected, hammering the edge of his hand into the man's throat, seizing his shirt and putting him between himself and Marianne. The man gasped and Sam jammed the soldier's own gun up against his throat, holding him like a shield. Bracing himself for the man to fight back, to respond, face-to-face with his mentor. The young man froze.

"Now, I don't want Junior's brains all over me and neither do you," he said to Marianne. "I want us to walk away from each other again. If you've killed…anyone here, well, just let me know who you took care of, and I'll go on my way and you go on yours and we need never mention each other's names. But I'm not freelance anymore, Marianne, and if you kill me, my colleagues will be relentless. They will come after you and they're not as nice as me. This time you will be dead."

He could feel the young man trembling slightly. Maybe this was his first job. Maybe he was reconsidering his career choices. Thinking of his family, whether this was worth his life.

Then he felt the cool of another gun at the back of his head.

"Do you bring your pair of underlings everywhere?"

"*Underling* is a harsh word," the voice behind Sam said. Female, Scottish accent. "It's vaguely insulting."

"Step back or I kill him," Sam said.

"Let him go," the Scottish woman said. "Or I kill you."

"No," Sam said. "I don't think Marianne wants me dead quite yet." He hoped those weren't his last words. The young man mumbled something in German.

Marianne smiled at him. "I had flash cards made for my students. Your face is on one."

"I hope it's a good picture."

"You're older now."

"If you kill me," Sam said, "none of you will be leaving the US. Ever."

Marianne kept her gun aimed at Sam. "Sam. Let him go, and let's talk. Or we both shoot you."

He released the young man, who stepped away with attempted dignity and took back his gun from Sam. Straightening his shoulders and now staring at Sam.

"I assume Bolt's not here," Sam said. "Or you'd be showing me his body and we'd be parting with a handshake."

"He is not," Marianne said. "But the reward for him is substantial, and we won't be able to collect it if you get to him first."

"Reward? That sounds like he's supposed to be gift wrapped." Did her client want Bolt alive? He'd imagined the orders were to kill Bolt on sight. Why would they want him alive?

Because…Bolt knew something or had something and they had to be sure he hadn't given it or hidden it.

"You said Carlos Cortez is CIA?" Marianne asked. "Makes sense. This house is fitted like a safe house. Cameras, plenty of food in the fridge and pantry for a man who is often traveling internationally. Outside locks on the bedroom doors, to keep someone inside. This is where you and your colleagues are to bring him, yes?"

Sam now regretted his little fib. "If he's staying here… then why am I breaking in?"

"You just opened an unlocked door," the Scottish woman said.

"I don't want you interfering with my work," Marianne said. "Bolt is worth ten million to me. I could retire, Sam. I could…not do this anymore."

"And I thought you loved your work. Kids, did you hear that? Teacher wants to retire."

Marianne said nothing. He saw what might have been a flash of remorse in her eyes. She wanted to wait and surprise Bolt in what she thought was his own safe house. And Sam was too much trouble to keep captive for long. She would kill him, perhaps with a tinge of regret, but she would kill him.

"I suppose it's too much to ask who you're working for," he said. "I imagine the Russian government has sent its own people. Are you going to kill them, too?"

"I'm deniable," she said. "If something went wrong."

"I'm pretty sure there's an actual Russian operative here hunting him as well. You, I'm guessing, are working for an elite who wants Bolt dead for some reason."

And then the front door opened, with a creak and Karen's voice, loud, like a warning foghorn. "I just want to know where my daughter is, Dennis, and you have to tell me…"

Past her he saw Dennis Gandy standing in the door-way, in shock, Karen behind him.

"Run!" Sam yelled.

Gandy and Karen both turned and fled.

Sam slammed the back of his head into the Scottish woman, spun, and shoved her into the soldier, who was trying to raise his arm to fire at Sam, but hesitated as his partner was in the way. Marianne was behind them both, screaming orders at them, but they ignored her. The soldier launched himself at Sam, who blocked his punches and managed to deliver a slamming blow to the man's chest that staggered him. The Scot landed on Sam, fingers going for his eyes, and he threw her off him into the soldier.

"Stop!" Marianne yelled. She leveled the gun at Sam. He stopped.

"I'll deal with him. Get Gandy, now!" she ordered.

The two exchanged a look.

"Now!" Marianne yelled. The two underlings obeyed, hurrying out the front door.

"Your kiddos were slow on your orders," Sam said. "I'd rethink those two; they're going to mess this up for you."

"Desperate, aren't you?" She could shoot him. She was out of his reach but she wanted information. He would get maybe another five seconds.

"Let's help each other. Who hired you?" he said.

"Are you working with Dennis Gandy?" she asked.

"Of course not."

He heard two shots from the front yard, the screech of car wheels revving. *Karen, run.*

"I'm going to see if Bolt's wife is lying dead in the yard, because if she is, it's huge news and those two clowns will make finding Bolt much harder." He turned and started walking away. And she acted in haste, running up to him, within reach. He spun, slamming a fist into her chest and wrenching her gun from her. In the living room window, he saw his car, with Karen at the wheel, zoom past. She was clear.

And he had no ride. No fast escape.

So he turned, grabbed his gun from the floor, and ran out the back of the house.

43

Austin

H<small>EY</small>," D<small>ANIEL SAID TO</small> J<small>AMES</small> as he went into the room.

"Shut the door," James said.

Daniel did.

"What's on the disc?" James asked.

"Mostly static. The video cuts out for several minutes, then returns to normal."

"What?"

"I think maybe it got erased or messed up."

"Oh," James said. "Maybe you picked up the wrong one. All that risk for nothing."

"Maybe so." He sat on his sleeping bag. "Thanks for sticking your neck out for me. Being the distraction and all."

"Sure," James said.

"You know," Daniel said, because mothers were on his mind, "Leonic is going to be a great mom. I mean not just to the baby. But to you." He didn't want to say, *Because your own mom is a mess.*

"She's all right," James agreed.

"She's more than that." Then he asked, because he

thought he should, "When was the last time you saw your mom?"

"It's been a while," James said, his voice going toneless. "There's still a court order in place." Now James wasn't looking at him. "I told you not to bring that up."

"If you give Leonie a chance...since your own mom—"

"Stop it. Just shut your mouth," James said suddenly, shoving Daniel, knocking him to the floor.

Daniel got up and pushed back. "Just give her a real chance..."

"She's not my mom and she never will be!" And then James barreled into him, knocking him back to the floor, and the boys struggled against each other until Leonie and Matt ran into the room and separated them.

"What's going on?" Matt demanded. "What the hell, guys?"

And neither boy would say. The silence grew uncomfortable. Leonie and Matt just looked at each other. "This isn't like y'all. At all," Leonie said. "I want to know what this is about."

Neither boy spoke. Their gaze met in mutual agreement. They remained silent.

"Well," Matt said, uncertain how to salvage the moment, "you need to shake hands and apologize." They did so begrudgingly.

"Sorry," Daniel said, not meaning it.

"Sorry," James said, the same. "I have homework to do." He activated his tablet.

Daniel grabbed the briefcase. "I'll work downstairs."

Matt and Leonie exchanged another look. "Dinner will be ready in a few," Matt said.

What did the static on the video mean? Who was capable of doing that to mask their entrance into the school?

He needed answers. So he needed to see Clarice again.

*   *   *

"I'm going to work on my project at the Coffee Haus," Daniel announced. "If that's okay. That's where my project partner wants to work."

Matt and Leonie looked at him, and then at each other. He could see them calculating that maybe it would be good for Daniel and James to have a break from each other.

"I'm doing a math project with Millicent Grant and she does her homework there because her brother practices drums at night." He pulled a fact of a friend's life out of the air to make an excuse for the trip. It was so easy to lie sometimes.

"Um, sure."

"Just let me be sure she can be there," he said. "Excuse me."

He texted Clarice's number. Could you meet me at the Coffee Haus on Old Travis Road in thirty minutes? I want to talk. I want to know more about my mom.

And the answer, quickly: Yes, of course.

Leonie drove him to the coffee shop. She parked the car and put a hand on his arm before he could open the door. "I've got some errands to run at the mall, so I'll pick you up or Matt will when you're done. Just text us, please."

"I think I'd like to go stay at my grandparents'," Daniel said. "It would be best."

"Your father wanted you with us," Leonie said.

"Matt and James can't want me there now."

"Of course they do. Matt cares about you and James is your best friend. I don't even remember the last time you got crossways enough to fight. What's going on with you two?"

"It's nothing," Daniel said.

"Is this about your mom? James has lost his mom, too, in a way. Since he can't see her until she's sober."

He wasn't going to say anything about James's mom. It would only make things worse. "He has you," Daniel said. *Which is what I was trying to tell him. He gets you as a mom and he doesn't even appreciate you.*

"So do you."

"It's not the same. It's never been the same since you married Matt," Daniel said, and he hated himself for saying it.

"Don't you want me to be happy? I love Matt."

He nodded. He thought he was about to cry again, and he couldn't do that. "Yes. I want you to be happy. James and I will be fine. But I wish you'd let me go stay at Nana's."

"She has her hands full with your grandfather. Plus, we want you here. Even James."

"No, he doesn't. He doesn't." Daniel opened the car door.

The Coffee Haus wasn't too busy. Daniel sat down at a table closer to the front, with his backpack. He'd put the photos of his mom inside and left the old briefcase at Leonie and Matt's house. His stomach was in knots from arguing with Leonie but she didn't understand.

Daniel glanced around the coffee shop. He didn't see anyone he knew, but…wait. In the back corner, on a laptop, was Ms. Dorridge, the school counselor. She had her gaze on the laptop, concentrating. A book and an open notebook next to her.

He got up and walked over to the counselor. "Hey, Ms. Dorridge."

She glanced up, smiling as though caught at something. "Daniel. How are you?"

"Fine. How are you?"

"I'm good, thanks. Working on my novel." She almost sounded embarrassed. She gestured at the laptop. He could see the book on the table was titled *Write YOUR Novel YOUR Way*.

"Oh, that's cool." He'd had no idea she wanted to be a writer. It was weird to him when he saw teachers or adults from the school out at restaurants, like they had existences entirely out of the classroom. "What is your book about?"

She blinked at him. "It's a family drama." She smiled. "Not about school stuff."

He wanted to say he was caught up in one of those, but then he didn't want her asking, yet again, if he was okay or did he want to talk or did he need help. "Oh, that's cool," he repeated, sounding entirely uncool, shifting to his other foot. "Sorry to have interrupted your writing."

"No, that's fine," she said. "How's it going?"

"Fine." He nodded. "I should get back to my table . . . and let you write."

She nodded. "Daniel, you know, if you ever need to talk to me . . ."

Were counselors required to say that? He thought if she wanted to be sure he never talked to her, that was the way to do it. But she was being polite. "Sure," he said. He went back to his table and sat down.

Two minutes later Clarice entered. She sat down across from him, and she risked a smile. She put her phone on the table, next to her purse.

"I'm glad you texted me."

"I thought we should talk," he said, trying to sound more grown-up than he felt.

"I do have some stuff to tell you since I saw you . . . Do you want hot chocolate or something? Or do you want coffee?" As if unsure if someone his age drank coffee.

"Lemonade," he said. "Please."

She nodded and went and ordered for both of them. She glanced back at him, as if wanting to make certain that he didn't leave the table. He turned back to the table and watched the room, wanting to be sure none of his dad's friends were in the shop—he and Dad had run into other parents they knew here—except Dad didn't have a ton of friends; he kind of kept to himself.

Clarice's phone buzzed. An incoming text. Even upside down he could see the name: SAM CAPRA.

Dad was texting Clarice. He couldn't help himself; he turned the phone around to read the preview of the message:

I'm sorry to hear about your cancer. But I cannot allow you to talk to D until I talk to him alone. I don't know how to make him understand about his mother.

Daniel's breath caught in his throat. He could see the number in the text; it was Dad's. What was there...to make him understand?

"Daniel?"

Clarice, back with their drinks.

"My dad is texting you," he said.

She sat down. "Yes. I contacted him after I saw you. His cell is the same number it was back when they were married. I told him I'm sick. I have at most a few months, Daniel. Your dad may not want me around but he's not heartless."

"You didn't tell him that we had talked."

"I didn't want him to be angry. I thought if he knew I was in Austin, he'd be open to me seeing you. He's not, though, not yet."

"What is this message she left for me?"

"I heard from a friend of hers, a while back. A friend in Miami. Who said he had found a recording that your mom had left for you. But she encoded it."

Miami. "Why would she do that?"

"Because she didn't want your father to see it, presumably. And whatever she was going to say to you she wanted to be private."

"Did she know she was sick?"

"No one knew, according to your dad." Clarice stopped, but her expression showed she wanted to say more. "But I never saw her medical records."

"My dad is in Miami."

"I'm sure that's a coincidence," Clarice said.

"No, it's not."

Clarice was silent, then said: "Did you look at the pictures?" As if leading him away from the thorny thoughts. *Let's talk about something else and then come back to the hard question. That your mom left something for you and maybe your father knows about it and is keeping it from you.*

"Yes."

"So what do you want to know about your mother?"

Someone willing to tell him all. For a moment he felt dizzy. "Um. Okay, what was she like? Like, when she was my age?"

Aunt Clarice frowned, as though disappointed by the question. Then she smiled. "She was tough. Toughest kid I ever knew. I mean, maybe you're tougher, I don't know you yet." She was blunt. Unlike Dad, who would not be blunt but sometimes wouldn't answer questions. Blunt wasn't bad.

"Tough how?"

"You know her parents died. I...I wasn't in touch with them much. Her parents were a wreck. Her mom—my sister—was an alcoholic. She mostly ignored Lucy. Her father was the opposite, a religious man. Religious nut, if I'm being honest."

"How did they die?"

"Barbara fell down some stairs, drunk on box wine. She'd been home from rehab for three days. Lucy found her." She hesitated for a moment. "My brother-in-law— your own grandfather—wrote me a letter, just saying that 'the sinner was dead and rotting in hell.' That was how I found out my sister was dead. Lucy's father didn't like me. Had that in common with yours." She took a sip of her coffee.

It was a lot to process. Daniel decided it was best to keep asking questions. "What...what did Barbara do, like, for a job?"

"She taught high school English and writing. She... she was very talented." She cleared her throat.

"And my grandfather had my mother."

"With Barb gone, Bob got involved with...a weird church. I was living in Phoenix. I went up to Minneapolis twice to see Lucy, and she seemed scared, broken." She took a deep breath. "When she was thirteen, your mother ran to me in Arizona. She didn't want to go back." She sipped her coffee. "You don't need to know details. It was a bad scene."

No, he didn't want to know details. He wasn't sure now he wanted to know any of this.

"Your grandfather Bob...he vanished. I think he got involved with bad people and they got rid of him."

What did *bad people* even mean, Daniel wondered. Had his mother known criminals? Pedophiles? His skin felt cold.

What kind of life had she had before Dad came into her life?

"So Lucy came to live with me in Arizona. The judge said Bob had abandoned her, since no one knew where he had gone, so I got custody. Her only living relative." Her gaze was steady on Daniel's.

"You said there was an uncle."

She flicked him a smile. "Yes. I meant my brother and I." She cleared her throat. "I waited for her to tell me what all she'd been through, and she didn't want to talk about it." She tapped fingers on the table. "Do you know what it's like to live with someone who's silent about their life?"

Yes, he thought. *I do. Dad.* Instead, he asked: "She never told you what happened?"

"How do you ask if someone was abused? By her dad, or her idiot father's colleagues in his crazy church? Lucy said she had nothing to say. So I let her be quiet about it and I got her into a good private school. She got a scholarship—she was very smart, she had great grades, but she was sneaky."

"Sneaky?"

"She was both book smart and street smart. She'd make friends with rich kids, and somehow she always had money—money hidden under her bed. She didn't have a job. I think she found out things on kids they didn't want their parents to know and they'd give her money to stay quiet. Like she was a little spy."

Daniel had thought when Clarice talked about Lucy, it would be all about what a good student she was, what a good mother she must have been, all the sweetness and light that could pervade a memory. He felt a sudden surge of anger. Why was she telling him how bad his mom's life was? He didn't want to know that. He wanted to know happy, nice things.

Didn't you want the truth?

He took a long sip of his lemonade. It tasted a little off, like maybe it was going stale. But sipping it gave him time to think about his next question. "So then she, what, went to college?"

"Yes. Again, on a scholarship, because she was smart as hell. She majored in computer science and she took a bunch of Russian language courses. I thought that part was a waste. She studied all the time; she could have met a nice boy there."

"She did meet a nice boy. My dad."

"Yes. Well. That was later." Her lips thinned as if there were words trying to creep out from her mouth. "I figured she would go off to a lucrative software job in Silicon Valley or Austin or Boston or stay in Phoenix; there are high-tech companies there. She went to Washington DC, though." Clarice shook her head. "They sent an uptight guy in a suit to ask me a bunch of questions about her past, and that was hard—talking to a stranger about Lucy's past. I didn't tell them anything bad. I guess I gave good answers because she got the job."

She stopped talking and Daniel didn't know what to say, because this was crazy, so he took a sip of his lemonade. "So she went to DC."

"Yes. For this very hush-hush consulting company. I don't know what that even means, what they did. Then...she told me about six months later she'd met a boy, I mean, a man, and she intended to marry him."

"Were...you at the wedding?"

"Yes. They got married by a judge, they did it fast because Sam's parents got a chance to come back from Africa and only *their* schedule mattered, mine didn't, and so I had to book a last-minute flight, which was not cheap." She said this as if feeling the pain from an old wound. Her lips thinned again.

"You don't like him."

"He was smart. He had a good job. Nice-looking. But there's something about him...He had secrets. I could tell it. You can tell it, too, can't you?"

He didn't want to answer that. "What did you think he was keeping from you?"

"What he kept was Lucy. She only came to visit me

twice, once with him, once without him. And then she wouldn't call me."

Daniel's brain began to swim. None of these were secrets; it could have just been Lucy—Mom—asserting her independence. And maybe Aunt Clarice didn't like that. But he said nothing. The weight of her words, her complaints, made him feel tired.

"And then they moved to London. She called me a little bit more, from London. Then she got pregnant. With you. I was so happy. I thought—with you coming, they'd come back to America. She still called, we'd talk, but I could tell something was wrong." Her voice grew harsh, and she took a hard, steadying breath. "Something was wrong. She was scared. I'm sorry, Daniel, I think it was something to do with your dad."

"You can't say that about my dad." His voice rose slightly, but then he didn't want people to hear this. No one was sitting right near them. He glanced behind him. Ms. Dorridge was still staring at her laptop, lost in her own thoughts.

He turned back to Clarice.

"She just told me once, on the phone . . . she said, *I fell in love with him and I didn't mean to*."

"Like . . . she married him for another reason?"

"Yeah, and came to love him. And then . . . she called me, just once, for a minute, and said she was fine but she'd left your dad and she'd left her job and she wouldn't be in touch for a while; she said she had to figure out her life." She swallowed. "Left him? With you about to arrive? I told her to come home to me; she said she couldn't. She thanked me . . . for taking her in. It all had the tone of a final good-bye, Daniel, and it broke my heart . . ."

She took a deep breath. Daniel thought, *She . . . left Dad?* That couldn't be right.

Clarice said: "Her due date came and I couldn't reach her, I couldn't reach your father. I called the FBI, the London police, no one would help me. And then I get an e-mail from Lucy, saying she's fine, she'll be in touch soon, you've arrived and you're fine. She sent a picture of you, her holding you. She looked sad, though, not happy."

From her pocket she pulled a photo and slid it to him.

"I have this picture," he said tonelessly. "It's the only one of me and her together."

"You're a newborn there," Clarice said. "You don't have other pictures with her?"

Daniel shook his head.

"I look at this picture a lot. I notice she's got on a patient bracelet, right? To match her to you so she doesn't take home the wrong baby. I zoom it up because I want to know where you're at, or where you were. The words— they're in French. It says *nom*, not *name*. You were born in France. Or some country that spoke French."

"France? No. I was born in New York." Dad wouldn't lie about that, would he? "They were working in New York."

Clarice stared at him. "I guess the hospital was just fancy, then."

Daniel didn't know what to say.

"So I e-mail her back, repeatedly. Silence. The name of the consultancy—it doesn't have working phones any-more. I call. Nothing. Like the company has shut down. Weeks passed. Then I got a short phone call from your father. He said Lucy had died suddenly, of an undiag-nosed heart condition. He said you were fine." She folded her hands on the table. "I screamed at him. I said you had all vanished, no one would tell me anything, Lucy had been hiding from him. He said no, that wasn't true,

I was mistaken. They had separated briefly but gotten back together before she died.

"I wanted her body back, to bury with her mother, and he wouldn't give it to me." Her voice rose slightly. "I tried to find him, and you, and I couldn't. It was like a shut door."

Clarice stopped, suddenly looking exhausted and spent. She had not raised her voice, but she touched at her throat for a moment as if she had shouted.

She took a deep breath. "This is all news to you, isn't it? Sam's parents never told you any of this? That he didn't even let me, her only relative, attend her funeral. Or tell me anything. Or let me see you."

"Why did you say her grave is empty in that text message?"

"Because there's not a record of a casket buried there. Your uncle got the paperwork for me."

"Dad said her ashes are buried there."

That stopped her. "She didn't want to be cremated. She told me that once. And most people scatter ashes, they don't bury them."

"She must have changed her mind."

Clarice took a deep breath. "I'm sorry I said that, then, but it doesn't change what's happened. Because there's still a big secret he's kept. I think it's this message."

Daniel said nothing. He felt exhausted.

"He let me see you, just once. He came out to Arizona for a day. He didn't even spend the night. But I got to hold you, and feed you your bottle, and see Lucy's sweet face in yours. He brought a very official-looking medical file that outlined Lucy's heart condition that came out of the blue. Doctors and clinics, and scans and . . . I think he knew I was suspicious as to what had happened. I asked him why they separated. He said because he'd bought a bunch of bars without telling Lucy. She got mad, left him for a bit, but then came back and they were fine. I had no idea where he'd gotten the money for these bars. He still have them?"

Daniel nodded.

"And then . . . then . . ."

"What?" He was afraid to ask.

Her voice wavered a bit. "He took you from my arms and then Sam handed me a check for a quarter-million dollars. He said it was Lucy's life insurance through the consulting company. He wanted me to have it, because Lucy was my family, but . . . the price was that I stay away from you."

It was like Dad was trying to ensure nothing from his mom's life could touch Daniel. He felt suddenly cold, not from the lemonade.

"I took the money. I needed it. It was Lucy's, after all." She steadied her voice again. "After a while, I went to New Orleans. I didn't tell Sam that I was coming. I found the house where he and you were living. There was a woman there. Well, two. He's a new widower and who are these women? I watched for two days, like a cop on a stakeout. One woman's the one keeping you now, clearly a nanny. I approached her, when she was sitting on the park bench with you. I just said how cute you were. She looked at me like I might be a threat; she was on guard the moment I got physically close to y'all. But I at least got to see you. I thought maybe Sam had shown her my picture, warned her about me."

"That's Leonie. She was my nanny. She's great."

"She's the one I saw with you at the cemetery. Remember, she's on your dad's side. Not yours."

Daniel didn't know what to say.

Clarice went on: "So I went back to your house. I saw Sam with another woman there. Blond. Talking to him on their porch when I drove by. When I drove back, they weren't there. So I parked down the street and snuck up to a window. I didn't risk peering in; I could hear them talking. She had an accent. Maybe Russian, or Eastern European. He called her Mila."

"I don't know anyone named Mila," Daniel said.

"My point is that they were living in Europe, your mama ended up dead suddenly, your daddy gave me a 'keep your mouth shut' payment, and then he's got this other European woman in his house."

He had to defend Dad. He had to. "Maybe she was just a friend. He owns bars in Europe. He knows people there."

"Men and women can't be just friends."

"I'm friends with girls," Daniel said.

"You're a child. It's different. I left before they could notice me. They went in a back room. A bedroom, probably."

"I guess if you had asked him, he would have known you were spying on him. After you took his money."

Clarice's smile was a bit crooked. "Who offers your mom's family hush money? Who tells them to stay away from you? He did *something*. He's hiding something about Lucy. And you and I both deserve to know the truth."

"So why reach out to me now?"

"Two reasons. First, I have multiple myeloma. It's a blood cancer; there's no cure for it. Treatments, yes, but not a cure. I don't have forever." Now Clarice's voice wavered.

"He kept me from you. This was my only chance to get you to talk to me."

"I'm sorry you're sick." Daniel didn't know what to believe. What to think, what to say. He had only wanted to know what his mother was like. "I don't want you to say any more about my dad."

"Sure, baby. I understand."

"And don't call me baby. I'm not a baby."

"No, you're not. I called Lucy that. I...I'm sorry." She swallowed hard. "Why, Daniel, would he not tell me about what was going on with Lucy before she died, those weeks where I never heard from her, and after? Not even have me at her funeral? If he didn't like me, I was still her aunt. Why?" She leaned forward. "And that's the second reason. This message. You could help me with that."

"I don't understand."

"So I got this note from a man in Miami. He knew all sorts of stuff about Lucy. He said they were friends and she had sent him a book from London. Now I want you to listen to me carefully, because this might be hard to understand. She sent him a book all those years ago, but he never read it. He wasn't interested in it. He put it up on a shelf or in a box, and only recently did he find it again and open it. In the last part of the book, she'd cut out the pages and she'd put a disc there, with a note that said, 'For my son when he is old enough to understand. Listen to it alone.'"

"Why didn't this guy reach out to my dad?"

"He said he knew your father and...he thought it best to reach out to me. And I'm guessing that whatever she left on this recording is something she wanted you to see, and maybe she thought your dad wouldn't let you see it."

"Who is this man?"

"He said he worked with Lucy, he knew her, she'd sent this to him. But it asks for a password."

"I don't have any way of knowing," he said.

"I think," she said slowly, "that if you and I talked to your father together, he'd have to tell us what happened, and he'd have to know how to view the recording. He'd have some idea what the password was. But he can't keep the message from you if he knows we know about it."

Daniel said nothing for a moment. She was right.

"We could call him," Daniel said. "Together. Right now."

"I think he could say no to you over the phone. I don't think he could say no to your face."

"So we should wait for him to come home."

"The message is in Miami. Your father is there. We could just talk to them both."

"I can't go to Miami. I have school tomorrow. And Leonie wouldn't let me go."

"We could fly there tonight. Or early tomorrow morning if you will cut school. We have access to a private plane. We can fly there directly, be there in under three hours."

"A private plane?"

"It belongs to a client of my brother's."

"I . . . I can't. Dad would freak out."

"He's going to freak out anyway. Look, he was relatively calm when I reached out to him. I think he knows your mom is on your mind."

He stared at her. "Because you sent me texts and that note. How did you get it in the school anyway?"

"I pretended to be a grandma, bringing something a student forgot. I got in after the school opened and looked in the binders until I found your name in one."

"How did you avoid the video? How did you know I was in choir?"

"My brother, he's clever about computers and cameras and such. He jammed the cameras. It doesn't matter. We didn't want to be caught, and have the school talking to your dad before we could talk to you."

"I don't have clothes or a bag and Leonie won't let me go."

"We can get you whatever you need in Miami," Clarice said. "But I'm not going to pressure you. It has to be your decision. Like I said, you're in control."

He didn't know what to do. He should call Leonie. He should call his grandmother. He should call his dad.

And listen to them tell him what they'd told him for years, which was nothing. He'd learned more about his mother in the past half hour than in thirteen years. Dad had shoved Mom's past into a dusty corner where he was forbidden to look.

Daniel had always been the good boy. The one who followed the rules, practiced hard, studied, did what his father told him to do.

"You'll get in trouble if Leonie or Nana calls the police," he said.

"Here," she said, her voice softer. "Do you want to call him? He probably won't talk you out of it." She pushed her phone toward him. "Since he just texted me."

"No. He'll tell me not to come and then I can't."

"What would you like to do, then, Daniel? You're in control."

Being in control was a new idea to him. "Leonie or Matt will be expecting to pick me up soon. She'll freak if I'm not here. But she'll call Dad, and he'll call me and tell me not to come." He paused. "I told her I wanted to go stay with Nana and Papa. James and I . . . we kind of had a fight."

"That's a shame," Clarice said.

"I could text her and tell her that I'm going to Nana's," Daniel said slowly. "She'll probably call Nana, though."

"I'll handle talking to Leonie for you," Clarice said. "I know what to say."

"She doesn't know you."

"I think she'll listen to me. I don't want to burden you with her reaction."

"Okay," he said. It felt like jumping off a cliff.

"Shall we?" She held out her hand to him.

He took it, although it was weird, but it seemed rude not to, and he glanced back at Ms. Dorridge. She was a witness; she would see him leaving with Clarice. Maybe she would tell someone. But she was staring at her laptop, sipping her coffee.

Clarice led him out the door. The night air was cool on his face.

"Aunt Clarice..."

She was already sending a text, tapping at the phone as they walked across the lot.

"It means the world to me that you call me that," she said softly. "There's someone I want you to meet."

"Who?"

"Your uncle. He's helped me. We didn't want to overwhelm you with both of us talking. He's in the car."

"Uncle," he said, like it was a new concept. He noticed Clarice had neatly swept up his backpack and had it over her shoulder. In the car she was walking toward, he could see a man sitting at the wheel, a laptop open next to him.

She opened the backseat door, and after a moment's hesitation, he got inside. Clarice shut the door. She still had a phone in her hand.

The man at the seat shut the laptop. He turned to face Daniel.

He was older, his hair full gray. He stared for a long moment at Daniel. "Hello, Daniel. I'm so pleased to finally meet you. I'm your uncle Mark."

He offered his hand and Daniel shook it. "Hi," Daniel said.

Clarice had gotten in the passenger seat. "Did you call the airport?"

"Yes, everything's ready," Uncle Mark said. He gave Daniel a crooked smile.

*   *   *

The text from Simone Capra's number came through right before Leonie was leaving the mall to go fetch Daniel. Hey Leonie: Daniel called me and asked me to pick him up at the Coffee Haus. He asked if he can spend the night with us, I said fine. I'll handle getting him to school tomorrow, he's got spare clothes here. He said he'd had an argument with James. I'm sorry to hear that. We're glad to have him, though. I will let Sam know he's staying here.

Leonie read it. She texted Simone back: D doesn't have his gear for practice tomorrow. I can bring his bag in the morning with James.

Simone: That would be great. He said he's not feeling well so he might miss school tomorrow. He might just need a little grandmother time. Alex has been better the past couple of days and Sam worries about me dealing with them both but I'm fine.

Leonie took a deep breath. Daniel's been upset lately. A lot of talk about Lucy. Asking questions. Thought you should know that.

Simone: Thx for telling me. And give my best to James. I'm sure the boys will work it out and be fine. Talk soon!

Leonie stared at the phone, frowning. She moved her thumb over the screen to tap and call Simone, then stopped. Daniel must need some space. That was clear. Or maybe he wanted to talk to his grandparents about his mother. They didn't know the truth about Lucy and her treason and so could not slip or do damage. Maybe this was best kept in his actual family. She could do more damage trying to run interference.

She just didn't want that boy hurt, and there was no way for him to know the truth and not be hurt by it.

Leonie took a deep breath and sent a text to Daniel's phone: Your nana let me know you're staying with her tonight. You OK?

A minute later, an answer: Y. Because typing "Yes" was such a lift for a middle school boy.

She waited, but there was nothing more. Typically terse boy-texting.

She switched to Sam's number and wrote him a message: Daniel staying with your parents tonight. He asked to. Him and James not getting along but it will be fine. Sorry. Your mom said it was ok and she'd call you later.

She sent the text. There was no answer.

Give Daniel space, she thought. Tomorrow was another day.

44

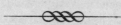

Kɪʀɪʟʟ ᴅʀᴏᴠᴇ ʙᴀᴄᴋ ᴛᴏ ᴛʜᴇ condos, wondering exactly how the hell he was going to break the news of Val's betrayal to Illya. He parked in the underground garage and took a deep breath.

There were several considerations. First, Illya had been fooled. So Kirill had been fooled. This was Illya's fault; he had let her inside the circle. Val had somehow managed to pass a full vetting and that was no easy feat. She must have had help. So likely she worked for another government.

Probably the UK. She had lived in London, been married to a British man.

Kirill got out of the car. He took a deep breath. This was going to be...problematic. He thought of Duderov, Bobo, his mother, all trying to tell him what he would need to do to survive this.

He could kill Illya and blame it on Val. Say he'd only talked with her on the plane. But then there was the fact of the meeting with the real estate agent, with his Russian contacts. Had he said anything? And Maria. Had Illya told Maria? She was pregnant. He did not think he could kill a pregnant woman.

He suddenly didn't want to kill anyone, except Markus, who was the root cause of all this misery. And all the misery of his life.

He went inside. He stopped at the ground floor. The lobby was expansive. Beyond the windows was a lush pool area full of his countrymen who had the money to escape the cold. He scanned the crowd. Illya was not among them, but Maria was, sitting at a shaded table, reading a magazine.

He walked outside, to Maria's table. "Maria. I'm looking for Illya."

Now she seemed to know who he was. "Yes. He's upstairs, resting." She lowered her sunglasses and looked at him. "Did you . . . do what you needed to do?"

He wished Illya had kept his mouth shut. He probably thought Maria could be trusted when the sorry truth was no one could be trusted. "I hope so, soon. I'll need Illya to have the plane ready."

"You should tell Val."

That's the problem, he thought.

"One of the planes isn't here, but the other one is," she added helpfully.

"How are you feeling?" It seemed rude not to ask.

She ran her hand down the swell of her belly. "I'm fine. Where is Val? I thought she was helping you."

"She had other business to attend to," he said.

Maria said, "Well, Illya is upstairs if you need him."

He nodded and went back inside, and took the elevator up to the penthouse. Val had given him the code.

He exited the elevator into a huge foyer, with stunning ocean views. He called out, "Illya?"

"Here."

Kirill walked through the foyer and found Illya sitting on a couch, his laptop open, notes spread beside him. He looked tired.

"Did you find him? Do you need my boat to go dump the body?"

"Is Val here?"

"No."

"Then she has betrayed you."

Illya blinked. Then laughed. Then stopped laughing. "What do you mean?"

Kirill explained the events of the day. "You think she took Amanda Bolt."

"I know she did. She got her alone and she got her to leave with her, and she has not contacted me."

"It's…it's not possible. We checked her background; it was all fine."

"Then she's been turned against you since you vetted her."

"Val is loyal."

"No, Illya, she is not. She has taken Amanda, to use as bait to draw in Markus."

The elevator pinged and Kirill turned, waiting, half hoping it was Val with Amanda in tow, saying, *Sorry but I had to play it this way, it's all fine, I didn't use you.* But it was Maria, with her bag and her magazine and her oversize ridiculously expensive sunglasses.

"Maria," Illya called. "Have you heard from Val?"

"No," she called back.

"Leave her out of this. You can't tell her everything," Kirill whispered. Illya nodded.

"If you hear from her, let me know," Illya said.

"Uh, all right," Maria called back. She had gone into the kitchen. They heard her pour water and then she announced, "I'm going to go lie down," and they heard her head down a hallway.

"Where would she go?" Kirill asked.

"But Val can't have…"

"Illya," Kirill said. "Think. We have to assume the worst."

"But why would she…"

"She might be a British agent. Or working for someone

else who wants access to what Bolt stole from you." He kept his voice down.

"I own multiple properties in Miami. She knows them all and has access to them all."

"Give me a list and send your security team to each one and see if she's there."

"It doesn't seem likely she would hide where I could easily find her."

"Are you willing to risk it? You know how her mind works."

"I thought I did..."

"...so where will she go?"

"If she's working for someone else, Kirill, they will have set up a safe house," Illya's voice was hoarse. "Surely you see that."

"Could she be working alone?" That was a more appealing possibility, because it meant he could more easily get control of this situation again.

"Why would she?"

"To force something from you. She knows about the financial network map. Maybe she wants to sell it to you. This might be criminal, not political."

"After all I've done for her," Illya said, bitterness in his tone.

"We have to work together, Illya," Kirill said, thinking, *Until we don't.* "We're both in trouble because of this. You brought her into Russia, you brought her inside the inner circle. We need to stay united."

Illya nodded after a moment, but Kirill thought, *He's not trustworthy. He'll throw me to the wolves at the first sign of trouble for himself.*

Illya called her. There was no answer; it went to voice mail. Illya said, "Val, we're concerned about you and where you are. Please call me as soon as you can. I simply want to know that you're all right." He ended the call.

"Maybe...maybe Amanda took *her*. Maybe Markus reached out to Amanda, and so the next time someone new with ties to Russia approaches her, she grabs Val to see what she knows."

Illya wasn't accepting the truth, Kirill thought, that Val had played them all. "She bought a house in your name in Coral Gables."

"Yes, she mentioned that. She said she would handle it and the reselling of it." He acted like this was no big deal. "Do we have Amanda Bolt's phone number?" Illya asked. "You must have been briefed."

"Yes."

"Then call her."

Kirill tried the number. No answer. He got Amanda's voice mail. He left no message.

"I'm going to check out the house," Kirill said.

"She won't be there."

"We'll see," Kirill said. "I want you to understand if I catch her, I'm bringing her back here. She has to be questioned."

"No, not here. I own a house nearer Fort Lauderdale. It's not...busy with people as it is here. More secluded. No one will hear her." Illya's voice had suddenly turned sour. Kirill could see his rising anger at the betrayal. Val was dead to him now. "Do you want to take one of my security men with you?"

"No. I'm used to working alone." And he should have stayed with that plan. But he had liked her so. He would not make that mistake again.

Kirill left. Illya watched him leave, and then walked out onto the balcony. He slid the door shut behind him. He produced another phone from his pocket, one that had a singular use. He called the one number in it.

Four rings, and then a woman's German-accented voice answered. "Leave message."

"I am going to need to expand your contract, Marianne. I need our original agreement taken care of"—Bolt, dead—"and then two additional agreements. I'll quadruple your payment. I'll tell you when next we talk."

He hung up. He leaned against the railing. He had built all this. This high-rise condo, the second down the beach, the resort in the Keys, the timber. He'd built it because he'd been given so much by Morozov. He could not lose it now. He could not fail. Maria's and his baby was coming soon, and he had no intention of losing his fortune or his freedom because of a lying bitch who'd pretended to be his confidant and friend and a spoiled Russian thug.

As soon as Kirill called that he'd found Val, Illya would call Marianne and her team.

Maria called for him to come rub her feet. He walked toward the bedroom, pushing down panic.

It would all be okay. It had to be.

45

Kɪʀɪʟʟ ᴄᴀʟʟᴇᴅ Bᴏʙᴏ ᴡʜɪʟᴇ ᴅʀɪᴠɪɴɢ. "I need some assistance."

"What?"

He had to be very careful how to phrase this. "I think I saw someone I recognized near Amanda Bolt's job. In a car. A British operative. Do we have any pulse inside MI6 that can tell me if they've deployed a team after Bolt?"

"Why would they? He betrayed America."

"And gave us the names of at least four UK assets, all of whom met untimely and sudden ends," Kirill said. "They could want Bolt as much as we do."

"They would tell the Americans if they knew he was in Miami. They wouldn't mount their own operation on American soil."

He had to convince Bobo. "I'm sure of it. I need to know if you've got any source in British intel. I need to know what level of op they're mounting here."

"English spies running around Miami. This is not a James Bond movie. Although that one with Bond in Miami, I liked it."

"Bobo, do you want me to find Bolt before they do? Because they won't kill him." He steadied his voice. "They'll pick his brain, and they'll get him to talk. We can't have it."

"I don't know...I'm not sure any sources we have would know."

"Find out." He cleared his throat. "I'm suspicious of Valeria Garrison."

"Illya's aide."

"Yes. She's...acted oddly. You said she was vetted."

"Yes. The widow."

The widow. "Bobo. Did we have anything to do with her husband's death?"

"Of course not."

"He was helping Illya set up a network of accounts and shell companies, was he not?"

Kirill could hear the soft hiss of Bobo breathing. "Yes."

"Did we silence him?"

"It was an accident."

"That's what Val told me but is it the truth?" He steeled his voice. "Did we kill her husband?" Because... then there was her motivation. A long game of revenge, cozying up to the man who had pulled her husband into a global scheme to move and hide money, all for the entitlement of the inner circle around the president.

Bobo said nothing, and that was the answer.

"She knows, then."

"She could not have known."

"Why would you let her remain close to Illya?"

"He felt bad about her husband. He wanted to take care of her. I think...perhaps at one point he had feelings for her."

Oh, these fools, Kirill thought. Bobo and the Dude, both. They wielded enormous power in Russia, and they thought that made them smart and untouchable, and they had no idea how they could be brought down, by one man's carelessness. They thought they were invincible. It was odd, he'd been told he took too many risks, but these were the clowns dancing on the tightrope. They just didn't realize it. He forced his voice to sound calm. "Let us assume, Bobo, that she knows. Assume the worst, and Bolt's actions are opening up a chance for her to take revenge."

"Then maybe she's operating alone. Not supported by the British."

"I need to know." He nearly then told him that Val had Amanda Bolt. But he was afraid of what Bobo might do. Kirill could fix this.

"Fine. I'll find out. Your mother is here. She wants to speak to you."

Kirill wasn't sure he could bear to talk to her. But he had to.

"Darling," Sonia Timofeyevna said. She sounded exhausted, and his heart wrenched.

"Mama."

"Are you all right?"

How many operatives had to check in with their mothers? He took a deep breath. "I'll be fine. How are you?"

"I miss my son. I miss my husband. I want you both back."

"I'll find him, Mama." He was sure Bobo was listening.

"I believe in you."

It was like she was sending him out onto the football pitch, or off to take a difficult math test.

"You can do this, Kiryushenka."

"Mama…" He wanted to come home. He wanted to come home and sleep in his old bed and have Mama cook meatballs and *golubtsy* and potato pancakes and cherry cake. Childish, he told himself. Talking to Mama was making him weak. "I know I can. I will." He made his voice like steel. "Put Bobo back on."

"Here he is. I love you."

"I love you, too."

He waited. He heard Bobo say, "Yes?"

Kirill made his voice steel. "Find out what I asked you. You are not going to sit there and hold my mother's hand and act like her friend and then not give me what I need. You can put a team of SVR operatives on the next oligarch's flight to Miami and put them under my command. If you've already got resources on the ground in the States, then send them to Miami, or I call Morozov on his direct line, and yes, I have it, and I tell him you're holding back from hunting for Bolt. I need resources. If I need to kill every single person here who might even suspect Bolt is back, I will do that. I'm telling you the landscape here has changed and we have to act with force to get him back."

"Calm down, Kirill. You can't be a battering ram in America. You have to be a knife."

"Let's compromise. I'll be a machete." He hung up.

Kirill drove through the traffic to the Coral Gables house that Val had bought, seemingly on a whim, a lifetime ago.

There was a light on inside. He parked. He got out of the car.

The front door opened.

He saw Val standing there. She stepped out onto the lawn, showing him her empty hands. That meant nothing; she could have a weapon hidden in the small of her back. He wanted to talk to her before he went for his gun.

"Let's talk out here," she said.

"Who are you?" he said. "Why are you doing this?" Even though he suspected he knew the answer—he wanted to hear the words from her. He tried not to think of the taste of her skin, the slight grin on her face when she was riding him in the bed, her hands on his shoulders, the intelligence and daring in her eyes that he'd found instantly appealing.

"Look down, Kirill," she said.

He saw the red dot appear instantly on his jacket. A sniper. He glanced around—where were they hiding? The house's upper floors, or the roof.

A second dot appeared on his shoulder. He wondered if there were more, on his head, where he couldn't see.

She had a team here.

He raised his hands, in surrender, to show they were empty.

"I'm surprised you're here," he said.

"I knew you'd come, and I want to talk to you. Face-to-face. It wasn't a conversation for phones."

"Where's Amanda?" he asked.

"Safe." She walked toward him.

"And you'll use her to pull in her father. Which means you have a way to contact him."

"This isn't the part where I reveal all my secret plans, Kirill. I don't do monologues."

"I don't want to die because someone did something stupid to hurt you back in London. Surely we can deal."

"Put your hands up," she said. She frisked him thoroughly, as one little glowing red light stayed on him. She took his gun, and the knife at his ankle. She touched him with care, the way she had their single night together. He felt a fool.

She ordered him into the house, and she followed him through the door. Inside was a big man, military haircut, broad shoulders. He said nothing to Kirill.

Some furniture had been delivered. Chairs, a table. Tall lamps. Heavy curtains, to cover the windows.

Val gestured him toward a chair, and he sat.

"I'm here to deal," he said.

"Odd. You don't appear to be holding any cards," Val said.

"You have Amanda. She's not worth much if you don't have a means to contact her father. The fact that he's not here suggests he either doesn't want to fall into your trap or you haven't been able to reach him." He kept his voice steady. She had shaken him and he couldn't let her know that. "And my people could anonymously call the FBI and tell them you're holding an American citizen against her will, and they'll descend on you like hornets."

"First of all, are you sure it's against her will? She may have decided to cooperate once I explained what we were doing. Second, I give them your photo and name and that Illya helped you, and both of you will be in American prisons for a very long time. Or shipped home to Russia to face a disgrace I don't think you want to deal with." She raised one hand from the armchair, cupped it. "Rock." She raised her other hand, did the same. "Hard place." She clapped her hands together. "You."

"And you're running an illicit operation on American soil. They will look very badly on that."

"The diplomats will have a chat, and if we give the Americans what we learn from Bolt, forgiveness will come fast." She paused. "Do you think they'll forgive you, or your mother, back in Moscow?"

That made him pause and he made sure to steady his voice. "Why are you doing this?" he asked.

"I don't owe you an explanation."

"If we could work out a deal—let's say Bolt gives you information you want—and you give him back to me, then we each get what we want and we part ways, undamaged. And I can take him home to my mother, which might be the most terrifying punishment for him."

"Information I want? Like the financial map."

He wished he could dial back the past two days and start over. Wished he'd kept his mouth shut and stayed alone in his bed. "I know Illya's been moving money around to mitigate the losses if Bolt talks."

"Oh, sure he has." She shook her head and smiled.

"He's going to be very upset with you."

"He already was. Did you know he's hired a German contract killer to eliminate Bolt, even with you looking for him? Of course, that was before he knew you were hunting Bolt—but he didn't call her off. He hired them in a panic. And I suspect he wants more than Bolt dead. Like, anyone who could talk about the map. That's you and me now. We're his loose ends, Kirill."

"He wouldn't dare."

"Of course he would dare. A man protecting billions in wealth dares anything. That's why the deal right now between us isn't about Bolt so much as it's about you."

His gaze flickered to the big man, standing in silence. "What, are you going to kill me right now? I came here in good faith."

"No, Kirill, I'm not going to kill you. I'm going to offer you a job."

He watched her, to see if she was joking. "Why?"

"Because I don't think Russia is going to be safe for you to return. There's going to be a scapegoat for this. It might be your friend Bobo. It might be your mother— yes, I know about her. A former Miss Russia with two husbands in intel work is hard to keep a secret. I think I would like her. But I'm terrified that the scapegoat is going to be you. You're young, you're expendable, and unlike Bobo and Duderov and the rest of the circle, you have no power. If you don't bring back or eliminate Bolt, they'll say you failed because he's your stepfather. That you let your emotions get in the way. That you were try- ing to spare his life to satisfy your mother."

"None of that is true. They know me and they know—"

"Kirill, please don't be naive. The good life you had in Russia is over because of this. I can see it, but you can't. I can have you on a plane to London in less than an hour and we can offer you a better life than what you can expect in Russia."

Kirill's hands gripped the chair. "You want me to be like Bolt. A traitor."

"I want you to live."

Kirill couldn't speak.

"Would you wait outside, please," she said to the guard. He gave her a cautionary look but stepped out and closed the door.

Kirill found his voice. "You want me to live. Because you care. You're a whore who slept with me to get me to lower my defenses."

"Why am I the whore and not you?" she said. "I slept with you because I wanted you. Because I actually like you."

He shook his head. "You're still playing me."

She gave him a slight smile. "I didn't *have* to do it. You were already trusting me, relying on me." She gave him an enigmatic smile. "You remind me of a very good man I once knew. At one time he was my closest friend. A basically good guy caught up in a very complicated, shades-of-gray world where good people sometimes make compromising choices."

"Your husband?"

"No. Someone I knew before." She pulled slightly at her lip. "You're kind of the Russian version of my friend."

He didn't care about her friend. He had to somehow find out where Amanda was. "If that's your motive for you causing all this carnage, we didn't kill your husband."

"*You* didn't kill my husband, Kirill, yes, that I know." She raised an eyebrow. "Or did you? Did they send you to London to drive the car? They send you where the difficult jobs are. Maybe that was a harder one that it looked. Snuffing out a defenseless man's life."

"Russia didn't do that." He shook his head. It was his duty to lie but he knew she would see through his denial. Damn Bobo and Illya for killing her husband. They had awakened a demon in this woman, hungry for revenge.

"Consider my offer. We'll take good care of you, Kirill."

"We took good care of Bolt and look where that got us." He felt sweat trickle down his back. This was his situation: being offered defection, because it was now a legitimate choice for him. He'd boarded Illya's plane confident and sure that he could find his stepfather and handle him. Now this. He steadied his voice. "People pretended to be Markus's friend. But no one likes a traitor. No one ever trusts him. He's shown you what he is."

"What you will be is what you decide to be. Markus betrayed a democracy; you're saving yourself from a country run like a criminal ring."

"That's not us," he said. "That's not true."

"You don't even believe that. That's my offer. You could join us right now. I think if you keep working this, your own country will kill you."

"No, thank you." The shame of it. What would Mama say? He could not imagine abandoning her to the tender mercies of the circle if he failed. They would take their revenge on her.

"We could get your mother out as well," Val said. "I'd do that for you."

"You couldn't." He thought, *Just get up and walk out. Stop listening to her.*

"We tell her that we need her here, to talk to Markus, she'd come."

"The Americans won't let her into the country."

"I can get her a UK passport under a new name and we can get her here. I swear it to you. All you have to say is yes, Kirill." She leaned forward. "Have a life and be free of these people."

He could hear the tremble in his own voice and fought it down. "They'd destroy me, and they'll destroy you. Do you know what it is to have a billionaire want you dead? The money they can spend on their vengeance is endless. If someone fails, send another. They only have to get it right one time." He shook his head. "Do you think they will not all be coming after you now, Val, or whatever your name is? Illya, especially? It's no way to live."

"My offer stands if you change your mind. But know once we have Bolt, we're not staying for you. We're not helping your mother. We move on. Don't get left behind, Kirill."

He stood. He could kill her right now. Her team would kill him in return but he could make her pay for the betrayal, for the ridiculous pain he felt, before he died.

"You could try," she said softly. "Others have."

Kirill Antonov turned and walked out into the dark Miami night.

46

<hr/>

Sᴀᴍ ᴡᴇɴᴛ ᴏᴠᴇʀ ᴛʜᴇ ʙᴀᴄᴋ fence. He heard Marianne yelling. He heard another shot. She'd had another gun on her.

He ran through the back neighbor's yard, through the gate, to the next street. Through another yard, over another fence, this one with a loudly barking dog. He covered the yard in seconds, the dog furious and chasing him, and then went over another fence, into a vacant lot where a foundation was being poured. He stumbled to the next street.

Karen had taken the car. And the police would be asking questions if Marianne's trainees managed to hit Gandy and left him for dead, or if someone in the neighborhood heard and reported the muffled gunfire.

He couldn't stay on the streets—the pair might be roaming the neighborhood, looking for him, to introduce him to a bullet.

Sam slunk through the neighborhood, putting seven streets between him and the Cortez house. Calling a rideshare meant staying in one spot, and he wasn't willing to stand on a residential street corner and wait out in the open, or put an innocent driver at risk. He also was unwilling to put Paige in danger by driving over here to pick him up.

He'd gone from hunter to hunted with one mis-step. He should have called for reinforcements, and he shouldn't have taken Karen to the house. And now if Gandy was dead...

But killing Dennis Gandy in the street wasn't going to get them Markus Bolt. Marianne and crew needed Gandy alive to talk, and so did he.

But Paige had gotten him Gandy's cell phone number. He tried it.

Four rings. Then an answer, a voice, panicked, clearly driving because Sam could hear the rush of the wind. Maybe he had a car window down. Or maybe it was shot out.

"What do you want?"

"Dennis. There are bad people after you."

"I know that."

"I'm very much against the bad people."

"Who is this?"

"My name doesn't matter. The woman and her team who are chasing you—wait, are they still chasing you?"

"Yes! Yes! Who is this?"

"I'm the guy they were holding at gunpoint when you walked in. I'm the guy who saved you with a warning. I'm Amanda's neighbor..."

"Oh," Dennis Gandy said. "I see you." And Sam turned and a car was barreling down the street, headed for him, Gandy's grim face behind the wheel, and then another car following.

Gandy zoomed past him. The car with Marianne's team shot past Sam as he took cover behind a minivan parked in front of a house. Then their car stopped.

And Sam thought: absolute stupidity, because Gandy had to be more important to them than bagging Sam. If they were making a mistake, he needed to seize the moment.

Sam charged at them.

The passenger side opened, the soldier rising, confident and sure, smirking now, aiming, and Sam leaped into him before he had his arm up, feet first, slamming him back into the V formed by the door and the body of the car. He slammed the soldier's head against the roof and shoved him aside, pulling the gun from his hand.

But then he realized the man had been shot.

From the driver's seat, the Scottish woman had fired at Sam, but hit the soldier in the side and he went down. Sam fired back at her but the clip jammed, so he slammed a punch into her head as she fired again past his head, deafening him. He shoved her out the driver's door onto the road. He revved their car forward and then the control console began pinging, because the key fob wasn't in proximity. In her pocket, presumably.

He stopped the car and then he saw that Gandy had stopped, half a block up, watching.

And then backing up. Sam slammed into reverse, putting distance between the pair and Gandy, watching the wounded soldier stagger around, kneel by the stunned woman, pull the key fob from her pocket.

Gandy got out of the car. He moved with assurance, a man on a mission.

Sam got out of the car.

"I can help you," Sam yelled. "I can—"

And then Gandy had a gun out, and he fired at the soldier, who dropped, and then he fired at the Scot, who jerked, her shoulder hit, and then he swung the gun toward Sam, who had retreated into the car.

"You," he said in that odd, reedy voice. "The neighbor."

And he took that step forward to be sure of his shot.

Sam drove backward, the bullets hitting the windshield, Gandy standing straight and emptying the clip and then racing back to his car.

All gone wrong. All gone horribly wrong. Two bodies in the street, maybe one dead, maybe he'd been spotted, his abandoned rental back on the street.

No choice. He headed back to Carlos Cortez's house.

If Gandy had been setting it up as a safe house for Bolt, it might contain information on where Bolt was now. Or a clue as to who else was helping him.

He pulled up to the house. His car was still there, unmarked by bullets... Karen had come back for him. He had told her not to, but she had.

No neighbors standing in yards, gossiping about gunshots seven streets over or any odd noises made ten minutes earlier.

He parked and got out carefully, because Marianne might still be in the house.

He crept through the open front door. He heard Karen's voice: "Where is my daughter?"

Marianne: "I told you, I don't know."

Sam stepped into the den. Karen was holding a gun on Marianne, who was sitting in a large chair.

"Sam."

"Karen, would you go to the front of the house and let me know if the cops arrive?"

"I don't think anyone called them," Karen said. "They had suppressors on their guns."

"I need to talk to her."

"And I need to know where Amanda is."

"I don't think she knows. Please."

Karen gave Marianne a poisonous look, then handed him the gun and went to the front of the house.

"Someone shot at me as I went over the fence. You missed."

"I was only trying to wing you."

"Your protégés left you behind. They didn't look trustworthy."

"I *vetted* them."

"The guy's dead and the woman's wounded. I stole their car."

Marianne's lips thinned.

"I didn't shoot them. Gandy did."

"Gandy."

He could see she didn't believe him. "If I'd killed or wounded them, I wouldn't be here bragging about it to you. Now. Listen to me, Marianne. I think Gandy might be more than a Bolt-obsessed computer geek. Who briefed you on the situation you were entering?"

She said nothing.

"If it was the client, I would suggest you abandon your contract. Because they're either not aware of what you're up against or they're not being honest with you."

Her phone started to ring.

Sam said, "That's probably Scotland calling. She took a hit in the shoulder."

He could hear sirens rising, a few streets over. Of course. A body had been left in the street.

Marianne said in a tight voice, "May I answer the phone?"

"No. I realize you're restarting your business, but you chose poorly with those two. Overconfident and brash."

"They reminded me of you and your old partner. The Moldovan."

"She's not my partner. I haven't seen her in ten years. Karen!" he called.

Karen appeared in the doorway.

"I need to search the house. They might have planned to bring Amanda here." He handed her the gun. "Watch her."

Karen nodded.

He made his search quickly. The sirens in the distance

were not getting louder but more numerous. First the bedrooms. Locks on the doors, so someone presumably could be secured within. Locks on the windows. No telltale extra clothes, though, the closets were mostly empty, with extra clothes from Carlos Cortez.

Nothing unusual. Except in the upstairs bedroom, on the bureau, there was a stack of books for teenagers, fantasy and science fiction novels. He recognized one as a book Daniel had read for a class last year. He went to the stack, looked at the titles.

An odd choice if for the safe house, Sam thought. Then he remembered Amanda's poolside reading. A thick fantasy novel. Were these books for her? Had they intended to bring her here?

He went back to the den. Marianne's phone was ringing again.

"Who's your client? Let's keep this civilized. I don't want to hurt you, but I will, and you know it."

Marianne sighed. She said, "A private Russian citizen."

"Who?"

"I don't know his name. One phone call, the rest was handled via secured text and e-mail. And payment through a numbered account."

Any number of private Russian citizens in the elite circle might want Bolt dead.

"I have worked for Russians before, so it would not be hard for one of them to be able to reach me." She shrugged. "But sorry, I don't have a name."

"Your team is down. Go home."

"But I need the money, Sam." She looked at Karen. "Don't you want your ex dead, Mrs. Bolt? For you, for your son?"

"I don't need my son discussed by a contract killer," Karen said.

Marianne was unfazed. "Don't you want him dead before he reaches your daughter?"

"You said you didn't know where he was or she was," Sam said.

"I don't, but I can help you find them. What are you going to do with me, Sam, call the police? You don't want attention to your little fixer operation here."

"I could kill you and dump the body in the bay."

Her insouciance vanished. "I know things."

"But not anything useful to us. Like your client's name. Stand up."

She did, and he bound her hands with the zip ties. "Where will your Scottish lass go, being hurt?"

"I've no idea."

"Wrong. You always have a rendezvous point if things go wrong. And if someone needs medical attention, you've got a resource ready."

Marianne said nothing. Sam called Woodruff. "I need a detention hold for a prisoner. It's at Grayson Cortez's son's house." He gave him the address. "It's Marianne. One of her team is dead and the other is wounded and running. She's been hired by a Russian citizen to eliminate Bolt. She says not the Russian government." He gave a fast status update.

"Grayson Cortez," Woodruff said slowly. "I know who he is. He's an intel asset I can activate in Miami. He's a good interrogator. We'd have her talk to him."

"What if his son is wrapped up in this?"

"Carlos is out of town for extended periods," Karen said. "I think Dennis is using the house because he knows this."

"That's Karen Bolt yelling at me?" Woodruff asked.

"Yes."

"I promise you Cortez will help you. He knows his duty to this country. Report in later."

Sam could circumvent Woodruff. He could call the FBI. But that would explode everything; he'd be done in the intel world. Over and done.

He looked at Marianne. She looked at him. His choices were nonexistent.

"Karen, will you call Cortez for me, please?"

47

<hr/>

Austin

IT FELT VERY, VERY REAL to Daniel when they got on the plane.

Weirdly, Aunt Clarice took his hand again as they walked toward the plane. He let her. What would Dad do when they got there and he saw Daniel standing with his aunt? He might ground Daniel, like, forever. Or worse—he would give him that look that said, *I am so disappointed in you.*

But Dad...Dad had disappointed *him.* Could it not go both ways? He stepped away from Clarice and she let go of his hand.

Uncle Mark went aboard and then he was followed by two pilots, who had been doing something outside the plane. Uncle Mark spoke to them in a very low voice, practically a whisper. The pilots glanced for a moment at Daniel.

"Are your clients, like, millionaires?" Daniel asked Uncle Mark.

"Several times over," Uncle Mark said. "I help some very wealthy people manage their money."

"Oh." That sounded like the kind of normal dad job he thought Dad should have. Maybe Uncle Mark could give Dad a job, once Dad calmed down.

They went aboard the plane. It was so cool and Daniel tried not to show how impressed he was. "Sit, Daniel." Clarice gestured to a plush leather seat. He sat. He automatically buckled into his seat, as if he were on a commercial flight. Clarice opened him a bottled water from the bar and handed it to him. He still had the dry, slightly off taste from the lemonade in his mouth.

"Are you all right?" Clarice asked him.

"Yes. What did Nana say?"

"We played a little trick on Leonie," she said. "Don't be mad. I texted her as your grandmother. So she thinks you're at Nana's, and Nana thinks you're with her. That way they won't get in trouble with your dad."

He stared at her.

"I'm being honest with you about what I've done," Clarice said. "I think there have been enough secrets, don't you?"

She glanced at Uncle Mark, who was studying Daniel intently.

"Maybe I should call Dad," Daniel said. "I don't want him to worry." He was starting to panic.

The plane's engines powered up. It started to move.

Daniel nearly got out of the seat then. But the door was closed and the plane was moving. He told himself to calm down. It was a white lie, wasn't it? Dad would understand. And Dad would have to explain himself.

"Listen to me," Clarice said. "Your father will not be mad at you, or at me. When we tell him . . . it'll be best if you're there, too, so he knows you know more about your mom than he's ever told you. We can have a real conversation. I know you love him. I can tell he's been a good father to you, because you're a great kid."

"A stellar kid," Uncle Mark said.

"Okay," Daniel said after a moment. "When I see Dad, we can sort this all out." But his throat felt dry.

Uncle Mark was still staring at him. His breath had gotten heavier and he seemed to force a smile to his face. And he seemed to sense Daniel's simmering panic. "May I show you something?" He tapped on an iPad, moved his finger around, opened a picture, and filled the screen with it. He handed it to Daniel.

It was a picture of Uncle Mark—younger, but clearly him—and his mother, sitting next to each other on a park bench. She was noticeably pregnant, eating an ice cream cone, a book on her lap. The photo was slightly crooked, as though taken on a phone at an angle.

"That's the last picture of her and me together," Uncle Mark said. "We met in a park in London when I had a business trip there. She's pregnant with you. See how happy she was? She's smiling."

It wasn't much of a smile, and maybe what she was happy about was the ice cream. That's what Daniel thought but he decided not to suggest that. She wasn't looking at Uncle Mark. The picture made him feel better; there were all those pictures of Mom with Aunt Clarice, no reason to fake those, and now one of her with Uncle Mark.

"My dad's not in the picture," he said.

"She didn't tell your dad she was meeting me. He wouldn't have approved."

"Why?"

"He wanted her to himself. He didn't like us, as a family." Uncle Mark shrugged. "He could be a little possessive about her. I'm sure it was just because he loved her so much."

It made Dad sound like a bad husband. "I'm sure he had a reason," Daniel said, because he felt he must say something in Dad's defense.

He looked at the picture again, his finger tracing his mother's face.

"You look like her," Uncle Mark said. "You're a handsome kid."

Daniel blushed furiously. He glanced up and Uncle Mark was still studying his face. The plane had risen and now evened out from its ascent, and he couldn't undo any of this now. They were going to Miami. He was going to miss school tomorrow and the tournament this weekend and Leonie and Nana would be so mad at him.

Well, they shouldn't have kept all these secrets. He wasn't the one who had created this situation. That thought made him feel a little better. He looked at Uncle Mark; Aunt Clarice had closed her eyes and was taking deep, calming breaths.

"Where do you live?" Daniel asked.

"Mostly London and Florida. I have a home in Moscow; I have a number of Russian clients."

"Is it a Russian client whose plane this is?"

"Yes. How did you know?" His smile twitched.

"It sounded like you spoke Russian to the pilot."

"How did you know that?" The crooked smile returned.

"I know a few words. My dad taught me."

"And how does your dad know Russian?" A very slight edge in his voice, but his smile had turned friendly.

"I don't know, he travels a lot. He owns, like, thirty bars. I don't remember if he owns one in Moscow or not."

"Clarice said you got good grades and play basketball. Smart, handsome, athletic, you're just a little golden boy, aren't you?" But he said it with a smile.

"No. I'm just me."

"I admire your modesty about your accomplishments."

Uncle Mark, Daniel decided, was a little strange. But this had been the weirdest day of his life, so whatever.

"Do you have kids?" Daniel asked him.

Uncle Mark seemed not to hear. He said nothing; he didn't react. Then his mouth crooked back into his odd smile. "Kids. Yes. I have two. A daughter and a son. They're quite a bit older than you; they're grown."

"So they are my mom's cousins."

"And your cousins as well."

"Are they in Florida?"

"My daughter is."

"What's her name?"

He hesitated before he answered. "Amanda."

Another relative he didn't know about. "Will I get to meet her?"

"If we can convince your dad to let you know your family."

Daniel sipped from the water bottle Clarice had handed him. He felt very tired. It had hit him all at once. "Uncle Mark?"

"Yes, Daniel?"

"I'm glad . . . I'm glad you and Aunt Clarice talked to me. I want to know my mom."

"She loved you so much. She told me that on that bench. Her hand on the swell of her pregnancy. 'I love him already,' she said."

This was not something Daniel had heard much before, from anyone other than Dad. It made Mom more real. Her own uncle.

He took another sip of the water and then the heaviness fell over his eyes and the bottle slipped from his hand.

Markus Bolt caught it before it hit the floor.

48

Miami

Lᴇᴛ ᴍᴇ ɢᴇᴛ ᴛʜɪꜱ ꜱᴛʀᴀɪɢʜᴛ," Grayson Cortez said. "You've taken over my son's house, and you have a hired killer as a prisoner in it."

"Yes," Sam said. Cortez listened as Sam and Karen described the evening's events. Cortez took a deep breath. "So you've committed felonies, witnessed a murder, and have one hired killer wounded and on the run, and you think this woman has the information that could find us Bolt."

"Again, great command of the situation," Sam said. "You're an interrogator. Interrogate her."

"I am no longer one and I have no oversight here. And this is my son's house!"

"Take that up with your son and his choice of friends. In fact, we should talk with your son, because if he was letting Gandy use this as a place to hide Bolt, he may know where any backup safe house is. On the other hand, I am empowered to charge you with the responsibilities and protections of being an operative of the Federal Intelligence Analysis Office."

"I don't even know what that is."

"Section K. The fixers," Karen said. "The cleaners of messes. This qualifies, Grayson."

"I cannot be involved in this," Grayson Cortez said.

"Grayson," Sam said, "your son may be entirely innocent, or he may be involved in this deeper than we know. Dennis Gandy killed someone today. Your son may have given him comfort and support in this operation."

"He would not!"

"But he could have. It could be argued. Now maybe if this all breaks open, and you've helped us, the authorities will realize your son was not really involved."

"You're a damn extortionist."

"He's a fixer," Karen said. "Talk to her, Grayson. It could disentangle your son."

"And your son, if he knows where else Gandy might hide Bolt—we need to know that, Grayson."

"I'll talk to him now."

"And I'll listen," Sam said.

Grayson called his son. He got Carlos's voice mail and asked him to call back immediately. "He's in Argentina, Peru, and Brazil on a banking trip. He's gone for at least two weeks. Gandy must have taken advantage of his absence."

"I hope so," Sam said. "But we need to talk to him, Grayson."

"And what about this hired killer? Who I am supposed to interrogate?"

"Don't worry. I'll be there to protect you."

Cortez made a noise in his throat. "I don't need your protection. She's restrained?"

"Yes, with zip ties."

"Grayson. The government isn't going to press charges if we can find Markus. This is the biggest moment of your career," Karen said. "Step up to it. For me, for yourself, for your son. For Amanda. Maybe this woman knows where she's being kept."

He glanced at her. "Fine."

Sam had moved Marianne to one of the upstairs bedrooms. "A man's going to ask you some questions," he said. "And then you'll be turned over to the authorities."

He eased her back into a chair. "Marianne, I will tell them you cooperated, and it will carry weight. You haven't killed anyone since you've been here, have you?"

"No," she said.

"What we care about is Bolt and your Russian client. Deals can be made. I'll help you."

She stared down at the floor. "Fine."

Grayson Cortez entered the room. "Sam. If you'll wait outside."

"Are you going to torture me?" Marianne asked, almost conversationally.

"Good lord, of course not," Cortez said. "We're just going to have a talk. Sam, privacy, please."

Sam stepped outside. He stayed close to the door, like a kid listening at the keyhole.

"I think we can make this simple," he heard Cortez said. "Who's your client?"

"He's Russian. I told Sam this already. I don't know more than that."

"What area code was the phone they used?"

"Miami, but that means nothing."

"What do you know about Dennis Gandy?"

She let a few seconds tick by. "He knew Bolt in childhood. He is obsessed with the case."

"What clsc?"

"We knew he would be a possible contact for Bolt. More likely than his daughter. She would call the FBI," Marianne said.

"What else do you know about Gandy?"

"He's a software programmer. He lives in Atlanta. But he spends a lot of time here."

"You seemed to have gathered this profile rather quickly since Bolt's departure."

"It was what I was given by the client. I gathered nothing. But it was apparently correct. Gandy must be quite a bit more than a software geek if he killed one of my people."

Sam heard a noise downstairs. Sobbing. He went down the stairs and found Karen trembling, crying. She'd been holding in her emotions and now they were getting released.

"I need to know that she's okay," Karen said.

Sam sat next to her. "Do you think Bolt would hurt her?"

"Not physically. Emotionally. She's been through so much. She finally got to a good place. And what helped her move forward was the idea she'd never have to see him or talk to him again. Now this, and whatever's happening with Roberto..."

"Which I think is more Roberto's problem than hers. He's involved with bad people, Tara said, so she knows about it. Maybe she's their watcher to be sure he behaves. Either he's using the courier service to move illicit goods under cover of regular deliveries, or he's cleaning money. And Amanda doesn't know about it."

Karen took a deep breath. "My poor girl."

"Is there anything else I should know so we can find her?" Sam asked.

Karen shook her head. "Why is Markus causing all this chaos now? Why? If I had only stopped him years ago..."

He saw guilt cloud her face.

"Karen," he said. "You know none of this is your fault."

She didn't look at him.

"It's not your fault."

"If I had just seen what he was capable of back then . . . my son would still be alive. And my daughter wouldn't be in danger now."

Sam took her hand, and she let him, and she squeezed his fingers hard.

"It's not your fault," he said again. "He alone is responsible for how he deceived you, how he deceived the Agency. How he deceived your children."

The lights went out.

Sam stood up in the darkness.

"Behind the couch," he said to her, and he saw, in the faint gleam of moonlight from the window, a man charging in for them and Sam parried his fist, slammed a punch into the man's rib cage. He stumbled but kept charging and tackled Sam, knocking over the couch. Karen cried out. The man landed a hard punch across Sam's jaw that stunned him.

Then grabbed him and started squeezing his throat. Strangling him.

Sam slammed a knee into the man's groin, gouged an eye, and the man cursed in Russian, and then Sam heard another voice, saying in Russian to move out of the way.

Sam saw, in the moonlight from the window, three more men rushing into the room. One of the men raised his hand, aiming at Sam, and Sam saw a weapon. He felt the Taser needles pierce him and then the electricity hit him like a wave, and he writhed on the ground. Karen had time for a brief scream and then Sam didn't hear her anymore. He tried to focus in the darkness and then he saw one of the men check a syringe against a suddenly bright flashlight. The two men held him down and he felt the slide of the needle and he knew nothing more.

PART FOUR

49

Miami

Sᴀᴍ ᴏᴘᴇɴᴇᴅ ʜɪs ᴇʏᴇs. Hɪs whole body ached. Morning light crept through the closed blinds. He lay on the floor of the living room, but he was bound, with zip ties, his hands in front of him. His ankles were bound together. Lying next to him was Karen, bound the same, still unconscious.

He crawled into the kitchen, managed to get on his knees, and pulled out a silverware drawer. He found a steak knife and sliced through the bonds lacing his ankles together. Then, carefully, he twisted the knife and slowly cut the ties holding his wrists together. He managed to stand, the feeling rushing back into his hands. He took the knife and he cut Karen's bonds. She was still out. He checked her; her pulse was steady and she appeared uninjured.

He searched the ground floor. The back door lock had been picked; he'd been careless not to hear the intrusion. There wasn't damage elsewhere on the first floor; they'd even put the couch back into place.

But he'd heard them speak Russian.

Why didn't they kill us?

He went upstairs to the room where Marianne had been questioned. The door was open. Cortez lay bound as well on the floor, still breathing. Sam cut his bonds. The sleeve of his shirt had been torn free and there was a piece of paper taped to his arm. It read, in English:

> Do not pursue this matter further.
> Your target is being handled.
> It is our problem. No longer yours.
> For your own safety and our mutual respect.

Marianne was gone. Of course she was. They had come here to free her. The wounded Scotswoman must have contacted the Russian client. They had moved faster than he thought they would be able to deploy an intel team on American soil.

"Grayson?" He patted the man's cheek.

Slowly Cortez opened his eyes. "Sam? What?"

"We were attacked. They took Marianne."

Cortez took several deep, steadying breaths. "We're not dead...because of the press it would generate. Bolt's redefection, or whatever you want to call it, that story hasn't broken or leaked yet. If they leave three people dead, including Bolt's first wife and a former intel official, the story blows up. The connections back to him are immediate. Bolt is back in the news and then they're trying to explain where he is. It makes a leak far more likely. They want this handled in silence, same as us. Because they're scared."

"They have an intel squad already here."

Cortez shook his head. "I don't think so, Sam." His voice was still thick with the narcotic. "I saw them... they were in suits. They sedated us both and I heard them talking—I think they were not military or intel. I think they are private security. Russian, yes, but brought over here with the elites. They're the bodyguards of the rich guys in Sunny Isles."

"Called together to do this?"

"Yes. Or ordered. If Marianne had a wealthy client, it could be his team, and maybe some borrowed from his friends."

"But very dangerous. They committed multiple felonies."

"These guys are well paid, and if they were in danger of arrest, the Russians would fly them out."

"I wonder if Marianne is still alive," Sam said.

"They risked a lot to save a mercenary."

"Or they didn't want her talking," Sam said. "Her odds might not be good right now. Shame, with her just back from the dead." *Or*, he thought, *there was something else here they wanted. Something we hadn't found.*

Cortez rubbed his wrists. "I try to pay attention to which Russians are spending the most time here. In case the government wants to try and recruit one as an informant. But I didn't recognize any of those guys."

"There must be files on these guys."

"Possibly," Cortez said. "On the elites, yes, but they change their security teams, move them around."

It was the wrong answer. Of course there were files on the elites. But the intel world would have information on the men and women who worked for them as well.

Are you lying to me? Sam thought. *Why would you?*

Cortez got unsteadily to his feet. "Karen..."

"Downstairs, unconscious, but all right."

"I don't think they'll be back," Cortez said. Sam showed him the note.

"How polite," Cortez said. "No mention of Marianne."

"They're protecting their hunt of Bolt. Which means they want to take him alive. There's a reason for that, that it's not kill on sight. He knows something or he has something they want back."

Cortez said nothing. "They wouldn't have trusted him with any secrets."

"Then he stole some. He used his skills over there and got something valuable."

"And why would he come back then? The Russians are after him, and Gandy is helping him, it seems."

Karen came up the stairs to the bedroom, groggy, blinking at them. She grabbed Sam's arm. "What happened?"

"They knocked us out and took Marianne. So either they've taken the operation over or they're freeing her to work for them. Or eliminating her as a loose end."

"I…I…" Karen blinked at Sam again, glanced at Cortez. "Did Marianne tell you anything useful?"

"No," Cortez said after a moment. "I tried to convince her she could make a deal with me, but she didn't buy it."

"Let's think it out," Sam said. "Her Scottish partner called the Russians and told them where she was—or her doctor did. She needed medical attention. The doctor that Marianne would have directed them to in case of need must be Russian. Maybe tied to the client. They'd need to be a resident here; they might not need a license to practice here if they're strictly black-market support. They would call the Russians if the Scot didn't."

"And call which Russian? Did the Scot know who the client was? The doctor must have," Karen said.

"This is all interesting conjecture," Cortez said. "But it doesn't get us Bolt. We've got to find him faster than they do."

"I've asked for more resources," Sam said.

Cortez looked at Sam. "I'm going to need you all to clear out from here. This is putting my son at risk when he returns."

"Your son needs to tell us where else Gandy might be."

"I'll talk to him, but I don't think Gandy asked Carlos if he could stash a traitor here."

"Then find where that could be."

Cortez's lip thinned. "I'll see what I can find out."

"Gandy. He's not just some programmer. I saw him shoot two people. He's either a dangerous sociopath or he's trained."

"He's not Agency; he hates the Agency."

"His father stole money."

"He doesn't believe that," Cortez said. "His father... his father told Dennis that Bolt was framed."

"That's where this obsession comes from?"

"Yes. The Agency believes that Bill Gandy's embezzlement over time was made easier by Bolt helping Bill cover up his theft. They looked out for each other. When Bolt defected, Bill Gandy was at risk of discovery. He killed himself." Cortez coughed. "But Dennis has always believed his father's rather self-serving lie. And if Bolt was innocent..."

"Then Dennis could believe his own father was innocent. That's why this matters so much to him." A son destroyed by his parent's betrayal. Dennis had turned into a conspiracy nut and murderer. Allan had killed himself. Amanda had been drawn to a criminal. Daniel...no. Daniel would never be this way.

"So Dennis might have reached out to Bolt or been in touch with him."

"Yeah. Markus must have recruited him from Russia, fed his paranoia. Genius, actually."

Sam wondered, for a moment, if Cortez didn't want him to find Bolt. Gandy, Karen, Amanda, Allan, the Cortez family—they'd all known each other back in their old neighborhood. Friendships, entangled with professional relationships.

"I'm going to find Karen a safe space to stay," Sam said. "I don't think there's much else we can do here." He glanced over at the bureau. The books he'd noticed before. The Russians had left them. They just seemed an oddity here if this was to be Bolt's hiding place. An unanswered question.

He went back to the stack.

"Sam, what is it?" Karen asked.

Before he had just picked them up without opening them. Now he paged through them, wondering if something had been hidden inside them. Nothing. Except there on the title page.

Handwritten, in a tight, dense hand.

Daniel—I hope these bring you comfort. Don't be scared. It will all be okay.

A lance of ice went through his heart. He closed the book.

"Sam?" Cortez said.

His phone. It wasn't in his pocket. He ran down the stairs. In the mess of the room, he spotted it, lying screen down on the floor.

A text, sent an hour ago: I have your son. Tell no one. You will bring Amanda to me.

50

⚬⚬⚬⚬

SAM STARED AT THE SCREEN. A number he didn't recognize. Karen and Cortez came down the stairs. He realized he could not let them see—he could not let Karen know he was to trade her daughter for his son.

He saw there was an earlier text from Leonie, about Daniel staying with his parents. He put the phone in his pocket.

He still had the inscribed book in his other hand.

"Bolt...likes these books. It was in a profile that was shared with me. We had a record of his Russian wife ordering them from a British bookstore. Minor detail but reinforcing he was to be brought here." The lie was so easy.

"Are you all right?" Karen asked.

"Yes," Sam said.

"You have a black eye, by the way," Karen said.

"I'm fine. Grayson, find out what you can on Gandy's possible locale. Karen—I have a place you can stay." He could put her at the safe apartment above his bar, for now. "We can regroup there and hopefully figure out where he's taken Amanda."

"Sure," Karen said.

They got into Sam's car, Karen driving because she had the keys from earlier. She drove back to Grayson's house, where Grayson went inside and Sam gave her directions to the bar. Karen gave Sam his keys and got in her car and headed out.

Alone in his car, he tried to call Daniel. No answer. It might not be true. Leonie would have called him.

He called Leonie. He kept his voice calm. "Hey. Just checking in."

"Oh, we've had some drama. The boys aren't getting along. So Daniel decided to go to your parents'. I guess your mom hasn't called you yet."

A thin reed of hope. "She hasn't, but she knows I keep weird hours. Are you all okay?" He had a sudden thought that maybe Leonie had been threatened.

"We're fine."

"Okay, let's talk later." He hung up and called his mother. She answered on the third ring.

"Hi, Sam, how are you?"

"Great, how's Daniel?"

"Uh, I guess he's fine. We haven't seen him since he's been at Leonie's but I talked to him."

"Oh," Sam said, his stomach sinking. "Oh, okay. Mom, I think I'm going to have him fly out here." He had to avoid his mother and Leonie realizing Daniel was missing and calling the police. *Tell no one.* "Just so he and I can have some time together. I'll talk to his teachers about it."

"Oh, all right." He forced himself to stay calm while Simone gave him an update on his father's condition— physically, doing better, but to her annoyance, he kept bringing up topics from the past that Simone felt were best left forgotten. Their marriage had not always been happy. Sam knew this; sometimes his parents had strayed, but they always stayed together. Still, it wasn't a history Sam wanted Daniel to know. He opened his laptop to send Leonie a text, telling her the same—that Daniel would be joining him in Miami, it would be a good break for him, and Sam would coordinate with his teachers. He told his mom he loved her and hung up.

Then he let out such a primal scream that he was sure Grayson heard it in the house. But the man didn't come out to the front door.

There. Done. Put that all aside, in the back corner of his brain, and focus on what he needed to do to get his son back.

Somehow—Bolt had Daniel. Sam wondered if Bolt and his helpers were familiar with the history of those who had kidnapped Daniel as an infant. It had not gone at all well for them. But Sam was older and operating alone, and another life was at stake. He could not just hand Amanda over to them.

There had to be another solution.

He summoned up the file on Bolt that Woodruff had given him. There was a sample of his handwriting there. Sam studied it. It wasn't the handwriting in the book. But it seemed familiar to him. He couldn't place it.

If he told Woodruff they had Daniel, Woodruff would immediately yank him off the assignment, and there was no time for another operative to come in. And they might not make Daniel the priority. He couldn't let Woodruff know.

This was father to father, a problem he alone had to fix.

He texted Daniel, knowing they would see it. I love you. I'll see you soon.

Then he took a deep breath. He didn't know who had Amanda. But maybe Sam could lure him out and end him without involving her.

He texted a reply to the demand: If you harm him, I'll kill you. Tell me where and when to meet.

He waited for an answer. Nothing.

Somehow that was worse.

He sped toward the bar.

51

Paige wasn't at Amado, and she wasn't upstairs. She might still be at home. He texted her: Can you help me? 911 level emergency.

He closed his eyes. Think.

Bolt had Daniel and was demanding Amanda.

The Russians (or someone) had Amanda and would use her to draw in Bolt.

If the Russians got him first, Daniel was useless to them. They might kill him. Or use him as bait to seize and silence Sam, to ensure he didn't recapture Bolt.

He could not fail.

On the bar camera he saw Karen enter, holding an overnight bag, and he went downstairs and brought her up to the apartment. "There's a bedroom through there, with a bath," he said. "It's soundproofed so you won't hear the bar too much."

Karen set down her bag. "I saw one of their faces. I was lying there, they'd Tasered me, they'd given you a sedative, and they'd stormed up the stairs and taken out Grayson and brought Marianne down. She tore the balaclava off one of their faces and yelled at him. I saw him, his flashlight was up toward his and her faces. Right then one of the other guys gave me an injection and that was the last I saw."

"Did you recognize him?"

"No, but if I saw him again..."

Sam called Woodruff. "I need any and all photographs you have of the personnel used on security details for the wealthiest Russians living here."

"Why?"

"I have a possible ID on one who may be helping Bolt."

"Yes, give us a few." He hung up.

Sam made them toast and scrambled eggs, with hot coffee. Cooking calmed him. He kept his phone in his pocket, waiting for a reply. They ate and Sam's laptop pinged when Woodruff's info came through. There was a link to a secured site of photos. Some were passport pictures; others had been taken on the street or in nightclubs.

They started paging through each picture, Karen halting to study the features while they finished their quick breakfast. She'd shake her head and they'd move to the next.

"Hey," Sam said. "You didn't tell Cortez this—that you saw one of their faces. Why?"

"I don't know. I just didn't. He didn't need to know. He's a civilian, as he keeps saying. But are any of us? Especially at a moment like this?" She sipped her coffee. "He's more worried about protecting his reputation than helping me find Amanda."

And so he had to ask, because if he had to bring them Amanda, he had to find her first. "Amanda left willingly with that woman," Sam said. "Would she respond to a simple invite to see her father if they could prove to her he's here?"

"No. She wouldn't. Not without calling me."

They kept looking at faces. Sam kept waiting for his phone to vibrate. No response. No further demands. No further instructions.

They finished eating. Karen kept looking. Sam thought, *Daniel. He must be so frightened. What does he think has happened to him? Why he's been grabbed? How are they getting him here for the exchange?* They could have driven him in but it was a day's drive, at least, from Austin to Miami—so maybe Daniel wasn't here yet. Maybe he was bound and gagged, lying in a car trunk, terrified, praying for his dad to come save him...

"Him," Karen said.

Sam glanced at the screen. A picture of a man, big-shouldered, hair shaved short, walking out of a storefront with a beautiful young woman with dark hair, wearing a tight dress and a lot of gold jewelry.

"That's the man I saw."

Sam looked at the photo's tag. "Pavel Vladimirovich Rustov. Says here he has worked for both Piotr Iskov and Illya Markarkin."

"Iskov is in London. He stopped coming to Miami regularly a few years ago after a couple of minor run-ins with the police," Karen said.

"How do you know that?"

"I keep tabs on them," she said. "It's like a hobby."

He glanced at her, as if expecting she would say more.

"So this Rustov works for Illya Markarkin?"

"That woman is Markarkin's girlfriend. I don't know her name, but I've seen her photo before. I saw them once at a restaurant here, a nice one the elites frequent. Cortez took me there."

"What is your relationship with him?"

"It's none of your business." She was staring at the picture of Rostov and the girlfriend.

"Everything connected to this right now is my business."

"It's hard to date after your husband commits treason. It's just...a constant thing that hovers over your life. Grayson understood. When I needed...understanding,

I didn't always have to... explain. Or answer questions. Or justify what I didn't know or didn't do," Karen said. "I guess you don't understand. Your wife's treason was kept secret."

"It's hard to date, period," Sam said. "Illya Markarkin. Where's home for him in Miami?"

"He owns a ton of property here but none of it is in his name. It'll all be through front companies. It could take days to sift through the possibilities." And Sam didn't have days. He stared at the photo again. Behind the girlfriend, on the storefront glass, there was a stylized stork carrying a bundle. "That store. It's a maternity store?"

"Yeah, Expect Greatness... it's high-end. It's not that far from here, actually. Super posh."

"She's not carrying any bags, though."

"No. They probably delivered to her. Lots of Russian wives and girlfriends who are expecting stay here and give birth in the US, so their child will have citizenship."

"Delivered. So they'd have her address." He reached for his phone, googled the store's number, called. His Russian accent was persuasive. "Yes, good morning, this is Pavel Rustov, with Illya Markarkin's office. Yes, hello. Yes. Do you have current address for Mr. Markarkin's account? Our last order for Maria, not delivered. What is address you have?" He listened. "That is correct, though, okay. So maybe problem is in mail room of building. Okay, thank you." He hung up. "I have Illya's address."

"And what do we do with that? Go in with one gun blazing?"

"No," Sam said. "I need to do something first."

52

Daniel opened his eyes. His mouth felt gummy and dry. He blinked and realized he was lying on a large bed, the covers down, his shoes off but otherwise his clothes in place. Not on the plane anymore. He wiped at his eyes and sat up.

Behind him was a wall of glass, looking out over the ocean. Florida. He blinked again and tried to remember—he'd been on the jet, drinking water, and he'd passed out. He didn't normally fall asleep drinking water.

They had drugged him. His heart sank.

The bedroom door opened, and Aunt Clarice came in, a nervous smile on her face. "Good morning. You slept like a rock!" She spoke in a tone of false heartiness.

She shut the door behind her.

"Yeah," Daniel said. "That's unusual for me."

"I brought you some hot chocolate."

He sidled away to the other side of the bed and stood as she set down the hot chocolate on the bedside table.

"Are you hungry? I can make some eggs."

"Where am I?" he said.

"Oh, this belongs to a friend of Uncle Mark's. We're staying here. Isn't the view gorgeous?" She was doing that thing adults do when they're being really hearty and friendly because they have news you don't want to hear.

"Yeah, great," he said. He looked at her. She looked nervous. "Aunt Clarice, what's happening?"

"We're going to meet your dad very soon," she said.

He felt in his pockets. His phone was gone. "Where's my phone?"

"You can have it back in a while."

"Give it to me right now. I want to talk to my dad."

"Soon," she said, nodding. "I promise, sweetheart. Please don't be mad at me."

"This is a kidnapping." He kept his voice steady, but he felt a white-hot panic surge up in him.

"Of course it isn't. I'm your aunt, and your family loves you very much. We just have to be careful. Because they'd be tracking your phone so we need to have it turned off entirely."

"Who's they?"

"There's a lot about your mom you don't know, honey. That your father never told you. She was in a dangerous line of work. And some of that is still happening, and we have to protect you while we help you understand—"

Daniel ran, shoving past her. Past the door she'd just come through. A hallway. He sprinted down it and there was a living room, fancy, with a huge couch and a giant of a man sitting on it, and he stood up as Daniel tried to run past him.

"Hey, kid," he said. "Stop this."

He grabbed Daniel's arm.

Dad had taught him how to defend himself if someone tried to grab him or start a fight with him. He had thought it dumb because he was most likely to get into a fight at school, and he wasn't going to actually punch another kid; what Dad had taught him was more about what to do if someone tried to grab him and pull him into a car.

He remembered it all.

Three sharp, hard punches, to stomach, heart, and throat, and the big man's eyes widened in surprise and then he smiled and seized Daniel's hand and pulled him over the back of the couch.

"Don't hurt him," Clarice yelled.

The man had both of Daniel's hands in his crushing grip and he leaned close to Daniel. "Now you're gonna be a good boy, or we're gonna have a real problem." His voice was low, hard, accented.

Daniel tried to head-butt him, like in the movies, but he only hit the man's cheek.

The man grinned. "Little fighter. I like that." He put an arm around Daniel's throat and squeezed.

Dots danced in the air for Daniel. He couldn't breathe.

"Stop, please stop!" Clarice yelled.

"I want you to listen to me very carefully," the man said. "I'm in charge of your security. That means we're gonna be friends, and I'm gonna forgive this little outburst of energy, and you're gonna do what you're told. Because you pull this again, we're gonna have a problem. And you don't want to have a problem with me, because I'm not gonna view you as a kid but as a young man who needs to learn a lesson. This is all to protect you." He carried Daniel, still with his hands in one grip, the other arm around his neck, but easing off the pressure, and took him back to the bedroom.

"Daniel, please, don't be this way. Please," Clarice said. "I promise you'll get to talk to your father soon. I swear on a stack of Bibles."

Daniel suddenly thought he would cry. He had never been so scared. But he didn't want to cry in front of them. The big man dumped him on the bed and Daniel stayed there, facedown, on the mattress.

"Good boy," the big man said. "That's what I like to

see, Daniel. Mind your aunt and me, we'll be fine, and you'll be with your dad soon."

Daniel lay on the bed, not looking at him or Clarice.

The door shut again.

"Daniel. Look at me," Clarice said softly.

He didn't.

"I know this is hard to understand, but it had to be this way. You'll understand soon enough when we see your dad."

"You're a liar," he said into the pillow.

She sat next to him and put her hand between his shoulder blades. "A lot of people haven't wanted you to know the truth about your mom."

"I'm hungry," he said.

"I'll bring you some breakfast. Toast and fruit. You don't have to worry about it being drugged."

He said nothing. He had decided to say nothing more. After a moment she said, "The chocolate is fine to drink, Daniel. And I would never hurt you."

She got up and went out the door. And when she shut it, he heard the click of an automatic lock. He was trapped.

He kept the tears at bay. He took a deep breath. He thought: *What would Dad do?*

He had to find a way out. There was just one guard but he was big and lumbering and Daniel thought he could outrun him, maybe. And Clarice didn't look athletic to him.

He had to get away from them. If he could get away, he could find someone to help him, to call Dad for him.

53

AMANDA HAD SLEPT HARD; VAL had not slept well and had checked on her multiple times through the night. The safe house was a short-term rental that Terrell had pointed her toward—available on short notice, leased now for a month, although Val hoped they would need it for only one night. Terrell had scrubbed it from the online catalog.

The two other former MI6 agents she'd pulled onto her team were eating in the kitchen, one having gone out for breakfast tacos and returned. Val only wanted coffee.

She picked up Amanda's phone. She'd taken it last night after Amanda fell asleep. She'd cracked the simple password code with a breaker—she wanted to see who was trying to reach Amanda and who Amanda might reach out to. She said she didn't have a way to contact her dad, but Val wanted to be sure that Amanda didn't warn her father. That she wasn't lying or acting to try and protect him. It was a slim chance, but one that she could not risk. Not if Val could find Bolt first, and she would.

There was a message from Roberto on the voice mail. From 2:00 a.m. She played it:

Where the hell are you? I cannot believe you have left me to deal with this alone. There was a Russian dude looking

*for you. And your mother and our new neighbor came to
the office and then to our apartment, and that asshole isn't
what I thought he was. He's involved somehow; he hit me. I
need to know who these people are trying to buy the business
because they're going to make trouble for us. I need them
to go away. If you're with that Valeria bitch, tell her to stay
away from me. We can't have this attention, all right. And
let me know you're okay. Jesus, what has happened to us? I
love you. I want you to know I love you.*

Val listened to the message again. Amanda's mother
was a complication, as she might contact the police if she
thought her daughter was missing. And who was this
neighbor? Just a nosy bystander or someone involved in
monitoring Amanda for her father?

She took the phone to the bedroom. Amanda was up,
brushing her teeth in the adjoining bathroom.

"Did you sleep well?"

"Surprisingly," Amanda said. "I think I've been
exhausted, and I don't…I don't always feel safe with
Roberto. That's been a hard thing to realize. I love him,
we've been together for a while, but…"

"It's not what you still want."

"No. But we're working together, work life and love
life all intertwined…"

"I've been there. It can be…a challenge." She handed
Amanda a cup of coffee. "You have a voice mail on your
phone you should hear."

"You listened to my…how did you access my phone?"

"We're British spies, we can do stuff like that," Val
said. "We wanted to see if your father had reached you.
Listen."

Amanda listened to the voice mail. She made a face of
frustration when Roberto mentioned her mother.

"I don't need my mother involved in this. I need her

out of this mess." She took a deep breath. "She thought she was being watched and I thought she was imagining things. The Russians were watching her."

"Or possibly someone else. Tell me about this neighbor."

"Sam."

Val let her face betray no emotion. "Sam?"

"Uh, yeah. He only moved next door to us this week. Tara got the immediate hots for him. He owns a bar over in Coral Gables."

"He owns a bar," Val repeated, slowly, as if digesting each word. "What's his last name?"

"Uh. Something French." She thought for a moment. "Sam Chevalier." Amanda stared suddenly at Val. "Are you okay? You don't look okay."

"I'm fine. Absolutely fine. We're running out of time. I want you to call Dennis. We need to find out if he's hiding your father. If Dennis has your dad, my team can grab your father and this is all over."

"Wouldn't Dennis have said this before...that my father was here?"

"Maybe he wasn't here yet."

"Where else in America would he go? His family is all here."

"I don't know," Val said honestly.

"You look shook. Is it this Sam guy?"

"I promise you I am not shook. I have never been shook. Get showered and dressed, and we'll call Dennis. And we'll go see this...Sam." Val made sure her voice was steady.

54

It had been a long night. Illya had gathered his expanded security team and sent them to attack Bolt's so-called safe house, and they'd brought back a German woman hired by Illya to spy on Amanda. Kirill was back at the high-rise by the time the team returned.

"Why didn't you tell me you had an insider source?" Kirill said.

"Because it didn't concern you," Illya said.

"Of course it did—she could have been another set of eyes for me..."

"She reported to me, and I would have told you what she knew. Let it go," Illya snapped. He seemed to be getting less timid about asserting himself; the Val situation had clearly unnerved him.

Kirill had not told Illya about his discussion with Val; he didn't want Illya to know about Val's offer. If Illya told Bobo and Duderov, they might immediately decide to pull him from the case. They might fear he was tempted. It was best kept a secret.

"Does your German woman know where Bolt is?"

"No. But she says the Americans know he's back; they sent one of their fixers to try and find Bolt. He's found Bolt's ex-wife, but not Bolt."

"Yet the Americans have not said anything to the press."

"They're like us; they want to find him first. They want to spirit him to one of their facilities and not worry about his legal rights, of which he has few, but he still has some," Illya said. "I wonder if Val is working with him."

"I don't think so," Kirill said. "I think she bears her own grudge." Kirill drank down some of his coffee. "But where has Bolt been? Why wasn't he already in that house, or why does he need to move from his current hiding place?"

"All I care about is where he is now, and we have no leads as to where he's hiding. He's not at the house Val bought from that idiot real estate agent—I sent a team there this morning. It's empty."

Kirill nodded. He didn't want to talk about the house. Of course Val had abandoned it.

"We need to know where she would hide Amanda," Illya said. "The boyfriend could call the police at any time..."

"He won't," Kirill said. "His business is dirty. I think he's cleaning money for someone. Presumably not any of our countrymen. He doesn't want police there asking him hard questions. But she'll start being missed, either by the employees or her friends."

"Then what do we do?" Illya said. "She's our only way to draw him out."

"Assuming he even cares enough about Amanda," Kirill said. "He doesn't have a great history with his loved ones. Ask my mother."

"You realize if Val escapes, we're both ruined," Illya said, as if it were somehow Kirill's fault.

"Yes, I'm aware." He had heard nothing about any possible UK informant from Bobo or the Dude. He would have to improvise...

Improvise.

He had assumed that Val's team was already established in Miami upon arrival. But what if they weren't? What if they, like he was, were improvising? Taking each day as it came. The team could have been staying in a hotel, awaiting word from her before acting. And then she had acquired one property, for ostensibly another reason, and used it to keep Amanda there until Kirill showed up and it could serve as a meeting ground before they abandoned it. On his last job in Japan, he'd stayed not in a Russian-owned safe house but in a last-minute online vacation rental, under an assumed name.

Could she not have done the same?

He called Bobo again. Looking at Illya as he did so.

"Do we have any informants inside the major online housing rental companies?"

"I would have to check," Bobo said after a moment.

"Put out an information request, with a suitable payment. I'm looking for anything in Miami metro rented by a UK national, in the past two weeks, for the next two weeks. They might have been interested in more secluded property, with security built-in and a lack of nosy neighbors."

"Or rented by Dennis Gandy," Illya added, leaning toward the phone. "That's the connection Marianne found that was using the house we raided."

"We'll check there, too, and I'll let you know," Bobo said.

Kirill ended the call. "There's a whole network of people willing to provide data that we can't easily access," he told Illya. "Bobo has several dozen of them—at banks, airlines, security companies, and he can put out a request and offer some money, and if they can find out without leaving a self-incriminating trail, they raise their hand."

Illya said nothing.

"To them it's not treason or betrayal of their nation; it's just answering a question Bobo put to them, that can't connect back to them very easily. And maybe it pays for the private school tuition, or the new car for the wife, or the medical bills for the grandparent. People are so easily bought."

"So we wait?"

"We find Val. We find Bolt. And we make them both pay for all this chaos."

Illya waited for Kirill to go to the kitchen. He went to the room where Marianne was attempting to make contact with her understudy. He closed the door, and knelt close by her to whisper.

"Who are the other two?" she whispered. "You said on the voice mail."

"Valeria Garrison, my assistant, and Kirill. They know too much and they're a danger to us both."

"He's an FSB operative, yes? That is expensive."

"I think if you find Bolt, you'll find them soon behind. Or all together." He cleared his throat. "Bolt's daughter, Amanda, may be with Val. She can't be allowed to talk."

"You're buying a massacre," Marianne said. "I'll just kill everyone and send you the bill."

"Like I said: quadruple the payment. That's more than fair."

She stared at him, uncertain. She had failed thus far and lost a team member. Maybe he should hire someone to clean up her and her team, which so far had not yet found Bolt or the financial map. He pushed the thought aside. Deal with the immediate threat first, which was Bolt, and then Val and Kirill.

Marianne nodded. "I'll let them do the lifting of finding Bolt, then I'll take care of them."

Her phone pinged. "That's my associate calling," she said.

He nodded and left before Kirill came looking for him. It would be okay, he told himself again.

55

GRAYSON CORTEZ ANSWERED THE DOOR, and without Karen in tow, Sam decided to act as he felt like.

"Really, I don't know where Gandy is and I haven't had time to find out anything—"

Sam slammed Grayson Cortez back into the entryway and shut the door. He didn't remember hitting Cortez this time, but he had, Cortez gagging and trying to breathe. Sam leaned down, grabbed Cortez's collar, and pulled him toward the kitchen.

He got Cortez a glass of water and poured it on his face, as the man still didn't appear ready to take a drink. Cortez sputtered.

Sam knelt by him.

"I want you to listen carefully," Sam said. "Bolt has my thirteen-year-old son and he wants me to bring him Amanda."

"Why wouldn't he just grab Amanda? Why involve you?"

"Because I am watching her. He clearly has a contact in American intel to know I'm on the job and this is his way to get me to stop doing my job."

"Or you were spotted."

"Your son gave over his house to a man who may be actively shielding and abetting a traitor. A man who killed a hired killer in the street. How's that going to look for you?"

"I told you Carlos doesn't know anything about what Gandy is doing."

"I need to know where Gandy is, Grayson, and right now I'm remembering every indignity you visited on me in that prison and I'm thinking how scared and afraid my son is and if you don't tell me where Gandy is—"

"I swear I don't know."

"Get up." Sam yanked him to his feet. "Both our sons are in serious trouble and you're going to help me with mine. And maybe I'll help you with yours. I want you to text Gandy. Reach out to him. Tell him you need to talk to him. Here's his number."

Cortez thumbed his phone. "All right, Sam, all right. I've texted him. No answer yet."

"There's an Englishwoman who convinced Amanda to leave with her. Are this Englishwoman and Gandy working together?"

"I have no idea."

His phone pinged. A text from Paige: I haven't found leverage against Gandy yet. But digging into his medical insurance records you should know he has been admitted to mental health institutions twice in the past five years. Both times for violent outbursts in the workplace when he was cautioned about visiting conspiracy theory websites. He beat up a manager but the man declined to press charges.

"Gandy's unstable."

"He's not been well since his father died," Cortez said. "I've tried to help him."

"He's violent."

"When his beliefs about his father's innocence are challenged, yes."

"Was his father innocent?"

"Not at all."

"I need to know if he's connected to the English-woman or if she's got her own angle."

He was mad at himself for not thinking to place a micro camera at the exit where the vans were. That way he might have seen her face.

He called the office. He lucked out; Tara answered.

"I need your help," he said.

"I can't help you," she said. "I warned you to stay out of this."

"If you want Amanda found and no police involvement taking a hard look at what's happening at the courier service, answer a question for me. Is there a security camera in the back parking lot, where the trucks are?"

56

Amanda called Dennis Gandy. No answer. She left a message while Val listened. "Dennis. I understand there may be a chance that you know where my father is. That he's here in town. That maybe that was why you were reaching out to me and not telling me." She cleared her throat. "So, if that's true, then I need you to call me back and talk to me." She hung up.

Val said, "He may think it's a trap. You could have the police waiting for him."

Amanda said, "I'll try to get him to trust me. He's tried to do everything to get me to meet with him; well, here's his chance."

Amanda's phone buzzed again. Her mother. "My mom has to be worried sick," Amanda said, reaching for the phone.

"It might not be best to talk to her right now."

"Why?"

"Because if you tell her you're possibly meeting your father, she may want to come along. Or talk you out of it."

"But do you really need me?" Amanda said. "Aren't I just bait to draw Dad in?"

"Do you want to see him?"

Amanda's gaze met Val's. "I have some things to say. He went to all this trouble to sneak into Miami, run from the Russians, he must have an important reason. Maybe he wants to apologize. Turn himself in. Make it all right. But that's a pipe dream." She took a deep breath. "Sam. You think he was sent to watch me."

"Yes."

"But he didn't try to grab me or force me to come with him. He could have. He didn't."

"I doubt those were his orders, unless you were in imminent danger."

"We could go to his bar. If he can help..."

"I would prefer not to. We're not supposed to be here, Amanda. I'm at your mercy when this is over. You could call the police, the FBI, and they'll arrest me and my team."

"I wouldn't do that to you, ever," Amanda said softly.

"When this is done," Val said, "we're going to take your father away. And if we can keep that we've captured him a secret, we will. He will be debriefed in London. He will tell us what he knows. He will give us something very valuable he stole from the Russians. And then we'll go public, and he can stand trial in London for the British agents he betrayed. And...and if he knows who killed my husband two years ago, we'll take that cooperation into account."

"Your husband. Oh. I'm so sorry."

"I've been trying to find out for two years and I haven't succeeded yet. But he might know. Someone might have bragged about it to him." She turned away. "I'm just telling you because we're taking him with us and I want you to be ready for that. You might change your mind when you see him."

"I hate him," she said. "I won't change my mind."

"He's your father."

"He drove my brother to suicide. He ruined my mother's life. He..." Amanda shook her head. "I won't change my mind. Can I text my mom?"

Val handed her back the phone. "You're not my prisoner, Amanda."

"I know." She tapped out a message to Karen and showed it to Val: Mom, I'm fine. I'm safe. Please don't worry about me and I'll be in touch soon. Goodles boodles.

"What's the last part mean?"

"It's a private joke between us. I couldn't say *good-bye* when I was little, so that's how Allan taught me to say it. It's a family joke. That way she knows I'm texting her."

The phone beeped. Karen: WHERE ARE YOU?

With a friend, Amanda texted back. I'll have more stuff to tell you soon. I can't talk more right now. Go home and stay safe. She handed the phone back to Val. "I'll tell her it's about Dad if I don't stop. Do you think she's safe?"

"It might be better if she stays with a friend, and not alone."

She handed the phone back to Amanda, who texted: Go stay with Grayson or one of your friends. Just so you're not alone.

I AM YOUR MOTHER AND YOU HAVE TO TELL ME WHERE YOU ARE

Love you, Mom. Talk soon.

Then the phone buzzed. Val looked at the number. "It's blocked. Like spinning the wheel of fortune to see who it might be."

"My dad. It might be my dad."

Val waited, and Amanda hit the speaker button and answered the phone. "Hello."

"Amanda." The soft, scratchy whisper of a voice. "It's Dennis."

"Hi, Dennis."

"Where are you?"

"Where are you, Dennis? I think that matters more. And is my father with you?"

"Why would you think that?"

"Because a Russian," Amanda said, "came to the office trying to talk to me and saying that Dad was back here. And since you're his advocate, I thought you might know if that was true or not. Is that why you keep wanting me to meet with you? To take me to my dad."

He was silent. Val gestured and Amanda muted the phone. "Be insistent. He's going to be concerned that you're taping him or coming with police."

Amanda nodded and unmuted the phone. "If he's with you, I deserve to know it."

"Why would you believe some random Russian?"

"Because this dude looked like a government sent him. And why would they make up such a story? It's insane to think he'd come back here, but I wouldn't put it past him. If he had a good reason."

"I'm going to give you an address and I want you to come alone."

Amanda glanced at Val, who nodded. "All right."

"Don't bring Roberto."

"I won't."

"And don't bring that neighbor of yours. The new blond one. I don't like the look of him."

"I barely know him, so no, I won't bring him, Dennis."

"Don't talk down to me, Amanda. I'm the one running this show."

Val arched an eyebrow.

"I'm not talking down to you."

"And don't bring that loudmouth Tara."

"Tara's at the office. I'll be alone."

"Okay. The address is 14 Dove Wing Way. I'll see you in exactly two hours. Don't be early. Don't be late. And don't be with anyone else."

"Fourteen Dove Wing Way," Amanda repeated. "All right. I'll see you in two hours." She hung up the phone. "I'm shaking. I'm literally shaking."

"It'll be fine."

"What do we do? I mean... I can go alone. I can."

"This is what we'll do," Val said.

Kirill's phone rang and he answered it.

"Mr. Smith?" a bright, chirpy voice said.

"Yes," Kirill said. That was the name he would be phoned under if one of Bobo's contacts found a match.

"My pleasure, Mr. Smith! We have a match for your customer service inquiry. I do want you to know that this call is *not* being recorded for customer service excellence. A Dennis Gandy did indeed rent one of our properties this very morning, in Miami, at 14 Dove Wing Way. It's in a charming area full of high-end mansions that are available for leasing."

Kirill said a quick thank-you and hung up. He looked at Illya. "Get your German and her helper, if you still trust them, or I'll go in alone."

57

An Englishwoman taking Amanda with her.

Sam called Woodruff. "Is there any chance the British are running an operation here to grab him?"

"They wouldn't. Not without telling us."

"There's an Englishwoman who has Amanda. She was followed by a Russian who apparently was waiting in the car. So I'm thinking a UK agent has penetrated the Russians and is making a move to cut loose and take Amanda, or there is a British team here, diplomacy be damned, and the Russians are hot on their trail."

Woodruff was silent for several moments. "It would be an international incident for them to do this."

"Do you have a trusted source on the British side, someone who'll tell you, so we can minimize the damage? If they have Amanda, then maybe they'd work with us."

"It seems that they and the Russians are doing a better job than you are," Woodruff said.

Sam managed to control his voice. "I've followed your orders. You wanted me to watch over her; that's how I even know who she's with. They have to have resources on the ground, a safe place to take her. We need to see if any home rentals have been done by UK nationals here. They might have rented more than one. Any property that could fit the standards for a safe house—not heavy traffic, privacy, neighborhood demographics."

"I'll see what I can find out."

"Pressure them. It's better we know now than later. We can forgive them now if they help me." Woodruff ended the call. Fifteen minutes ticked by while Sam waited. It felt like an eternity.

Woodruff rang back. "I'm told there's a chance there's an off-the-books team on the ground in Miami. Three of them, including two agents who were dismissed in the past year. And the Brits are not happy with them at the moment. They would rather we take them in than FBI or local law enforcement."

"Personnel?"

"They wouldn't say. They won't say until their team confirms you have contacted them."

"Why were two dismissed?"

"They broke protocol on an assignment. They think whoever's ringleading promised them their jobs back if they helped on this mission."

"So even riskier to their long-term careers."

Woodruff cleared his throat. "Apparently a personal vendetta against Bolt is involved. Very unprofessional if you ask me. But you understand. They lost some people when he defected; he exposed part of their network."

"I understand." *I understand*, he thought, *that this Englishwoman has put my son in danger.*

"It was also promised to us that Bolt has information that we will be very interested in," Woodruff said.

"Is this intel his ticket back?"

"Of course not, but we want whatever intel he has to offer. Once it's proven."

But then why have me bring him Amanda? He could just offer the goods in exchange for meeting with her. But she might not agree. She might go public. Bolt didn't want to risk not seeing his daughter after all this, and he was willing to use Sam's son as a pawn.

But why Daniel? Why him?

Lucy, meeting with Bolt before both their betrayals, and meeting with him afterward. They were connected somehow—traitor to traitor.

"When you've secured Bolt and the intel, call me immediately."

"Are we sharing with the British?"

"If we must. If we can secure the information without them, the better."

"Where might I find these intrepid Brits?"

"They tapped into a sleeper bank account last used in an overseas operation a year ago; it was supposed to be closed and it wasn't. It paid for a house rental, and that tipped my contact's office. The address is 104 Pierrepaul Drive. That's all they're giving us."

"I'm going there."

"Sam, perhaps assess if they're close to grabbing Bolt. If they have his daughter, they may know more than you. Let's not rush in and put losing him at risk."

My son's life is at stake.

Tell no one.

Sam could not be silent, not with a team preparing to go hot. They might not have full reconnaissance. It was a greater risk to stay silent. But his next few words could gamble with Daniel's life. The hardest words he'd spoken in years. "Bolt may have a hostage. A child. Their team needs to know that before going in. They can't go in with guns blazing."

"Who?"

"My son." He had to force out the words.

Shock from Woodruff. "What? How?"

"He has him. I don't know how, or why. Bolt has an old connection to Lucy—his wife told me. They met before his defection. I don't know more."

"Sam. When were you going to tell me this?"

"Well, now, apparently, now that I know armed Brits have more information than I apparently do and a bigger team." Sam flying solo had been Woodruff's call and Sam couldn't keep the bitterness out of his voice.

Woodruff's voice was steel. "And what has he asked you for in return for your kid?"

"He wants me to bring him Amanda."

"Well, that helps answer the motivation to come home. He wants to see his daughter."

"There has to be a reason he's grabbed Daniel. It was an enormous risk for him, on top of all the others he's already taken. Why?" Karen. Telling him about Lucy meeting Bolt. What had been between them?

"You're off the case."

"You cannot. You cannot. You don't have anyone else to put in here."

"I can have another operative on the ground in three hours. You stand by and be ready to brief them."

Sam hung up. There was no point. He wasn't going to spend time arguing with Woodruff while a rogue team went into a house armed where his son might be.

He called Paige. She answered on the first ring. "Sorry I overslept."

"Hey. Is Karen still there?"

"She is not."

"Damn it. Can you get me details on a safe house at 104 Pierrepaul Drive? The Brits are using it as a base. I need to know who owns it, where it is, what's the surrounding neighborhood like."

"Give me a few," she said before ending the call.

He called Amanda's phone. No answer. He texted: Amanda I must speak to you. About your dad. Please, PLEASE call me back.

No answer.

He called Karen.

She answered on the first ring. "Your daughter is likely at a house at 104 Pierrepaul Drive. I'm heading there right now. She's about to be taken to see her father and I need her to not go." *Because I have to take her myself.*

"She won't answer."

"Text her that you know she's with a British team. And that you have the address. Tell her to wait for you so you can come with her. If she's going to him, I need to go with her. Not the Brits. He has my son."

"What?"

"He has my son. He's thirteen. His name is Daniel."

"Oh, Sam."

"Would he hurt a child?"

"Markus would do whatever he had to do to protect himself. Let me try."

"Don't mention my son to her. Just tell her to say nothing to the Brits and to wait for me."

He raced through the streets. He had a gun, loaded, and a knife he wore at his ankle. He zoomed through a red light, honking well in advance of the crossing, and the Miami drivers got out of his way. He thought it would be his luck to be pulled over by a policeman but there was none. He forced himself to slow down as he entered a residential area.

His phone pinged and he answered. It was Paige. "The address is on a cul-de-sac on the water. It's been on the market recently and is currently leased through a service. The houses around him are also investment properties—the owners are shell companies. So they could be vacant; it might be a good place to go unnoticed if no one's in residence other than the staffs. There's a pier. I'm looking at a satellite image right now. Two boats docked there, but I don't know if they're with the house. I'd assume so."

"They will know I'm coming," Sam said.

"Yeah, you don't really have cover. There's some large hedges for boundaries by the house on one side, the side closest to you as you approach—there's only one road in and out to the cul-de-sac. There's also a guard station you're going to have to get past."

"What's the owner's name?"

"Nigel Wyngarde. But those guards generally know when people are around or not, and they accept deliveries. You might have to just plow through the gate."

"I'd rather talk my way through."

"Good luck, golden tongue."

He had turned down the sole road that led to the waterfront. It was surprisingly narrow, with dense vegetation growing alongside, a wall of green to shield the adjoining property from the road. He could see the guard's hut and the lowered bar. He slowed and rolled the window down.

"May I help you, sir?" The security guard was young, maybe twenty, with a boyish face and a briskness in his voice. The kind of guy who wanted to do a good job. Sam really didn't want to hurt him.

Sam had lived in London for a year when he had been with CIA Special Projects and had twice had to pose undercover with an English accent. He thought it might work well enough to get past this guard. "Hello, I'm going to the Wyngarde house. I'm expected."

"The house is closed down, sir."

Sam presumed that meant the staff wasn't there. Maybe Wyngarde had knowingly loaned his house to the UK spies, queen and country and all. "But there are some folks there right now, expecting me."

"I haven't been notified, sir."

"Because Mr. Wyngarde might not want a record of

my visit," Sam said enigmatically. "The rental service has allowed some guests there now, yes? Some of my fellow countrymen?"

The guard said nothing, but Sam knew he was starting to believe.

"Well, Mr. Wyngarde would like for me to make sure there is nothing untoward going on with his guests. He accessed his security cameras and saw some troubling behavior. I'm from the embassy and he called and asked me to check it out."

"I . . ." The guard's training had not quite prepared him for this. A story that was vaguely suspicious yet also oddly plausible. "Do you have some ID, sir?"

"I'll show it to you but you're not writing down my name on your little clipboard, please." Sam gave him a UK passport with his picture and a false name. The guard studied it and handed it back. "All right, sir."

The bar rose, and Sam drove through.

He didn't park at the Wyngarde driveway. There were five mansions on the cul-de-sac, all on the water, and he parked one house over, hidden by the large hedges. He wanted to be close when the Brits resisted him. He hurried down the hedges, coming closer to the lapping water. He crawled through the hedges and ran quickly across the driveway, headed for a door.

He tried the knob. Unlocked. Shouldn't be. Bad sign.

Maybe Marianne and the squad who hit the Cortez house had already made it here, if they'd gotten past the young guard. They could have come in by water.

He really hoped these people were still alive, especially Amanda.

Sam pushed the door open. A mudroom, tiled floor, a doorway opening to what looked like a massive kitchen, the lights dimmed.

He listened for a sound, an indication of anyone in the house. He heard nothing. He pulled his gun. Steadied it in front of him.

He moved toward the kitchen, through the doorway, an empty breakfast nook with a view of the water on his right, two teacups still sitting on the table, a large kitchen cabinet that blocked his view on his left.

The fist slammed into his forehead. He staggered to the left, raising the gun. The man—bigger than Sam, dark hair cut military short—seized Sam's gun hand, twisting it hard. Sam powered a blow into the man's stomach—it was like rock—and then the man wrenched the gun from Sam's grip. Before he could raise it, Sam threw himself into the man, shoving him hard against the kitchen counter. The man didn't have a good grip on the gun and Sam knocked it free. The weapon fell into the sink.

Sam pressed his advantage, three hard blows into the bigger man's throat, a dreadful rat-tat-tat, and the man staggered to one knee. Sam saw the second man just as he launched at Sam. Wiry, head shaved, holding a Taser. Sam threw the bigger man in his path and used him as a shield. The bald man hesitated, and Sam dumped the big man, vaulting over him, landing on the bald man, who yelled. Sam landed only one punch and then slammed the man's head twice down on the floor. He pulled out a zip tie and bound the guy's hands before he could recover.

The big man seized Sam from behind and wrapped hands around his throat. Sam tried to power back and head-butt him, but couldn't. Sam reached up, pried open the cabinet door as he couldn't breathe. Grabbed whatever was there. Felt metal. Brought it down on the man's head. It was a cookie sheet. He hit him again with it. No effect.

"Who are you?" the man said. He kept squeezing Sam's neck, which didn't make it any easier to answer.

Sam shoved the cookie sheet against the big man's face. He pulled up his leg and freed the knife from under his pants. He slashed at the man's forearm and the man let go. Sam could have stabbed him cleanly then but refrained, powering another fist to the man's face and then throat, and the man staggered back. Sam lurched toward the sink, where the gun lay. They had to talk to him. They had to help him.

Sam seized the gun and whirled, aiming.

And staring at a woman he had thought never to see again.

58

THERE MILA—HIS FORMER PARTNER, HIS former friend—
was, standing in front of him, gun leveled at him, saying
words that weren't registering.

"Drop your weapon, Sam," she ordered again.

"Mila," he said.

"Mila Cebotari is dead. Mila Court is dead. I have
another name for the moment."

"Mila," he said again.

"Sam. Drop your weapon, right now. And kick it over
to me."

He did.

She ordered the big man to cut the bald man free.
Sam stayed still.

The last time he'd seen her was late at night on the
M7 road leading to Moscow. Their car pulled over, a
tense confrontation between him and his brother and
Mila, who wanted Sam to come with her. To leave his
brother—who had attempted to assassinate the Russian
president—and come with her. She was his partner in
the post-espionage career he'd found, his ally, his best
friend.

He had chosen to stay with his brother, which meant
leaving her.

What she had said to him on that dark road:

Give your son my love. Tell him I love him.

When he had watched her walk away in her evening gown along the dark road, toward a distant café where British intelligence would retrieve her, a core deep inside him, past bone and heart, broke.

Now they stared at each other. And the big man got up and slammed a fist hard into Sam's face, and he went down.

"Stop," Mila said. "He's a friend. Or he once was."

Sam's head was ringing, his jaw feeling pounded. "Mila...why are you chasing Bolt? This isn't your fight."

"I don't have time to explain to you. We'll leave you here, and when we're done and wheels up, I'll notify a contact in American intel that you're here. Sorry our reunion cannot be sweeter."

"Mila. Bolt has Daniel."

For a second she gave no answer. When Daniel was an infant, Mila had risked her life more than once to help Sam save him. She had called him *puişor*, a Romanian endearment, played with him, cared for him, loved him.

"That's even beneath you, using him that way."

Sam was stunned. "I'm not using him. Bolt has him. I swear."

"Your son is in Austin. How would Bolt get there? He's lucky to have made it to Miami. He's not traveling on a domestic airline or driving four days there and back."

"He has him."

"Because you are here pretending to be her neighbor."

"Well, technically, I am her neighbor. I did rent the apartment."

"Sam. You cannot have him. Amanda is cooperating with us."

"He wants me to bring him Amanda in exchange for Daniel."

"Why?"

"He wants to see her."

"He has something I need," Mila said. "Something he stole."

"Okay. I'll get it for you when I get Daniel."

"We're three, you're one, and you're a beaten-up one right now."

"Your guys aren't looking so hot. Are you the two who got dismissed from MI6?"

The two guys in question glared at him. But they hadn't said anything, letting the conversation between Sam and Mila spill out. She was clearly the one in charge.

"British intel knows you're here," he said. "My handler has been poking the nest over in London. They're not happy with you. You help me, my boss and I will say you were working directly with us the entire time." He was off the books as well, but a unified front would sound better to Mila's bosses. They could smooth out details later. When he had Daniel back. "Mila. Please."

"Always on the bended knee for help," she said. "Always asking for my assistance."

"You wanted my help once," he said. "The first time we met. You tracked me down while I was on the run for my life"—he glanced at the two Brits—"and you asked me to help you."

"It was both ways."

"It's Daniel. *Daniel.* I'm sorry we parted on such bad terms. That's not his fault."

"Thank you for alerting us to his presence. Of course I'll retrieve him for you." Her voice shook ever so slightly. More than ten years since he'd seen her but he could read her still.

"Whatever you're after from Bolt, it cannot be worth more than my son's life."

"He's lying," the bald man said.

"Take me with you," Sam said. "Just take me with you. You can do whatever you want with Bolt. I don't care. I only care about getting Daniel back."

"Why would he take him?"

The next words were hard to say. "Lucy went to Russia. When she was pregnant with Daniel. I've seen the photos of her meeting with Bolt there. She pretended to be a friend of Bolt's son. They were both traitors. Maybe they were working together and it was never discovered. Maybe he's after what brought them together."

"Maybe. Or something else." Mila's words felt like a hammer.

"Daniel is my child. There were DNA tests when we recovered him, Mila, and I'm going to get him."

"Sam." Amanda stepped into the kitchen, pale, looking shocked. "Your son. I'm sorry. But you lied to us about who you are."

"I was sent only to watch over you. To find out if your father had contacted you. Or was trying to."

"And why didn't the FBI or the CIA sit me down and tell me he had escaped Russia?" Amanda asked.

"*Escaped* is an interesting word, since he ran there and betrayed us to begin with. We didn't want you to know, if we could recapture him."

"I would have known eventually. He would have faced trial."

"Maybe. Maybe not."

"Oh, so we're lawless now."

"He has something Mila clearly values—he's trying to buy a ticket back. But he destroyed lives other than just yours. You're going to call me lawless when he's kidnapped my son?"

"It's not mutually exclusive."

"Maybe worry about why your boyfriend is frantic over anyone looking at his financial records. Who's he fronting for?"

"No one."

"I think we're going to find he's cleaning money for some people. And your name's on the checks and the lease and what have you, next to his, and your British friends are not going to be able to help you with that when the police are suddenly interested. But I can."

"What, are you two fighting for my loyalty?" Amanda said, but her voice shook.

"Mila, what do we do with him?" the big man asked.

She stared at Sam. Her former partner, her former friend.

"Decide, please." Sam stared back at her. *We meant something to each other once. We were partners, friends. Your friendship helped me move past my wife's betrayal. I helped you move past the tragedy of your past.*

Will you help me now? Or was my choice back in Russia to walk away from you too much?

Amanda said, "If my father is out there and I'm really going to see him, I want as much protection around me as I can have, Val. Or Mila, or whatever your name is. What are you, Sam, CIA? Something more back corner?"

"Something like that. And I won't be running back to Britain."

"How dare you…" The bald man started forward and Sam stuck out a hand for him to shake. He didn't. Sam gave him a wry smile.

"Listen, I want you all to get back to Britain without issues. But you need someone here to help smooth this out domestically for Amanda and her mother. That's me."

"Your son being there is emotionally compromising," the bald man said. "You will not be focused on anything else."

"Tell that to Mila." Sam meant that he'd rescued his son before, but she looked at the two men and then at Sam, pain in her eyes. She had lost someone she had tried to save once.

Sam took a deep breath. "If you don't let me come, there is no one in the world I trust more to get Daniel out safely than you. You know that." He could hardly look at her; he thought tears might come to his eyes.

The silence ticked away for twenty seconds. It became uncomfortable.

"Fine," she said. "Come with us."

59

Fourteen Dove Wing Way was a reclusive choice for a safe house, even more so than the safe house where Mila had hidden Amanda. It sat at the back of a larger set of mansions, also with water access. Sam wondered where all this money came from.

He rode in the car with Mila and Amanda, Mila driving. He had been put in the backseat. The two operatives were following them in another car. Sam waved farewell at the surprised young man as they went past the guard hut.

"How is Daniel?" Mila asked unexpectedly. "I mean... what kind of kid is he?"

"He's great. He loves basketball, he's playing on his school team. He sings in choir. He struggles a bit with math. He...he's kind. He doesn't know...about his mother." He didn't want to say much more in front of Amanda.

"Sam's wife committed a crime similar to your father's," Mila said, as though it weren't a buried secret. "Only hers was not public. She died."

Amanda glanced back at him. "I'm sorry. I'm sorry you and your son went through it."

"Mila is leaving out quite a bit," Sam said. "Maybe we can stay focused on our plan."

"My team will take up cross positions outside the house. You will take Amanda to the yard and have them bring out Daniel. Then the exchange. As soon as you have Daniel, you will return to the car. You will not be asking Bolt about Lucy, Sam. You will not converse with him. You get Daniel out, free and clear, and we will handle the capture."

"He'll have guards. Someone sent a team. And Marianne is looking for him, too. She could interfere."

"You said she's down her team."

"Gandy killed one and hurt one. But she's working for a Russian; they could give her resources. You know she's dangerous."

"Perhaps a person who is bought can be bought again."

"You know how she is about her teams. Like they're her kids. But these two weren't very respectful to her." He took a deep breath. "I'm briefing you en route to what could be a shootout. Are you sure we're ready for this?"

"Yes," she said. He looked for her to look at him in the rearview, but she did not.

"Amanda. Are you going to be okay with your dad?" Sam asked.

"I have to be, don't I?" She glanced back at Sam. "I'm not going to let him see that he's continued to hurt me. I'm not going to let him *win*."

"Let's review what we're doing, again so we're clear on the game plan," Mila said, iron in her voice.

Mila turned the car into the Dove Wing Way cul-de-sac. The second car had peeled past; her guys, Bald and Big, would approach on foot, from opposite sides.

She stopped in front of the house.

Amanda and Sam each got out, keeping their hands where they could be clearly seen.

The front door opened.

Dennis Gandy emerged. He wore jeans and a dark shirt, sunglasses, and he was holding a gun.

"Hello, Amanda," he called. "I'm sorry it came to this. Hello, Sam. I was always suspicious of you."

"Where is my son?" Sam called. He and Amanda began to walk onto the expansive yard.

"He's safe. He's fine," Gandy said.

"Bring him out here," Sam said.

"He's not here at the house. He's safe, where he doesn't have to hear any conversations that a child shouldn't."

"I brought you Amanda." Something cold shifted in him. They were going against the agreement.

"Dennis, where is this boy and where is my dad?" Amanda said. She glanced at Sam. And then he saw her gun. She'd tucked a gun into the back of her jeans.

Hell.

"The boy is fine. And Sam will get him as soon as we've reached an agreement. Bolt has something to offer, and I want you to promise him safe passage and a meeting with your bosses. He's not arrested; he's not charged."

"I don't have the power to offer that."

"You'll figure it out, Sam," Dennis said. "Make that deal for him. I will serve as witness."

What did Bolt have that would earn him such treatment? Woodruff would not agree to this, but if Daniel wasn't here, then maybe this was a chance for Sam to learn more and find something to use as leverage.

"I'm not making any calls for you or Bolt until I have my son. If he has something of value, then he doesn't need to involve my child or Amanda."

"Why are you doing this, Dennis?" Amanda said.

"Because my dad wasn't a bad guy. He wasn't a thief. Bolt can prove I'm right. My dad was framed. The money Dad was accused of stealing from the CIA... someone else stole it. A Russian."

"Dennis, my father's lying to you," Amanda said, her voice wavering. "He's a very good liar. He's using you."

"My dad was innocent, and maybe he didn't kill himself." He raised his hoarse, whispery voice, like it was going to be heard around the world. His deepest hope, given strength. "You weren't willing to talk to your dad but I was...we were right."

"Dennis," Sam said. "Okay, your dad was right. Where is my son?"

"I told you, he's safe. Talking to Bolt will reassure you on that front. I feel you need to hear his authenticity."

Authenticity. Of a traitor.

"Let's you and me and Amanda go inside." Dennis Gandy stared at Mila. "She can wait out here. There's a gun trained on you, so don't try to leave. Just wait here."

Sam glanced at Mila. She didn't like this, being shut out, because she wanted whatever it was that Bolt had.

"I'll give it to you," he whispered. "I don't care about it."

"Ask him who killed my husband," she said. "Do that for me."

Her husband had been killed by the Russians? What had happened? But he simply nodded.

Dennis gestured toward the door, and Sam and Amanda followed him in. Sam could see that Amanda was shaking. He put a reassuring hand on her shoulder.

They followed Dennis into an expansive entryway, with a marble floor, and large, ugly gilt mirrors on its walls. The next room was a giant den, done as through straight out of a magazine, with no family pictures or personal touches. The air smelled slightly stale.

"Well?" Amanda said, her voice shaking.

Dennis walked toward her. She pulled the gun from the back of her jeans.

"Amanda, please don't," Dennis said, like she had put

a glass down on the table without a coaster. "He's not going to come in here with you waving that around. Do you even know how to use it?"

"Yes. I learned after Dad defected. I didn't feel safe. Grayson taught me."

Dennis held out his hand for the gun. "We're just talking. Talking. Okay?"

She glanced at Sam. He nodded. She surrendered the gun. Dennis took it and put it on a far table. "Sam?"

"I have a knife and a gun and I'm not surrendering either."

Dennis nodded. He produced a phone and tapped a button. He held the phone out toward Sam. "Put Daniel on, please."

"Dad?" Daniel's voice.

It was a knife in his heart. "Hi, son," Sam said. He kept his own voice steady.

"Are you coming soon?"

"Yes. Very soon."

"Okay. I—" And then the phone was apparently taken from Daniel. Dennis tucked his back in his pocket. "The weapons, please. Put them on the floor, then step away from them."

Sam obeyed. Dennis gestured, and Sam and Amanda moved toward the center of the room. "All right," he called.

The door opened. Markus Bolt stepped through. He looked uneasy. He looked at Amanda and said, "Hello, darling," and then glanced at Sam. Seemed to study him for a moment. Then said, "Sit down, please, and let's talk."

The bald agent didn't like this at all. He thought Mila had lost her mind. But he'd been willing to follow her orders because she'd promised to get him back on active duty, his record expunged of some mistakes and problems. He didn't know what else he might do other than the work he'd done for MI6. Go mercenary, but he wanted to be close to home, not off in some trouble spot.

He moved carefully between the massive houses, walking along the fencing. He turned a corner and saw a woman. Her arm was in a sling. She wore a sundress. He hesitated, because if he started waving a weapon in this neighborhood, the police would be called. But he kept his pistol behind him, his hand on it, assessing her.

"Ma'am, don't be concerned, I'm private security with the house across the way and we're just conducting a sweep—"

"Aw, you're British," she said with a Scottish accent. "Sorry."

The bullet hit him in the back of the head, and he fell forward. Marianne signaled at the Scot and they both moved as planned, separating, hunting the next target.

The Scottish woman turned and walked to the edge of the house and peered around. At the end of the cul-de-sac, four houses away, she could see a woman standing by a parked car.

They'd watched the woman turn into the cul-de-sac and the other car with the two men park nearby. The other operative was here, moving among the houses, out of sight.

One down, two to go.

Sam and Amanda stood by the couch.

"I'd like to give you a hug, Amanda," Bolt said.

"Well, I don't want one from you," she said. She was crying quietly. Her resolve was wavering in the shock of seeing a man she had thought she'd never see again. "The pain you have caused…"

"I know. Well, I'm sorry for that. I guess this is my apology tour. But I am sorry. And I do love you."

She made a choked half laugh. "You've kidnapped a kid and you claim to be making apologies. I can't even... Allan killed himself because of you. The shame you brought on us..." She stared at him. "But look at you. You're nothing now. Nothing."

"Amanda, I had my reasons."

"I don't care about your reasons."

"I undertook a job that could take years," he said quietly. "And the job is now done."

"What?" Sam said. "This is your story? You were on a job? A deep cover one? No one will believe that." He glanced at Gandy, who was staring at him.

"It was a mission I gave myself. Sure, I had taken money from the Russians. But that let me earn a way in with them. And then, once I got to see them so regularly, to realize their pull on the world and its money, then I also realized I couldn't simply sit and do nothing in Russia. I had to act."

"No," Amanda said, shaking her head. "And now you're back asking politely for forgiveness? No."

"I'm dying," Bolt said. "Incurable illness. Nothing to be done. I wanted to come home and see my children."

Children. Plural. Sam stared at him. The unthinkable rising in his chest. He had to ask. He had to know.

"You knew my wife. Lucy."

"Yes. I knew Lucy. I saw her in Miami. I saw her in DC. She came to see me in Russia." A little, knowing smile. "What a surprise she turned out to be. I think now our mutual interest was in leverage that could keep us alive. I think her bosses told her I was of interest to them. Imagine owning someone inside the Agency who's been dealing secretly with the Russians. She wanted intelligence I had access to and she was willing to pay me."

Every word a stab. A twist of the knife.

"And why did she come see you in Russia, then?"

"Oh. A couple of reasons. The first was that she wanted to know information from Russia; if I could access it, she was willing to pay. "

"And the second?"

"That's more private. There was a letter from Allan. Disowning me. Expressing all the anger I supposed he wished he could say to my face. I did write him back. With a suggestion I came to regret."

Amanda stiffened.

"And she had some...other information for me." He stared at Sam.

"I can see the lie you're trying to tell. It's not possible. Whatever happened between you and Lucy...you are not Daniel's father."

"Of course not, Sam. I'm yours."

60

G ET UP," THE MAN HAD said, standing over the bed. He wouldn't tell Daniel his name—the same guy who had easily manhandled him when he tried to escape—so Daniel called him "Bradley" because he reminded him of a bully back at Lakehaven Middle School.

Daniel got up.

"Follow me," Bradley said.

He followed him. They walked out to the den, where Clarice sat, trying to read a book. It didn't look like she'd made much progress. She seemed nervous and unhappy.

"Hey, Aunt Liar," he said. He'd decided to go on the offensive.

Bradley shoved him to the couch.

"Stop that," Clarice said, and Daniel wasn't sure who she was talking to. She'd gone to a store and bought him clothes, jeans he hated and a shirt he wouldn't have picked out. He had been allowed to shower, with Bradley outside the door. Otherwise he had been stuck in the room, with the ocean view. He had rewatched some Marvel movies, wishing a superhero would crash through the window. Or just Dad. Why was it taking so long for Dad to come and give them whatever they wanted? Or to talk to Aunt Clarice.

Was Dad okay? What if Dad never came for him? What

would they do, just let him leave with Aunt Clarice? Uncle Mark had not been here.

"Your father is on the phone for you. You say nothing about where you are. You can ask him to come get you, so he cooperates, and all is well, yes?" Bradley said.

"Okay." Daniel took the phone. He heard a man's voice say: "Put Daniel on, please."

He let a few seconds pass.

"Dad?" Daniel said.

"Hi, son," Dad said.

"Are you coming soon?"

"Yes. Very soon."

"Okay. I—" And then Bradley pulled the phone away. He listened for a moment and hung up.

"I didn't get to talk to him." Daniel felt a sharp, hot anger rising in him.

"You'll see him soon." He stared down at Daniel. "Go back to your room."

"Why, Bradley?" he said very slowly. He had decided to start testing Bradley. These people were holding him for no reason he could figure out; everything to lure him to Florida—see Dad, talk to Dad, hear a message from his mother—had all been a pack of lies. And he was tired of the lies.

"Get your ass up," Bradley said.

Daniel didn't move. He glanced over at Clarice, who looked vaguely terrified.

Bradley seized him by the throat and held him up, above the couch.

Daniel started to choke.

Bradley rumbled, "I have some room, not much, but enough, on how I treat you."

Daniel stared at him, tried to nod.

"Put him down!" Aunt Clarice stood, her finger still holding her place in her unreadable book. "Now!"

Bradley glanced at her, glanced at him, and dropped Daniel back on the coach.

Daniel clutched at his throat. Making a gagging sound. Clawing at the air.

"You hurt him!" Clarice screamed.

"I barely…I barely squeezed." Bradley peered at Daniel, as if interested in what would happen next.

Daniel thrashed, tossing the pillows. He pointed at his throat.

"He's choking!" Clarice screamed. "Call 911!"

"We can't, you know we can't." Bradley flipped Daniel over, pounded on his back.

"That's not helping!" Clarice sobbed "Daniel, Daniel, please…"

Bradley turned Daniel back around to face him, and Daniel powered a kick of absolute force, precision, and fury right into Bradley's groin. Then again. The man stared at Daniel in frozen shock as he staggered and Daniel vaulted off the couch and ran straight for the front door.

He opened it and fled into the hallway, Clarice imploring him to come back. He saw an exit sign—in English and Russian—and he pushed open the door into a stairwell. He ran down the stairs. The floor numbers said 20, then 19. He heard the entry door above him wrench open. He kept running. At 15, he ducked out back into the floor's hallway, carefully shutting the door after him. There had to be a stairwell on the other side, in case of fire. But then he saw an elevator, two older women waiting for it, and it chimed and opened as he approached. He boarded it with the two women. They both were in floppy hats and bright floral swim coverups, murmuring to each other in Russian. One nodded at him and he nodded back.

He wanted to ask them for help, but they were

speaking Russian and Bradley had a Russian accent, so
he was afraid they might not help him.

They all got out at the ground floor, the two women
heading toward the pool, and Daniel deciding not to run
past the security guard at the front entrance, but just to
walk out calmly to the street. He glanced back. He saw
the other elevator door opening and Bradley and Clarice
coming out.

Now he ran.

He didn't know where in Miami he was and he didn't
know where to go. High palm trees lined the sidewalk.
He scanned the street. No sign of a police car. Not many
pedestrians; people were mostly in cars. He glanced
back.

Bradley was gaining on him, even hobbling as he ran,
a look of absolute rage purpling his face. Clarice behind
him, bleating Daniel's name.

Across the busy street was a coffee shop. People there
would help him. He dodged into traffic, cars honking at
him. He glanced back. Bradley and Clarice still pursuing. He ran into the Starbucks.

He heard people, at the tables, all speaking Russian.
Was he in Russia or Miami? He didn't like this. He ran
through the café, around the counter, to the back, and
out the door into the service alley.

He didn't hear the screams from the road.

Ten seconds, the Russian thug thought, *I'm ten seconds
away from him, and when I get him, I'm going to take this
little punk bitch upstairs and I'll show him what respect is
and what sore balls are, and if the boss doesn't like it, tough
because no one does this to me.*

And then the wail of brakes, hit too late, and a scream
and he glanced back. Clarice had gone over the front of
a car, over the windshield, down the back and behind,

another car braking hard to avoid her. Her scream cut off.

Damn this brat. Damn him. He couldn't leave Clarice in the street, and people were getting out of the cars, and as Bradley hesitated, two men in a pickup truck got out and grabbed him as the woman in their group rushed to Clarice, a phone already in her hand.

These, unfortunately, weren't Russians. "Why was that lady chasing you?" one yelled at him.

"No, that's not it," Bradley started to say. Screw this, the brat was more important and he couldn't be tied up talking to police. He started running and the men grabbed at him.

"You can't leave a scene," one yelled.

Bradley hammered a fist into one's face; the guy crumpled to the asphalt. The other man cussed at him, hit him, not hard enough to do damage, and then there was a police car arriving.

No, no, no. The boss would be so displeased. He had promised such a large payment, and now the little brat had ruined it all. He had to get out of here. Run, hide, the boss would hide him—

He stepped backward into the other lane, directly in the line of a speeding driver who was busy glancing at the chaos, and never saw what hit him.

61

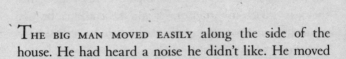

THE BIG MAN MOVED EASILY along the side of the house. He had heard a noise he didn't like. He moved around the corner and saw his compatriot's body on the ground.

"Two is down," he reported. And then a suppressed bullet caught him as well.

In her earpiece, Mila heard her colleague say, *Two is down*, and then the sound of a person falling.

Marianne's team was here and taking hers down. She felt a bright, hot anger.

But she couldn't leave Amanda. She ran for the side of the house.

Sam stared at him, and Bolt flexed a weak smile.

"Is this a joke?"

"No. I have enjoyed talking to Daniel. He thinks I'm his great-uncle. I'll leave it to you to tell him I'm his grandfather. But I'll understand if you want to keep that a secret."

"Again, is this a joke?" Sam was aware that Amanda was staring at him, then at her father, trying to absorb the news.

"My early work in the Agency took me to many

places. Your parents and I were all in Uganda around the same time, for several weeks. Your brother—I'll just say he seemed a troubled kid, even at an early age, and there was a strain in the marriage. I met your mother at a reception at the embassy; we became friends."

"That's a lie. She's never mentioned you to me. Knowing you."

"Well, no, she wouldn't. People suddenly didn't talk about their connections to me when I headed to Russia. But she got pregnant in Uganda—I know it because they came back to America for you to be born. She told me she wanted nothing more to do with me, it had been a mistake, we were both married, and we didn't have a future together. She wanted to stay with Alex. But she told me you were mine."

"You're lying," Sam said. It couldn't be true, it couldn't be, this was just a ploy to unnerve him. His father was Alex Capra, a good man who had devoted his life to helping others, not . . . this broken, damaged husk.

Amanda made a noise in her throat.

Bolt continued: "I kept tabs on your family. When you applied to the Agency, I added an endorsement letter to your application. When Lucy reached out to me all those years ago—her criminal employers were aware of my passing information to Russia, before the CIA was, and trust me, having criminals know what you're doing is somehow worse than the government knowing—my countermeasure was to expose you as my son. If I went down, I could take down you as well. Which would bring her unwanted attention and possible exposure. That made Lucy pause. We negotiated. Then Lucy got into her own trouble, and she wasn't my problem anymore. She vanished."

Silence fell upon the room. Sam took a deep breath. He could play this a couple of ways. Argue more about it, or act like he was accepting it. He could feel the weight of the stares against him: Bolt, Dennis, Amanda.

"Daniel is a fine young man. He calls me Uncle Mark, although he knows right now that everything is not quite as it seems since he was sedated on the plane, he hasn't seen you, and he's confined to a bedroom with a large Russian guarding him."

"Get his name out of your mouth," Sam said. The plane? How had they gotten him here on a plane? It must have been a private jet. Bolt had more resources and help than he had imagined.

"So, son, what I need from you is for you to let your bosses know I'm surrendering, but on my terms, which they will accept. Or Daniel and I might have to have a little chat about his dearest mommy."

"I didn't think you could sink lower, Dad," Amanda said. "I was wrong."

"What are your terms?" Sam asked.

"I have information that will be key to national security. A financial map of all the hidden accounts of the Russian elite, all over the world. You want leverage over them? I can give it to you. They don't know the map exists. I stole it from Illya Markarkin. Your friend Valeria's employer."

"Illya's assistant—did you kill her husband?"

"No. I did not. But I know who did, and I'm happy to share that information with her. Later. She's after me for the map."

"You expect me to believe you've memorized the details of hundreds of accounts and front companies."

"I have an eidetic memory. It's part of what made me such a good spy. I have enough of it memorized that you tip over a few, you'll find the rest. Enough to handcuff them."

"And your price for this?"

"I'm kept in a safe location, not prison, but a safe house. A nice one, with a view. My medical needs during my illness are tended to. Dennis stays with me, and after I'm dead, he can write the book he wants to write that really tells my story, how I went to Russia on a mission of my own and came back a hero and burned the billionaires down, while leaving out the details about you and Daniel. You and Amanda spend time with me. I would like to see Daniel as well but I understand why you might not permit that."

Amanda made another half laugh.

"And I'll give you everything. They kept me like a pet. A trophy. But they were sloppy. They're so rich, they're careless. I collected information like an insurance policy, in case they ever turned on me. I can gut that inner circle. We have to move quickly, before they discover Illya screwed up and let me get this information and they start shifting their money around. But I need . . . forgiveness."

Sam glanced at Amanda, waiting for her to speak, but she said nothing. "I won't ever forgive you for dragging my boy into this. And Amanda's forgiveness is hers alone to give."

"How long do you have?" Amanda asked.

"Maybe six months. Less if the Russians find me."

And Sam saw the way it would play out. His offer was too sweet to refuse if it was real. He would not be forgiven, but he would be tolerated. Taken care of. And Dennis would normalize this, rewrite the history when he was allowed to see his antihero as a hero, a man who repented his sins and bought his way back into grace. He felt sick.

"You sent the Russians after us at Cortez's house?"

"No. But they know I'm here. I forgot one little detail in my dance when I left Russia: a phone I used to contact Dennis here. So they've sent my stepson Kirill after me.

He's a very good FSB operative, and I'm not sure if he'll kill me on sight or tie me up and take me home to his mama. He reminds me a bit of you, Sam."

"You don't know me."

"Yet…I feel like I do. I've read about you, of course. Your files, first at the CIA, and then what meager scraps the Russians collected on you. And of course Lucy told me so much." He attempted another smile. "I'm not asking that you like me. I'm asking that you talk to me. Call Woodruff, agree to my ask, and I'll reunite you with Daniel."

"A father who kidnaps his own grandson," Sam said, letting Bolt's fantasy spin out. "What an example."

"Even if you don't talk to me or help me, I got to see him. I got to talk with him. I spoke to him as an adult. I think that was a new experience for him."

"Are you really going to critique my parenting?"

"Not at all. He's an extraordinary young man. He certainly has your bravery."

He wondered how Bolt knew that. Daniel must have fought back. He pulled out his phone. "I'll call now." He glanced at Amanda; she had her eyes closed.

"Please. Put it on speaker," Bolt said.

He did.

"Sam." Woodruff, answering.

"You're on speaker phone," Sam said. "I am sitting with Amanda Bolt and…her father. He would like to surrender to you, with qualifications." He listed out Bolt's demands. He did not mention his assertion of parentage. Woodruff did not interrupt or speak.

"Does he have your son?"

"He does, at an undisclosed location."

"Let me speak to him," Woodruff said.

"No," Sam said. "Whatever you say to him you say to me."

"All right. Mr. Bolt. What is it you want?"

Markus repeated his demands, including more details on the financial map. Woodruff listened. "I'll see what I can do."

"One other item," Markus Bolt said. "I would request a private meeting with Grayson Cortez."

"For what reason?" Woodruff asked.

"Closure," Bolt said.

"He won't agree to that," Amanda said. "I know him."

Sam thought that was odd—wouldn't the man who was fascinated by traitors *want* to speak to the famous one who got away?

"I appreciate your insight, Amanda," Bolt said. "Then you can't give him a choice about it. I have one thing to say to him, just one, and then I'll be done."

Silence.

"Fine," Woodruff said. "I'll grant your demands for your cooperation."

Sam heard a noise. Like a distant, muffled shot.

"Thank you," Bolt said.

"I think we need to go, and now," Sam said.

Mila entered the huge house at the back, through an unlocked door. Neither of her teammates were responding. They were down, likely dead, and she fought down the surge of anger and regret she felt. She held her Glock in her hand.

The room's lights were off, but there was light from the windows looking out over the expansive patio. She listened. She heard voices, raised. Including one she recognized from the times he'd visited Illya in Sochi.

Markus Bolt.

She moved toward the voice.

*　　*　　*

Kirill, Marianne, and the Scot moved toward the house. The younger woman was favoring her shoulder.

"Are you able?" Marianne whispered. The woman's wound looked like it might be bleeding again. She'd been tended by a doctor referred to by their client, off the books.

"I want Gandy," the Scot said. She moved ahead of Kirill and Marianne, who let her. Sometimes you had to let even a wounded bird fly. She remembered, though, what Sam had said about not trusting this one.

Marianne glanced at Kirill, who shrugged. It was foolish to volunteer.

"There's a panic room we can go to," Dennis said quietly. "All these mansions have them."

"And we do what? Go in there and have them wait us out?" Sam said. He wasn't particularly interested in being locked up with Dennis. He had shot Marianne's soldier with a cold, determined look on his face, not the panic a civilian might have shown. He was emotionless in a concerning way, blind to all moral considerations other than his agenda.

"We could put in Amanda," Dennis said. "I can stay with her and you can get Bolt out."

"No," Amanda said. She grabbed her father's arm; it was the first time they had touched.

"We need out, which way?" Sam said.

"Back puts us against the water," Dennis said. "There's a side door, least used, let's take that."

Sam led, pulling Bolt behind him, Amanda close to her father, Dennis in the rear, watching as they moved out of a hallway and into a massive designer kitchen. The side door was just beyond the kitchen and a small office used by the mansion's chief housekeeper when in residence.

They moved quickly, Sam shepherding them into the side office.

Dennis stopped. Glanced back. Grinned at the woman who emerged from the main hallway, a gun leveled at him.

"I spared you, you're wel—" Dennis started and then the woman shot him, a bullet right through the throat. She didn't see another woman emerge from the opposite entrance, leveling, firing, catching her in the head. The woman dropped.

Bolt shoved Sam and Amanda toward the door.

Kirill, behind the fallen Scot, stared at Mila.

Mila met his gaze, aimed at him, but didn't fire at him. "Come with me, Kirill," she said.

He shook his head. And then Marianne burst from behind him in the hallway, firing at her, driving Mila into retreat.

Marianne glanced to her left. The kitchen was empty now.

Choice—chase Bolt or that woman who shot her student. She glanced at Kirill. He could have shot the woman and didn't. Something odd. And he was heading in the direction Bolt had gone. Fine. He could kill Bolt and his merry band, and she would still get paid.

Because Bolt was only part of the job.

She took off after the Moldovan woman. She did not glance back at her dead protégé.

62

———⟨⟨⟨⟩⟩⟩———

SIDE DOOR, AND OUT. AMANDA was sobbing because Dennis was dead and she had seen him fall. Bolt had an arm around her, clutching her close, keeping himself between her and what might follow. They were running for the car Mila had driven. Sam remembered she'd left the keys in the car—so anyone could start it if in need and not be trapped if they were making a hasty escape like now.

Ten feet away from the car and he heard a man's voice order them to stop. Sam whirled and he saw the pistol's laser sight on the Russian's weapon. He saw the red dot on Amanda's forehead. The Russian stared at Sam. "You cannot shoot me before I shoot her. Drop your weapon." His English was excellent. This must be Kirill, the stepson.

Sam did. Amanda steadied herself. She stared at Kirill.

"It's rude to aim a weapon at your own stepsister," Bolt said in English.

Kirill glanced at Amanda, as if seeing her as a person for the first time. The red dot didn't waver.

"I don't want to hurt Amanda. You've hurt her enough, I'm sure," Kirill said. "So down to business. Mama wants you home." He spoke now in Russian, but Sam understood it.

"I miss her smile," Markus Bolt said in English. "They sent you to use you."

"You've mistaken me for a negotiator. Now. We can do this a vicious way or an easy way. Those women in there are hired killers to take you out. The Americans are going to imprison you and then kill you. Treason doesn't get a hall pass. You come home with me, back to my mom, back home, you're going to be under house arrest, but you'll be in a house. Not prison."

"Don't you want to ask me where it is?" Bolt said. He smiled at Kirill but he glanced at Sam.

"What?"

"My ticket home. The financial map."

"Where is it?" Kirill said.

"I gave it to the boy," Bolt said.

The boy. Sam's heart froze.

And then gunfire erupted from the side of the house behind Kirill, two women—Mila and Marianne—spilling out of the house, both struggling to gain control of one pistol locked in both their hands.

"Amanda, run!" Sam shoved her and she sprinted toward the neighboring house, just trying to get space and trees and fence between her and Kirill's gun. "Go! Go!" He spun, to pick up his gun, and Kirill launched into him, a powerhouse kick that felt like it nearly tore Sam's arm out of its socket. And then a fist, hard against Sam's throat. He went down.

Kirill aimed his gun down at Sam.

"Get in the car, Markus, now."

Bolt stared at Sam. And then he obeyed. "Don't kill him. Please. His son needs him. I'll do as you ask."

Something in those few words swayed Kirill. He didn't pull the trigger and end Sam. "I've left your friends alive," Kirill said. "So you will cooperate."

They got in Mila's car and Kirill steered away.

Sam got to his feet and sprinted toward the two women, still locked in combat.

"Marianne!" he demanded. "Stop!" He pressed his gun against her head; Mila had her by the throat. The gun they'd fought over lay in the grass.

Marianne stopped.

"Were you sent here to kill us?"

"No. Bolt is the contract," she said.

"Well, he's gone. Go deal with your wounded."

"She's dead. This bitch killed her."

"This bitch will kill you," Mila said.

"You should have killed him," Marianne said. "Ended this."

Mila zip-tied her arms behind her back and shoved her into the grass.

"Who hired you to kill him?"

She said nothing.

"Who hired you? Tell me and you live. Lie to me and you die. I'm only taking your first answer, Marianne."

"Illya Markarkin," Marianne said.

"I would know if he did. I'm his former assistant."

"Yes, Illya, because he wanted back something Bolt stole."

"Kirill was to kill Bolt."

"He might balk. He might fail. And if he did not, I was to eliminate Kirill. Kirill, and you, and anyone who knew about what Bolt stole from Illya—a flash drive with some financial data on it, I don't know what the data is—but no one in Russia could know it existed, much less than Bolt stole it."

Sam knew she was talking to bargain for her life. Leave her here, with two bodies in the house and two more in the neighborhood, and she would cut a deal with the FBI and the police.

Sam yanked her to her feet. "Where's the car y'all came in?"

"Sam, what are you..." Mila started.

"She's coming with us. I want Kirill to hear what she has to say. Marianne. A boy. Did you see a teenage boy at Illya Markarkin's?"

"No. Just him, his girlfriend who's very pregnant. I think she's the one who called me and hired me."

"He wouldn't be there," Mila said. "Illya wouldn't give shelter to Bolt. He wants him dead."

Sam dug in Marianne's pants pocket, found her keys. They ran down to her car.

"You're right," he said. "This neighborhood is weirdly empty."

"It's full of Russian investment property," Marianne said.

They got into Marianne's car, Marianne and Mila in the backseat, and Sam drove.

"Use my phone to call Amanda, let's find her."

I gave it to the boy. These people—Kirill, Illya—would be after Daniel now. No. No.

"She's not answering," Mila said.

Maybe too scared. He couldn't blame her. She'd found out she had a Russian assassin for a stepbrother and an American spy for a half brother.

"Can we get to Illya?"

"He's beefed up his security," Mila said. "Especially after he knows I betrayed him."

"You're not getting within a mile of him," Sam said.

"You are not the boss of me. He hired Marianne and her people and they killed my friends. He's mine."

Marianne made a coughing noise.

"You. Marianne. You hear about contracts that go out."

Marianne didn't look at her.

"You ever hear of one two years ago? Philip Garrison. A banker in London, run down by a car."

Her husband, Sam thought. The one she mourned. This was why she was chasing these people. Vengeance.

"Cars are inefficient," Marianne said. "I don't use them."

"Which is why they're generally considered to be accidents, not murder, even when unsolved."

"We're focusing on Daniel now. On the living," Sam said.

Mila shot him a look but she went silent.

"I need Bolt to tell me where my son is, and so if Kirill is taking Bolt to Illya's, we're going to Illya's. Agreed?" He looked in the rearview at Mila. She nodded, after a moment.

Sam turned to Marianne. "And you're going to help us."

63

DANIEL RAN PAST THREE MORE streets. He saw, of course, yet another Starbucks. He walked in. First table was two women, speaking Russian to each other. But the next table was two older men, laughing, one speaking loudly in a New York accent that Miami hadn't had time to fade.

He went to the men's table.

"Sir," Daniel said. "Excuse me. I need to call my father to come get me and I lost my phone. Could I borrow yours for just a moment?" And suddenly he heard this hitch in his voice, like he might cry if the man said no. He didn't want to say, *My aunt and my uncle kidnapped me and drugged me on a plane and have been holding me hostage in a building full of Russians.* That was insane. Dad was dealing with these people. Maybe Dad was in trouble with the police, too, if this was known. He glanced toward the front of the café, sure that Clarice or Bradley would be there at any moment.

"Okay, son," the man said. "You sure you're all right?"

"Yes, sir. I just need to call. Please."

"Why don't you tell me the number and I'll dial it for you?" Like he was worried Daniel might run out the café if he handed him the phone.

He started to say Dad's number. But. But. Dad was

with the bad guys right now. If he called Dad...maybe that wasn't good. Maybe the bad guys would hurt Dad for Daniel running.

The bar. He didn't know the bar's number but he said, "My dad owns a bar called Amado on the Miracle Mile but I don't know the number." He knew the manager's name was Paige.

The man googled the bar name, tapped the number. "Who do I ask for?"

"Sam Capra. If he's not there, Paige. Please." He steadied his voice.

"Yes," the old man said. "Is Sam Capra in?" He listened. "Okay, how about Paige?"

Please, Daniel thought, *please*. He glanced back toward the door. What would he do if Bradley came in?

"Hello. There's a young man who wants to talk to you. Hold on." He handed the phone to Daniel, pulled out a chair so Daniel could sit. He sat.

"Hello? Paige? This is Daniel Capra."

"Hi, Daniel. Paige had to step out for a moment. This is Karen. I'm a friend of your dad's, I'm staying at the apartment above the bar. Are you okay?"

"Yes." He couldn't say he'd been kidnapped, not in front of these guys. "I'm alone and I lost my phone, can someone come get me?"

"Yes, sweetheart, I'll come right this second. Where are you?"

"I don't know. A Starbucks. In a Russian neighborhood."

"In Sunny Isles?"

"Is this Sunny Isles?" he asked, and the man nodded and gave him a nearby intersection for reference. He repeated it to Karen.

"Okay, I'm on my way. Stay there. Do you feel safe?"

"Not really."

"Whose phone is this?"

"A nice man let me borrow his."

"All right. You wait there. I'll be there in like thirty minutes."

Too long, he thought, *too long*. But he didn't know what else to do. This was America, a man couldn't grab him from a coffee shop full of people. He would scream his head off.

"Thank you. Do you know where my dad is?"

"Not right this second but I'm coming to get you and we'll figure it out."

She knew maybe she couldn't call Dad, either. Not until he was safe.

"Thank you," he said, but she had hung up. He handed the phone back to the man. "Thank you, sir," he said. "She's coming to get me."

"You sure you're okay, son?"

"Yes."

"Do you want to sit with us while you wait for your ride?" the man asked gently.

He nodded. He offered Daniel a drink but Daniel said, *No thank you, sir*, and nearly added his most recent beverages had all been drugged, so he was just fine. Daniel turned the chair toward the door, so he would see if Bradley entered. No Bradley. No Clarice. He heard a howl of police sirens. The two men started talking about the Miami Dolphins and if they would be good again soon.

64

YOU DRIVE," KIRILL ORDERED HIS stepfather. "And don't try anything, or I'll plant a bullet in your head."

"That would upset your mother." Bolt slid into the driver's seat as Kirill slid into the seat behind him, gun firmly aimed at the back of Bolt's head.

"She lost one husband and got over it," Kirill said. "Who is this boy you gave the financial data to?"

"The American operative's son," Bolt said. "He's here, under my control."

"You pulled a kid into this? You piece of garbage." Kirill did not want to have to kill a kid. He was sure, in fact, he couldn't do it. A kid wouldn't understand the financial map. Just take the file from him.

"Oh, and the kid's aunt and a very desperate hired Russian thug." Bolt seemed a bit amused. "I can vouch for the kid, he'll say nothing. None of them know anything about the files."

"Why did you do this?"

"I'm dying."

"I know."

"And I wanted to see my children before I died. Have time with them."

"Such a noble gesture, Markus. You'll make Mama cry." *Hit a bump in the road*, he thought, *and the gun will go off. I'll tell Mama it was an accident, I tried. But I need the files. And then we'll go to Illya's plane and this is all done. I'll take you home to Mama and then Mama can come visit me in Moscow and I never have to see your lying face again.*

"I do love your mother," he said unexpectedly.

"Don't talk about her to me."

"I never meant to hurt your father."

They had never discussed Kirill's father. Kirill forced himself to take a deep breath.

"It's easy to blame me," Markus said. "I'm the easiest bad guy in the world to blame. It's very strange to be a defector, Kirill."

Kirill wondered if Bolt could somehow know of Mila's offer of refuge. He couldn't. But Bolt was the devil—who knew what he knew? "I'm sure it is," he said, because he had to say something.

"Have you ever been the new kid at school, Kirill? No? It's a challenge. Everyone looking at you, judging you, wondering whether or not they should befriend you. I had done them a great service, giving them those names, destroying the informant networks that were hurting them. And hurting your country."

Kirill thought Bolt was waiting for a thank-you, but Kirill stayed silent.

"And the cool kids want to be near fame, or at least notoriety. So everyone wanted to be my friend, all while privately loathing me for being a traitor. I was their show dog for a while. Your father was the one who was kind to me. Took me under his wing. Warned me, correctly, about some of the president's associates that I should not get too close to. He took me home to have dinner, to meet your mother and you. Do you remember that?"

"Yes."

"And I knew I wanted to be with her the moment

I laid eyes on her, and I could tell she was intrigued with me. I could pick up on the cracks in the relationship between them. You know that's part of what we do, read the room, see the potential weaknesses. I remember thinking, *Oh, I've one real friend here, this nice man, so I'll stay away from his wife.* And you were a very charming child, Kirill. I liked you from the beginning."

"This won't keep me from shooting you," Kirill said. "If I so choose."

"I don't know what your father was told," Bolt said. "If it was your mother who told him it was over because she wanted to be with me or the president's people who said he had to step aside and let your mom and me be together. But it wasn't me. It was never me."

"Val," he said, using her alias, "thinks you know who killed her husband in London."

"Oh, it was Bobo behind it, but I assumed you knew that. Illya still thinks it was an accident. His affection for Val was real. She's very likable, don't you find?"

"Not particularly."

"And have you told her it wasn't an accident?"

"No."

"It's a very bad look for Illya, that. Letting her inside his business, his life. He might not rush back to Russia."

"He's not as bright as he thinks he is," Kirill said. *Great*, he thought, *now you're agreeing with Markus*.

"Oh, that's true of many people who have risen high in the world. He's rich because he's Morozov's friend, not because he's some genius captain of industry. This is who you work for, Kirill. A circle of former spies where one got lucky and made them all rich. Does that sound like a system of government?"

Markus could crack jokes with a gun at his head. Maybe he had ceased to care.

"Are you really dying?"

"Yes. That should put a smile on your face."

"I work for Russia. Not billionaires."

"But that's who they are now."

"You worked for them, too."

"I did, and haven't things turned out well for me? Let me ask you a question."

Kirill waited.

"I understand you aiming your gun at Amanda—it stayed Sam's hand. But would you have shot my innocent daughter, just to hurt me?"

"Shut up."

"I didn't realize you were on this descent to cruelty."

"Where are we going?"

"Sunny Isles."

Kirill couldn't keep the disbelief out of his voice. "That's the last place you would go."

"I lost the place I originally was going to stay, so I decided to hide in plain sight. Illya had his hit team scouring all of Miami except one of his own buildings."

The sheer nerve, Kirill thought.

"I'm going to share something with you, in exchange for a promise. It's a simple favor."

"No promises."

"I suppose you have the upper hand and I'll have to trust your good nature. That contract kill team, that woman Marianne. They're here not just to kill me. They're here to clean up all the loose ends. That would include you."

"Wrong," he said.

"You know about the map. How do you think Morozov holds on to power if it's known the financial networks could be compromised? Marianne will try to kill you as soon as you have the data."

"No," he said, a little less certainly.

"Why is she here, then? Why? No one else knows to hire her, except Illya."

"Bobo or the Dude could have hired her."

"And not told you there was another player gunning for me? It puts you both at risk. Does that sound like correct operational protocol to you, Kirill?" He met Kirill's gaze in the rearview mirror. "I'm sorry this is our first heart-to-heart talk, at gunpoint, on the run from killers. I should have asked you to go have tea when our lives were calmer."

Kirill considered. Bolt had a point. But Kirill was an agent of the Russian government, he should be untouchable, Bobo's golden boy... and the stepson of a traitor, who had now betrayed the country that had paid him good money and taken him in. The stink of Markus could affect him once Markus's latest betrayal was known.

"So in return for what I just told you, you'll let the American boy go," Bolt said. "He knows nothing; he can't hurt you. Swear it."

Kirill said nothing.

"I'm not asking you, I'm telling you, Kirill. I've just done you a favor that might save your life."

But Kirill said nothing. He thought, *What is this mission turning me into?*

65

A WOMAN WALKED INTO THE coffee shop and noticed Daniel immediately. She made a beeline for him. She was older, in jeans and a faded blue shirt. By the time she'd gotten there, the sirens had stopped.

"Daniel?" she said.

He nodded.

"I'm Karen." She smiled at the two men and offered her hand to them. They shook hands with her. "Thank you for watching out for him."

Daniel didn't stand. He'd already gone off once with someone pretending to be his friend, his aunt, and doing this again suddenly felt weird. "Where's Paige?" He had not met Paige but he at least had heard her name.

"She's helping your dad. So I came alone. I thought we'd just go back to the bar and wait for your father. My daughter is with him right now, so I'm expecting they'll be in touch really soon."

"All right," he said. He got up and he thanked the men again and he followed Karen out to her car. She drove a Mercedes and she opened the door for him.

"How do you know my dad?" Daniel asked as they headed toward Coral Gables.

She didn't answer right away. "Well, I know him from the bar."

"Do you work there?"

"No, just a regular."

"He's not at this bar that often."

"I know, but I know Paige, and so I've seen him every time he comes through."

"Okay."

"Daniel."

"Yes."

"Were some people holding you prisoner?"

He had been surprised she hadn't asked before, but he hadn't volunteered the information. "I came here with my aunt Clarice and my uncle Mark."

"Oh. Are you close to them?"

"I never met them before this week. Aunt Clarice showed me a bunch of pictures with her and my mom. She raised her."

"Oh, that's nice. And your uncle...Mark?"

"He wasn't in most of the pictures. He left me in the condo with Aunt Clarice and Bradley."

"Who's Bradley?"

"He was supposed to keep me inside the apartment, but I got out. I don't know his real name. I just called him Bradley because he reminded me of someone."

"Clever boy to have gotten away," she said.

"I just faked being hurt and they bought it long enough."

"Where was this apartment?"

"A few blocks away in a high-rise on the beach. It was full of Russians."

"I'll bet it was," she said. Her voice cooled.

"What do you mean?"

"That town, a lot of Russians moved there. They have their babies there so their kids will be American citizens." He could see she was gripping the steering wheel. "So tell me about Uncle Mark."

"Why?"

"I'm wondering if Sam mentioned him to me."

"I don't know. He said he lives here sometimes. He has a daughter named Amanda and he helps rich people manage their money."

He could see Karen's mouth tighten. "What does he look like?" she asked.

"Like, old. Gray in his hair. Medium tall, I guess. He's just a guy."

"With one of those faces you can forget," she said.

"I guess." Why was she asking about Uncle Mark?

Her phone beeped. She answered it. "Sweetheart. Are you okay?"

She listened; Daniel couldn't hear the voice on the other end.

"Okay. Is Sam with you?"

He kept himself from reaching for the phone. He wanted to hear the sound of his dad's voice as never before.

"What?" Karen said. Something wrong. Something very wrong.

Karen listened.

"All right. All right. Go to Grayson's house. Please be careful." She put down the phone. On the opposite side from where Daniel sat in the passenger seat.

"What's happening?" he asked.

"That was my daughter. Her name's Amanda, too." She tried to give him a reassuring smile. "I don't know that the bar is safe to take you there," she said. "Some people are after your father. We're going to go to a friend's house."

"No," Daniel said. "I'm not going to somewhere else where I don't know anyone. Take me to a police station then."

"If the police know what your dad's involved in, he'll be arrested."

That couldn't be true. Dad wasn't a criminal.

"Can I borrow your phone to call him?" Daniel asked. "I just want my dad."

"I know, honey, and I'm sorry. He's not in a place where he can talk to you right now," Karen said. "I know this is hard, because this Uncle Mark guy lied to you, and now you're thinking that I lied to you. So I'll take you where you want to go. But the bar might be dangerous because people could be looking for your dad. So I will take you to a mall, or a park, or any place you feel safe while we wait."

"Wait for what?"

"For your dad to call you, honey," she said.

He didn't know what to do. "What friend did you want to go to?"

"He's someone who has known your dad a long time. He probably knew your mother."

"How?"

"That's up to your dad to explain, not me."

"My fake uncle," Daniel said, and he said this with a sneer, "said my mother left a message for me. I guess that was a lie, too."

"Maybe not," Karen said. "Maybe this friend would know. His name is Grayson Cortez."

"Fine," Daniel said. "Let's go to your friend's house."

66

"WELL, WELL," THE MAN SAID at the front door. "Who have you brought me here?"

"This is Daniel Capra," Karen said. Her voice was tight.

The older man looked at Daniel at first with surprise and then a soft smile. "Hello, Daniel. My name is Mr. Cortez. It's a pleasure to meet you." He offered his hand and Daniel shook it. Karen steered Daniel into the house and Cortez shut the door behind them.

"I'm delighted to meet him, but why is Daniel here?" Cortez asked.

"He was staying with his aunt in Sunny Isles and he decided to leave."

"Sunny Isles."

"She got me on a jet here with my uncle and then they wouldn't let me see my dad or leave," Daniel said.

"His uncle Mark, who he had not met before," Karen said.

Five beats of silence. Cortez glanced at Daniel. "Uncle Mark? And your aunt's name is Clarice, is that right?"

"How do you know that?"

"I'm familiar with your parents'…history."

"Their history," Daniel said slowly. "Uh, okay." He didn't know his parents had a history. It sounded ominous.

"Are you hungry?" Cortez asked.

"I could eat," Daniel said. He had only nibbled at what Clarice had given him, still afraid they would drug him again.

"Sandwich? Ham and cheese?"

"Yes, sir, thank you."

Cortez went into the kitchen and quickly made a sandwich. Daniel and Karen sat on the couch.

"It'll be okay," Karen said again.

"I need to talk to my dad," Daniel said. "Please."

"I told you, he's not where he can talk right now."

"Why is this happening?" His voice rose.

"It's his place to tell you, not ours," Cortez said as he brought Daniel his sandwich and an unopened cold can of sparkling water. Daniel popped the tab and drank.

"You said their history. Mark and Clarice said there was a message from my mom for me. I don't understand. Was that just a lie to get me here?"

Cortez glanced at Karen. "No. It's not just a lie. She did make a video for you."

"Why haven't I seen it?"

"Your father didn't know about it. I never told him. It was intended for you."

"Have you seen it?"

"Yes," Cortez said.

"They said it was passworded."

"It is, but I guessed the password. It was your birthdate."

"How did you know my birthdate?"

"Like I said, I'm familiar with your parents. Clarice really is your great-aunt." He looked at Karen, who said nothing, but put a reassuring hand on Daniel's back.

Familiar with wasn't the same as knowing them. "Why did they bring me here?"

"To force your father to help them, I assume," Cortez said.

"Help them with what?"

Cortez took a deep breath. "Your father owns a number of bars."

"Yes, I know."

"Those kinds of businesses are attractive to some bad people," Cortez said.

Daniel bit into his sandwich and stared at him. "What?"

"People who have lots of money they need to clean, to be able to account for, and a bar is a good way to do that. A group of thirty bars, owned by one man, is even better. So they want to take over his bars."

Daniel saw Cortez and Karen exchange a look and he wondered if the man was lying to him. But it sounded like something that could happen. Bradley was a thug, and Mark was . . . sneaky. Off, in some way. "Why doesn't he call the police?"

"He doesn't want the police involved for a few reasons."

"Do you have this message she left for me?" Daniel asked suddenly. At least Clarice and Mark had told him one truth.

"How did you know about it?"

"Clarice and Mark told me."

"And how did they know about it?"

"They said a friend of Lucy's found it in a book."

"Your mother sent it to a friend of hers here in Miami. A man named Terrell, who had helped her before. He gave it to me, long after your mother sent it to him. He didn't know what to do with it, but he knew that I knew your mom. I communicated with people about it when I received it." He glanced at Karen. "Somehow . . . Mark knew about it. He must have had someone contact her friend Terrell. Maybe pay him to talk."

Awkward silence in the room.

"Don't show that video to him without his father here," Karen said. "Don't, Grayson."

"I have the right to see it," Daniel said. He thought Dad might just say no. He had controlled everything that Daniel knew about his mother; this was his one chance. "Please."

"Excuse me," Cortez said. He got up and went down a hallway.

"Be careful what you wish for," Karen said.

"Is it all bad?"

"The truth doesn't always set you free," Karen said. "I know this from bitter experience."

Cortez returned. He held a disc, slid it into the player. A key entry appeared, and Cortez used the remote to select numbers that matched Daniel's birthdate.

His mother appeared. She looked very young. She looked scared. She wore a shapeless sweater and a coat; the room she was in was dark. It looked like it might be a cheap hotel room.

"Daniel...Hello. I don't know if you'll ever get to see this. I hope you do. I need you to know why I'm not with you right now. It's not because I don't want to be. It's because I am trying to keep you safe.

"My work is dangerous. I can't go into detail, and you're too young to understand, but I work to help defeat bad guys. I got involved in being undercover before I knew I was pregnant with you and then I couldn't easily get out of it. So I can't be with you right now...or maybe ever.

"Your dad doesn't know. I have to protect him from it. I have to protect you from it. So you may not always hear nice things about me. People doubted my ethics at times. But I'm your mother, and I love you—I love you more than I ever thought I could—and I want you to know that. I'm sorry I'm not...the typical mother. The first time I held you, I realized you deserved better than me…but I want you to know what I was doing was important work to me. And I tried my best. Your dad loves you and I know he'll be a good father. I love you." She seemed to stumble over, even be surprised by, those last three words.

The video ended.

Daniel swallowed. He stared at the screen. Then he said, "So she was…what, a cop of some sort?"

"She worked for the government. I can't say more than that." His voice was neutral. Karen made a coughing noise and Cortez shot her a look.

"So she was doing something dangerous and then died from her heart problem?" Daniel's voice shook a bit.

"It wasn't a heart problem. She was shot."

Daniel took a deep, shuddering breath. "Why would he lie to me?"

"Because she was on a mission. He doesn't know details. The government covered up her death as a heart issue. They had their reasons, years ago."

"So my mom…was a hero," Daniel said.

He looked at both the adults. Karen stared at her lap.

"And my dad kept that from me?" Daniel asked.

"He didn't know all the details," Cortez said again. "Her work was secret, even to him. He had to go along with the government's story. Don't be mad at him."

"That's not fair to her," he said. *Your father has so many big secrets.* "And Clarice and Mark knew this? That's why they said he was lying."

"Technically that's true," Cortez said.

"How did they know if my dad didn't?"

"Mark was one of the bad guys," Cortez said.

"But this was thirteen years ago," Daniel said.

"Bad guys don't always go away."

"Who killed my mom?"

"We'll never know," Cortez said.

"Was it this Mark guy?"

"I think Mark manipulated your aunt—she is your real great-aunt, obviously—and got her on his side by telling her your mother's death from a heart condition wasn't what it seemed."

"He made her suspicious of Dad."

"Yes. It was cruel," Cortez said.

"You sure know a lot about this," Daniel said.

"It was my job once to study these kinds of cases like your mom's, to prevent them from happening again. I worked for the government, too."

"And my dad . . . he just owns bars, right?"

"Yes," Cortez said.

Like Dad could be some sort of government operative. That was clearly ridiculous.

"Can I watch again? I've never seen her talk before. Never heard her voice."

"Of course," Cortez said. He pressed a button on the remote.

The video started again. Daniel felt Karen take and squeeze his hand, and then she got up suddenly and walked into the kitchen, as if she could not bear to watch.

He stared at the screen and, for only the second time, listened to his mother's voice.

67

TWO MINUTES AFTER KIRILL AND Bolt arrived, Sam pulled into the condo parking garage. There had been an accident of some sort farther down the street—one ambulance pulling away, without sirens; another one roaring past them, sirens blaring. One dead, one alive, Sam guessed.

"This feels like driving into the heart of darkness," he said.

"There's my car," Mila said. "Bolt and Kirill are here."

"How can we get up without being seen?" Sam asked.

"Penthouse elevator," she said. "I have a master access code. He may have only changed the regular code."

"Up we go," he said. She entered the code; it worked. The doors opened to an empty elevator. They got in.

"Bolt talks first. He tells us where Daniel is. Agreed?" Mila nodded.

Marianne closed her eyes and then reopened them again. "You and your son and this bitch are as good as dead," she whispered.

"I wonder how your employer will view you bringing us back here?" Sam wondered. "If we're dead, you're dead."

"You spared my life before and I spared you at Cortez's," Marianne said. "We're even right now."

"I don't know that you spared me as much as missed," Sam said. Marianne said nothing.

The elevator rose.

Four floors below the penthouse, Kirill kept his gun on Bolt as Bolt opened the door. They entered, Kirill careful to keep Bolt between him and any possible threat.

"Pyotr? Clarice?" Bolt called. No answer.

They went through the condo. Empty. One room had a bed that had been slept in and clothes for a young teenage boy, with price tags attached, hanging in one closet.

"No one home. That's troubling," Bolt said.

"The police and the ambulances a bit down the street we saw," Kirill said. "Could be related."

"I don't see how that could have anything to do with us. May I make a phone call?"

"Keep it on speaker," Kirill ordered. Bolt had been in this building all along. His own condo was only a few floors away.

Bolt called a number: Kirill could see on the screen the number was for Clarice.

No answer.

He tried another number: no answer.

"How did you give the data to the boy?" Kirill said. Because if the boy was loose, so was the data.

"I put the flash drive in the pocket of the new jeans his aunt laid out for him. I didn't want to keep it on me while out and about and I didn't want it lying on the table. It would ensure his father came to me."

"Why would that matter?"

"He and I had issues to discuss."

"His aunt? You've pulled a whole family into this?"

"It's a story not of interest to you. The boy is not here. They've taken him somewhere."

"Or maybe the Americans knew about this and have rescued him and they have the file."

"Or Illya found out I was hiding here in his own building. That seems far likelier. I bought this through a shell company..."

"They're not answering, so they're either incapable or they're dead," Kirill said. "Let's go upstairs and get your flight home arranged, Papa," he said, making the last word a twist of the knife.

The elevator to the penthouse opened.

"Where the hell have—" Illya said, rushing forward, and Mila had the gun leveled at him.

"Where's the security team?" Mila said.

"With Maria—in the other apartment. I moved her for her safety and kept the team with her."

"Don't lie, Illya," Mila said. She didn't believe that Illya would sit here alone, unprotected.

"I don't want her to hear what you might say," Illya said. "They could be bought. What do you want?"

Sam stepped out of the elevator with Marianne. Illya shook his head.

"Where's my son?" Sam said.

"I have no idea who you are or what you're asking." Illya glanced at Mila. "What do you want? You show your face after you betray me? After everything I did for you?" He spat at her, his mouth trembling.

"Bolt is coming for you, along with your charming stepson," Mila said. "Now, I can help you, Illya, for the sake of our friendship..."

He made a dismissive noise.

"...and the fact you're about to be a father."

This silenced him.

Sam gestured a hush to Mila. He pointed at Illya. He

gestured at the bound Marianne to sit on the floor by the elevator and she obeyed. He started moving through the apartment to clear it.

Mila kept speaking, in case anyone was listening: "I'm going to make the same offer to you I made to Kirill. Defect to the UK. Come with me, and I'll protect you. Maria, too, if you want. You're going to lose a lot of your money, but you'll be alive and you'll be protected. Russia is over for you as soon as the rest of the oligarchs learn you had their financial details and let them slip into Western hands. You're done."

"No. No. You suggest I be like Markus, a traitor? No." Illya at least wasn't shouting out a warning, but that could be to let anyone waiting for Sam maintain their defensive posture.

Sam moved through the kitchen. Quickly. He saw three glasses in the sink. He pulled a carving knife from the magnetic hanger over the grand oven. He moved through a hallway, past a bedroom, and he could see another door, barely open.

"I suggest you consider my offer," Mila said.

"You are the worst liar I've ever known, and that's saying a lot," Illya said. His voice broke.

"Don't cry," Mila said. "You don't fool me."

"I trusted you so much, Valeria, and now you bring this American to help kill me..." And his voice rose, like a warning.

Sam kicked in the partly open door. It bounced off the heavy man who had been hiding behind it. He fired his weapon through the wood, the bullet passing above Sam's shoulder, a suppressor muffling the shot.

Mila turned and ran toward the sounds. Illya ran to the elevator, jabbing the button, Marianne screaming at him to cut her loose, him ignoring her.

The elevator doors opened.

*   *   *

Sam was shorter than the Russian, by a head, and he slammed his fist, with three fast blows, driving the Russian back into the desk. The man raised the gun and Sam whirled, hammering the weapon with a roundhouse kick, the bullet firing into the office bookshelf. Sam grabbed the gun, they fought for it, and then Mila came up behind the Russian, jammed her gun into the back of his head, and fired. The man dropped.

"Pavel. He was always nice to me," Mila said and turned around, hurrying back toward the den.

68

THE RIDESHARE DRIVER DROPPED OFF Amanda in front of
Cortez's house. She shivered as she headed for the door.
She knocked, hoping that Cortez knew where she was.
Her father— here, *here*, and touching her and talking
to her, almost like nothing had happened—felt like a
punch to her brain, her soul, and she wanted her mother:
her aggravating, bossy, sometimes distant mother.

Grayson Cortez answered the door. "Amanda," Cortez said.

"Is my mom here?"

"Yes, she is, come inside."

He shut the door behind her. And locked it.

"Mom?" she called out.

Her mother walked out from the kitchen, relief paint-
ing her face.

"Oh, baby," Karen said. She ran toward Amanda,
embraced her in a hug.

"Mom, Dad is here. In America. Here."

"I know. I know."

"And Dennis is dead. I saw him get shot. A woman
shot him and then she got shot." She took a huge gasping
of air. "I saw it. And then Dad's stepson, he's a Russian
killer, he aimed a gun at me, but then my new neighbor,
he fought them and I ran...I ran, he told me to run..."

"Sam?"

"Yes."

"His son is here. Your dad had him held but he got away."

"Oh, thank God," Amanda said. "Sam saved my life."

Karen wouldn't release her daughter from the hug. "His son's had a hard day. He's resting in a back room."

"Where is Sam?" Cortez asked.

"I don't know, Mom. He saved me and I don't even know if he's okay...I ran, I just kept running. Dad said Sam was his son. That can't be, can it?"

"What?" Karen paled.

"That Sam was his son," Amanda repeated.

"That can't be true," Cortez said. "Although...it would explain a lot."

"What do you mean?"

"Sam...has a checkered history. Like your father."

"Has he betrayed anyone?" Amanda asked.

"His wife did, and he managed to avoid blame. Now his dad's a traitor. Oh, my," Cortez said. "This is a lot to take in."

"Dad's dying, that's why he came back. He's dying. He wants to be put up in a house and be able to see me... and Sam. And just die, peacefully, and he has something he says the government will want..." She stopped. It was as though the shock and exhaustion were starting to settle in.

Karen said, "I'm going to try and call Sam now." She found his number and pushed it.

69

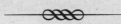

THE ELEVATOR DOOR OPENED. KIRILL and Bolt stood there before Illya.

Bolt winked at Illya.

"You found him," Illya said. "We can put him on the plane right now. Do you have the files?"

"No. He doesn't have them," Kirill said. He stepped out of the elevator.

Illya mouthed, *Val is here. And a man.* As a warning.

Kirill yanked Illya into the elevator, pushing Bolt back as well. The doors closed. "Bolt was hiding here, inside your building, with the American operative's son. Where would they have gone?"

"There...there was an accident. Two people hit by cars. Down the street. The security guard in the lobby called me up and told me about it. He tells me about anything odd that happens."

"Was the boy hit?"

"No. He said a man and a woman. He wasn't sure they survived. He said they were chasing a boy." Illya's voice shook. He stared at the gun.

"Then the boy got away. Where would he go?" Kirill asked.

"He would try and find his father."

"I'm not sure he knows that his father is an operative. It's not the thing you tell your children."

"You're not going to get the files. You can't find the boy," Bolt said.

"Kirill, Val is upstairs. She is working with the American. We force her to tell us." Illya punched the buttons. The elevator began its descent. "I will just get out of your way and you can deal with them."

"Illya, why did you hire the German and her people to kill Markus?" Kirill asked.

"I…"

"You hired them from the plane, didn't you? Once you told me about the financial map, you put yourself in danger. I needed to know it because when I killed him, I needed to retrieve it for you. But you weren't going to trust me to keep your secret. Your very embarrassing, damaging secret. And I would have, Illya. They're not here just to kill Markus but me."

Illya was not a good poker player. Mila's theory was right. He started babbling an apology, an explanation, a justification, a word wave that washed over Kirill. He fired the one bullet directly into Illya's heart and he collapsed, sliding down the wall of the elevator.

It stopped at the floor Illya had pressed, where Maria and his security team would be. Kirill glanced at Markus, who wasn't moving, just watching.

The doors slid open, no one in the hallway. Kirill leaned over and hit the basement button.

"They'll be mad at me for this," Kirill said. "Bobo, the Dude. All of them. The circle is untouchable."

"You killed a guy who's put all the Russian elite in danger. They'll forgive you."

Kirill put a steely look on his stepfather. "Where is the data, Markus? Where is the boy? "

"I'm not going to tell you that. He's my grandson."

"I don't believe that you're that man's father or that kid's grandfather," Kirill said. "I think this is another scam of yours, a ploy for sympathy. And you've used that kid to draw in his father for whatever reason."

"The American has known Val much longer than you have."

"Anyone who knows Val has known her longer than I have," Kirill said.

Markus Bolt crooked a smile, as if he'd heard something extra in Kirill's voice. "They worked together for years, I happen to know. Not always staying inside the lines. I wonder what their feelings are for each other."

"That's not my concern."

The elevator reached the garage and they got out. "Well, no flight back via Illya. Perhaps you'll let me stay here and avoid the inconvenience."

"There are many private planes. Bobo will get us on another one."

"Not without the financial map. They want that back more than me."

"You're here, you're cutting deals. You've been on the ground for a while. You might have said something that the boy heard. He'd know a place to go."

"He doesn't know I'm his grandfather. He thinks I'm his great-uncle."

Kirill shook his head. "There's something so deeply wrong with you. I could never say that because it would upset Mama, but it's true. You're so broken."

"Well, I didn't just kill a man in cold blood, but you say what you like."

Kirill ran through the possibilities. "Cortez. This

Cortez guy. He's ex-intel, right? He's got connections. I think that's who you made your deal with here. He's got ties. Come on, let's go."

Bolt watched his stepson's face. So much emotional turmoil for Kirill. He was very careful not to smile.

70

K<small>AREN SAID,</small> "S<small>AM</small>?"

"Yes."

"Are you all right?"

"For the moment."

"Daniel is with me. He's safe."

"What?"

"He called the bar and I talked to him. He says he got away from his aunt and he got to a Starbucks and borrowed a phone and so I picked him up."

"Oh, thank God. Thank you, Karen. Where are you?"

"Grayson's house."

"All right. Is Daniel okay?"

"Yes. He's had a rough time of it; I put him to bed to rest. We've tried to be circumspect about what he's heard—not reveal anything about you. But he has seen a recording of his mother that Cortez had. Lucy sent it to a contact here and he brought it to Cortez and he's had it for a while. She paints herself as a hero. Just so you know."

Why did Cortez have this? Fine, Sam wasn't going to worry about that right now.

"Amanda is here, too," Karen said. "She's badly shaken."

"Thank you, Karen, I'm on my way."

"Is this true? That Markus is your father?"

"Not now, Karen, take care of my son, I'll be there as soon as I can be." He caught up with Mila and ran out to the elevator. Illya was gone. He must have fled. Marianne was still zip-tied, lying on the floor.

Mila summoned the elevator. He glanced at Marianne.

The elevator doors opened. Illya lay dead, crumpled in the corner.

Sam checked his pulse. He was gone. He pulled Illya's body out onto the floor. "Your employer is dead, Marianne, so I don't think you're getting paid. I'll leave you here and you can explain yourself to his girlfriend and his security team."

She said, "It was Kirill and Bolt. Illya got in the elevator with them while you two were fighting the guard."

Mila stood over Marianne. Holding her gun. Marianne closed her eyes and waited for the bullet.

"Thank you for the information. I appreciate it and that's helpful to us. I think Illya's people will deal with you, and it will be worse than a bullet in the head. Don't come at us again, Marianne." Mila turned and walked away and Sam shook his head at Marianne. She closed her eyes.

They got in the elevator and headed down. Sam called Karen back, away from Marianne's hearing. "Karen, there could be a flash drive in Daniel's pocket. Can you check? If so, it's the files that Markus wants to use to buy his entry back. It's probably passworded."

"Yes, I'll check."

"Call me back. Markus and his stepson are loose, and if they have any sense, they'll be heading for the airport to get the hell back to Russia. But they could be looking for these files, and if they show up at the house, don't let them in."

"I have things to say to my ex," Karen said.

"Let us get him into custody."

"Grayson and I can handle that. We'll take him."

"Kirill is FSB. He's dangerous. They've just killed a man."

"Amanda says he's Markus's stepson."

What a family reunion Markus had engineered. "Apparently. He's supposed to take Markus back to Russia."

"Then he and I are in agreement," Karen said, and she hung up.

71

Kɪʀʏᴜsʜᴇɴᴋᴀ," ʙᴏʟᴛ sᴀɪᴅ, ᴜsɪɴɢ ᴛʜᴇ familiar form of Kirill's name that he wasn't allowed to use, "if you will allow me to make a call, I would like to apologize to your mother before I get shot. Because I'm pretty sure that, no matter what happens, you're going to shoot me."

"I'm not."

"Out of sensitivity to your mama? That's sweet but I don't buy it. You've wanted me out of the way for a long while. As long as the financial map doesn't fall into Western hands, you don't mind me dying."

Kirill wasn't sure he believed Markus would call Mama. He could be trying to call someone else, an ally here, a paid helper.

"No," Kirill said. He was driving now, Markus sitting next to him, with a calm that disturbed Kirill. "How long do you have?"

"Six months, maybe a year if I'm lucky. And if you don't kill me."

"I'll let the disease do that and I'll hope it's painful."

"I will actually miss you, you know. I will miss your mother. You and I can say good-bye but she and I didn't get a chance."

"I am putting us on a private jet. I already texted Bobo; he'll arrange it."

"And Val? Are you going to let a spy who infiltrated someone like Illya's life go unpunished? You really do need to know what she knows."

"She's not the priority, you are."

"I didn't tell everyone every reason why I came back. Sam and Amanda. Yes, I wanted to see my children. Yes, I wanted to die at home. Yes, I wanted to make up for the pain I caused, which I can't, but I can try. And I wanted to kill Allan's murderer."

"What?" Kirill's voice was a short snap.

"My son, Allan. I know who killed him."

"How?"

Bolt didn't answer.

"Who killed him?" Kirill repeated.

"I'll tell you. Will you please let me call your mother?"

"No. No."

72

∞∞∞

Karen walked into the darkened bedroom. Daniel was out, under the covers, snoring slightly. The poor kid. At least he felt safe here. She stared down at him. He looked younger than thirteen, his face slack with sleep. In the days that followed Markus's defection, she had often been unable to sleep—chewed up with guilt, with regret that she hadn't killed him, with anger toward him, and with a sick worry of what would happen to her and the children. It was going to define their lives.

They would always be the children of a traitor.

It would be the same for this boy if the word got out. She felt a sudden, odd protectiveness toward him. He would have it better than her kids. Amanda's life had gotten scrambled, and if she could get a better footing, maybe she'd be happy. And Allan...The shame had stolen Allan from her. That she could never forgive. That she still wanted to punish Markus for.

She looked at the sleeping boy's face, the lock of dark blond hair across his forehead. Looking for a trace of Markus, an echo of Allan in his face, if what Markus claimed about Sam was true. She reached out to touch his cheek, gently, with a mother's care. He hadn't had a mother. She stopped herself. It would scare him if he awoke and she was brushing back his hair like he was a baby. He was a brave, daring kid.

She saw the brand-new jeans he had worn lying on the covers; he'd taken them off before crawling under the sheets. She dug into the pockets. And felt it then, a flash drive. Small, silver. She laid his jeans back down across the bed.

This was it. Markus's ticket home. His hall pass to all his demands, on Amanda's time and of comfort from the inevitable pain of his illness, and amnesty for his crimes.

All his hopes, in the palm of her hand.

Karen Bolt took a precautionary step for insurance. She put the drive in her pocket and went back to the den. Cortez stood there, lost in thought.

She said, "Sam is on his way. He's worried Markus is coming here, too, with his stepson. I think Amanda and Daniel should leave."

"And go where? It would be better if we could stay together," Cortez said. "Safer."

She gave him a measured stare. "A Russian assassin is possibly coming here with my traitor husband, so you understand why I want Amanda and Daniel gone."

"They stay, Karen. Let's get Sam here."

Amanda was in Cortez's backyard, on the phone. She had tried to call Roberto; there was no answer. She left a short voice mail, saying she was fine, she was with her mom, she wasn't sure when she was coming back.

And she wasn't. She'd seen Dennis Gandy die. Someone she'd known for much of her life. Her father, impossibly, was back. She had made peace with the idea of never seeing him again, never wanting to see him again. Now he was telling her she had a half brother and a half nephew (was that a thing?) and that he was going to die soon and it was a lot. It was too much. She wanted to go back to her apartment and sit with Tara by the pool and drink wine and just not think.

Tara.

She had borrowed her mom's phone and she sat down on the patio furniture and she called the courier office.

Tara answered.

"Hey, it's me," Amanda said.

"Where the hell are you?" Tara said. "Are you all right?"

"Yes. I'm fine. What's happening there?"

"What's happening is that Roberto hasn't shown up and we're running it all on our own. What's going on with these Russians wanting to buy the company?"

"Yeah, I think they've lost interest," Amanda said. "I don't think that is still happening at all."

"Oh, good."

"Tara."

"Yeah."

"What's going on with the company?"

"What do you mean?"

"Why didn't Roberto want anyone looking at our financials? We're making a lot of money; what's the problem?"

Tara said, "That's not for me to say."

"I don't have time for the bullshit. What is it? What's Roberto involved with?"

"Hold on."

Then Roberto was on the phone. "Hey. You all right?"

"She said you weren't there."

"I just walked in," he said. But she could tell he was lying.

"What's going on with the company?"

"It doesn't concern you."

"It does. We took your laptop. If I take it to the police, what happens? What would they find?"

"Please, can we get together and talk about it?"

It felt like a pivotal moment, and Amanda realized she was done. "I'm not turning you in. I'll destroy the laptop. But you're buying me out. I don't want anything more to do with the courier service or with you." And it felt like a shackle slipping off her.

"I can't get out from under it. They're...I mean, they're not mobsters but they're...tough businessmen."

"We could have gone to the FBI, someone, anyone when they approached you," she said.

"I suppose. We're way more profitable now. And Tara...Tara is their person inside the office to keep an eye on things."

To make sure they didn't go to the police or sell to a curious buyer. Tara. No wonder she'd been digging at Sam, and nervous about Dennis Gandy. She'd thought Tara was a friend.

"Amanda, I'm not sure I can buy you out on my own—"

"I'm not asking, I'm telling you. This is what is happening. And if you make trouble for me, the Russians will come back." She could bluff, too. "I'm out and we're done. I'm sorry. I thought I loved you and thought you loved me. But it's not so."

Roberto was silent for ten long beats. "All right. I'll have the papers drawn up. I'll pay you something fair." His voice shook. "I love you. I do."

He didn't, because he hadn't told her this. She was so tired of men anchored by terrible secrets. But let him think that he had—she was shedding him, and despite the trauma of the past day, she felt a weight pull up from her shoulders. "I know. I just want you to be happy and safe."

"Amanda..."

"Good luck with Tara and get the papers drawn up.

Call me and cut a check and I'll come sign." Amanda hung up. She released a deep breath. So what would she do now? Visit her father as he died? Keep that huge secret? She wasn't sure. She needed to do something for herself.

She would call Sam. He would be able to help her. She hit the number to call him from the phone's recents list on the screen and then she stood up, facing the house. Then she saw the reflections of her father and the young Russian hurrying up behind her, in the patio windows. She had the presence of mind to slide the phone into her pocket, still active, hoping Sam could hear and would have the presence of mind to remain silent.

She turned to them. The young Russian—her stepbrother—smiled. "Hi, Amanda, I'm Kirill. We didn't formally meet before. My apologies."

73

I THINK WE JUST NEED A conversation, a calm one," Kirill, holding a gun, said. "There really is no need for bloodshed." He had walked Amanda back into the house, aiming the gun at her.

"Aim the gun at me, please," Bolt said.

"No one cares if you get hurt," Kirill said. "But no one's getting hurt. We're just talking. Quickly, but just talking."

He was in the den now, Bolt at his side, Amanda seated across from him.

Grayson Cortez watched them; he was standing by the couch, where he had been when they walked in. Before the men entered, Karen had gone down the hallway toward the bedrooms.

"Who else is in the house?" Kirill asked.

"Karen," Cortez said.

"And the boy?" Kirill asked.

"Daniel's asleep," Cortez said.

"Call to her to come out here. Just call, nothing else."

"Karen?" he called. "Can you come out here, please?"

After a few moments, Karen Bolt came into the living room. She held, of all things, a hammer. She stared at Markus Bolt.

"Drop that, please," Kirill said.

She dropped it.

"Hello, Karen," Markus said hoarsely. "You look well."

"You do not," she said. "You look like the absolute garbage you are."

"So this is what is going to happen," Kirill said. "The boy is going to come with us. Along with the data drive he brought. When we leave, you will not call the police, or any federal authorities. We're going to leave the country, maybe by plane, maybe by boat, not telling. Right before we leave, we will release the boy, with a phone, so he can call you. If you interfere or try to stop us, then he will . . . suffer."

"No," Amanda said. "I'll go with you. Not the kid."

"Absolutely not," Karen said. "I'll go with you."

"No, the boy," Kirill said. "Not negotiable. Markus, go get the drive from the boy and bring him out here."

"He's asleep, he's exhausted," Karen said.

"Then he's an even better choice," Kirill said. "He won't give us any trouble."

"Why?" Markus Bolt said suddenly. "Why can't you let me just come home and die?"

"Because it's what you want. I wanted my life as it was, and you ruined it. My dad is dead because of you, and you turned my mother into a stranger. So, no, Markus, you don't get to have hurt me, and all these nice people, and get your cozy little death." He turned to Amanda and Karen. "I apologize that he managed to get away from us and bring you pain. Not my wish. I understand how much you dislike him. I feel the same."

"We're not your friend," Amanda said.

"No, we're family," Kirill said with an unsettling laugh.

"But what about Allan?" Bolt said suddenly. "I need justice for Allan." He turned to Cortez. "You killed my boy."

74

Sᴀᴍ ʟɪsᴛᴇɴᴇᴅ. Hᴇ ʜᴀᴅ ɪᴍᴍᴇᴅɪᴀᴛᴇʟʏ muted his side of the phone when he realized what Amanda had done, and the conversation was muffled with the phone in Amanda's pocket, but he could hear enough.

"Kirill . . ." he said.

"Is a killer if he has to be," Mila said. "I don't think he would hesitate to kill any of them if he had to. It's his job. He wouldn't *want* to kill Daniel, but he would. I'm sorry this intersected with your life, Sam."

"We need a plan."

"I would suggest you let me go to the front door. Kirill will happily want to take me as a hostage instead of Daniel. The Russians want me for spying on Illya; I'm likely to be accused of his murder. You get to the bedroom window where Daniel is and get him out."

"I'm not letting you go with him," Sam said. "There is no way. He won't let you go when it's time."

"This is a failure for the Russians, Sam. I'm Kirill's ticket back with a win."

"I won't allow that," he said.

"It's not your choice, it's mine. I'm not letting him take *puişor*." Her old nickname for Daniel. But Daniel wouldn't remember it.

"You haven't even seen Daniel in years . . ."

"It matters not. He's not taking him." Her voice was steel.

Then they heard Bolt accuse Cortez of murder as they parked in front of the house.

Daniel stood in the darkness, pulling on his jeans and his shoes, listening. He couldn't hear all of what was said, but something about dying, and Uncle Mark's voice, and Karen telling someone he looked like total garbage, but there was a man with a Russian accent, and that was enough for him.

Uncle Mark and the Russians had found him again. He had to get out of here.

But he couldn't leave Karen behind. She had helped him; he had to help her.

He could crawl out the window and call the police. His phone was long gone but out of habit he stuck his hands in his pocket. He felt something in the deep pocket. He pulled it out.

A flash drive, encased in plain silver. He heard the man say something about files. Maybe this was it. He had what the Russian wanted. Someone must have put it in his pocket.

He had to do something. Now. He tiptoed toward the living room.

He remembered the flooring was tiled. That would help.

He had to be brave. Like his mom, fighting the bad guys. He started to inch forward toward the den, his heart in his mouth.

Sam and Mila went across the yard. Mila headed toward the front door; Sam headed toward the east side of the house. He thought that was where the bedrooms were likely to be; he remembered a larger kitchen on the other side of the house, close to the garage.

Daniel's life might depend on the right choice.

Sam went to the window. Peered inside. A master bedroom, bed made. No sign of Daniel. He went to the next window, a smaller one. Peered inside. A bed unmade, but no sign of Daniel. This looked more like a guest room, though.

He tried the window. Locked.

"I beg your pardon," Cortez said. He stared at Bolt. "Are you serious?"

"Absolutely."

"Is this part of your ploy?" Cortez said. "To create chaos for your comeback? No." He shook his head. "Karen. Amanda. He's lying. You know he's lying. All he does is lie."

"Why would I lie now, when I want America to take me back in? But if my wife or my daughter is going to be Kirill's hostage, then I want them to know, I want them to know the final reason I came back was to tell you... I know."

"And why would I do that?"

"You see, I brought back a little financial map of Russian money laundering. And you and your son's fingerprints are all over it. You have used Amanda's business and thousands of others, big and small, to clean billions. For the Russians. You don't study the ones living here for recruitment. Oh, maybe a bit, just for cover. But really you help them invest where they can't and hide the profits." He took a deep breath. "He wrote me about how dismal his financial prospects were, and I gave him a piece of advice. An e-mail. For someone who might help him. The name was Greg Hollister."

Cortez made a noise. "That's not my name."

"It's the same name," Kirill said slowly and clearly, "that you used when you checked up on Lucy Carrier's activities here. When you made sure the identity she used in Russia would not be exposed. With a payoff."

The room was silent, except for Karen starting to gasp and cry. Grayson stared at her in shock. "We're going to believe the Russians now? This is insane; you can't believe him. They want to tear me down."

"I'm telling the truth," Kirill said. "I have no loyalty to Markus, Mrs. Bolt." And Kirill thought, *Bobo's asset here isn't someone still inside the Agency. It's whoever is cleaning the money. That's more valuable than someone who sends a photo of a file.*

Bolt stared at Grayson. "I told Allan if he needed money, he could contact this Greg Hollister via e-mail. I knew it was an alias that Grayson had used on his little side deals. I kept my mouth shut about one crook making money on the side in the Agency with Bill Gandy; it wasn't hard to keep my mouth shut about two. So I think my boy eventually followed my very bad advice, and instead of taking care of him with a loan, or something normal and decent, Grayson, I think you tried to pull him and his failing business into your laundering network. Maybe you tried to pull him in close, tell him how much could be made. And he still said no. And then he knew too much."

"Allan killed himself," Cortez said. "We all know it." Karen moaned, her hand clapped over her mouth. Amanda hugged her mother.

"You have a thing against the children of your enemies," Bolt said. "Allan, Dennis, Amanda. Maybe I can't prove it. But I know it. *I know it.* And so do you."

75

THE DOORBELL RANG.

No one moved.

"It's Val," a voice called through the door.

"Karen, answer it," Kirill said. "Let her in. You don't run out the door."

"As if." Karen got up and answered the door. Mila came inside. She already had hands on her head. She wore a blazer over her shirt and jeans.

"I'm not armed. You can check under my jacket."

Kirill pivoted the gun on her. He moved forward to search her, running his hands along her ribs.

Daniel Capra stepped into the room, holding the flash drive aloft like a flame.

"Hey, mister," he said. Kirill turned toward him.

"You're looking for this?" Daniel's voice shook. He held up the flash drive.

Kirill turned toward Daniel, keeping the gun aimed at Mila. "Give me that."

Karen said "No, Daniel!"

Daniel dropped the small drive to the tiles. And then grabbed Karen's dropped hammer and slammed it down on the drive.

Kirill and Bolt both yelled and Mila flicked her wrist and a retractable baton slid out of her jacket sleeve. She snapped it and it extended. She whipped it across Kirill's chest and he yelped and staggered back. She brought it down on his arm, and he dropped the gun. He howled in anger and slammed a fist as she completed the swing, catching her between shoulder and throat. She staggered back.

Cortez bolted for the kitchen, Amanda and Karen following, Karen grabbing Daniel's hand, yanking him along. Cortez reached into the freezer. He yanked out a gun and pointed it at them. "Get in the pantry, now."

They obeyed and Daniel started to follow and Cortez said, "No. You come with me." He pushed the gun against Daniel's head; Daniel froze. Then Cortez slammed the door and jammed a chair under the pantry doorknob and Karen screamed and pounded on the other side.

"If you fight me, I'll shoot you," Cortez hissed at Daniel. And he yanked the boy toward the garage.

76

⌗

Sᴀᴍ ʜᴀᴅ ɢᴏɴᴇ ᴀʀᴏᴜɴᴅ ᴛʜᴇ house, peered through the back window, saw chaos erupting, Amanda running toward the kitchen side, Mila fighting Kirill. The back door was now locked—he kicked it in. Entered. Saw Markus Bolt kneeling on the floor, trying to collect broken bits of something on the tile floor. Not a threat.

He heard noises from the kitchen but saw Mila fighting Kirill hand to hand. He powered into Kirill, three hard slams of fist fast into the face, fueled by rage and adrenaline. But Kirill was younger, took the blows, hammered an uppercut that caught Sam.

"Daniel! He ran with the Bolts!" Mila yelled.

Sam lashed out a kick at Kirill, who blocked it with an arm. They both moved into flashing punches, parries. Mila seized the baton where it had fallen and hammered it into the back of Kirill's head and he dropped. She pulled zip ties from her jacket pocket and fastened his wrists and ankles while he fought for consciousness.

Sam ran for the kitchen.

"Thank you, Val, that's kind of you," Markus Bolt said. He was trying to gather the broken drive, cupping it in his hands. His ticket home, punched and destroyed by a teenage boy.

She ran past him. She could hear Amanda and Karen

inside the pantry, Karen screaming Daniel's name, the chair jammed under the lock. The door from the kitchen to the garage was open; Cortez's car gone; she heard wheels screeching and saw Sam running toward the car.

Cortez took Daniel. Dear God.

She reached for the chair.

"Not quite yet, Val," Bolt's voice said. She looked over her shoulder. He was aiming a gun at her. Kirill's gun. In the chaos, in her panic to be sure Daniel was all right, she hadn't secured it. But he had.

He gave her a slight smile. "I'd prefer my family not see this."

"Markus, you asshole!" Karen screamed through the pantry door.

"Dad!" Amanda yelled.

"Get back in here. Keep your distance. I'm sure you could beat the snot out of me, and I don't intend to let you get the chance. Drop the baton; you're quite a maestro with that."

She obeyed him.

"Back in here and sit on the couch."

She did. "Use your teeth and bind your wrists with one of those zip ties you brought along." She did. "Tighter," he said. "I'm an old cat, I've seen a lot of the tricks." She obeyed, glaring at him.

"Now," Markus Bolt said. "I want you to bear witness to what I'm doing for my country." He walked over to the groggy Kirill.

"Wake up." He prodded him with his foot. He smiled at Mila. "I used to have to do this when he'd oversleep as a teenager. His mother wasn't known for her discipline."

He started singing, in a terribly off-key voice, a Russian folk song, and Kirill nearly jerked awake, as though responding by instinct. Markus knelt by the young man.

"You're going to do what I tell you, Kirill, and later you'll realize I'm doing you a favor. I'm setting you free."

"What...what?" Kirill said.

"We're going to each make a phone call. I'm going to make mine first. Not sure they'll take a call on an American phone but I bet with this unsettled, uncertain situation they will." He almost sounded hearty. He slid a phone close to Kirill. "She'll listen to you."

"Who's she?"

"Your mom." Bolt glanced at Mila. "You know Kirill's mom was a Miss Russia? Someone like her truly loving someone like me, well, how likely was that?"

"Kirill told me," Mila said. She looked at Kirill, who looked scared for the first time that Mila had known him.

"What...what do you want me to tell my mom?" Kirill said.

"Good-bye," Bolt said.

77

Bolt tapped the screen. On speakerphone. Mila heard a man's voice answer suspiciously. "Yes, who is this?" he said in Russian.

"Hi, Bobo. It's Markus. I see you're answering my home phone. I figured you'd make my dasha your base of operations."

A stunned pause, then the man found his voice. "We're still searching it, Markus. You want to come back home?"

"It was never home. Is Duderov there with you?"

"Yes."

"Is Sonia Timofeyevna?"

"No, she's downstairs."

"Put me on speaker. You both can hear what I have to say. One moment." Bolt put the phone call to Bobo and Duderov on mute and tapped the other phone. It rang. A woman answered.

"Sonia, sweetheart? It's Markus. I am here with your son."

"What...Kirill?"

"Yes, Mama," Kirill said faintly.

"Sonia, walk out of the house, and down to the pond." There was a large pond on the property, shared by the other dashas, at the bottom of an expanse of backyard. Sonia Timofeyevna liked to skate on it in winter.

"What? Why?"

"Because I don't want anyone else to hear this," Markus said. "Do as I say, please."

"Mama, do as he says," Kirill said. His mouth thinned.

Mila thought, *He's going to kill Kirill and make her listen*. She struggled against the bonds. Kirill was an enemy, but this was wrong.

They listened to her breathing, heavily, as she hurried down the pathway from the house to the pond.

"All right, I'm at the pond," Sonia said.

"Just stay there, hold on, I'll be right back." Bolt put the phone calling his wife on mute and unmuted the call to Bobo and Duderov.

"Thank you for your patience," Markus said. "I imagine you've torn my house apart by now looking for evidence of whatever secrets I took. Did you find anything interesting?"

"Not particularly," Bobo said. "Where are you? What do you want?"

"I just want us to talk. Hello, Duderov."

"Hello," another voice rumbled.

"I'm impressed you've kept this quiet," Markus said. "I must be quite the embarrassment."

"We can bring you back. I'm not sure the Americans will want you," Bobo said.

"I'm not sure I'm still in America," Bolt said. He winked—*winked!*—at Mila.

"But your family is. Do you think we cannot get to them?"

"And now you're desperate, making that kind of threat. The Americans would never, ever stand for it."

"There is someone closer at hand," Duderov said. "We'll kill Sonia if you don't come back."

"I took something from Illya Markarkin. A financial

map of all the shell companies, all the accounts overseas. Illya had built it for insurance but I've made it my own. I think a man named Cortez helped you create it."

"Markus..."

"You just threatened both my American and my Russian families. I can burn you to the ground."

An awkward pause.

"I'd like to continue this productive conversation. Will you hold one moment." He muted the phone and unmuted the phone calling Sonia. "Sweetheart, are you still at the pond?"

"Yes. I am." Her voice shook.

"I want you to know I'm sorry. I know all of this is hard on you. I know you probably didn't have much choice in spying on me. But I do wonder if you ever loved me."

"I did. I do," she said. "But you're not easy to love. Let me speak to Kirill."

"Just hold one moment, and I will." He unmuted the phone to Bobo and Duderov. "Good-bye, gentlemen." He hung up on Bobo and then called another number, pressing the keypad with slow deliberation. A phone number. Then more numbers: Mila realized Bolt was entering a code.

From Sonia's phone there was the sound of a distant but massive roar. "Markus! The house...it just blew up! My God! It's gone!"

"Sonia," Markus said. "They were going to kill you. They won't be able to now. They'll probably say I died in the explosion and blame the Americans. Play along, and you should be fine. Tell Kirill good-bye because I don't think he should come home. They might kill him. I'm sorry. I did love you."

"Mama, be careful...please," Kirill yelled.

"Markus!" Sonia screamed. "Don't you hurt my boy, please..."

"I won't. I promise you I won't hurt him. I'll make sure he's protected. I'll make sure he's safe."

"Good-bye, Mama," Kirill sobbed. Sonia screamed something Mila couldn't decipher. But a baying of pure pain and anguish.

And Markus Bolt hung up. He stood and patted Kirill on his cheek, where a heavy bruise was rising. "You might want to make a deal with the Americans or the British." He nodded toward Mila. "She needs a ticket back to London for her bosses' good graces and you're likely to be it. It's not so bad, being on the enemy side. You get used to it."

Markus Bolt smiled and went to release his ex-wife and daughter from the pantry.

78

CORTEZ SHOVED DANIEL INTO THE backseat, told him to stay down or he'd kill him.

Daniel stayed down.

Cortez's SUV revved down the driveway, past Sam's parked car, barreling toward the less busy part of his neighborhood, an expansive park. He roared down the street.

He had the boy. They'd have to leave him alone. If not... well, it would be unfortunate and ironic. Here he had studied the Capra family, and now the child would pay for the sins of the parents. Like Allan. Like Dennis.

He glanced in his rearview mirror: a car, coming up fast behind him. Sam Capra at the wheel.

"Your father is following us," Cortez yelled. He wasn't even sure why he said it, but he did, like the boy knowing that would change something. He needed to pull in Sam where there were fewer potential witnesses, kill him, kill the boy, and then there were plenty of people who would hide him. He had a few friends here in Miami, friends of his son as well, who could get him to South America. People who were likely on Bolt's financial map and would need Cortez's help as well.

There. A likely spot. He veered onto a side road that led deeper into the park.

*   *   *

Daniel lay on the leather backseat, bouncing as Cortez wrenched the SUV along the road and then swerved into a hard turn. Dad was following them. What the hell could Dad do? He couldn't fight these people; they were crazy and violent.

But he couldn't just lie here. What would Cortez ask Dad to do to get Daniel back? Maybe he had no intention of giving Daniel back. *You destroyed the drive, dummy, and maybe that was the bargaining chip.*

Daniel sat up. What could Cortez do while both hands were busy driving? Daniel had to do something.

"Get back down," Cortez ordered.

Instead, Daniel crawled over the backseat, into the SUV's storage area. He hit the button and the back window flew open. He could see his father in a car, closing fast, driving like a maniac. He worked the handle and the gate of the SUV fell open.

Then he heard the gunfire.

Cortez, trying to fire at Daniel while driving, going off the road onto the unpaved grass, the window shattering to Daniel's left. He screamed for his father and lay flat.

Cortez lost control, turning to fire at the boy, to stop him from jumping from the SUV. He pivoted his body to shoot and reflexively floored the accelerator as he did so. The SUV bounded off the road and down the lawn toward the massive pond. He fired and then realized his mistake and pivoted back around to regain control of the steering wheel.

Too late. They were off the road, and in the air.

He is shooting at my son, Sam thought, and he could hear Daniel scream *Dad* and then the SUV was airborne, off the grass, rocketing off an embankment. Sam could see Daniel's face blossom in fear as the SUV plowed into the water and rapidly began to sink. Sam slammed his brakes, dovetailing to the embankment.

Daniel tumbled out of the back of the SUV, into the water. Cortez wasn't still shooting but then Sam heard a yell, cut off suddenly. He arrowed into the water, swam toward the sinking SUV.

Sam saw Daniel go under. Maybe hurt or stunned from the impact. Sam dove, powering downward, finding in the dark water his son's shirt, his hair. He pulled Daniel close and swam back to the surface, breaking into the air. Daniel sputtered and coughed and closed his arms around his father like he'd never let go.

"I got you. I got you, baby," Sam said, swimming backward.

"Dad, Dad." Daniel wasn't crying but he was shivering, shaking. Holding on to his father.

Sam pulled him onto the grass. "Are you hurt? Are you okay?" He ran his hands along his son's arms, legs, cupped his face.

"I'm okay, I'm okay," Daniel said.

Sam scanned the water. No sign of Cortez. If he surfaced, Sam was going to have to deal with him, and right in front of his son. No.

"Can you get in my car?" Sam asked, and Daniel nodded.

Sam dove back into the water. Down, down: he found the gate Daniel had opened. He felt along the SUV. The driver's window was down. He could feel Cortez's shoulder, struggling, hands flapping. The seat belt release wasn't working; he was trapped.

He had tried to kill Daniel.

He felt for the man's face, felt the panic under Cortez's skin.

Sam put a hand on his jaw, on his throat, and broke his neck.

One clean motion, like he'd been taught.

The act, hidden by the darkened water from his son's eyes. He felt for a pulse on the floating wrist. None.

Sam Capra kicked up toward the light, toward Daniel.

He surfaced with a giant gasp of air. He swam, hard, for the grass. Clambered on. No one around. No one had seen it. He got into the car. Daniel sat shivering in the front seat.

Sam started the car.

"He's dead," he said.

"Dad . . . aren't we going to call the police? Or wait for them?"

"No." Sam wheeled the car around and headed back toward the Cortez house. "Not right now. There are some things I have to explain to you."

And he wondered this time, how much would be truth, and how much would be lies.

79

⬡⬡⬡

THE DAYS AFTER WERE DEVOTED to tidying and storytelling.

Woodruff's cleanup team had arrived from their waiting station in Fort Lauderdale. Bolt was taken into custody. The computers at the Cortez house had been wiped before Cortez was (eventually) reported missing by his friend, Karen English. The Cortez house had been cleaned up; at the Russian mansion the bodies of Dennis Gandy and the Scot collected as well. Neither body was ever found; Dennis Gandy was reported missing a week later by his fellow Bolties on their website, and his disappearance sparked a whole new set of conspiracy theories that would be discussed for the next several years. Marianne's other protégé, the German man Gandy killed in the street, was eventually identified as an ex-army soldier who apparently had come to Miami looking for trouble. The cell phone found on his body had already been wiped clean remotely. The investigation stalled.

The bodies of the two UK operatives were retrieved and returned to their country, for burial with honors.

There was another cleanup happening at Illya Markarkin's condo in Sunny Isles. Illya's body was hidden in a crate, per the instructions given to his girlfriend by Bobo's immediate and frightened successor, and flown back to Russia. Within three days it was announced that

Markarkin had died of a sudden stroke, at home in Russia. Another oligarch quickly bought the Miami high-rise and allowed Illya's girlfriend to remain there, as her due date was in a few weeks.

There was no mention, in any report from either side, of a German woman who was found bound in Illya's penthouse. Probably because Marianne was not still there when the guards discovered Illya and his body-guard were both dead. Marianne had vanished, again, into the wind.

A report out of Russia indicated that a mansion in a restricted area reserved for government notables had been destroyed in an explosion, tied to a gas leak. There was no accounting of deaths. Other reports, unrelated, in the intel community noted that Mikhail Duderov, a key associate of the Russian president, had fallen out of sight and out of favor. Longtime bureaucrat and Morozov aide Yuri "Bobo" Boborin was listed as having died of a sud-den heart attack. There was no mention of Markus Bolt.

Cortez's SUV was found in the deep pond at the end of the week—he died of a broken neck. He'd appar-ently been driving at high speed and lost control. He was memorialized as an author and a longtime government expert in the psychology of traitors.

Among the entries on the financial map of shell com-panies and money launderers were found connections to several overseas banks where Grayson Cortez's son served as a consultant and client. Among them was a local Miami courier service, already cleaning money for a Colombian drug enterprise. A Russian money laun-derer was taking a cut of the cleaned money from the Colombians and investing it, through a venture capital arm, into startup software companies from Estonia to San Francisco.

Carlos Cortez was brought in for an interview and,

after seeing just the part of the financial map that he could be tied to, immediately cut a deal and began to talk.

Roberto's laptop, turned over to the Section K hackers, showed a pattern of transactions that served as a template to start examining every front and shell company listed on the financial map.

Clarice had survived being hit by the car; the Russian thug did not. Witnesses said they appeared to be pursuing a teenager; people assumed he was a thief, or a purse snatcher, but no one had seen a boy matching his description, and he hadn't been carrying a bag. Clarice was in intensive care in a hospital in Miami, until a family member arranged for her to be flown to a private clinic.

In a rural part of northern Florida, a modest house was bought, and an older man moved in. He had a full acre, no neighbors close, but people did notice that the new resident never came out. One of the safe house's attendants locally spread the rumor that the new resident was sadly very ill. The local pastors who stopped by to visit and offer solace were gently rebuffed.

A young woman came to visit once, stayed three hours, and left. She walked back to her car as if a weight had been lifted from her shoulders.

The disc with Lucy Capra on it, talking to her son, was removed from the Cortez house long before the body was found in the pond.

80

———∞∞∞———

So," Sam said. He sat in the safe house above Amado, the bar beneath them quiet. He'd had Paige close it for the rest of the day so he could be alone with his son. "We have some things to discuss."

Daniel was on the couch, fed, showered, checked by a doctor sent by Woodruff, just happy to be with his father. "Yeah, I would say so."

Sam cleared his throat. "I'm going to tell you what I can tell you and ask you to trust me on the rest."

"Okay," Daniel said.

"First, Uncle Mark...he's not really your uncle."

"I figured."

"You know I own bars around the world. Bars often have financial issues. Mark and Cortez used to work for the government, in intelligence..."

"Like spies?"

"Like spies. And they both retired early, and in their work they got to know some...people who work outside the law. These people, they're bad guys, and they have lots of money they need to clean. Do you know what money laundering is?"

"No."

"It's when an illegal operation—think drugs—needs to be able to account for all the money they've made by breaking the law. So they have these legit businesses that serve as fronts. And they say on the accounts that the business is taking in more money than it really is. Way more, maybe millions more, because then the money appears to be legit and they can spend it. Understand?"

Daniel slowly nodded, remembering Karen's words.

"So Uncle Mark and Mr. Cortez, they were working with these bad guys and they wanted to take over my bars. And take over Karen's daughter's business because it could also be used to clean money." He didn't add that Roberto was already doing this—it had given him the idea for this cover story.

"So they kidnapped me because they wanted you to give them the bars. That's kind of what Karen said."

"Be their front, so to speak. Mark and Cortez pulled in Clarice because…Mark knew your mom from his work before and knew Clarice would help him if she got a chance to see you. You were leverage."

"I don't want to see Aunt Clarice again," Daniel said. "Ever."

"I understand. I don't think she's mentally healthy. And she had doubts about how your mom died, and there were things she couldn't be told."

"Because Mom worked for the government."

Sam nodded.

"Was she a spy?"

"I cannot tell you specifics. It's classified and I don't know what she did. But what Mr. Cortez told you, about Mom fighting bad guys, yes, that was true." It was true once. When she first joined Special Projects and met Sam. He was going to let his son have this belief. There was no one to counter it anymore.

"Were you a spy?" Daniel's eyes were wide.

"No," Sam lied. "They don't let spies marry each other."

"Oh."

"We can't talk about this," Sam said. "The agencies are investigating, but they don't want it known publicly what happened. So you can't talk about it. Not to your friends, not to your grandparents. Not even to Leonie. Can you do that?"

Daniel nodded, and for a moment Sam saw the man he would become, not the boy he was.

"Okay. You've been through a lot, though, and I can get you a counselor who understands."

"There's Ms. Dorridge at the school. She always wants to talk to me."

"No, I don't think she can help. The counselor we'll get will come from the people Mom worked for. You can be completely honest with them."

Daniel took a deep breath. "It's a lot of secrets to keep, Dad."

"Yes. And I'm sorry."

"Did Mom really die of a heart condition?" Cortez had said she was shot, and he wanted to hear what Dad said.

"No," he said after a moment. "That was why Aunt Clarice was suspicious of me. She was killed. But no one can know that."

"By a bad guy?"

"By a bad guy. I don't even know all the details. They can't tell me." He took a deep breath. *For his own good, for his own good, for his own good.*

Daniel wanted to say *she was shot*. But maybe he shouldn't. Dad carried so much.

Daniel stared at him. Finally he said, "All right. Can I keep the recording?"

"Yes. Of course."

"It makes it a little easier. Knowing she died a hero."

An odd look passed over Dad's face and then was

gone. "I'm glad. I'm sorry I couldn't have told you what I knew before."

"I wouldn't have understood. I really do now." And there it was, Daniel becoming his co-conspirator. Agreeing to the lie.

"All right," Sam said.

There was a knock at the door. Sam answered it.

Mila.

"I wanted to check on Daniel. And you."

"Sure." He let her in. She smiled at Daniel. When they had returned to Cortez's house, she had put Kirill in Karen's car and driven him to the house she'd bought from Terrell. A temporary safe place until she could get him out of the country.

"Hello, Daniel."

"Hi." Daniel looked at her uncertainly and Sam thought, *You'll never know all the times this woman risked her life to help me. To help you.*

"I'm Mila. I'm an old friend of your dad's."

Sam hadn't known what name she would use. She was back to her original one.

"Hey." He glanced at Sam.

"I knew Mila in Europe," Sam said.

Daniel gave her the look he sometimes gave when a woman came around Sam, smiling and talking down to Daniel.

"I used to take care of you," Mila said. "When you were very little."

"Like a nanny?"

No, like a guardian angel, Sam thought. *An avenging angel.*

"A bit like a nanny," Mila answered. "Although nannies have rules and are boring. I was no Leonie." Mila had disliked Leonie on sight and had never managed to learn to like her. "I was more like a very fun aunt. We used to play games. I called you *puisor.*"

"What's that?"

"I am from Moldova, and there we speak Romanian. It's a nickname for a sweet child. Which you were."

"*Puişor,*" Daniel said. "That's funny."

"Yes, it's a funny word. It would make you laugh when you were little. And I loved to make you laugh."

"Did you know my mom?"

"Not well. Only a little."

"But you know about these bad guys?"

"Yes. I can't say more." Mila glanced at Sam.

"Oh," Daniel said.

"I have to go now, but I hope I will see you again soon, Daniel, under happier circumstances."

"I'll walk you out," Sam said.

"Nice to meet you…I mean see you again," Daniel said. She touched his jaw lightly, and then she and Sam walked out the front door.

She had parked in front of the bar. "Woodruff sent me a team to guard Kirill. We're flying him to London tonight. I have a lot of explaining and apologizing to do. But I offered him asylum if he talks. I think he will. He can't go back. He failed too much. I feel oddly responsible for him."

Sam said nothing to that; it was her business. "What about who killed your husband?"

"I think Kirill can give us names."

"You realize he might have done it."

"I don't think he did. I have my reasons. But I think the orders came from his masters, or maybe Illya, and they're all gone now. And Cortez."

"Two years working for Illya. Mila, did you plan that…"

"Yes. It was like being in amber. It helped me mask my grief." She looked at him. "You know about that."

"Yes. What will you do now? Keep working for the Brits?"

"Yes. They've given me a homeland when I didn't have one. I'm in some trouble. I was supposed to get close to Philip because of his ties to the Russians; hence the Valeria alias. But Philip was a good man used by bad people. Loving him wasn't an assignment. He was funny and kind and he was what I needed after...after my life calmed down a bit. After all the chaos you brought to it." She gave him a half smile. "You would have liked him very much. I did love him, Sam...I married him because I *wanted* to marry him. And I think the Russians killed him because he might have become a whistleblower on them. I took the job with Illya when he offered; I wanted to find out who killed my Philip. But I was supposed to just send back information to MI6. Recruiting those guys to help me, coming to Miami...I went rogue then. I didn't think. And that was a terrible mistake." She cleared her throat. "I'll be disciplined. But I'm bringing them Kirill, so I'll be forgiven. Two years spying from behind the Russian border, I get a long vacation now. You?"

"You could come work for Section K. If the Brits are too hard on you." The words were out of his mouth before he thought them through. He could make it work with Woodruff.

"I need to take my punishment, Sam, but thank you. How do you like your arrangement with them?"

"I don't know. I'm on call when needed. It's not all the time, or even that often. But when they call me, they need me. As a fixer. But I'm not sure I can live a lie with my son. He thinks his mother is a hero, and I have to let him think that. It just feels like a house of cards. He doesn't know who Markus Bolt is. But maybe one day months or years from now he reads about him and sees a picture and thinks, *That's Uncle Mark*. I don't know how to deal with that."

"You'll figure it out. You'll give him a good life. He's a smart, resilient boy."

"I hate the word *resilient*. People said that to me after Lucy died. It's not real. You just go a day at a time."

"True. I'm glad he's okay. I'm glad you're okay." She seemed to want to say more.

"Are we okay?"

She stared at him. He couldn't stand the silence. He said: "I'm sorry we weren't in touch. That's my fault. I didn't think you would want to talk. And I wasn't sure what I could say."

"I didn't want to talk to you. Not then. Not for a while." She gave him a measured look. "We've both lost so much; maybe it was hard to be around each other until we figured out how to deal with it. Yes, Sam, we're okay. It was good to work with you again. Take care of that boy." She suddenly turned and walked to her car.

He watched her leave, so many words he wanted to say, but he just watched her go.

From the window above the bar, Daniel watched the woman named Mila walk away, wondering. There was something between that woman and his father, he could tell—something that made him a little uneasy. He turned away and put on the disc with his mom. It was a comfort to watch her, to understand more, to know the truth.

81

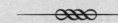

Northern Florida

"YOU SEEM SETTLED IN," SAM said to Bolt. He sat at a table across from him.

"Yes. I have a nurse, and a doctor, both of whom enjoy drawing blood in the most painful way possible to monitor my condition." He was in a plain upstairs bedroom that had been converted into a debriefing room. Bolt did not have access to the full house, but only the upstairs. There were guards stationed downstairs and near the house, with orders to shoot to kill should Markus attempt an escape. Or should the Russians attempt to reclaim him.

"You're not my father," Sam said.

"It was Uganda. I was there on Agency assignment, your parents were there, their first field deployment since your brother was born. The marriage was frazzled, and I was bored."

"There is literally no way that my mother would stoop to you."

"Have you seen my Russian wife? I am not without my charms."

"You're a petty little psychopath. I should know, I was married to one."

"The sweet Lucy."

"You're going to tell me why she came to Russia to see you."

He ran his thumb along his chin. "Do you think only countries try to recruit spies these days? Our excitingly new globalized world has moved beyond that, son... corporations, private organizations, alliances, and more."

"If you call me son again, I will break your larynx," Sam said.

"I actually was one of the people who suggested you and your brother for Agency service." He bit at his thumbnail. "I'd kept my eye on you. You were both ideal candidates, although I wasn't sure your brother could have passed the mental health assessments. Only you came to work at the Agency, though. I realized Lucy was working on the side for a criminal syndicate, in reviewing files, financials, and more. I thought she might be useful to me. I confronted her, and the little daredevil, she wanted to recruit me to spy for her criminal syndicate as well."

"The Nine Suns."

"Which were at the start a misbegotten attempt by the CIA to leverage criminal networks in the war on terrorism. A horrendous misstep."

"Why did she come to Russia, Markus?"

"One of her covers for the Nine Suns was as a Miami real estate agent, especially with the surge in Russian investment here; it felt like an opportunity for her employers to get financial dirt on Russian dealings for leverage. She hoped to recruit my son as leverage to get me to share what all I learned in Russia. He was a teenager then, and she was just out of college; I'm sure he was flattered by her attention. And she was his lifeline to me—a way, I guess, for him to have the chance to tell me off. So she befriended him, and brought me a letter from him. The implication from her was if I didn't go along, she could eventually pull him into working for them as well. I . . . I didn't want that for him. I couldn't protect him from afar."

"So you sent her information?"

"A bit. Enough oligarch gossip to keep her bosses interested and away from my boy. And then she stopped contacting me. No one else contacted me."

"How did you know Cortez killed him?"

"I didn't. Not for sure. Not until the moment I saw him and I said so. Because Grayson hated me. I was the traitor he never spotted. I was his white whale, the one that got away." He took a deep breath. "Bill Gandy and I were both misbehaving, let's say, but we watched out for each other—sort of a mutual aid society. Bill must have been terrified when I ran to Russia. I could see him going soon after that to Cortez, a neighbor, a friend, a dad with kids in the same class, who happened to be a guy who worked on finding traitors. Bill could have thrown himself on Cortez's mercy—making a deal with the guy he thought could help him. And I think Cortez killed him and took some of the money Bill skimmed and hid and that was the start, eventually, of funding the network of shell companies he, and then his son later, helped the Russians build. Suicide worked on Bill and so they did it for Allan. I feel certain he monitored Amanda and Allan. And so after Lucy's betrayal of the Agency, and him realizing this Terrell Carrier had given her a cover, he would have looked hard at the fake life and records of 'Lucy Carrier.' He must have learned she had been in touch with my son those years ago; he would have gone to confront him. The son of a traitor and the friend of another traitor? Allan would have been a psychological profile that Grayson couldn't resist. And by that time, Cortez and his son had built their money laundering network for the Russians, leveraging what Illya Markarkin and his British banker had assembled and that Illya started mapping as it grew. Allan was barely staying on his feet financially, and I assume Grayson offered him a chance to work with them. Allan would have said no and might have threatened to expose them. To make amends for what I'd done." He coughed and for a moment he averted his gaze from Sam. "So Grayson killed Allan and then covered it up as a suicide. All while pretending to stay friends with Karen and Amanda, because he had to; he couldn't drop them after Allan died. Too suspicious. And I'm guessing we'll find he was behind the loan to Roberto and Amanda's company. He didn't make the same mistake with Amanda; he didn't tell her about the laundering." He shrugged. "Literally no one else in the Agency would have gone to see Allan because of Lucy." He took a deep breath, as though dismissing the past. "Your boy is bold."

"What?"

"The drive he broke in front of Cortez and Kirill. It wasn't the one I used to steal the financial map."

Sam said nothing.

"Karen took the real one from Daniel's jeans and replaced it in his pocket with the blank one that Daniel smashed, some spare that she either had in her purse or found in Grayson's office. I noticed it wasn't the same, but said nothing. And Daniel's gutsy move drove Kirill over the edge, and that determined how the day played out. Which means Section K has the real drive, and the real map I stole, and so that's why I'm getting the deluxe guest treatment. I've finally done my nation a great favor. You all can really limit Russian actions now against us;

you know where all their money is, and if they move it, you'll know that, too. You're welcome." He put a hand up to his ear, as if waiting for cheers and applause.

Sam stood.

"I wrote letters to Amanda I never got to send. I wanted to tell her about you. So she wouldn't feel so alone."

"Amanda deserves so much better than you."

"So, no DNA test?" Bolt asked.

"I don't need one and I'm not insulting my parents by taking one. Whatever happened between you and my mother is between the two of you. I look in the mirror and I look like my dad, a man whose family were blond Northern Italians, and I look like his dad, too. I'm nothing like you."

"You're just like me. Full of secrets." Bolt flexed a smile. "I think you're the other side of the coin ... of me."

Sam said nothing. He wanted to punch him but he reminded himself Bolt was a terminally ill man.

"Well, if you aren't my son, at the least you were useful in helping me reach my goals here. Thanks for being a brain and muscles that got me what I wanted." He looked at the floor, then at Sam. And Sam could see that he wished it so; that Sam was his son.

"You're pitiful. You're going to die, alone, and in pain," Sam said. "I'm sure that will be a relief to Amanda and Karen. Think on that. They'll be glad you're dead. Thanks for being honest about Lucy, at least."

He turned and went to the closed door.

"Sam?"

He stopped and looked back at the traitor.

Markus Bolt smiled. "Keep all your secrets. Keep them close. It might end up being all you have."

82

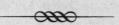

Austin

Sitting at her kitchen table, Ms. Dorridge checked the attendance records in the school database. Daniel Capra had been absent for two days recently, unexcused. Interesting. She had been surprised to see him sitting in the coffee shop with an older woman that odd night. They had been having an intense conversation. She wondered what it had been about, and if it would interfere with any of her plans for his father.

She hoped not. She still hoped she could have a chance to talk to Daniel. To earn his trust, to listen to his secrets, to know his mind.

And then to know his father.

The kettle whistled and she poured hot water over an Earl Grey teabag. The steam rose; the tea smelled fragrant. She closed her eyes and took a sip.

Then she walked down into her projects room.

And closed the door behind her.

Part of one wall was covered in photos of Sam Capra: at the basketball games, walking with his son in the neighborhood, leaving the grocery store. Close-ups of him. She liked his face; it was a good one.

In the dim light from the computer, she studied the photos. If Daniel was developing a tendency to be truant, then that was an opportunity to talk to him. If he had taken a trip with his father, it could still be an opportunity to hear about his travels. Middle schoolers always had issues and challenges, and it was important as his son's school counselor to be available. She just had to find Daniel's emotional need and use it. Become important to him. Trusted.

And then she could get close to Sam.

83

Virginia

Sam stepped into the hospital room. Clarice lay in the bed, both legs in casts, her face badly bruised, her cheek stitched.

"Hey, Clarice," Sam said.

She opened her eyes. Stared at him in fear. He pulled a chair close to her.

"Do you know where you are?"

"Hospital," she said.

"Not just any hospital. You're not in Florida anymore, in case you didn't realize. You're in Virginia. The CIA runs this one."

She said nothing.

"I'm glad you're alive. First, so I can apologize to you, and second, so I can warn you."

She swallowed.

"I'm sorry I cut you out of Daniel's life. I made what I thought was the best choice at the time. Because Lucy was every bit the criminal and traitor that your friend Bolt was, and I wanted nothing of Lucy to be near my son. I didn't want you telling him what a great person

Lucy was, or talking about her to him. I just wanted her...erased. Maybe that was wrong of me. But everything she did to me. To others. The chaos and suffering she caused..." He stopped. "I don't want to dim your positive memories of her. Those are yours."

"Sam, please, I'm sorry."

"I'm sure you are. You were in contact with a known traitor to the United States. You abetted him in his actions on American soil, including the kidnapping of my son. Those could all be federal charges." He let that sink in. "And you lied, repeatedly, to Daniel."

"Is he okay?" Tears brimmed in her eyes.

"Yes. He's okay. And he thinks now his mother was some kind of hero. Not some kind of traitor. I can live with that. But he can never know the truth."

"Sam. I'm sorry. Please."

"So let's talk about Bolt. I need you to explain how you got tangled up with him." He chose his words carefully—tangled—like they mitigated her guilt.

"He knew Lucy. He knew details about her life. He reached out to me via e-mail. He said...he said that he could have influence over you to let me see Daniel. Then he sent me a phone. I'm guessing he had someone here to do this for him. These...favors."

Dennis Gandy, Sam thought. His useful idiot.

"He called me. We talked. He said he had been framed, and had to run, and the same thing had happened to Lucy before she died. I thought of reaching out to you—but if what he was saying was true, then you might have been one of the people who...got rid of Lucy. I couldn't risk that."

"He played on your fears, Clarice."

"I...he wanted to know if I could prove to Daniel I was his great-aunt. That I had pictures of Lucy and me together."

"He needed you to prove his case to Daniel."

"Yes. And he'd said he'd pose as my brother," she said. She peered at Sam. "Why was he so intent on having contact with you?"

"He had something he wanted to tell me, face-to-face, and to tell his daughter, and using Daniel was one way to do it while making sure we didn't try and fight him back. You and Daniel are nothing but pawns to a man like him."

She had the grace to look shamefaced.

"Why? Why would you do all this?" Sam asked.

"Because you kept Daniel from me."

"That's…" He was going to say not enough reason, but clearly, to her, it was. It was.

"I could have helped you with him, Sam. If I knew everything."

"You couldn't know everything. It was classified. I'm sorry."

"How was I supposed to know that? She's unhappy, she's leaving, she's suddenly sick, and she dies? She didn't have a heart problem, did she? Did you kill her, did the Agency?"

"A very bad man killed her," Sam said. "A terrorist. She was trying to make right what she'd done, and he killed her." *No, actually, she's down the hall in a room where she's been for thirteen years. But you can't ever know that.*

"So she died doing good?" Her voice wavered.

"Yes." He forced himself to meet her stare. It might help her, to believe this.

"All right. All right. I'm here so I have to believe you."

"Your medical bills will be ruinous to you. But… the government will take care of them in exchange for your silence. As a favor to me. But the moment you talk about this, to anyone, those bills will be due." He hated saying this, but it was true. He was telling her the deal, not offering it to her.

"That's blackmail."

"Clarice, you're lucky you're not in prison. Or dead by the hand of Bolt or the Russians."

"Daniel..."

"...wants nothing to do with you. If he changes his mind and decides to see you, I'll bring him to you. But the decision is his now."

She sobbed. She regained enough composure to say, "You lie to him every day. And yet I'm the liar."

"Well, I didn't drug him and put him on a plane with a murderer, Clarice. I didn't hold him in a condo with a Russian thug as his guard dog."

"You drove me to this. You drove me to this because he's all the family I have left and—"

"You did this to yourself. You've poisoned the well with him."

"Does he even know I'm still alive?"

"Yes, of course he does. Of course he asked if you were okay. Good luck with your recovery. You'll get outstanding care. The doctors and nurses here are wonderful."

"Sam...please..."

He didn't want to say this to her. But he had orders from Woodruff, and she had to understand the gravity of having kidnapped his child. The CIA and Section K had less patience than Sam with someone like Clarice. "If word gets out that Bolt returned to America, and then you talk about him or me or any of this, you'll face a full set of federal charges for rendering aid to a fugitive and kidnapping across state lines. I'll make sure you have a good lawyer, but at that point, I cannot shield you. Because of the hurt it would cause to Daniel. He is my priority, and if he's also yours like you claim, then you and I are finally on the same side. In my line of work there are not a lot of second chances. I'm giving you one. I'm giving you your life back, Clarice. Do you understand me?"

She nodded. "You did good with him," she said. "He's a good kid."

He took it as sincere. "He is. If he wants to see you, I'll bring him to you. I do promise you that. Maybe give him time."

She nodded, tears in her eyes.

"Bye, Clarice."

She said nothing; she stared at the wall.

He closed her door. He looked toward the end of the hall. It was a long hall. He had been told before that was where her room was. He had not been to the hospital in all those years; he was no longer her husband; he had no rights to her information. The Agency had, for a while, set up a camera feed where he could log in and see her. Eventually a new doctor took it away, and Sam didn't object. Lucy was gone, in a hell worse than death, and she could do nothing more to him or his son.

He looked toward the elevator. And then back to the end of the hall.

Something made him walk forward.

He went past the nurses' station; no one stopped him. He kept walking. He wondered what he would do when he saw her.

Cry? Hold her hand? Remember how much he'd loved her? Tell her that Daniel had turned out to be a great kid? Fight the urge to smother her with a pillow?

He got to the door. He took a deep breath. He pushed it open and stepped inside.

The bed was empty.

ACKNOWLEDGMENTS

It can be a challenge to return to a series after a five-year break from it—but I really wanted to go back to the mysterious world of Sam Capra after some time away. I made the choice to move the story ahead ten years from when we last saw Sam—so his son Daniel could be an active character, and Sam could be one of those fascinating types who leads what seems a quiet suburban life but has a secret life in a dark, dangerous, unsuspected world. Thank you to those who already entered the "Capraverse" in the earlier novels, and welcome to the new readers who are just finding Sam and Mila now. I'm so grateful and glad you're here.

Many thanks to those who supported this book: Wes Miller (who read the book when it most needed his thoughtful guidance), Ben Sevier, Karen Kosztolnyik, Beth de Guzman, Matthew Ballast, Andy Dodds, Autumn Oliver, Joe Benincase, Morgan Swift, Jeff Holt, and the whole team at Grand Central; Peter Ginsberg, Holly Frederick, Sarah Perillo, Mahalaleel Muhammed-Clinton, Shirley Stewart, Eliane Benisti; my Miami consultants Paige McClendon and Marianne Fernandez; Meg Gardiner, John Q Smith, J. T. Ellison, Harlan Coben, and Daniel Stashower.

As always, my greatest thanks to Leslie, Charles, and William for their love, patience, and support.

ABOUT THE AUTHOR

@ Leslie Abbott

Jeff Abbott is the *New York Times* bestselling author of twenty-two novels. He is the winner of an International Thriller Writers Award (for the Sam Capra thriller *The Last Minute*) and is a three-time nominee for the Edgar Award. He lives in Austin with his family. You can visit his website at www.JeffAbbott.com.